praise for Trici

'"Masterful" is used a lot in reviews, but Tricia Stringer really is. With *Birds of a Feather*, she firmly takes her place as one of Australia's most accomplished writers.'

—*Better Reading*

'A book you can't put down ... Stringer's skill is in weaving the experiences of different generations of women together, with sensitivity and familiarity, gently showing how context can shape women's decisions ... A moving, feel-good, warm read about strong, loving women ... the exact book we all need right now.'

—*Mamamia* on *The Family Inheritance*

'... a polished family saga ... all delivered with intelligence, wit and emotion in equal measures ... Perfection!'

—*Better Reading* on *The Family Inheritance*

'Tricia Stringer is an intuitive and tender-hearted storyteller who displays a real ability to interrogate issues that affect families and individuals. *The Family Inheritance* is another gratifying read from Tricia Stringer.'

—*Mrs B's Book Reviews*

'This book is the equivalent of a hot bath or a box of chocolates, it's comforting and an absolute pleasure to immerse yourself in ... If you enjoy well-written family sagas, look no further. *The Model Wife* is perfect.'

—*Better Reading*

'Tricia Stringer's *The Model Wife* is a beautiful multi-dimensional family saga.'

—*Beauty and Lace*

'Tricia Stringer excels at two things: strong, empathetic characters; and finding an experience or emotion shared by many, then spinning that small kernel of commonality into an engaging novel. *The Model Wife* is no exception … Stringer's prose is warm and friendly. She pulls you in with an easy and flowing writing style that quickly has you absorbed by the action. It's easy to read, but that doesn't mean it's shallow.'

—*Other Dreams Other Lives*

'[A] heartfelt saga.'

—*Herald Sun* on *The Model Wife*

'I would highly recommend this novel and hope that readers will gain what I have from it. *The Model Wife* is a beautiful story with familiar challenges and a strength of a family who are connected via their life experiences together.'

—*Chapter Ichi*

'A well-written, engaging story of the everyday challenges of life and love … a wise, warm, and wonderful story'

—*Book'd Out* on *The Model Wife*

'Delivers a gentle satisfaction that makes it a great choice for a lazy Sunday afternoon read.'

—*Books + Publishing* on *Table for Eight*

'A witty, warm and wise story of how embracing the new with an open heart can transform your life.'

—*Herald Sun* on *Table for Eight*

'... a moving, feel-good read ... a warm and uplifting novel of second chances and love old and new in a story of unlikely dining companions thrown together on a glamorous cruise.'

—*Sunday Mail* on *Table for Eight*

'A wonderful story of friendships, heartbreak and second chances that may change your life.'

—*Beauty and Lace* on *Table for Eight*

'Stringer's inviting new novel is sprinkled with moments of self reflection, relationship building, friendships and love.'

—*Mrs B's Book Reviews* on *Table for Eight*

'... a really moving tale ... This truly was a delightful read that left me with that feel-good happy sigh ... be enticed by this tale of love and laughter, trauma and tears, reflection and resolution.'

—*The Royal Reviews* on *Table for Eight*

'This winner from Tricia Stringer ... is a light-hearted and easy-to-read novel with twists and turns along the way ... enjoyable and fun.'

—*The Black and White Guide* on *Table for Eight*

'Tricia has no trouble juggling a large cast and ensuring we get to know and connect with them ... captivated me start to finish; if it wasn't the wishing myself on board for a relaxing and pampered break from reality, it was connecting with the characters and hoping they managed to find what they were looking for. Definitely a book I didn't want to put down!'

'A heart-warming novel that celebrates friendships old and new, reminding us that it's never too late to try again … If you enjoy stories that explore connections between people and pay tribute to the endurance of love and friendship, you will love Stringer's new novel. *Table For Eight* is a beautiful book … If you're looking for a getaway but don't quite have the time or funds, look no further – this book is your next holiday. Pull up a deck chair and enjoy.'

about the author

Tricia Stringer is a bestselling and multiple award-winning author. Her books include *Table for Eight*, *The Model Wife* and *The Family Inheritance*, and the rural romances *Queen of the Road*, *Right as Rain*, *Riverboat Point*, *Between the Vines*, *A Chance of Stormy Weather*, *Come Rain or Shine* and *Something in the Wine*. She has also published a historical saga; *Heart of the Country*, *Dust on the Horizon* and *Jewel in the North* are set in the unforgiving landscape of nineteenth-century Flinders Ranges. Tricia grew up on a farm in country South Australia and has spent most of her life in rural communities, as owner of a post office and bookshop, as a teacher and librarian, and now as a full-time writer. She lives in the beautiful Copper Coast region with her husband Daryl, travelling and exploring Australia's diverse communities and landscapes, and sharing her passion for the country and its people through her authentic stories and their vivid characters.

For further information and to sign up for her quarterly newsletter go to triciastringer.com or connect with Tricia on Facebook, Instagram @triciastringerauthor or Twitter @tricia_stringer

Also by Tricia Stringer

Table for Eight
The Model Wife
The Family Inheritance

Queen of the Road
Right as Rain
Riverboat Point
Between the Vines
A Chance of Stormy Weather
Come Rain or Shine
Something in the Wine

The Flinders Ranges Series
Heart of the Country
Dust on the Horizon
Jewel in the North

TRICIA STRINGER

birds *of a* feather

First Published 2021
First Australian Paperback Edition 2021
ISBN 9781489270870

BIRDS OF A FEATHER
© 2021 by Tricia Stringer
Australian Copyright 2021
New Zealand Copyright 2021

Published by
HQ Fiction
An imprint of Harlequin Enterprises (Australia) Pty Limited (ABN 47 001 180 918), a subsidiary of HarperCollins Publishers Australia Pty Limited (ABN 36 009 913 517)
Level 13, 201 Elizabeth St
SYDNEY NSW 2000
AUSTRALIA

® and TM (apart from those relating to FSC®) are trademarks of Harlequin Enterprises (Australia) Pty Limited or its corporate affiliates. Trademarks indicated with ® are registered in Australia, New Zealand and in other countries.

A catalogue record for this book is available from the National Library of Australia
www.librariesaustralia.nla.gov.au

Printed and bound in Australia by McPherson's Printing Group

For Margie and Mandy

one

Eve Monk would never forget where she was and what she was doing the day she got the call to say her husband had been killed. She'd been packing the car, the bright orange Torana she and Rex had bought just after they were married. It was sixteen years old and Rex had bought several cars since but she loved the Torana. All that morning she'd been loading it with as many of the boys' things as she could fit, along with a few items of her own. She'd gone back inside to get the washing basket from the laundry. It was full of dirty clothes but they were mostly school uniforms and the boys would need them.

The phone was ringing at the other end of the house. She hesitated, not wanting to answer, but she always worried it would be the school. There'd been plenty of calls from both her sons' teachers over the last two years. No doubt after today those calls would become frequent again but it couldn't be helped.

"Eve!" a voice bellowed at her down the line.

1

"Spiro?" Her heart skipped a beat at the sound of her friend and business partner's voice. The trawlers had only gone out the previous night for the first fish of the season. She wasn't expecting them back for a few days. She glanced at the sky through the big kitchen window. There was no sign of bad weather.

"What's up?" She tried to keep the panic from her voice. She wasn't ready to face Rex. She'd hoped to have time to talk to the boys, explain why they were leaving their father and settle them in to their alternate accommodation before he returned.

"Eve," Spiro said again, this time more a moan followed by a shuddering sob. "Eve, I'm so sorry."

"Why? What's happened?"

"There's been an accident."

"Are you all right?"

"Yes."

"The boat?"

"It's fine. It's … Eve, it's Rex."

"Rex?" But Rex was invincible, always escaping harm although often creating it for others.

"We had some trouble with the winch and it fell. Eve, I'm so sorry. Rex was under it. The full force hit him on the head. There was nothing we could do."

Eve sagged to the stool beside the kitchen bench. "Are you telling me …"

"He's dead, Eve."

"Rex is dead?" The anger that had fuelled her mad packing spree all morning trickled from her as if she were a sieve full of holes, leaving behind tiny grains of sorrow bumping against the numbness inside her.

"We're over the other side of the gulf. The police are coming."

Spiro's voice went on and on but Eve could only hear the loud rushing sound in her head. Then Spiro was saying her name again.

"Eve? They're here. I have to go. I'll call you back soon."

"Okay."

"Should I phone Pam? You shouldn't be alone."

"I'll be okay." She ended the call and hung the phone back on the hook. Then reached for it again. She'd have to call Rex's parents. Their only son, their pride and joy ... they'd be inconsolable. She put the phone back. Not yet. She had to give herself a moment.

Today she'd finally made up her mind to leave her duplicitous husband but instead he'd left her. A strange sensation burbled deep inside her and rose up. She clapped a hand to her mouth but the force of it was too strong, squeezing between her fingers and erupting – a crazy cackling noise. She took a deep breath and forced herself to be calm.

Spiro had said something about a winch falling. Had he given her more detail? She hadn't heard everything. Once more she reached for the phone and once more she stopped. She had no idea where Spiro had been calling from.

She looked around the kitchen. The old navy jumper Rex wore around home was draped over the back of his chair and a packet of his cigarettes lay on the desk among piles of papers and envelopes. A bottle of rakija sat on the bench. A sticky ring remained beside it. He'd overfilled her glass and she'd had to lean down and suck up the first mouthful. Little signs of Rex were everywhere. Before Spiro's phone call she'd been stoically ignoring them, avoiding Rex's things and grabbing as much of hers and the boys' as she could. She'd wanted to be gone, well before he returned.

She hadn't been moving far away, just to a friend's beach shack, a temporary stopgap until she could sort things out with Rex. It was the washing that had finally done it. After the boys had gone to school she'd begun the mountain of washing that had been languishing around the house. She'd do anything needed if it related to their prawn fishing business but housework bored her. When she'd come to the pile of shorts and jeans she'd carefully emptied pockets. Arlo often had paper folded in his, covered in his scribbled diagrams and workings out, and Zac had his usual assortment of string, empty lolly wrappers and a plastic fishing float.

It was what she'd found in Rex's pockets that had sent her head spinning and her heart thudding. In one was a crumpled receipt from a motel in a town further up the coast. The date was from two nights earlier. The night he'd said he was spending on the trawler, getting it ready for the start of the season. He'd paid cash. And in the other pocket was a set of earrings wrapped in a scrap of paper. They were gold loop earrings for pierced ears. Eve didn't have pierced ears. There was a phone number scrawled across the paper. She dialled the number. A woman answered. Eve gasped.

"Hello?" the woman said again.

"Who is this?" Eve asked but in her heart she already knew.

"Eve?" The voice was little more than a whisper now.

Eve dropped the phone back on its cradle. Bile rose in her throat as she ripped the paper to tiny shreds.

Then she'd gone to their bedroom and started pulling things out of his drawers. Tucked at the back of one she found a box of condoms, open, with several missing. Eve had had her tubes tied a few years after Zac was born. They never used condoms.

All of the horror of two years prior had come rushing back.

The discovery that Rex had had an affair then had nearly destroyed her. The town had buzzed with gossip. The woman had been the wife of a local businessman, and friendships and families had been blown apart as everyone took a side. Rex had sworn it was a mistake and he'd never do it again. He'd begged Eve to take him back. Spiro had stood by them both, not taking sides but making it clear to Rex what a fool he was and to Eve that he would support whatever decision she made. The woman had left town and in the end Eve had stayed with Rex. They had two sons and a business together. She wasn't giving it up easily.

Time had eased her pain and she'd almost felt like they were a proper family again. Three nights ago they'd toasted the success of the new prawn season with two glasses of rakija. Rex's enthusiasm for the fishing season ahead had been infectious – his fervent mood had warmed her as much as the alcohol. They'd talked and laughed together and taken to their bed like young lovers. And the next night he'd been with someone else.

Discovering fresh signs of deception, realising he'd been with another woman, and who knew how often – it was too much. Eve felt old beyond her thirty-seven years. Already she was building another wall around her heart, cocooning herself from the hurt of his betrayal. It came easily, probably because deep down she'd never truly forgiven him.

But none of it mattered now, she realised. Rex was gone, and with any luck this latest treachery would be buried with him. Eve thought of Arlo and Zac and her heart ached. She had to protect them. It was bad enough they'd lost their father – at least they wouldn't know about this latest affair. They had good friends to see them through. Her best friends, Pam and Eric Paterson and Gert and Tom Belling, had stood by her last time and would help her again. Their children were all friends. Pam's two, Heath and Julia, and Eve's boys were especially close. She knew Heath looked out for Arlo, and Julia did her best to stop Zac spending too much time alone.

Eve rose from the stool and quickly sank back to it as her legs refused to support her. Her heart thudded in her chest. She sucked in a breath and then another as her lungs screamed for more. Her fingers gripped the edge of the stool and she forced herself to take deep, slow breaths. She'd felt like this after Rex's first affair too, but she couldn't afford to panic now.

The desk caught her attention and she focused on it like a lost traveller would a light in the dark. Built into a nook off the kitchen, it was their office. Beside it was the filing cabinet, one drawer half open and a pile of files stacked on top of it. Rex had a life insurance policy. She slapped her hand over her mouth as the realisation hit – Rex was dead and suddenly her financial situation was stronger than if she'd left him.

Between the insurance and the fishing she could continue to support her family financially. Eve did the books, the cooking for the crew, mended nets and generally filled any role needed. That could continue. They'd have to employ someone to take Rex's place. The measured deep breaths had succeeded in slowing her racing heart. Panic was useless. She had to think of her boys and their future.

She dragged herself from the stool and went back to her bedroom. She paused at the door, seeing the jumble she'd created – first from digging through Rex's things, and then the chaos she'd left as she'd wrenched her own clothes from the cupboards. Her lips trembled at the sight of his belongings strewn around. She'd been so angry, yet a small part of her had hoped if she left him he'd come to his senses, want her back, work harder to make them a family again. Now that could never happen. Rex was never coming home. Tears brimmed in her eyes. She stiffened and batted them away. What good were tears? She'd cried enough of them over Rex. She had to be strong now, for her boys and for the business that was their future.

Eve swallowed the lump in her throat and lifted her chin. She strode forward, tidied the mess and tossed the condoms in the bin. Then she unpacked the car, put everything back where it had been and, instead of preparing to tell her sons they were leaving their father, she prepared to tell them he was dead.

two

Present day

Every Thursday morning Eve drove her Holden Torana coupe
into Wallaby Bay. She parked it in the shade of the massive pines
on the edge of the supermarket carpark and walked the length of
the street to do her jobs. Because she did it at the same time each
week, she knew who she would and wouldn't meet. She always
called at the post office first, to check her mailbox and pay bills,
and the supermarket last, so that her dairy and meat items would
remain cool in the esky for the ten-minute journey home. Not
that the temperature was a worry today. The first week of June
had been cold, a sudden prelude to the winter that was to come.

In between the post office and the supermarket, Eve stopped at
the newsagency to buy the local paper. Terry, who only worked
behind the counter on Thursdays and was a Holden buff, asked
her if she wanted to sell her car, as always.

She popped in at the hairdresser to say hello – her tight curls
were trimmed every six weeks on a Tuesday so it was purely a

social call. Moira was halfway through an intricate updo for a young woman Eve didn't know. Eve asked, but there was no special occasion, the woman said, and then Moira had given her a quick rundown on the previous evening's local business meeting. Apparently there was a stalemate on what kind of plants should be put in the new garden boxes the council had installed along the street. Half the meeting wanted shrubs that would only need water and the odd prune, the rest wanted colourful annuals to brighten up the street. A decision hadn't been reached.

She stepped quickly past the op shop, keeping her gaze strictly ahead. There'd been a time when she'd loved to search through, looking for the treasures that could be found among someone else's cast-offs, but not now. She just had time to visit the fruit and veg shop before she met Gert. She loved the way Franco settled her apples and pears gently into her basket as if they were eggs being placed in a nest. Her last stop on the main street would be the cafe to get a takeaway coffee.

Once a year she visited her husband's grave on his birthday but that wasn't today. Today she was meeting Gert at their mutual friend Pam Paterson's graveside. It was the anniversary of Pam's death and Gert and Eve always met at the grave on this date, and again on Pam's birthday, to fill their friend in on local goings-on.

Eve was running behind schedule when she whipped into the Cinnamon Bark Cafe at the end of the main street. She had a quick chat to Dale and Brent who ran the cafe, more planter box discussions – they were on the side of colourful annuals. They made her coffee to take away and as she turned to go two women entered. They both paused, looked from Eve to each other.

Eve drew herself up, annoyed at the sudden race of her heart. "Audrey, Norma," she said with a nod as she strode towards the door.

Audrey stepped into Eve's path. Her finely plucked and pencilled eyebrows shot up to meet her lacquered fringe. "What are you doing here?"

"Buying a coffee. I believe anyone can."

"Well! There's no need for that tone," Norma muttered.

Audrey put a hand on Norma's arm and turned her sharp gaze back to Eve. "Haven't seen you about in a long time."

"I'm still here."

"Not coming back to help at the museum again?"

"Not likely."

"We won't hold you up then."

Eve stood her ground. She wasn't about to be dismissed by Audrey Owens. "What's happening with the prawn industry display?"

"No agreement has been reached about that."

"I wonder why?"

Audrey's look turned hawk-like. "Withdrawing your donation has slowed things, but others will come on board."

"No-one else in the industry will make a donation unless a proper plan is developed."

"Unless you allow them to, you mean."

"Each business is their own master, Audrey."

Norma sniffed her displeasure but Audrey's lips turned up in a cat-that-got-the-cream smile.

"That's so true," she said. "I suppose you've heard about Chrissie's engagement."

"No." Eve swallowed the why-would-she-care retort that sprung to her lips. She felt sorry for whoever was going to get

Audrey as a mother-in-law. Rumour had it that her other two sons-in-law danced to her tune. But of course Eve wasn't one to listen to gossip.

"Nicholas Colston." Audrey was beaming now and Eve could understand why. The Colstons were based in Port Lincoln. Ralph Colston was another pioneer of the local prawn industry. Three generations of the family helped manage their extensive fishing business. Audrey's youngest daughter was marrying into fishing royalty.

"Please give them my congratulations."

"Oh, the queen is giving her blessing, is she?" Sarcasm dripped from Audrey's tongue, her smile gone. "You've had your say for too long, Eve Monk. Your influence is on the way out."

Eve's cheeks warmed and her heart picked up speed again. She was aware that the tinkle-clink of cutlery on crockery and the mumbled conversations around them had stopped.

"Is everything all right here?" Dale had left the counter to stand beside them.

The cafe was almost silent and Eve felt the collective gaze of those seated around her press close, an invisible wall of condemnation. A horrible feeling of deja vu swept over her.

"It's fine," she said and strode outside.

She could hear Norma's complaining voice start up before the door even closed behind her.

"That was unfortunate," Eve muttered.

A young bloke gave her a strange look as he passed. She forced a smile to her lips.

Damn! Eve hurried across the road. Of all people to run into. It wasn't Audrey so much as the people observing that bothered her. She blew out a breath, adjusted her grip on her coffee and made her way back to her car. The adrenaline that had charged round her body was ebbing, leaving her hand shaky as she searched for her keys.

It hadn't always been like that with Audrey. While they weren't friends, Wallaby Bay was a small town and over the years they'd managed to move in different circles. Eve's volunteering had been devoted to the school council, the women's and children's hospital auxiliary, the hockey club and Meals on Wheels, while Audrey, with three daughters, had spent her time at netball and callisthenics. They had different friends and interest groups. And on the rare occasions they found themselves in the same place they had tolerated each other.

That was up until the previous year when Audrey had joined the local museum committee, a committee that Eve had held various positions on for over twenty years. Audrey's presence and interference had been difficult enough but then there'd been Audrey's unfortunate accident. Time might patch old hurts but in Eve's case they had never truly healed.

She reached the cemetery, determined to put today's confrontation with Audrey from her mind. There were better people to devote her time to. She drove right in and parked at the end of the row. Gert was already there. Eve took out her small folding chair and sat it next to her friend.

Gert had a few years on Eve's seventy but they and Pam had all arrived in the district in the late sixties, new teachers at their first postings or, in Gert's case, second. The three of them had married local men, seen each other through life's highs and lows. They were all widowed now; Pam and Eve both years ago and Gert only last year.

"You're early," Eve said as soon as she was settled. "Or am I late?"

"I visited Tom first," Gert said.

"How is he?"

"Much the same." Gert managed a smile that almost broke Eve's heart. Grief had taken its toll on her friend.

"No more suffering," Eve said softly.

"No more suffering," Gert echoed.

They both looked down at the headstone in front of them.

"We're here for a chat, Pam." Eve rested her flowers next to a small bunch of Gert's home-grown chrysanthemums.

Gert lifted her coffee in the air. Hers was in a proper china mug, filled from the thermos at her feet. Eve tapped her cardboard takeaway cup against it.

"Cheers." They both took sips then settled back in their chairs and chatted as old friends do, about family and mutual acquaintances and the last prawn run for the season, and ended up discussing the flower boxes in the main street.

"I wish they'd put a few out here," Gert said. The wind-swept expanse of the cemetery was barren of colour except for whatever people put on the graves, which often blew away, sometimes arriving back at the cemetery gate before the person who'd delivered them. At the moment, though, the breeze was gentle.

"It is a bit bleak." Eve looked across at the monolith marking Rex's grave. His parents had wanted it and now they were buried in equally grand fashion beside him. "I want my ashes to be scattered at sea."

"But then there's nowhere for your friends and family to visit."

"My family aren't here and I don't imagine anyone but you would visit me. By the time I go you'll be too doddery to come out here."

Gert huffed. "I visit Tom every week."

"He was a good man," Eve said. She'd certainly not wasted her life visiting her husband's grave every week. Her friends Gert and Pam had drawn the long straws with the men they'd married.

They sat in silence for a moment. Eve had thought to tell her story of running into Audrey – a hurt shared with an old friend would ease it – but Gert spoke first.

"I need to head off." She stood. "I've got a hair appointment in twenty minutes."

"No need to rush then." The cemetery was a five-minute drive from Moira's.

"I've changed hairdressers."

"Really?" Moira had been their hairdresser since she'd opened her salon at least twenty years ago.

"Don't give me that face, Evelyn."

"I'm not making a face." Eve's tone had risen a notch. Gert only called her Evelyn when she was taking her to task and that was becoming more common lately.

"Moira doesn't listen to what I say. I'm trying someone new and I don't want to be late."

Gert's fine silver hair had thinned in the last few years and the previous month Moira had suggested a pixie cut. Eve had thought it looked great, very Judi Dench–like, to which Gert had retorted she wasn't that old yet. Eve glanced at her friend. Her hair had a bit more growing to do if she wanted a different style.

"I'll call in tomorrow and see how you got on." Eve smiled.

"I'm going to Adelaide first thing."

"Are you?"

"It's the baby's first birthday. There's a big party planned," Gert said. "I'm sure I told you."

"Maybe."

Gert's two sons and their families lived in Adelaide. Between them they'd produced five children who ranged in age from the baby turning one to ten-year-old twins. Eve had always envied their proximity. She had one son in Darwin and the other in Singapore. They were good at keeping in touch but for all the information she got via the video calls with her teenage grandchildren, she may as well have been talking in a foreign language. She sighed. Perhaps she was.

"How about early next week?" Eve said.

"I'm not sure which day I'll be back."

"Coffee on Thursday then?"

"Yes."

"We'll meet at the Cutty Sark. Let's write it down."

Gert sniffed. "I don't need to write it down."

Eve drew her phone from her bag. "I record every appointment on here these days. It even sends me reminders."

"There's nothing wrong with my memory." Gert pinned Eve with a glare that dared her to say otherwise.

"I'll see you next week then." Eve's smile was a forced response to Gert's sharp nod. "Say hello to the family," she called as Gert strode towards her car. Never mind Judi Dench – with Gert dressed in a knee-length coat and sensible walking shoes, her chair in one hand and a large handbag in the other, she only needed a scarf on her head or a corgi at her side and she could have been a younger Queen Elizabeth.

Eve turned back to Pam's grave as Gert drove away. "Wish you were still here, dear friend. We're getting old, Gert and I. Perhaps I'd feel less ancient with you beside me." A little barb of sorrow jabbed inside her. She didn't miss her husband but there was still an empty space in her heart for Pam. And even though she'd been

gone for years, recently the space had become bigger. She longed
for Pam's gung-ho attitude and wise counsel.

"I'm worried about Gert. I know she's lost Tom but it's more
than that. Something's not right and I can't put my finger on it.
Oh, and I ran into Audrey and Norma on my way here. Still no
change on the museum committee and Audrey's ridiculous ideas.
That despicable woman continues to thwart me."

Two vehicles pulled up outside the cemetery. Doors banged
and voices carried as a group of people made their way through
the gates. Eve packed up her things. There were already enough
stories about her without adding talking to dead friends.

On the short drive back to the shops and all the way around the
supermarket, Eve tested the tiny festering hurt that Gert's abrupt-
ness had caused. Had she always been that way and Eve hadn't
noticed it, or was it a change brought on by the weight of being a
full-time carer and then losing her husband?

Eve couldn't pinpoint when the changes had begun but she
did remember the first time Gert had snapped at her. It was when
Tom hadn't long been housebound. One of their sons had come
up from Adelaide to spend a few days doing maintenance jobs
around the house and keep his dad company. Eve had suggested
she and Gert go out for lunch and a movie. She couldn't remember what they'd seen but she did remember shouting Gert lunch
at the pub and then Gert being annoyed because she'd been served
the wrong dish. She'd insisted she'd wanted chicken with bechamel sauce. Eve had been surprised when Gert had changed her
mind and agreed to the special the waitress had recited. That had
been chicken schnitzel with parmigiana sauce and the added extra
of pulled pork, caramelised onion, cheese and BBQ sauce. They'd
both groaned at the sight of it piled high on the plate.

"What is that?" Gert had exclaimed.

"The chicken special."

"It's not what the girl said." The young waitress had spent a lot of time explaining the menu items before the two women had settled on what they wanted and Eve had gone to the bar to order it.

"Yes it was."

Gert had drawn herself up and glared at Eve. "I know what she said and this is not chicken bechamel. You ordered the wrong thing."

Eve had felt terrible. In all their years of friendship they'd hardly had a cross word let alone berated each other so sharply. Eve had apologised, although she hadn't felt she'd needed to. After all, she'd bought the lunch Gert had asked for. Gert had pursed her lips and eyed the mountain of food. "It's too much," she'd groaned.

Eve had suggested cutting the meal in half and sliding it onto another plate. Gert's good humour had returned and the rest of the day had gone smoothly.

By the time Eve pulled into her driveway she was stewing over the several times recently that Gert had berated her over something small that had escalated to something big. The knot inside her made her feel as if she'd rather not meet Gert for coffee, but it was a whole week away, and a silly misunderstanding was not something to dispel fifty years of friendship.

The wind that often came up the hill from the bay had strengthened and was tossing the bushes in her garden as she walked the path from the garage to her home, shopping bags dragging at both her arms. Eve looked up at the weathervane at the top of the post in the middle of the yard. In the shape of a snapper, it pointed steadily south-west. She followed the direction of its snout, over the shrubs of her side garden, to the bay where white caps ruffled the deep blue water. The two prawn trawlers she and Spiro owned were safely moored at a pontoon in the marina so the wind wouldn't bother them.

Her gaze swept on along the shoreline. White sand edged the shallow water, which was a pretty turquoise colour today, and then beyond where the houses clung to the curve until the groin of the marina, the higher structures of the silos and then the wharf that pointed its long arm out into the bay. She never tired of this view.

The old house had been run-down when Rex had insisted they buy it. She'd wanted to live in town but he'd been in love with the property and she'd soon come to his way of thinking. Their business had done well enough for them to renovate, keeping the wonderful bones of the original building but with a more practical internal layout that made better use of the view.

Eve adjusted her handbag on her shoulder and moved on until she was protected from the breeze by the vast iron-roofed verandah. She reached for the screen door. As she gripped the handle and tugged, the bag full of food swung forward. The bottom of the door usually caught on the wooden doorstep but today it leaped open, her arm flung wide with it, and the combined weight of her bag and the shopping propelled her arm backwards. She gasped as a sharp pain jagged her shoulder.

"Damn!"

She dropped the shopping bag and clasped her shoulder until the pain eased. Taking a deep breath, she went inside with the first load and then back for the bag by the door.

"Should have made two trips from the car," she muttered and avoided using her right arm as she unpacked her shopping.

She turned her thoughts to the dinner she was planning for tomorrow night. She'd bought some herb-and-camembert-stuffed chicken rolls. Spiro and Mary were bringing a prawn dish for entree and Eve had also bought the ingredients to make a cheese-cake for dessert. She managed very well on her own, but it was always good to have something to look forward to.

By the time she'd put everything away, the pain in her shoulder was only a dull ache. She glanced at the bottle of rakija on the bench then at the clock. It was a little early for her nightly glass.

"Wine!" She clapped a hand to her forehead. She'd meant to buy wine while she was in town. She swept her keys from the bench and grimaced as her shoulder complained at the movement. She gave it a rub and headed for the door. More than anything she hated the waste of time and fuel in making two trips to town but it was better she went back today. She wanted to leave tomorrow free to prepare for her dinner guests. She always had stocks of rakija, the fruity brandy she had learned to enjoy when she had first met Rex. Spiro had introduced the potent drink to him and they'd delighted in initiating Eve but Mary had never liked it and preferred a light red wine. Something told Eve her dinner guests weren't coming purely for a social outing and she wanted to be on the front foot.

three

It was nine o'clock on a Thursday night and Lorenzo's Bar was humming. The pre-show diners were long gone, the après-theatre drinkers yet to appear, and the group celebrating Julia Paterson's birthday had taken over one of the large booths. Julia sat at the top of the U, with her colleagues seated along each side or on stools at the end of the table. It wasn't the cosy night in she'd imagined for herself. She'd been coerced by a couple of work colleagues who'd insisted they needed to celebrate the end of a project and the return to their previous research. They'd wanted a place with style and for them Lorenzo's, nestled in a narrow lane off Melbourne's East End theatre district, had style. Julia had given in and agreed to go only because they had the next day off.

The gift of an extra day to their weekend was a total luxury but after the year they'd had Margaret, their head of department, had said they deserved the break. The team had worked long hours tidying up the last lot of research for handover and then preparing to kickstart the original work they'd been doing pre-pandemic. They'd all be ready to begin again fresh on Monday after their long weekend.

The dimly lit booth suddenly illuminated. Julia frowned as a birthday cake with candles already alight was pushed towards her along the table, then glared around wondering which of them had decided it was a good idea to surprise her. Julia didn't enjoy birthdays. Not her own, anyway, and especially not those ending in five. Today she turned forty-five and she'd hoped to let it slide by without comment. The background music was drowned out as she was treated to a rowdy rendition of "Happy Birthday".

"Act happy." Geraldine, who'd worked with Julia for longer than the others, dug her with an elbow.

"Was this your idea?" Julia snapped, but Geraldine was saved by Kylie, another of their team, calling for her to blow out the candles.

Julia waved a menu across the flames, and managed to smile as her colleagues howled with excitement at her leaving one candle still alight.

"There's a boyfriend somewhere," Kylie cooed.

"Somewhere," Julia agreed and cut into the cake that it was now obvious Kylie had brought along.

"Where is Glen?" Geraldine gave her a questioning look.

"Work." Julia wasn't actually sure what Glen was doing.

"At this hour?" Geraldine raised an eyebrow.

"We're not married. We lead separate lives."

Geraldine raised both eyebrows.

"How come you're up this late anyway?" Julia asked. Geraldine had a husband who also worked long hours and a young family. She rarely attended social events.

"My mother-in-law's staying and she gave me the night off. It seemed like a great escape when she suggested it." Geraldine stifled a yawn. She was five years younger than Julia and looked permanently tired. "But I know I'll regret it in the morning when the baby wakes."

Cake on paper plates landed in front of them and they both bit into their slices as if their lives depended on it. Julia groaned. It was four-layered red velvet and the first taste was so divine she quickly took another bite. Around her almost everyone else had stopped talking to eat.

"You should make an honest man of Glen," Geraldine said through a mouthful of cake. "He's perfect. Divorced, has kids so won't want more, good job, good looks. What more could you want?"

"More cake?"

Julia shoved her empty plate towards Kylie, who was waving the knife over the remains of the large slab. Geraldine followed her example and then Kylie asked about Geraldine's kids thus saving Julia from answering.

What more did she want? She had no idea. Glen Walker had been her on-again, off-again partner for three years. He'd only met Geraldine on the rare occasions he'd been Julia's plus one at a fundraising dinner or an end-of-year function. She'd heard nothing from him today. Not that she'd even thought about him until Geraldine had mentioned him. To be fair, he'd rung the day before to ask her out for a late dinner on her birthday. They both had busy jobs and didn't see each other often during the week. It had been easy to decline, use work as her excuse. In truth she'd taken a tram to the city and bought herself some new boots, leather with no heel that would keep her warm and be good for walking. She'd thrown the old ones in a bin and gone straight from the shoe shop to Lorenzo's. It had been after eight when she'd arrived. The cake was her dinner.

Julia deliberately kept her work life separate from her love—
she corrected herself, personal life. Her relationship with Glen
was both complicated and not so. They were such a non-event as a
couple. She'd told him she needed space and he'd always given her
that. She'd said no to his recent offer of dinner and footy tickets.
They hadn't been out together for weeks.

It had been the footy that had brought them together, three
years earlier. She enjoyed his corporate box. If she was honest,
it was their mutual interest in football and the great sex that had
kept them together, but the sex had dwindled so that only left
football, and she wasn't sure she cared that much about that any
more either.

"Another drink?" Kylie called.

"No. Thank you for the cake but I'm heading home."

"Over the hill now you're forty-five." In a gap in the music
Foster's voice resounded around the booth.

A collective intake of breath whooshed within the group, all
eyes swivelling his way then back to Julia. Foster had been the
junior lab technician little more than a year – he'd come to them
straight from uni. He often spoke without thinking and wasn't
good with following protocol. He'd caused them more grief in
his short time with them than everyone else put together. It was
Julia's job to oversee his work and he'd been a thorn in her side
for the first few months. He'd been named Feckless Foster by their
head of research and the name had stuck, though never to his face.

Now they all waited on what Julia would say. *Idiot* was the first
word that came to mind but she chose to keep the peace and not
spoil what had been a pleasant evening.

"Cheeky," she said instead. "For that you can autoclave the
Eppendorf tubes for the whole lab on Monday."

Foster blanched. It was a job everyone avoided.

Julia gave Geraldine a shove with her hip. "Let me out."

The others shuffled around. Kylie handed her a shopping bag with the remains of the cake in a box at the bottom and someone pressed the flowers into her hands. She retrieved her small leather backpack from under the table and slid it over her shoulders. A chorus of goodnights followed her across the room.

As soon as the front door to her apartment block slammed shut, Julia removed her boots. Immediately her feet thanked her. It had been silly to wear them. She checked her letter box, took out a card and smiled as she noted the handwriting, then, juggling the flowers and cake, she walked up two flights of stairs to her second-floor apartment, her socks the only buffer between her and the cold terrazzo.

Nearing the top of the stairs she heard a noise. She was at eye level with the floor. Her neighbour across the hall was away; she'd been collecting his mail. She slowed, took the last few steps to the landing very carefully and peered around the balustrade. There was a man sprawled in a sitting position against her door, filling the space between wall and stairwell. A loud snoring noise emanated from his open mouth. Not dead then.

She stepped onto the landing and peered closer. A bunch of flowers lay beside him, and a bottle of red. She pulled herself upright and looked down at the dishevelled figure of Glen Walker.

"Oh, Glen," she said sadly and would have put a hand to her head, only both her hands were full. There was no way to get inside without disturbing him.

She put her bags and flowers on the floor and gently shook his shoulder. He lurched forward, his eyes opened and he briefly focused on her.

"Hi, honey," he mumbled. He always said it with a singsong chant that made Julia want to add "I'm home". She kept silent as he blinked and brushed at his chin then slowly folded sideways to the floor, curled himself around her legs and began to snore.

She eased her legs from his clasp and unlocked her door. Once she was inside she reached back for her things, cast one last pitying look over Glen and shut the door. Thankfully she'd never given him a key.

Inside her apartment she stripped off her coat, hung it in her wardrobe and tucked her boots at the bottom. In the kitchen she put the flowers in a vase then glanced at the bottle of red she'd got out that morning. It was the only thing, other than the flowers and the cake, on the compact bench. When she'd left home her plan for the evening had been to order in Mexican food, watch some catch-up TV and enjoy a few glasses of her favourite red. She took the cake box from the bottom of the bag. There was still a small portion left.

"What the hell." She shrugged and slid it onto a plate and opened the red.

Snuggled on her lounge with wine and cake on the coffee table, she picked up the envelope she'd tossed there on her way to her bedroom. Julia's brother, her sister-in-law and her two nephews had all sent texts during the day. There'd also been a couple from friends and of course Margaret, the head of their research team, had wished her well as they'd passed briefly in the corridor, but the only person who still sent a card for her birthday was Julia's godmother Eve.

Julia felt a pang of guilt as she opened it. When had she last communicated with Eve? She couldn't remember. Eve was her dead mother's best friend and as dear to Julia as her mother. Their last Skype session had to be more than a month ago and there'd been a text or two since then. Life got busy and time flew by.

She withdrew the card from the envelope and leaned closer to the table lamp, the only light she'd turned on in the apartment. Julia smiled. Besides the card there was also a letter. Something else Eve did that no-one else Julia knew bothered with, and that was to write letters. Most of it was small talk, about the weather, the fishing, a movie Eve had been to, but it was the ending that surprised Julia. Eve said she hoped everything was okay with Julia, that she'd tried to ring a couple of times, had left messages but she'd had no reply. Julia put down the letter. She couldn't remember a call from Eve. She slapped her palm against her forehead. There had been a call the night Glen had last taken her out.

They'd gone to some restaurant where everything was vegan. She recalled her phone ringing while she and Glen had been arguing over why he'd picked that restaurant. He'd thought she'd enjoy it because she'd said something about giving up meat. Julia had been horrified. "Of course I'm not giving up meat. I thought I was eating too much meat and needed to cut back and eat fish more often, that's all." Glen had totally misunderstood. They'd had a rather sad night – both of them in a huff and even though she'd been surprised when the food had turned out to be tasty, she wasn't a vegan and on the whole she hadn't enjoyed the night.

Julia had listened to Eve's message after Glen had dropped her home but it had been too late to call back then. The next week had been extra busy at work and she'd been late home each night, time had gone on and … she hadn't returned Eve's call.

She glanced at the time and realised once again it was too late to call. She made a mental note to phone over the weekend, folded the letter, slid it inside the envelope and stood the card up on the table.

The last sliver of cake teetered on the plate. Julia took a mouthful and washed it down with a sip of the pinot noir. The chocolate of the cake met the berry and cherry flavours of the wine in an orgasmic explosion on her taste buds. She flopped back against her couch then almost immediately sat up and repeated the process. She'd probably feel sick soon, being that this third piece of cake was the only food she'd had since a salad at lunchtime.

She was halfway through the slice when her stomach began to churn. She took the plate to the kitchen, tipped the remains in the bin and topped up her glass, ignoring the internal alarm saying not to. She hadn't drunk alone in a long time.

She took a defiant gulp of the tasty pinot. "It's my bloody birthday," she shouted. Not that she was celebrating this one but they did only come around once a year.

Her phone announced an incoming text and there was a thud beyond her outer door. She hunched her shoulders as if that would suddenly make her disappear. She'd forgotten about Glen.

There was another soft thud, then a gentle tap on the door. "Julia? Are you in there?" Another tap, a little louder this time. "Honey? It's Glen."

Julia rolled her eyes but kept her lips firmly pressed together.

There was a rustling sound, then finally the echo of footsteps on the stairs. She peered through the peephole. He was gone. Carefully she turned the lock and eased open the door. The flowers he'd left propped there toppled towards her and a small card slid with them. She snatched them up and, with the door once again secure, she got out a vase for the flowers. She only had two vases and her usual one already held the flowers from work. This one was crystal. It had belonged to her mother. The wording on the card was simple. "Happy Birthday Julia, love Glen." She tossed it in the bin, and thought about putting the flowers in too but she so rarely got flowers. She put them in the vase and sat them on the kitchen bench. Then with a pang of guilt she fished the card from the bin and propped it against the base.

With her glass of red in hand she paced. Glen turning up like that had unsettled her, or perhaps she'd already been on edge. If she was being honest, the lead-up to her forty-fifth birthday had been playing on her mind for days, weeks even. Most people anticipated zero birthdays, either with excitement or disdain. For her, zero birthdays had meant nothing more than another year older, but anything ending in five was bad luck. She wasn't super-stitious but it was inevitable. She glanced at the clock. A bit less than an hour until midnight, then this birthday would be done. Her phone pinged again, reminding her she had an unread text.

The message was from Margaret. *Sorry so late. Didn't want to spoil your birthday. Could you come in to work tomorrow. 10am. M*

The churning of cake and wine in her stomach met the surg-ing swirl of nerves in her chest. She sagged to a chair. Margaret had called her to work without the others before but that was when they'd been in the middle of some vital testing and she'd wanted to go over things, cross the t's and dot the i's. Julia was sure they'd done all that. They were ready to restart their pre-pandemic research on Monday.

Had they missed something? Julia's mind raced back over the previous week's work. As the second-in-charge she oversaw Fos-ter. She'd had to be tough on him for his lack of careful procedure when he'd first arrived but he was a brilliant researcher and once he had understood the importance of their recording and double-checking processes he'd been much better. Or so she'd thought, but a stuff-up wasn't impossible when it came to Foster. Just last month he'd missed recording a second test result that would have set them back months. Julia had been happy with his work since but perhaps Margaret had discovered something.

Julia frowned at her phone. She didn't think Margaret would call her in just to talk about him. Anyway, he'd been given tidying-up tasks the last few weeks, nothing he could stuff up. Now that she thought about it, they'd all been so focused on their final write-ups and clean-outs she'd only seen her boss in passing the last few days. Margaret had either been holed up in her office or out of the department altogether. Julia peered at the text, trying to read between the lines. Her gaze lingered on the word "spoil". Why would Margaret think a late-night text would spoil her birthday? Surely she meant interrupt. Julia knew there was no point replying or ringing. Margaret turned her phone off between the hours of eleven pm and six am.

Julia did a mental scan of their current situation. Money was short but it always was. Last year the funding for their original research on immune responses had dried up just as Covid-19 hit. The damn virus had saved them. Money had been thrown their way to use their research to explore those immune responses to Covid-19 infection. Perhaps they'd have to pare back staff now that they were going back to their original research.

Julia glanced at the clock again. Only forty-five minutes to go. It couldn't be something bad if it didn't happen on her birthday.

four

Lucy slid the dress up her body, over her arms and onto her shoulders. The satin lining slithered softly across her bare skin sending a shiver down her spine. She tugged the hem down and reached behind to catch the zip. It wouldn't come all the way up but it didn't matter. She smoothed the jade lace of the outer layer over her hips and stomach, and stood side on to take in her profile then twisted her head from side to side to inspect her hair. The hairdresser had done a good job. Lucy's hair was thick and hard to manage. Moira had tamed it, even if just for a while.

She glanced at the digital clock by the bed. It was nearly time to collect the kids. She undid the zip, stepped out of the dress and hung it back on its hanger, knowing it wouldn't get the same careful treatment later tonight when Alec took it off. It had been a lucky find at the op shop in the main street, one of several good buys she'd found there since they'd moved to Wallaby Bay.

Lucy cast a critical eye around the spotless house as she passed through the rooms and took her keys from the kitchen bench. They'd been lucky to get this place. It was small and basic but she liked it and the rent was cheap. Mr Flavel, who owned it, planned to knock it down one day so he didn't want to spend money on it, although he was happy to pay for any minor fixes they did themselves to keep it liveable. Lucy already had a list of repairs for Alec to tackle while he was home. A fizz of excitement bubbled in her chest as she picked up her bag and keys. He'd be here tonight.

The kids were staying with their grandparents overnight. Their bags were already packed and in the car. She was delivering them straight from school. Alec's parents always offered to have the children on the first night of his return home.

Kon and Helen Nicoli were the main reason she'd agreed to move with the children to the town where Alec had grown up. The move had been so Alec's parents could support her when he was away but as it turned out she was being just as much help to them. His parents had run a fish and chip shop down by the jetty for years. They'd retired last year, just before Lucy and the children had moved and before Helen's diagnosis of rheumatoid arthritis. Then there'd been Kon's hip replacement and, more recently, cataract surgery. Lucy didn't like to add to their load by leaving the children with them for any length of time but they both insisted. They were the kids' only grandparents and their mutual adoration was great to see but Lucy had to keep a balance for normalcy. Helen and Kon would turn her children into spoilt brats if she let them have too much access. And she was determined never to burden people with her children even if they were family. Noah and Poppy were her responsibility – a role she cherished yet was often weighed down by.

She was later than usual arriving for school pick-up and all the close parking spots were taken. She'd hoped to slip in to wait outside Poppy's classroom but instead had to walk from the other side of the schoolyard past groups of parents gathered in little clutches outside rooms.

She liked Wallaby Bay, loved their rental house just over the sandhills from the beach, but she hadn't managed to make many friends since they'd moved and the school drop-off always left her feeling like a bug under a microscope. She'd thought after almost six months she'd have blended in but obviously not, by the way the group of women waiting outside Poppy's classroom were looking at her. She smiled. They smiled back and turned away. A few of the mums from Noah's class had been welcoming and the staff were great, but this group of women kept her firmly at arm's length.

The siren blasted and the classroom door burst open. Lucy caught sight of Poppy's tousled curls in the gaggle of children who surged out. Her daughter had her dad's curls but they were Lucy's blonde, while Noah's hair was dark brown like Alec's but thick and straight like Lucy's.

"Mummy, Mummy, can Jaylene come and play at our house?" Poppy flung an arm around Lucy's leg, her backpack dragging on the ground beside her.

"Not this time." Lucy smiled at the little girl who was two steps behind Poppy. They'd only just started having play dates. Jaylene was the youngest with three much older siblings. She and Poppy got on very well. Sadly, Lucy didn't feel the same enchantment for Jaylene's mother, who was eyeballing her from the other side of the lockers.

"Ohh!" Poppy wailed.

"You're going to Pappouli and Yiayia's house, remember?"

Poppy gasped. "Oh yes!" She turned back to Jaylene. "I'm sorry, I can't play today."

Jaylene's big round eyes narrowed briefly, heightening her resemblance to her mother. "Okay." She stuck her thumb in her mouth and turned away.

"Hey, Mum." Noah rushed up beside her. "Why is your hair like that?"

Lucy put a hand to her head and brushed the gold-and-pearl clasp Moira had slipped into the side of the updo. She'd forgotten about her hair and the make-up she'd applied just before she'd tried the dress. Wearing jeans and one of Alec's daggy jumpers, she no doubt looked a bit overdone for school pick-up.

"I've got a dinner date and you're going to your grandparents' place."

She felt Noah study her as they made their way back across the schoolyard. She opened the car door. He stopped beside it, staring up at her.

"Dad's coming home, isn't he?" he said.

"Daddy! Daddy!" Poppy screamed as if Alec had suddenly appeared.

"He gets in late. You'll be asleep at Yiayia's," Lucy said as she fought to buckle her squirming daughter into her seat. "You know he'll be home for two weeks."

"I'll be at school."

"Dad will pick you up tomorrow. Then you'll have the whole weekend together."

"Yay!" Poppy screamed.

"Poppy!" Lucy snapped. "That's too loud in Mummy's ear."

A set of soft arms slipped around her neck as she finally managed to click the seatbelt into place. "Sorry, Mummy."

Lucy felt an instant pang of guilt. She was eager to drop off her children so she could go home and prepare for Alec's arrival. Noah's large brown eyes were locked on her across the seat but he said nothing. Lucy extricated herself from Poppy's sticky clutches and glanced down.

"What's that green stuff on your hands?"

"We made slime." Poppy held up her hands for Lucy to see.

Lucy lurched back. "You'd better wash your hands as soon as you get to Yiayia's."

Poppy chattered all the way to her grandparents' marina home, full of what she'd been doing all day. Both children had settled well into their new school and were happy there. Lucy pulled into the driveway and glanced at Noah in the rear-view mirror. He was looking out the window now, his silence a heavy weight on her heart.

The front door of the house flung open and Kon loped across the short space to the car before Lucy had time to stop the engine. He opened Noah's door.

"Hey, mate, how was your day? Guess what I've got for us?"

"What is it, Pappouli?" Poppy cried, undoing her seatbelt in far less time than it had taken Lucy to do it up.

"This is just for the men, my little Poppy, but your yiayia has something special for you inside too."

Poppy barely kissed Lucy goodbye in her rush to get inside but Noah didn't undo his seatbelt.

Kon looked at Lucy and raised his eyebrows as she walked around the car.

"Noah knows his dad's coming home tonight but I've told him Alec will be very late."

Kon patted her shoulder and took Poppy's backpack and the overnight bag from the back seat. "Your dad is going to be so jealous," Kon said as he walked back to Noah's side of the car. "He always wanted a remote-control boat. You and I will master it, then on the weekend you can show him how it works, hey?"

Lucy met Kon's gaze over the open door of the car. There was a brief pause then Noah climbed out.

"Okay."

Lucy bent down, squeezed him in a hug and planted a kiss on his cheek. "Be good and—"

"Look after Poppy, I know, Mum."

He hefted his school bag onto his back and went inside.

"They'll be fine, Lucy."

"I know," she murmured. The guilt of farming out her children battled with the blissful anticipation of having her husband to herself for twenty-four hours. She had to remind herself they were staying with their grandparents and she wasn't going to be at work. If they needed her, she could be there in a flash.

Kon patted her shoulder, which was nearly her undoing.

"Helen's been cooking all day," he said. "We'll catch up with you on the weekend so you can help us eat some of the mountain of food she's made."

"Thanks, Kon. Ring me if you need."

"We won't need."

Lucy glanced towards the door, the guilt stabbing harder.

"Say hello to our boy when he gets in but don't worry about anything else. You enjoy yourselves." Kon winked. "Now get going. We'll see you on the weekend."

Lucy reversed the car from the drive and headed back towards town. She had one more stop to make. She wanted a bottle of wine to go with the steak she was cooking for dinner. Noah's hangdog look stayed with her until she reached the drive-through bottle shop. She hated bottle shops, never knew what to pick. Alec was the one who usually bought any drinks but there was nothing left from his last trip home.

The guy behind the counter gave her an appraising look as she got out of her car. She was once more conscious that her hair and make-up looked over the top with her sloppy jumper and jeans. She gave him a brief smile. "I'm looking for red wine."

"Plenty here, love." He waved a hand towards the back wall.

Lucy spent several minutes picking out bottles, reading the labels, putting them back. Other customers came and went, then a bottle of wine appeared in front of her.

"If you're looking for shiraz, the local winery makes a decent drop."

Lucy glanced around. The older woman who'd come into the hairdressers earlier and wanted to know the reason for her special hairdo was waving a bottle of wine at her. Lucy glanced away from the woman's piercing look. The label on the bottle had an outline of Yorke Peninsula on it.

"I don't think I'll get shiraz." Aware her voice had come out sharply, she added, "But thank you."

"Clare Valley's the next closest and they make some good reds." The woman was not to be deterred.

Lucy had been desperately trying to remember the type of wine Alec had bought last time he was home. They'd both enjoyed it. "I'm looking for a temperkeno."

She winced as the woman frowned. It wasn't the right name but it had started with temp and rhymed with dough. They'd giggled over how hard it was to say once they'd finished the bottle.

"Do you mean tempranillo?" The woman pointed to a higher shelf. "There are several here that were grown and produced in the Clare Valley. I always like to support local if I can."

Lucy examined the different labels. None of them looked the same as the one Alec had bought but who knew where that had come from? She plucked the cheapest one from the shelf.

"Are you a local or a tourist?" The woman was studying her closely now.

"Neither," Lucy said and took a step away.

"Fair enough."

Once more Lucy regretted her churlish response. "My partner grew up here."

The woman's sharp gaze drilled deeper. "Who's that?"

"Alec Nicoli."

"Oh yes, I'd heard he'd moved back to town. You're living in the Flavels' beach shack, aren't you?"

"Yes." Lucy took another small step away.

"Moira did a great job with your hair. It looks very pretty." The woman's eyes sparkled suddenly and her lips turned up but revealed clenched teeth so her smile was more like a grimace. "I'm Eve Monk. I live out along the coast a bit further than you. I've known Kon and Helen since they opened the shop. I knew Alec and his brothers too, of course, but I haven't seen them since they were at school. The older two live interstate, don't they?"

"Yes."

Eve raised her arm, winced and lowered it to her side again. "You've got some little ones, haven't you? When I last saw Helen she was so excited to have you move close. How's she managing with the arthritis? Dreadful disease. Such a shame." Eve paused. "Sorry, I didn't catch your name."

"Lucy."

"Welcome to Wallaby Bay, Lucy."

"Thanks."

"Only we have so many strangers pass through our community, being that we have such a beautiful beach. It's always nice to know who the blow-throughs are and who's a local."

Lucy nodded again.

"Anyway, I'd best be off. Nice to meet you. Hope you enjoy the tempranillo. I'm a shiraz gal myself." Eve plucked another bottle from the shelf. "But one of my guests likes pinot noir so that's what I've come for. Enjoy your night."

"Thanks, you too," Lucy said but Eve was already striding away. Lucy turned back to the shelves. Thank goodness. The thing she hated most about living here was how everyone wanted to know who you were and how you were connected to the town. If Lucy had a dollar for every time she'd been described as Kon and Helen's daughter-in-law she'd be a rich woman. She was pigeonholed by who she was connected to, not who she was.

She rolled her shoulders and kept studying the shelves. She also needed some red to make the jus for the steak and it would give Eve a chance to pay and leave before she got to the counter. Who knew what other questions she'd ask if they were lined up side by side at the check-out?

Lucy picked out a bottle of merlot. The label described raspberry flavours with a super smooth finish. It sounded delicious. She glanced behind her. There was no-one waiting at the counter. She took her two bottles and paid.

Later that night they were curled up on the couch, Lucy's head nestled against Alec's chest listening to the reassuring thud of his heart. They'd only had one glass of the tempranillo before he'd eased her out of her dress and they'd taken to the bed. It was always like that the first night he was home. They missed each other so much and sex was one of the first ways to reconnect. Then she'd cooked the steak, they'd eaten it and finished the red, filling each other in on everything that had happened over the three weeks since Alec had been home last. They'd cleaned up the kitchen together and now, sated with food, wine and sex, they were both too lazy to go to bed.

Lucy was drifting in a sleepy stupor and startled when her phone pinged. She groped around on the floor, found it and checked her messages. "Fred's offering me a cleaning shift tomorrow morning at the motel."

"But it's my first day home."

She twisted to look up at Alec. "It's only a few hours and there're a couple of things need fixing here. You can work on them while I'm gone."

He groaned.

"Fred knew you'd be home, that's why he's asking. He knows I don't like to work early shifts when you're not here for the kids."

"Go for it."

She sent a quick reply and put her phone back on the floor.

"I've been offered work on a new project," Alec said.

"I told you something would come up." She gave him a gentle poke in the ribs. He'd been worrying because his current job was nearly finished and he hadn't found anything to replace it.

"It's offshore and a lot further away than where I am now."

Lucy sighed. That would mean travel time would eat into his off time. "I guess you have to go where the work is." They'd made the decision not long after Poppy was born that Alec would take on FIFO work while the kids were little. Lucy had stayed home with them full-time until last year when she'd gone back to nursing part-time. That had been a disaster so they'd decided to stick with the plan of Alec working away for a bit longer. Only trouble was, the work had started out closer to home when Poppy was a baby, but these days it was all in remote WA.

"They're offering family quarters at the nearest place I'd be flying in and out of."

She sat up. "Where?"

He grimaced. "Port Headland."

Lucy lurched up straighter and slipped off the couch, a worn mat the only thing between her and the wooden floor. "Bugger!" She rubbed at her butt and stood up. "The kids have only just settled into school here. I'm not moving them again."

Alec swung his legs to the floor. "But if I take the job, I'll have even less time at home. At least I'd see more of you and the kids if you moved to Port Headland."

"You'd still be gone weeks at a time and what would we do then? Stuck up there, not knowing anyone. It was bad enough moving to Wallaby Bay but at least your parents are here. Up there we'd have no-one."

He slumped back against the couch. "I know. I just hoped …"

"You won't have to do it forever, Alec. Once we've got a bit more behind us, we can get our own place, and I'll get more permanent work eventually …" Lucy bent to collect their empty wine glasses so she didn't have to look at the question on his face. "It's late; we should go to bed." She rinsed the glasses and sat them in the drainer with the rest of their dinner dishes. Then remembered she hadn't rinsed the blender. Alec being home had distracted her. She filled it with water and pressed the start button.

She jumped as a pair of arms slipped around her waist. She hadn't heard Alec move over the noise of the machine.

"Sometimes I think you love that Thermomix more than me," he mumbled in her ear.

She stiffened and pressed the stop button. "You didn't mind the red wine jus I made with it for your steak."

His lips trailed down the back of her neck. "It was delicious like you," he murmured.

A tingle rippled down her spine, her momentary angst over the blender forgotten.

The kisses stopped and Alec pulled back. "You've got green stuff on your neck."

She lifted her hand and felt something dry under her fingers. Then she remembered Poppy's sticky hug. "I suspect it's slime." She turned in the warm cocoon of his arms.

"I think we should take a shower and wash that off." His lips tugged gently at her earlobe.

Lucy thought about the small shower cubicle with its mismatched tiles and low water pressure. "I've got an early start, Alec."

"I won't keep you up late." He grinned and slipped his t-shirt over his head before he took her by the hand and towed her to the bathroom. She'd be tired tomorrow but the smouldering look he gave her blew any practical thoughts clear away.

five

It was a chill wind that blew Julia to work Friday morning. There'd been no time to put up her umbrella against the sharp shower that sent pedestrians scurrying as she stepped away from the tram shelter. It was over before she'd made the other side of the road but it had been enough to dampen her coat and frizz the swirl of fringe that poked from her knitted hat. She lowered her head into the wind and hurried the block and a half to her building.

Inside, the heating was cranked up and she tugged off her hat, releasing her thick curls. They were springier than ever in the damp air, and she dragged them back from her face as she crossed the tile and glass foyer towards the lift, stripping off her coat.

By the fifth floor she was alone in the lift, and when she stepped out the corridor was empty. She paused as the lift door hissed shut behind her. For a floor that normally housed at least fifteen occupants it was eerily quiet when no-one else was around. She continued to the little kitchen, made herself a coffee and went on out across the corridor. She planned to collect her notebook and have a quick look around the lab before she met Margaret.

She lifted her swipe card to enter the lab and startled at a voice behind her.

"You're here, good. Come on down to my office."

Julia blew out a breath and turned enough to see her boss at the other end of the corridor. "Good morning, Margaret," she said brightly. "Awful day outside ..."

Margaret had already disappeared back into her office. For an over seventy-year-old who walked with the aid of a stick, Julia always marvelled at the speed with which Margaret could move. Julia felt the dull ache down her left leg that sometimes bothered her on cold days – some occasional stiffness and a slightly lopsided gait were the legacy of an accident twenty years ago. Maybe she'd need a stick by the time she was Margaret's age. Julia grinned and imagined using it to poke annoying research assistants.

"What's happening?" she asked as she entered the cupboard-sized room Margaret claimed as an office. In her capacity as head of their research team, Professor Margaret Crouch was the only one to have her own space. Julia eased herself onto the one vacant chair, her knees jammed against the back of a filing cabinet, and lifted her gaze to meet Margaret's.

Her boss's grey hair was swept away from her face into its usual low chignon clasped at the base of her neck. She never wore make-up unless there was a formal event, like a fundraising dinner or a presentation evening. Some days she looked anaemic, no doubt due to years of indoor work under artificial lighting, but this morning, sitting rigidly upright, her hands clasped in front of her, she was so pale she was almost ghostlike.

"We need to talk." She moistened her lips with her tongue.

A small wiggle of fear wormed its way to the pit of Julia's stomach. "About?"

"It's not good news, I'm afraid." Margaret cleared her throat. "There's been a huge funding cut and—"

"No!" Julia shoved back her chair and leaped up, knocking her knee against the filing cabinet as she stood. She groaned at the pain but her eyes were still locked on Margaret's lips as if she could still the words she didn't want to hear.

"Our research has been canned."

"No." Julia slipped back to the chair, her hand around her throbbing knee.

"I'm so sorry." Margaret's face was not only pale, there were mottled shadows beneath her eyes.

Julia swallowed her shock, reached a hand across the desk and gripped Margaret's, still clasped together on the desktop. "This was your baby, Margaret. You must be … how … when did you find out?"

Margaret acknowledged the sentiment with the slightest of nods then slipped her hands to her lap. "Seven o'clock Wednesday night. I was called to a meeting."

Julia slid her own hand back. That was as close to emotional contact as either of them would muster. "I'd heard a few whispers but …"

"I knew there'd be cuts but I didn't think it would be us, not when we're so close."

"Can't we fight it?"

"I spent all day yesterday on the phone and meeting with people. It's done and dusted. There's been a shift of focus, a major restructure, and we're a by-product. But at least our research will continue. The university will take over the whole project. I've been told to pack everyone up next week."

Julia sucked in her cheeks, clasping the warm skin between her teeth. It was her equivalent of a stiff upper lip. She'd developed the skill after her first lambasting by a misogynistic science professor during her first year at uni. It had served its purpose then and many times since. She never gave in to tears and the lump that formed in her throat served as a platform to keep her voice steady.

"You're sure there's nothing more that—"

"Nothing." The resignation on Margaret's face left no doubt she'd tried. "I was hoping you'd help me tell the team."

"Of course. Will the uni need some of our people?"

"Possibly."

For a moment the lump in Julia's throat mellowed in a glimmer of hope. The previous year, their work on tuberculosis, HIV and immune response had been redirected to include the immunopathology of Covid-19, but if they could go back to their original focus … "That's a positive."

"If you're prepared to move to Queensland."

Julia groaned. She'd become so used to meetings via Zoom she'd momentarily forgotten their collaborators were two states away.

"I'm fairly sure they'll want some of the team but you and I are top-heavy to their requirements."

Julia thumped the desk and swore.

"I've already done a fair bit of that … ever since they told me."

"You should have rung me. A problem shared."

"It was your birthday. There was nothing more you could have done anyway."

"Hell!" Julia put her head in her hands. She thought of Geraldine, her young family and the large mortgage they'd just taken on, and two of the men on their team who were the sole breadwinners for their families. Research was always a risky business, not well paid – you did it for the love not the money. Usually you looked for a new job when you could see the current one was drawing to a close but this was so sudden. "This will be a financial blow as well as a research one."

"Some of the younger ones have got families who might tide them over but the rest of us … unless you've got a benefactor to support you, you'll need work, and sooner rather than later. I've been doing my best to find possibilities for them."

Margaret's gaze shifted to the folders on her desk. Julia pondered their future. She'd be able to find research work, perhaps not what she'd been working on for the last four years but her credentials were good. Margaret's were excellent, but she'd invested so much time into their current research she'd narrowed her options.

"You'll get something too," Julia said.

"We both know no-one's going to want an ageing head of department who hasn't kept up with the technology. If the truth be told, I'm looking forward to a change. I'm fed up with constantly begging for money."

Julia shook her head. "But it's so sudden."

"We would have been shut down a year ago if it hadn't been for Covid-19. It saved us for a while. Now that there are bigger players focused on the immune response aspect, our team is no longer required. I'd hoped we had garnered enough interest in our original research over that time, at least to get some more funding and we could go back to the way things were pre-Covid."

"Except we can't and we're not. We've been usurped." Julia thrust back into her chair. "It's not bloody fair."

Margaret looked at the laptop screen in front of her. "I've just had an email about taking some of our supplies off our hands."

"Let me guess. Bill Russell."

"Correct first try."

"Word travels fast. The bloody vultures are circling already."

Lucy opened the door to room five, her last for the morning, and clamped a hand to her mouth. She cast a quick look around the small motel room to check there wasn't a dead body before stepping back out into the cool air and taking a deep breath. According to her cleaning sheet, the occupant of the room had vacated in the early hours and yet the room still stank of bad body odour and vomit.

She took the can of Glen 20 from her trolley, sucked in a deep breath and sprayed the room, then after another gasp of fresh air she opened all the windows and went back outside. Thankfully there'd been no sign of actual vomit but in her quick dash to wrench open the bathroom window she'd caught sight of the toilet and bile had risen in her throat. She gasped in more fresh air, sank to her haunches and pressed her back against the brick wall.

In the short time she'd been cleaning motel rooms she'd come across some gut-turning sights and putrid smells that had rivalled what she'd seen in years of nursing. Mostly she enjoyed the physical labour and the lack of responsibility other than doing a thorough job. And the extra bit of income meant she could buy groceries and clothes for the kids and more of Alec's money went to savings, which brought them nearer to getting their own place.

A willie wagtail landed nearby and hopped closer, its insistent chatter berating her idleness.

"Okay, boss," she said and got back to her feet. The busy little bird stabbed at a moth with its beak and flew away. Lucy tied a clean cloth around her face, pulled on a fresh pair of gloves and steeled herself to go back into the room.

By the time she'd finished it was clean and fresh again but she felt filthy. The fetid smell had invaded her nostrils and stayed. Thank goodness she could go home and shower. She shuddered as she climbed into her car. Even though she'd worn gloves and washed and scrubbed her hands, unseen grot probably clung to her clothing. She pushed away the thought of it transferring to her car.

Safely back in her own driveway, she made straight for the back of the small holiday shack that was temporarily home. Inside she stripped off and stepped into the bathroom only to find Alec standing in the shower fully clothed. His surprised look changed to a perky grin. In her haste to rid herself of the filth she'd forgotten he was home.

"What are you doing?" They both spoke at once.

"I need a shower," Lucy said.

"No can do, babe. I've turned off the water."

"Why?" Goosebumps prickled her skin and she grabbed a towel and wrapped it around her.

"You wanted me to fix the leaky shower." He stepped out. "The head is so corroded I can't put it back. We need a new one. Now that you're here I'll take the car ... or I could delay." He reached for her but she flinched away. "I'm filthy. How long will you be?"

"Depends if the hardware store has one. I might have to go further, to the plumbing supplier."

"Why did you have to do it now?" Lucy hopped from foot to foot. It wasn't just the cold but an urgency to get clean that built inside her, agitating and gnawing like a living presence. Alec never understood the importance of keeping clean, even after all the chaos of the last year.

"You had it on the list for me to do." His reply was sharp like hers.

She swallowed her annoyance. "I'm sorry. I had a grotty job to do this morning and I felt like a hot shower."

"I could drop you at Mum and Dad's while I'm at the shop."

"No." Lucy was not going to ask his parents for anything more. They already did enough. "I'll be fine." She shivered. Now that she'd stripped and had stopped moving, the cool air was chilling her through.

Alec rubbed her arms. "Get dressed and I'll make you a tea before I go."

"Thanks."

She washed her hands and arms with sanitiser. In the bedroom she pulled on the trackpants and jumper of Alec's she'd worn the day before and made the bed he'd still been in when she'd left earlier that morning.

When she came out he was sitting at the table looking at his phone, two mugs of steaming tea in front of him. She sat opposite him. He put the phone down and passed her one of the mugs.

"Sorry," she said.

"What for?"

"My mini meltdown. The last room I cleaned was disgusting."

"I wish you'd stop doing the cleaning."

"It's good money."

"It seems such a waste when you're a trained nurse. You desperately wanted to get back into it last year when Poppy started kindy. Dug your heels in when I suggested you wait another year."

Lucy glanced at the Thermomix on the counter behind him then swallowed her guilt with a sip of tea. She could never tell him the whole reason for her avoidance. It had been her own selfishness that had pushed her to work earlier and it had gone all wrong. If she couldn't forgive herself she couldn't expect him to.

Alec reached out a hand, perhaps thinking her silence meant she was pondering his suggestion to start nursing again. "I know work's hard to find at the moment," he said. "But if you went back nursing, Mum and Dad are more than happy to help look after Poppy and Noah when I'm not here."

"They've got enough on their plate now without having to juggle children and my roster."

"Noah and Poppy are their only local grandchildren. They don't mind."

"Anyway, it's not that easy. There's a glut of nurses here."

"I didn't know you'd even checked."

"I'm not totally idle when you're not home."

He frowned. "I'd never call you idle, Lou, but it's crazy you working as a cleaner when you're a fully qualified nurse."

"Nurses are plentiful at the moment."

"At least you've made the first step and put your name down."

"I didn't say I'd put my name down. I asked a few questions, that's all." She wrapped her fingers around the mug, absorbing its warmth. "Let's not talk about it. We just go round in circles."

Alec's gaze lingered on her. She could tell he wanted to say more but he swallowed the last of his tea and stood up. "I'll go and get this shower head."

"Don't forget to keep the docket."

She huddled over her tea as he backed out and drove away. Ever since her car had been stolen when they'd been living in Melbourne, they'd decided to stick with one car while he was working FIFO. He flew into Adelaide and caught the bus to Wallaby Bay and usually she and the kids drove him back to Adelaide for the return journey. It was a reassuring routine she'd become used to. Reassurance and routine had become her mantra, her main reason for moving to Wallaby Bay. A shiver ran down her back. Creating security for her family was the only thing that mattered.

She swallowed the last of her tea and stacked the cups in the sink, along with Alec's breakfast dishes. Now that she was warm and had different clothes on, she didn't feel quite so desperate for the shower. She cast a look around her tidy kitchen and smiled when her gaze rested on the glossy green fiddle-leaf fig. Outside there was a gap in the clouds and the plant's tall frame was bathed in a shaft of sunshine.

"You like that spot, don't you, Zig." She took a cloth, gently wiped its leaves then stood back to admire it. "There you are, nice and fresh. Wish I could say the same for me."

Lucy rubbed her hands up and down her arms. She looked in the fridge and tried to distract herself by deciding which of the recipes she'd already shopped for would be their dinner tonight. The ringtone of her phone pulled her up. It was faint, then she remembered it was in her bag in the laundry where she'd dumped everything on her way in.

Her heart skipped a beat when she saw 'School' on the screen.

"Hi, Lucy, it's Harmony from the school. Now please don't panic. Nothing serious."

Harmony's voice was as tuneful as her name and Lucy immediately let out the breath she'd been holding.

"I've got Noah here with me. His teacher has sent him because he says he's not feeling well. He does look a bit flushed."

"I'll be right there."

"Don't rush. He's fine with me until you get here."

"Thanks, Harmony. I won't be long."

As soon as Lucy ended the call, she remembered she didn't have a car. She jabbed at Alec's number then jumped as she heard a low rumble behind her. His phone was vibrating on the table.

"Bugger!" She paced around the room. She'd have to ring his parents. She hated having to ask them for unexpected help. They were good people but they'd see the kids every day if she let them and that was too much. They fed the kids with so many treats they were too full for dinner, bought them toys or whatever took their fancy. Lucy knew Helen thought she was too strict but she had to be both father and mother most of the time and letting the children do whatever they wanted made life difficult.

Kon answered her call immediately. "Yassou, Lucy, we were just talking about you. It's so good to have Alec home. He's having a cuppa. Would you—"

"Is Alec at your place?"

"Yes, he stopped in to get some tools and his mother insisted he eat some of the cake she made for the—"

"Kon, I need to talk to Alec. He left his phone at home."

"Of course."

There was a muffled swishing sound and then Alec's voice. "What's up?"

"It's Noah. Harmony from the school rang to say he's not well. You have to go and pick him up now."

"Really? I haven't been to the hardware shop yet."

"You need to go now, Alec. He's with Harmony at the front office." There was a rustling sound again and muffled voices. Lucy could feel the tightness in her stomach extending up into her chest as if her insides were a marionette puppet being drawn up by strings.

"Mum said he was fine this morning."

Helen probably fed him Froot Loops for breakfast and sent them to school with sweet treats in their lunch boxes. And now Alec was wasting time at his parents while Noah might actually be coming down with something. Lucy swallowed her annoyance.

"Kids get sick quickly, Alec. Please get him and bring him home to me."

"Okay, okay. I'm sure he's fine but I'll go and pick him up. You'll have to wait a bit longer for your shower."

"Just hurry and get Noah, please." He would have been gone all morning by the time he finished talking with his parents and then went to the shops but she saved herself from spitting that into the phone by ending the call with a jab of her finger.

Eve peered at the sallow face in the mirror. Dark eyes stared back at her. She winced and then turned away from the haggard old woman she'd become. This morning she felt a hundred instead of seventy. The previous evening she'd taken ages to go to sleep. It had been difficult to find a position where her shoulder didn't ache. It didn't feel so bad this morning but she couldn't say as much for the rest of her. She swallowed. The barbed wire still prickled her throat even after two cups of tea and some porridge, and the crick in her neck and slight headache still lingered. Even though common sense told her she'd probably slept heavily in the one position and snored, giving rise to the symptoms she'd woken with, she couldn't go ahead with tonight's dinner.

The chicken could be frozen and she hadn't started on dessert. She glanced at her kitchen clock; it was mid-morning – not too late to cancel. Whatever it was that Spiro and Mary wanted to discuss over dinner could wait. Mary would probably be relieved not to have to come anyway.

Spiro didn't answer her call. She tried Mary's phone. It rang a long time. With a sense of relief Eve waited to leave a message when Mary's voice cut in sharply.

"Hello, Eve."

"Mary, how are you?"

"Fine."

"Looks like a blow coming. I guess Spiro's battening down the hatches."

"He's off somewhere. Why are you ringing? It is tonight we're coming for dinner, isn't it? Spiro reminded me this morning."

Eve was used to Mary's sharp edges but today they cut easily through her resolve. "It was to be but I'm feeling a bit off-colour."

"We shouldn't come then."

"I'm sure it's nothing but best not. I'll reschedule when—"

"I've got another call incoming, Eve. I have to go."

Eve was left holding a silent phone. She'd been determined not to let Mary get under her skin but she was too late. She clicked her tongue. Some days it was difficult to cope with the knowledge that Spiro, her business partner and friend, had married a woman who disliked her so much. Eve had lived her life reluctant to use the word hate but these days she was more realistic. She was sure hate was a better word for the way Mary felt about her.

"Damn!" She marched across her kitchen and scrubbed the one cup and plate she'd used at breakfast. She'd learned a long time ago to banish self-pity from her life and had mastered the art of not letting Mary one-up her, but today she was at a low ebb.

Outside the rattle of a downpipe and the whoosh of trees announced a strengthening wind from the north. In the distance she heard a thud. She hung the tea towel and listened. It came again. Something was loose outside.

Eve had very few maintenance jobs left to be done on her small property. Over the last year since she'd stopped her volunteering and committee involvement, she'd kept herself busy going over every inch of her house. Zac had come from Darwin twice to help her.

First she'd emptied cupboards and then she'd started on the building itself, patching cracks, painting walls. Zac had done the ceilings. She'd gone on to sand and varnish any exposed wood, and even re-tiled the laundry. Outside she'd pulled everything out of the garage and the old boatshed. Zac had been there with his wife and children that time. They'd had a happy week sorting through more than thirty years' worth of accumulation. Eve had only put back what she deemed useful. The rest had been stacked behind the shed, taken for scrap or to the dump once Spiro and her neighbour, Pete, had gone through it for anything they wanted. She'd kept herself so busy there was little left to do.

She lifted her head and listened as the thud came again. Obviously something wasn't right outside. It was times like this she missed her old dog, Merc. He'd been a companionable presence for seventeen years and his loss a year ago had been but one more change in her life that left an empty space she couldn't fill.

Eve went outside and followed the path to the back gate, listening for the sound. It came again, a hollow blow accompanied by a screech of metal. A movement across the yard caught her eye. One of the big wooden doors to the boatshed was shuddering in the wind. She hadn't been in there for weeks but Spiro sometimes used it – perhaps he hadn't latched it properly. The catch was difficult to put back in place. She headed towards it.

The boatshed had been a barn. It was made of stone and was as old as the house. It had been a part of the original farming property when Eve and Rex had bought their subdivided portion thirty-five years ago. Rex had done up the old shed with its huge doors and high roof line. He'd put down a cement floor and used

it for boats, nets, motors and everything in between that went
with commercial fishing. There were no boats now but Spiro still
used it to store nets, flat packed prawn boxes, preservatives and
other gear they needed for the business.

Eve reached the door just as it flung back. Leaves and debris
whirled on a strong gust that propelled the giant door against her
shoulder. The force of it and the accompanying burst of pain sent
her stumbling backwards. She clutched her arm then sank to her
knees as her usually strong legs turned to jelly. Nausea pushed up
her throat and erupted as a scream. The sound was lost in the roar
of the wind and the clanging of the giant door.

six

Lucy had barely brought the car to a stop before Poppy leaped out and ran for the back door shouting, "Daddy, Daddy!"

"Slow down, Poppy," she called but she was wasting her breath. If Noah was resting again, he wouldn't be for long with all her noise.

When Alec had brought Noah home from school, they'd come into the house laughing and joking. Noah's temp had been up a little and he'd looked flushed so she'd made him go to bed in spite of his protests. By the time she'd allowed him to get up and eat a late lunch, his temp was back to normal. He'd said he was feeling better but he only picked at his sandwich and she'd sent him back to bed. He'd objected but when she'd stuck her head in last, he'd been absorbed in the latest Weirdo book. Alec had fixed the shower and was working on the loose hinges of the front screen door. With him home she'd been reassured enough to head to the street to do a few jobs before she picked up Poppy.

She'd just made it to the back door, weighed down with bags of shopping and Poppy's school bag, when the little girl came flying out the door. "Daddy's not here." Her bottom lip wobbled.

"Dad's probably just outside somewhere. I told you Noah's not well, so he's in bed." Lucy propped the screen door with her foot and heaved her load inside. The beach shack was small, only two bedrooms and a kitchen–living area with the wet areas attached across the back. It didn't take her long to find neither Noah nor Alec were inside.

"I'm hungry," Poppy whined.

"Have a banana." Lucy pulled a cloth bag from the shopping.

"No."

"There're apples or some strawberries in the fridge." Lucy unpacked the rest of the groceries.

"I don't want fruit."

"Fine." Lucy wasn't in the mood for Poppy's tantrums. She was wondering where Alec and Noah were. Had Noah got worse and Alec found a ride to the doctors? Surely he'd have rung her.

"There they are!" Poppy called. She was kneeling up on the window seat pointing towards the beach. While the shack was basic it was in an excellent position, only one house back from the beach on a side road and built at an angle across the block. Apart from the large pine tree on the front fence line they had almost uninterrupted views to the beach and bay.

Lucy moved to the window beside Poppy. Two figures huddled on a rocky outcrop, one tall, one short, and from their stance they appeared to be fishing. Lucy's poor mood deepened. What was Alec thinking, dragging a sick child out fishing? It was sunny outside now and the earlier strong winds had abated but there was still a stiff breeze across the bay.

"Can I go to the beach too?"

"No."

Poppy wailed her displeasure.

Lucy flicked the kettle on to make herself a cup of tea. "It's getting cold. They'll probably be back very soon." She tried to give her daughter a hug but the little girl pulled away and flopped to her bottom. "How about I whizz up a banana smoothie?"

Poppy straightened up. "Can I have chocolate on top?"

"A little. Empty your school bag and wash your hands first." Poppy shot off to do as she was asked. Lucy felt bad about the bribery but a little sprinkle of Milo on top of the healthy milk drink was a small price to pay for peace.

A while later she and Poppy were on the window seat in the sunshine, sipping their drinks in between Poppy's attempts to read aloud her latest take-home book. Lucy's annoyance at Alec had abated a little as she enjoyed some one-on-one time with her daughter, playing with her soft curls turned golden by the afternoon light. The concentration on Poppy's little face as she sounded out a word was so cute and then a confident nod would follow as she said it. Poppy had grown up fast now that she'd started school. So different to the frightened little girl she'd been the previous year.

There was a thud outside the back door and Poppy shot off the seat.

"They're back."

Lucy grabbed the large smoothie glass that teetered after Poppy's rushed departure. Luckily it was nearly empty. She swallowed the last of her tea then followed her daughter outside. Alec was scooping Poppy into a hug and Noah was putting the fishing rods away.

Lucy shivered in the cool air after the warmth of the window seat. She wrapped her arms around herself and leaned on the door frame. Alec met her gaze over Poppy's head.

"Noah brightened up and the tide was right so we thought we'd chuck in a line."

Lucy shook her head. "He shouldn't be out in the cold."

"He's fine," Alec said.

"We've got enough fish for tea, Mum." Noah held the bucket up triumphantly.

"And we all love fish for tea, don't we, Popsicle." Alec put Poppy back on the ground and she squealed in delight as he tickled her. The three of them laughed then turned as one to look at Lucy. She knew she'd lost this time.

"I'd better peel some potatoes to make chips then," she said and with one last querying look at Alec she retreated inside. The casserole she'd started could wait until tomorrow.

Eve swallowed her nausea as the doctor prodded at her shoulder. After getting back to the house she'd sat and hoped the pain would go away but it hadn't so she'd tried to lie down and that had been agony. Admitting to herself she might need a medical opinion, she'd rung the surgery and managed to get an appointment with her doctor for late in the day. Driving herself there had been the difficulty. Now the pain was so intense she could hardly keep from moaning.

"I suspect you've torn your rotator cuff," Ryka said.

Ryka Sandeep had been Eve's doctor for several years. Eve liked the woman for her thorough, matter-of-fact manner on the rare occasions she needed to see a doctor.

"That sounds serious."

"And your blood pressure is higher than usual." Ryka had insisted on giving Eve a full once-over before she looked at her shoulder. "That's probably because you're in pain. I'll write you a script for that."

"I don't need painkillers."

"I'm not forcing you to take them but it will take a while to get a specialist appointment."

"A specialist?"

"We won't know until you've had tests but given your lack of arm movement and the amount of pain you're experiencing, I would expect you're going to need surgery."

"Now?"

"Oh no. It's elective but I don't think you'll get better without it."

"Are you sure surgery is necessary?"

Ryka sat back in her chair. The direct look in her dark brown eyes softened. "You shouldn't be worried about having the surgery, Eve. The end result will be much better than living with it as it is. But, before we get ahead of ourselves, I'll organise some tests and a referral to an orthopaedic specialist." She began typing at her computer. "Do you have a preference?"

"Preference?"

"For a specialist?"

Eve shook her head. "I've never had trouble with my shoulder before." Even as she said it she realised that wasn't quite true. She'd injured her shoulder after Rex had died. She'd done a lot of manual labour in those days, proving she was up to as much physical work as the men. Some physio and heat packs had eventually fixed it, but that shoulder had always been her weak spot. Spiro had convinced her there were other roles for her that were just as important in their partnership. That had been a long time ago.

"Jock Campbell consults at the health centre," Ryka said. "He's as good as any."

"Are you sure it won't just come good with physio?" Eve leaned back in the upright chair and the sharpness of the pain made her gasp.

Ryka raised her eyebrows as she handed over a script. "Get the script filled. Strapping the arm will help, one of the nurses can do it for you, but you'll need stronger painkillers than paracetamol in the interim." She stood up. "Jock will want some imaging done before he sees you. His receptionist will be in touch once he has the referral. We'll let him be the one to decide if surgery is necessary or not."

By the time Eve was being ushered out by Ryka her head was in a spin. How was she going to manage everyday tasks, housework, shopping, even dressing herself? And if she had surgery that would be a few weeks of invalidity. Her heart thudded loudly in her chest. She swallowed, trying to moisten her dry mouth. It was a rare feeling for Eve but she recognised that strange sensation that was alarm building inside her. She had lived her life never having to rely on anyone. It irked her to ask for help.

She was so caught up in her thoughts it took her a while to refocus and sort the payment. Once that was done she turned away from the counter and almost bumped into a woman coming in the door.

"Hello, Eve." Norma Banks swept her beady gaze over Eve.

Eve tried to pull herself up straighter. "Norma."

"I heard you weren't well."

"Nothing to worry about," Eve said grandly and glanced around, looking for Audrey. The two were rarely apart. How unlucky to run into her again so soon.

"I saw Mary at the supermarket." Norma waited to see if Eve would elaborate. She didn't. "Anyway she mentioned you'd cancelled dinner. I hope it's not the flu." Norma took a small step back. "I've had my injection of course but there're no guarantees and we don't want—"

"Mrs Monk?" The nurse saved Eve from further grilling. "You can come through now."

"Oh, you need the nurse." Norma peered around Eve. "And it's Jess, isn't it? I heard you'd moved back to town, and a new bub on the way by the looks of it. Isn't IVF wonderful?"

Jess's face went pink from her cheeks to the top of her forehead and she turned to lead the way to the treatment room.

Eve gave Norma a brief nod and followed.

"You take care, Eve," the woman called after her. "Get well soon."

Eve gritted her teeth. Of all people to meet. She should have just told Norma she'd hurt her shoulder. There'd be another much juicier story circulating around town about her before she knew it. She'd have Covid-19 by dinner time.

Eve shook off thoughts of Norma then gasped as her arm brushed the door frame on the way into the treatment room. That's if she could stomach the chicken roll she'd kept for her dinner. The scratchy throat and headache had long gone but the nagging pain from her shoulder made her feel mildly nauseous. She might have to fill Ryka's script after all.

Jess's colour was returning to normal by the time they settled in the treatment room and she gave Eve an encouraging smile.

Eve smiled back. She recognised the young woman now. She'd grown up in Wallaby Bay and had been in either Arlo or Zac's circle of acquaintances.

"How's Zac?" Jess said. "I haven't seen him for several years. Is he still in Darwin?"

Zac's age then. Eve nodded. "It's nice to see you again, Jess. Are you back for a while?"

"Yes, my husband's a builder. An opportunity came up for us to move here and ..." She put a hand to her baby bulge. "I'd like to be closer to Mum and Dad."

"Family can be a great help."

"Doctor says you need a sling?"

"I've given my shoulder a bit of a bump."

"More than a bit, by the way you're holding it. I'll try to be as careful as I can."

A short time later Eve's arm was neatly strapped to her body and the pain had settled to a dull ache.

"This is only to help keep you comfortable while you're moving around. You shouldn't keep it on all the time. Do you have someone at home who can help you, Mrs Monk?"

"I live alone."

"How will you manage? I assume you're right-handed?"

Eve sighed. "It won't be easy but I'm sure I'll be fine. I've done for myself for a long time."

"The simplest of tasks can be difficult with a damaged rotator cuff. I can organise some home help for you."

Eve stood up. "That won't be necessary. Thank you for this though."

Jess glanced at her watch. "You've missed the chemist now."

"I'll fill the script tomorrow."

Jess opened the door then paused. "How did you get here?"

"I drove." It was out before Eve thought about it.

"You really shouldn't be driving."

"I'll be fine, Jess. Thank you for this." Eve indicated the sling.

"I hope you feel better soon."

Outside the doctor's surgery the sun was low in the sky and a chilly wind blew along the street from the sea. Eve got herself back into her car then took a moment to rest and let the pain settle again. She looked at the gear stick. She hadn't told Jess her car was manual. It had been difficult to drive herself to the surgery but she'd managed to hold the wheel steady by pressing her legs up against it when she needed to change gears.

Eve took a breath and fiddled with the keys. It was so awkward trying to do it with her left hand. They slipped from her grasp and she slapped the wheel in frustration as they hit the floor.

"Damn!" Eve swivelled, felt around for her keys then she tried again. The key slid into place.

A few minutes later she was stopped on the side of the road, watching in her side mirror as a tall policeman approached. What on earth did he want? She'd just turned onto the road leading up the hill to her house when she'd heard the whoop of a siren behind her. She'd glanced in her rear-view mirror to see the flash of the police car's lights and had pulled over.

With her left hand she managed to reach across and wind down the window.

"Hello, officer." Once upon a time she'd known all the local police but these days their station was in the next town and there'd been so many changes. This young man was a stranger. He studied her with a steely look but Eve was not one to be intimidated. He looked young enough to be her grandson. She smiled sweetly. "What can I do for you?"

"Do you have your driver's licence?" he said.

She took her phone from her bag, juggled it in her left hand as she selected the app with the fingers of her right and stabbed in the PIN. Eve startled as another officer, a woman this time, moved up the other side of her car, inspecting it closely. The policeman handed back her phone as the woman walked around the front of the car and placed a hand reverently on the bonnet.

"I'd like you to do a breath test, please." The man-boy at her window held out a large yellow machine.

"I haven't had a drop to drink," Eve defended herself.

"You were driving erratically."

"Might have something to do with that sling, Troy." The woman had come up beside him and waved a hand towards Eve's shoulder. "It is you, isn't it, Mrs Monk? I recognised the car."

Eve stared as the officer leaned down and lifted her sunglasses onto her head.

"Lisa? Lisa Green?"

"That's me. Only it's Lisa Thomas now."

"I haven't seen you since ..."

"The night I drank too much and threw up all over your front verandah." Lisa chuckled.

"I was going to say since you left school."

"That's so sweet." Lisa patted the door frame. "I'm amazed you still have the Torana. She's in good nick, although the two back tyres are showing a bit of wear."

"Tyres are booked to be changed next service,' Eve said. "I've got a good mechanic looking after her for me."

Troy cleared his throat, the breath test kit still in his hand.

"I don't think we'll need that," Lisa said.

"But—"

Lisa waved a hand at him and turned back to Eve. "What did you do to your shoulder?"

"Torn rotator cuff."

Lisa leaned in, glancing around the interior. "And this old girl is a manual with no power steering. Might explain why you took that last corner erratically."

"You shouldn't be driving if you're injured," Troy said sternly.

Eve's heart skipped a beat. She wouldn't be able to survive if they stopped her driving. "I didn't realise there was a law against driving with your arm in a sling."

"There's not," Lisa said.

Troy's young brow creased. "But if you can't drive safely, you're a danger to yourself and other road users."

"That's right, constable," Lisa said.

A vehicle came down the hill, slowing as it drew closer. Eve didn't recognise the car. She closed her eyes and hoped it was tourists or there'd be more gossip spread about her and she hadn't even made it home yet.

"I should get myself off," she said.

"You can't drive," Troy said.

"We've established there's no law against driving with my arm in a sling." Eve huffed. "You surely don't expect me to walk."

Troy straightened. He was a good head taller than Lisa and she was close to six foot. "Driving a motor vehicle requires you to be in control of your vehicle at all times."

"I am in control."

"I tell you what, constable." Lisa patted the car again. "How about I drive Mrs Monk home?"

Eve frowned. "That's not necess—"

"I don't think—" Troy spoke at the same time.

"That way we know she'll be safe, along with everyone else." Lisa looked at Troy, who still hadn't put away the breath test kit, then at Eve. "And I'm sure she'll agree to not drive again until her arm is better."

Eve opened her mouth but closed it at Lisa's wink.

"I suppose that would work," he said.

"Great." Lisa opened the door and reluctantly Eve got out.

Once they were both settled, Lisa wound up the window.

"Hell, that's hard work. No wonder you've wrecked your shoulder."

"It's not wrecked."

Lisa continued winding. "Long time since I've wound a window."

"What about driving a manual?"

"Oh yes. I can still do that." Lisa lowered her sunglasses to her nose, started the car and moved off up the hill without a falter.

Eve was annoyed. Even Zac bunny hopped the Torana when he hadn't driven it for a while.

"Thanks for agreeing to this, Mrs Monk. Troy hasn't been in the job long. Technically he could have thrown the book at you, as they say. You can be fined for not being in control of your vehicle, you know." Lisa chuckled. "But that would have created a lot of paperwork and wouldn't have done anyone any good, would it? He's still got a bit to learn about community policing."

Eve turned her gaze to the scattering of bush they passed on the side of the road. She hadn't actually agreed to be driven but Lisa had skilfully manoeuvred the situation so that both Eve and the young constable could save face. It was kind of her but Eve wasn't usually so easily manipulated. The shoulder had worn her down. The pain of it nagged at her now. She adjusted her position in the seat.

"You still run Wallaby Bay?"

Eve snorted. "I don't run Wallaby Bay."

"You always knew what was going on when I was a kid. Helped a lot of people, I remember, and kept others on the straight and narrow." Lisa laughed harder as she turned into Eve's driveway. "Reckon that's why the local station closed. No need for a police presence here."

"Things were different when you were a girl." Eve wondered if Lisa meant her comments as a dig or to be kind. It was so hard to gauge behind those dark glasses.

"The region has certainly changed but not the good people in it, I'm glad to say. You were kind to me when I lived here. Having me out for weekends, treating me like family when my own was dysfunctional."

"You were a good mate to Arlo."

"And look at him now. A fancy banker in Singapore. He always did like playing with numbers. Would you like me to put the car in the garage?"

"No, by the gate here is fine." Eve turned to Lisa as the car rolled to a stop. "I assume I can still do what I like on my own property."

"Sure. But perhaps don't drive into town again until you're out of that sling." Lisa lifted her sunglasses again and smiled. "It'd be awful to hear you'd had an accident."

Eve had been about to give the young woman a lecture on how she managed on her own but decided against it. They both got out of the Torana.

"Great to see you again, Mrs Monk," Lisa called over the roof. "Take care."

She waved, climbed into the police vehicle and young Constable Troy drove them away.

"Thunderation!" Eve hissed.

Lisa had as good as told her not to drive again until her shoulder was fit enough. Eve marched around to the driver's side, then stopped. Instead of moving the car to the garage she removed the keys. The ache in her shoulder had become unbearable. She closed her eyes, drew in a long breath then walked as steadily as she could inside. She'd dealt with many things on her own and she wasn't going to let a damaged shoulder or a zealous young constable defeat her.

seven

It was midday and Julia was still in the t-shirt and trackpants she'd worn to bed. She'd convinced Margaret to go out for a meal the previous night and they'd had a few consolatory drinks. When Julia had returned home she'd kept drinking. It seemed the only thing to do.

Of course she'd known she'd couldn't escape turning forty-five without some kind of disaster. It had been happening on every birthday ending in five since she was fifteen. That was the birthday her dad had died of cancer. On her twenty-fifth birthday she'd been walking home from work, got hit by a car that swerved to miss a dog and spent months in rehab learning to walk again. And then on her thirty-fifth birthday her mum had died. Pam Paterson's official death certificate had read heart attack due to complications of diabetes but Julia was sure it was more about working herself to an early grave. She'd kept teaching and working the farm after her husband had died and until Julia's brother, Heath, was able to take over but Pam hadn't slowed down. She'd kept up her community commitments, her teaching and helping on the farm until the day she died. And to top it off, Julia's

70

long-term relationship had ended. Tim hadn't left her on her actual birthday. No, he'd waited until she was back in Wallaby Bay, working through the quagmire of arrangements, paperwork and clearing out that had followed her mother's sudden death. The bastard hadn't even been brave enough to say it to her face. He'd rung her when she was a whole state away and grieving.

Now she was feeling maudlin. The previous night she'd marked each of her significant birthdays with a toast, but she'd run out of red and had started on the bottle Glen had brought on her birthday. When she'd eventually fallen into bed she'd slept heavily and woken late with no desire to do anything but be a slob. Thinking about anything serious like a new job was beyond her. She'd put her heart and soul into the research that had just been snatched from her grasp and her head was still in it. She couldn't imagine what she would do next.

There was a knock on her door. At first she didn't move and then she remembered her neighbour was due back today and she'd been keeping his mail. She swept up the small pile from the top of the microwave and opened the door.

"Glen." Julia resisted the urge to shove the door shut. She didn't want company.

"You are home." Oblivious to her cool response, he stepped inside, brushing a kiss across her cheek as he passed her. "I've been trying to catch up with you since your birthday."

"I found your flowers and the bottle."

"Yeah. Sorry I missed you." He moved through to her lounge and flopped on her couch. The same couch she'd been curled up on happily nursing her morose thoughts before he'd interrupted her. "I'd had a terrible day at work, a few of us met for drinks after, ended up not far from your place. I thought we could have snuggled up on your couch with some takeaway. When you weren't home I sat for a while and must have dozed off. Combo of fatigue and one too many drinks wasn't good. It's funny, I dreamed you'd come home. Woke up stiff as a board with a sore shoulder." He rubbed at the spot. "You must have had a late one."

"It was a late night, yes." Julia kept her response vague, not wanting to let on she'd found him on her doorstep and ignored him.

He patted the couch and because she was tired and not up to an argument she sat. He pulled her in close. "How was your birthday?"

"Just another day."

"I wanted to make it up to you and take you out for dinner over the weekend. Tonight if you like or lunch tomorrow."

"I don't feel like celebrating."

He patted her arm. "Every birthday's a celebration, Jules. The alternative's no fun."

She pulled away, annoyed at his positive spin. Glen worked in advertising and he usually had that glass-half-full approach no matter what. She'd never explained to him her many reasons for disliking birthdays. He knew about the accident, of course, he'd asked about her scars the first time he'd seen her naked, he knew her parents were both dead but he didn't know each terrible event had happened on her birthday, and he knew little about Tim.

"I'm really not in the mood. My birthday present was our research project being closed down."

"Oh, Jules. I'm sorry. That's tough." He patted her leg.

She resisted the urge to push his hand away.

"Can you pick something else up?"

She flung herself to the other end of the couch and folded her arms. "You don't just pick up another research project. That's been my life's work for the last four years and we were finally making some headway just before bloody Covid. Then we got side-tracked. Now that others have taken over the Covid-related aspect of our research we were hoping funding would be redirected to our original research and we could go back to examining general immune response in HIV and tuberculosis, but instead we've been shut down."

"I'm sorry."

She turned away from his concerned gaze. She was still too angry and she didn't need his sympathy.

"If you don't want to go out, I can order in some Mexican and we can watch something on TV."

Her traitorous stomach rumbled at the thought of her favourite takeaway. "There's nothing on TV."

"We could stream something. You pick while I organise the food."

He pulled out his phone and started scrolling.

Julia sighed and reached for the remote. Glen's subscriptions to streaming channels could be accessed from her TV. She rarely watched them unless he was here. She stabbed at the buttons. She didn't want a soppy movie or a crime series, and not the *Star Wars* movies that were his go-to chill-out viewing. She scrolled down to TV shows. Perhaps she could spend all weekend binging on something. She shook her head, dismissing title after title until finally her finger stopped on *Doc Martin*. She hadn't watched it for years. She selected the first season and pressed play.

Glen stood up. "Coffee or wine?" he asked.

"Coffee, thanks," she said, distracted by the appearance of Martin Clunes on the screen. Some of the tension Glen's arrival had brought eased. Even though Portwenn was nothing like home, something about the small beachside community reminded her of growing up in Wallaby Bay and that brought its own happy memories.

⟶

Lucy relaxed into the cushions of the wicker outdoor setting and felt her drooping eyelids close. Below her, at the bottom of Kon and Helen's marina garden, Kon, Alec and the two children were on the pontoon manoeuvring a remote-control boat. The drone of its motor was like a gentle mantra adding to her drowsiness. While Alec was away she didn't always sleep well. And since he'd been back her sleep had been broken, the first night getting used to him being in her bed again and the second she'd been up and down to Noah who'd had a nightmare and been restless. Now, with a full tummy from Helen's delicious lunch and the sun warming her weary body, she felt the lethargy of sleep drawing her down into its comfy cocoon.

Poppy screamed and Lucy shot to her feet, heart racing. At the same time Helen stepped outside carrying a tray of afternoon tea.

"Squeals of excitement," Helen soothed.

Lucy checked Poppy was still on the pontoon, her hand firmly in Kon's, and lowered herself back to the chair. Alec and Noah were both focused on the boat being controlled by the remote in Alec's hands.

Poppy squealed again as the boat did a three-sixty in front of her and Kon's deep laugh followed.

Helen sat the tray on the small table beside Lucy, easing her crippled fingers from the handles. No matter how many times Lucy offered to help, Helen would have none of it. Only on the rare occasions when Lucy's visit corresponded with a bad day for Helen's rheumatoid arthritis would she allow help with anything.

Helen poured the coffee from the old metal pot. "Kon says he bought that boat for Noah but the men are having as much fun as the children."

"Big boys' toys." Lucy reached for the cup Helen offered. "Thanks."

She nestled back into the chair, shaking her head at the plate of cake Helen held out. "Lunch was amazing as always, thank you. I couldn't eat another thing."

"I made the biscuits for the children. You can take the extras home with you. They're not the kind that can be made in a blender."

Lucy kept her eyes firmly on the group at the pontoon. Helen often tutted over her penchant for using her Thermomix – a sign of domestic failure on Lucy's part. It was so much more than a blender and using it was so quick and easy. Rather than biscuits, she preferred to make slices for the children's snacks. She could blend the ingredients and have a slice in the oven in no time at all and hers usually included honey rather than the large amounts of sugar Helen used.

Below them on the pontoon Alec gave up the controller to Noah, who was finally getting a turn at manoeuvring the little boat.

"Noah seems okay today," Helen said.

"Yes. He didn't sleep well last night but he doesn't have a temp or aches and pains any more."

"That's good. They both love having their father home."

Poppy squealed again. She'd escaped Kon's hand and Alec had scooped her up onto his shoulders.

Helen leaned forward, watching a moment just as Lucy was, then they both sat back.

"Alec says he's got a new job."

"Yes."

"It's a long way away. Such a shame he can't find something closer."

"He's chasing the good money while he can."

"I wish we hadn't spent so much money on this place." Helen waved her hand at the roof above her.

Lucy shook her head. It was a lovely home but modest in comparison to many others on the marina. "You and Kon worked hard all your lives. You deserve this."

"We should have kept more to share between the boys. Alec wouldn't have to take these far-away jobs. You two could be running the fish and chip shop."

"We don't expect you to give us a handout. And I'm sure the others don't either." Both Alec's brothers were older and already had places of their own. "And Alec and I aren't certain what we'll do once he stops the FIFO. You know we weren't necessarily going to take over the shop."

Helen gave her a surprised look then turned away. "It's a pity the people who took on the business didn't keep it going. Another empty shop and such a prime position. We could still be running it until you and Alec ..." She tsked. "That bloody virus and then this disease." She held up her crippled hands. "It robbed us. If only ..."

"It's done now, Helen. We can't change it." Lucy hated going down this path of what-ifs. When Helen was feeling down she kept revisiting the hurried closure of their business. The people who'd leased it hadn't been able to make a go of it and had eventually given up.

Helen and Kon were hoping Alec and Lucy would reopen it. They'd talked it over a lot and Alec had drawn up some business scenarios but they weren't sure that was what they wanted. And if they did end up taking it on, they were agreed they had to purchase the property. Helen and Kon needed the money from the sale for their retirement. "You've got this lovely home and I know the arthritis can be awful but you manage so well."

Helen inhaled deeply and smiled. "I'm lucky my Alec found such a wonderful woman as you. And that you've moved here. It's good to have some of my grandchildren close."

Lucy smiled but inside she squirmed. Sometimes Helen's adoration was suffocating. Lucy had no family of her own. Her world had been one where she'd had to make her own way and then she met Alec. She'd let him in, and then Noah and Poppy, of course. Her little family was all she needed.

Poppy squealed again and once more both women looked towards the water. At least Helen understood a mother's concern for her children. Alec didn't say it exactly, but she knew he thought Lucy fussed over them too much.

"It's a shame you work for that dreadful cleaning company." Helen offered a plate of cake. Lucy waved it away.

"It's not dreadful."

"Fred Howard's name has been associated with some bad deals. I've got a friend who worked for that man and she's told me a few stories. I don't like that you work for him."

Lucy shrugged. "I hardly ever see him. He rings me about the jobs and I do them, usually with one of his regular cleaners. He pays well and on time. And he only calls me when Alec is at home. Not many jobs would be so accommodating."

Helen shot forward. "You should go to the doctor's surgery."

"I'm not sick."

"With your resume, I mean. When I was there yesterday, Jess, one of the nurses, was talking about going on maternity leave soon. She went to school with Alec. She works part-time and evidently they can be a bit flexible with hours." Helen leaned closer, warming to her topic. "The job would be perfect for you."

The coffee soured in Lucy's stomach. "I can't, Helen. Not while the kids might need me at any time. Look at what happened yesterday. Noah had to be collected from school."

"We could do that for you and have the children after school if you needed."

"I'm happy with the current arrangement. Maybe when Alec comes home for good I'll go back to nursing. When he can help more."

Helen stiffened, her gnarled fingers curled at her knees. "You know Kon and I love having the children."

"I don't want them to wear out their welcome." Lucy forced a smile, knowing she'd come across a bit abruptly.

"They're our grandchildren, not strangers," Helen said. "They're always welcome here. Besides, what else do we have to do?"

Helen and Kon had worked seven days a week for so long they were struggling with retirement. A dose of guilt added to Lucy's already squirming stomach. Everyone was so keen for her to go back to nursing but after the pressures of the previous year the passion and satisfaction she'd always felt for her work had evaporated. "I was hoping you'd look after them the day I take Alec back to Adelaide for his flight. I've got a few jobs to do in the city."

"Of course." Helen brightened. "You know we would have them any time." Another of Poppy's shrieks drew their attention towards the pontoon. Kon was retrieving the boat from the water. "Looks like they've had enough of that." Helen waved as the men and children made their way up the garden steps. "Come, come! Afternoon tea is ready. There's cake and biscuits."

"Biscuits!" Poppy squealed and started up the steps as soon as Alec placed her on the ground. Noah walked at a more sedate pace beside his dad. He was so like Alec, but somewhere during the last year his sparkle and confidence had been replaced by a more serious boy, a much quieter child who always seemed to be watching for someone or something. And Lucy couldn't help but feel it was all because of her. She definitely couldn't go back to nursing, or any kind of regular work, not yet.

Eve sat in the stiff chair, careful not to lean back too far. It was the only place she'd found peace from the nagging pain in her shoulder. She'd slipped the sling back on and taken some paracetamol. If she just stayed upright in the dining chair she could remain comfortable but she dreaded the thought of the long night ahead, if the previous one was anything to go by. She'd hardly slept for the pain, and this morning the thought of driving her car into town to have the script for the painkillers filled had been enough for her to break out in a sweat. Not because the police had warned her off driving but because of the extra pain she knew it would cause.

She'd rung Spiro to see if he'd come out and collect it for her but he and Mary were halfway to Adelaide. Pete, her neighbour across the paddock, hadn't answered her call. He was probably off fishing. And Gert was in Adelaide. There were others she could call but she'd run out of energy.

The sound of a car door jolted her awake and she gasped as her sudden movement sent a fresh wave of pain through her shoulder. She must have been dozing. Once upon a time Merc would have alerted her as soon as the car turned onto the track that led into the house yard but these days she often didn't know she had visitors until they knocked on her door.

Eve struggled to her feet, and out along the passage. She was surprised to see Jess beyond the screen.

"I have got the right place," Jess said. "I wasn't sure."

"What brings you out here?" Eve pushed open the door.

"I hope you won't think I'm being nosy but I was worried about you. My husband and I were out for a drive and we weren't far from here."

Eve glanced at the car parked beyond her back gate. She could see a shape through the window.

"I couldn't stop thinking about you with your injury and being on your own."

"That's very kind, Jess, but I'm managing."

The young woman gave her an assessing look. "Really? You're very pale. Aren't the painkillers helping?"

"I don't have them." Eve sighed. "I didn't get into town this morning."

"Oh, you poor thing."

"Sorry, I shouldn't have you on the doorstep." Eve tried to distract her. "Would you and your husband like to come in for a cuppa?"

"Thank you, but we won't stop. We're heading to my mum's."

Eve had a sudden pang of loss. She hadn't expected visitors but now that someone was here …

"It was very kind of you to check on me, Jess, but please don't worry. I'll be fine." She went to lift her arm just a little to prove her point and a pain ripped through her that was so sharp she yelped with the force of it.

Jess eyeballed her from the doorstep. "The chemist near Mum's is open till mid-afternoon. Give me your script and I can have it filled and drop it back to you on our way home."

"I don't want to cause you any trouble."

"It's no trouble. It won't fix your arm but it might help keep you comfortable. I bet you hardly slept last night."

Eve pursed her lips. Lisa yesterday and now Jess – it seemed she was continuing to be bossed about by the younger generation.

"My aunty tore her rotator cuff last year and luckily I was able to help her." Jess tipped her head to one side and smiled. "You can't go the whole weekend feeling miserable."

"You're sure it's not out of your way?"

"I wouldn't offer if I didn't mean it."

Eve stepped back into the passage. "Come in while I fetch it."

Jess followed her along the big wide passage that ran the length of the house into the kitchen. "What a lovely kitchen ... and that view."

"Best outlook in Wallaby Bay, I think. It's certainly easy to keep an eye on the weather from here."

"I love old stone homes when they've been beautifully restored like this one. I'd like to buy one in town but my husband hates renovating. He wants to start from scratch and build something new."

"Old houses are a lot of work." Eve took the script from her purse and handed it over with a fifty-dollar note. "Perhaps one day you can stop and have a cuppa. I could show you the rest of the house."

"I'd love that." Jess waved the script in the air. "I'll be back with this in the late afternoon. We're going out for dinner or I'd stay then."

"Perhaps we can make a date when you come back?" Eve was warming to the bright young woman and she only realised how much she missed company when there was actually someone in her house. She followed Jess outside. A man was peering in the window of Eve's Torana, still by the back gate where Lisa had parked it.

"That's my husband, Chris. He's a sucker for old cars."

"Hi, Mrs Monk." He waved as he walked back to his own vehicle. "Cool car."

"My sons keep telling me I should replace it with something modern but I can't bear the thought of parting with the old girl. She was the first car my husband and I bought after we were married. The local mechanic keeps her well-tuned."

The young couple got into their four-wheel drive.

"I'll call back with this later," Jess said, brandishing the script.

Eve gave an awkward left-handed wave as they drove off. She looked at the Torana then turned and made her way back inside. The ache in her shoulder nagged at her again. Just for a while she'd been distracted enough to ignore it.

eight

The sound of her phone woke Julia from a deep sleep. She flung out a hand and bumped the reading lamp but couldn't locate the phone. She groaned and dug her fingers into her neck as she rolled to the edge of the bed and sat up. Grey light filtered in around her blind. She had no idea what the time was. She glanced at the empty bed behind her. Glen had stayed over last night and she'd had one too many drinks again. That had to cease.

The phone stopped. She flopped back against the pillows trying to remember what day it was. The phone started again.

"Damn!" She rolled over. From the floor, the bright screen flashed at her. She plucked it up and peered at the name, caught sight of the time as she answered and her stomach roiled. It was Monday and it was eight o'clock. She'd promised Margaret she'd be there by seven.

"Hello, Margaret."

"Where are you?"

"I'm running late."

"I was worried. Most of the team are here already."

Julia swivelled her feet to the floor and gripped her head as she waited for the room to steady. "I won't be long. Can you get them to gather up their notes?"

"That's what they're doing. I've said we'd all meet at eight thirty."

Julia dashed through the kitchen. Last night's dinner dishes were still piled on the sink. "Hell!"

"What's the matter?"

"Nothing." She'd forgotten about them. "Can we make the meeting eight forty-five? I'll be there soon."

She glanced over the mess once more. Glen had come over again last night and had cooked lasagne. They'd shared a bottle of red and started on a second before tumbling into bed. He'd stayed all night. He'd promised to clean up before he left.

"Bastard!" she muttered for the second time that day. She vaguely remembered him trying to wake her earlier and she'd sworn at him to leave her be.

Bloody Glen and his promises. Just as well the sex had been surprisingly good last night. Julia had been desperate for it and had shut out the knowledge that Glen had to take a pill to have sex with her. There wasn't a pill to take for that blow to her ego. She turned her back on the mess and headed to the shower.

By lunchtime she had a headache and was ready to go home again. Her day had only gone from bad to worse. It had been after eight forty-five when she'd entered the building that would soon no longer be her workplace. Everyone had been waiting, crammed into the biggest lab. Margaret had delivered the bad news as gently as she could, but there was no easy way to tell people they'd lost their jobs.

There'd been anger, tears, dismay – the full gamut of emotion. Feckless Foster had been excited at the prospect of some time off. He, of course, still lived with his parents rent-free and wasn't worried about not having a job for the time being. "Something else will turn up," he'd said with a clueless shrug of his shoulders while all around him devastated colleagues were trying to come to terms with no work.

After that it had been hard to muster the energy and the interest to pack up. By twelve Margaret had suggested they all go home and start fresh tomorrow and she'd left to attend a meeting. Julia was the last to leave. She'd just swallowed some paracetamol and was gathering her things when her phone rang. It was Margaret.

"Are you still in the building?" she asked.

"I was about to leave."

"I've been talking to the powers that be and there might be an opportunity for you."

"What is it?"

"Can you head down to level one?"

"Now?" All Julia wanted to do was go home and shut her eyes.

"Yes. The meeting room."

"What's this involve?"

There was no response. Julia glanced at her phone to see the call had ended. "That's very Hercule Poirot of you, Margaret," she muttered. Nevertheless, she wrapped her scarf around her neck with more energy than she'd summoned all day. Her interest was piqued.

She took the stairs down to the first floor. There were several rooms on level one for conference-sized gatherings but only one was called the meeting room. It was tucked into a corner of the building with one small window that looked directly at the office block opposite. There was no-one in the corridor and the door to the room was shut.

She opened it and immediately thought she'd misunderstood Margaret's directions. Seated at one end of the table, smiling brightly, his hands clasped together over a folder, was Bill Russell. Bill was Margaret's counterpart in a different research unit. He was loud and brash, open about poaching whoever and whatever he needed for his department, often politically incorrect but escaping censorship by playing the "I was mis-understood" card. He was Margaret's complete opposite, yet somehow he always seemed to attract the big funding and his department was advancing well with their research.

"Julia, hello." He jumped up.

She made a point of looking around the small room as if there could be someone else hidden somehow. "I thought Margaret would be here."

"Can I get you a coffee or a tea?" He picked up his phone. No doubt his hard-done-by assistant was waiting for his call.

"No ... thank you," she said, swallowing her contempt for the man.

"Please sit." He waved to the chair opposite his.

Julia gritted her teeth. She could simply turn around and walk out but she was officially out of work as of tomorrow and there was no point in getting on the wrong side of Bill. Research work at her level in Australia was incestuous. She perched on the edge of the chair and tugged her scarf away from her neck.

"What's this about, Bill? I was expecting to see Margaret."

"It was Margaret who suggested I talk to you. She set up this meeting."

Julia found that difficult to imagine but she remained silent.

"I'm looking for someone to head up the side project that's come from our latest research findings."

Julia laughed then.

He raised his eyebrows.

She met his look. "You're serious." She'd come in expecting to be talking something over with Margaret and instead Bill Russell was offering her a job. The same Bill Russell who both she and Margaret thought a buffoon. A man who delegated everything to his staff and then took all the credit when any progress was made. The heating in the room was stifling. She pulled her scarf right off.

"I was about to go searching for the right recruit but, as Margaret pointed out, with your experience and the work you've been doing, you'd be perfect."

"Working in your department?"

"It's not the same responsibility or salary that you had but it would keep you in the field and who knows what it might lead to." Bill leaned back in his chair, put his hands behind his head and gave her his best condescending smile. "I can't say too much about it yet but if you were interested, I could give you more detail."

He'd obviously taken her silence to imagine she could be. She waited another heartbeat. "No, thank you, Bill." Not if it was the last job on earth, but she didn't say that out loud.

He lurched forward, the smile gone. "Have you got something else already?"

"Not yet." She stood up. "But thanks for the offer—"

"What will you do? These sorts of jobs with such a prestigious department as mine don't come along very often."

"I'm taking a break."

"What?"

"A holiday. I haven't had one for over a year." Julia hadn't planned to take a holiday at all but the idea was suddenly appealing.

"I thought you were the kind of person who didn't worry about that when there was a new challenge to be taken."

"I am, but everyone needs a chance to recharge."

"If that's all you want I can give you a few days before you start but I need someone soon. By this time next week."

"No thanks, Bill." Julia hooked her scarf back around her neck. "I'll be gone for two weeks, possibly three." The thought had come to her that she should go back to Wallaby Bay. Visit her brother and his family, drive a tractor, walk on the beach, stay with Eve. Julia could do with some mothering. If she was going that far she might as well make a decent break of it.

"Julia?"

She turned back.

"I made the offer as a favour to Margaret and to you. I won't be making it again."

"That's all right, Bill." She smiled. "I wouldn't expect you to." She closed the door on his open mouth and strode back down the corridor. What on earth had Margaret been thinking? Julia would talk to her later but for now she was keen to book herself a seat to Adelaide as soon as possible. She'd been drifting, rudderless since Margaret had told her about the end of their research but now she had something to look forward to and a new purpose.

As soon as she was outside she found a spot out of the wind, took out her phone and scrolled to Eve's number. She still hadn't returned Eve's call. Now at least there'd be something of interest to tell her. Eve had been the one constant in her life, holding her hand through the toughest of times. They hadn't seen each other face to face since Eve's last visit to Melbourne more than a year ago.

Julia's finger hovered over the screen then she exited her contacts and searched for flights instead. Eve rarely left Wallaby Bay and Julia knew the family farm would be busy with seeding so her brother should be home. She'd book flights and surprise them all.

Lucy waved as Alec pulled up outside the new house she'd just helped to clean. Occasionally she got work with the team who did the final clean ready for the owners' first inspection. She always enjoyed those jobs. A brand-new house with no furniture was much easier work and it was always interesting to check out the layout and colour schemes. Unfortunately, she didn't get to do them very often. This one was on the marina, not far from Kon and Helen's place, so Alec had dropped her off and gone to have morning tea with his parents.

"Ready to have lunch," he said as she climbed in beside him.

"Has Helen been giving you food again?" she said.

"No. I'm taking you out."

"We can't, Alec," she groaned. "You have to take me home first. I'm all grotty."

"You look perfect to me. Besides, it will add another half an hour by the time we go home and you change." He turned the car towards the town.

"I stink," she wailed.

"You don't and we're only going to a cafe."

"Not many open on a winter Monday."

"The Cutty Sark is and it's a nice day. You can put on your jacket and we'll sit outside."

Lucy shook her head but made no more protest. She'd only had a banana for breakfast and after her busy morning she was feeling ravenous.

Alec found a park and glanced across at the building that had housed his family's fish cafe. The grand old structure stood alone on the low rise above the beach, all shuttered up.

"Have your parents been pressing you to take it on again?"

His lips turned up in a sheepish grin. "How did you guess?"

"It's got to be our decision, Alec, not theirs."

"I know, but we said we'd think about it."

"When we've got enough money behind us. They can't just give it to us – it wouldn't be fair for them or your brothers."

"We've almost got enough to get a loan now." They got out of the car. Alex lingered, still gazing towards his family shop. "Dad's suggested we rent it from them, rather than borrow the money."

"No, Alec. Whether the business is a fish shop or you start an engineering place it has to be ours. We've talked about that."

"I know." He turned his back on the building and threw an arm around her shoulder. "Lunch?"

"Lunch."

They sat in a sheltered spot in the outside eating area of the Cutty Sark. There was a stiff sea breeze but the sun was shining and it was good to be out with Alec even if she did wish she could have showered first. She rolled her shoulders, basking in the warmth on her back, and did her best to forget her grimy clothes, Noah's sullen face when they'd dropped him at school this morning and Alec's leave disappearing all too quickly.

They ordered fish and chips and drank coffees while they waited.

"I didn't think you'd be hungry after spending the morning at your mum's," she said.

Alec grinned. "I resisted temptation 'cause I knew I'd be taking you out. Mum had some interesting news, actually," he said.

"Did she?"

"She was back at the doctor's yesterday."

"Is she okay?"

"Yes, just collecting a script but she was chatting to one of the nurses there, Jess. I went to school with her. She's about to go on leave to have her first baby."

Lucy's tranquil mood evaporated. "Helen's already mentioned that. I don't want to work at a doctor's surgery. All those people coming in with their germs and complaints." And locked into shifts where she'd no doubt have to organise out-of-school care.

Alec put up a hand. "It's not that. Jess was telling Mum about Mrs Monk, who lives out along the coast. You know … in that old house on the hill overlooking the bay."

Lucy frowned. The name Monk was familiar.

"You remember that day last summer when Dad took us out in the boat? We went up the coast and you said that house had the perfect location."

"The big stone place all on its own facing back towards the town?"

"Yeah. Anyway, Mrs Monk's hurt her shoulder and has to have an op. She needs some home help and some nursing care."

Lucy gripped her empty coffee mug, the contents of which now soured in her stomach. "There're agencies for that."

"There's not a big pool to draw from here and Jess said they're all booked. They've been asking around for people with the right qualifications and Mum mentioned you. It would only be day-time hours and would suit you perfectly."

"And what happens when you're not here? We've got two kids, Alec."

"They'll be at school and you've got Mum and Dad for backup."

"You don't realise how much pain Helen's in. Some days it's a struggle for her to get out of bed."

Alec's shoulders slumped. "I know you don't want to burden them, Lou, but they love having the kids. I think it's a distraction for both of them. They hardly saw my brothers' kids when they were growing up. They live interstate and Mum and Dad worked seven days a week. Now that they don't have the shop, they want the opportunity to be more hands-on grandparents."

"It's not like I keep the kids from them. We go there for a meal once a week when you're not here and sometimes on weekends. And ... well, they're not my parents, Alec, they're yours. I don't always feel as comfortable there without you."

"I know it's hard for you to feel part of an extended family again." Alec reached across the table, removed the mug from her grip and took her hands in his. "My parents can't replace yours. They're not trying to, but sometimes I think your upbringing has left a few holes in your understanding of family."

She snatched her hands back. "Just because I was a foster child doesn't mean I can't be a good mother."

Alex reached out again and held her hands tight this time. "You're a wonderful mother, Lou." He spoke gently. "I'm not talking about your ability as a mother. I'm talking about letting my family get a little closer to you. All Mum and Dad want is for you to feel part of our family."

"I do." She glanced down at her hands wrapped tightly in his.

"It doesn't always seem that way to them."

"I can't help it, Alec." He came from the security of always knowing he was loved, safe, cared for and, as the youngest child, confident in his adored position. She'd been raised by a loving couple in her early years, not her parents but they'd been like parents in every respect and then they'd died. After that she'd lived with several families but never truly felt part of them. When she'd met Alec and then the kids had come along she'd vowed to herself she'd create a new family of her own. Alec and Noah and Poppy were that family and all she needed. She'd put that in jeopardy last year but never again. "I'm doing my best."

"I know." He grimaced and jiggled her hands in his. "This has come out all wrong. It was work I wanted to talk about. I want you to find a job that suits you. You're a good nurse."

"Was."

Alec pursed his lips and his big brown eyes held her gaze, muddy pools of tenderness.

"I know it was tough last year. Nursing through it all and losing people you cared about."

"It could so easily have been prevented."

"It's done now. You can't change the past but you need to get back on the bike, Lou. I hate to think of you spending so much time alone while I'm away and the kids are at school."

Lucy looked down at her hands clasped in his again. She'd worked in aged care and sadly several of her clients had succumbed to Covid-19. Dying was a regular occurrence with the demographic she nursed regardless of what else was happening in the world, but some of it could have been prevented if people had followed the protocols properly in the early days.

She glanced back at Alec, who was still studying her closely. There was more to her reluctance to return to nursing than watching people die and in that moment she wanted to tell him why; to lay the weight of her guilty burden on the table between them, but she couldn't. He already worried about them while he was away. Last time she'd gone back to work against his wishes. If she told him what had happened, it would just add to his load.

"I keep busy," she said brightly. "There's the odd bit of work for Fred, I volunteer at the school, help your parents when they need it."

"I know you do but ..."

"But what, Alec?" She pulled away from him again.

"Mum thinks the kids don't get out enough, see other people. You can't keep them cocooned forever."

"Did you tell Helen to mind her own business?"

Alec frowned and his shoulders drooped. "She's worried for you too, Lou. We didn't move here so you could hide away from the world."

"Is that what you think I'm doing? Hiding?"

Alec sighed. "Perhaps avoiding is a better word."

She stiffened, then seeing the softness in his look she forced herself to relax. Maybe their time apart honed his awareness but somehow Alec always had the ability to see her clearly, often understood her better than she did herself, except in this instance. If he knew what she'd done he'd be so upset with her. She couldn't bear the thought of it.

Their meal arrived and they both reached for a chip as soon as the waitress walked away.

Lucy was glad of the interruption. She waved her chip in the air then took a careful bite. "Yum."

"Not bad," Alec agreed.

"Don't be too enthusiastic."

"Not as good as—"

"Your parents' chips, I know. You tell me every time we have chips."

"That's because most places use reconstituted frozen ones these days." He looked off in the direction of the closed-up shop. "Mum and Dad cut up real potatoes."

She followed his gaze. She'd allowed herself to dream about the possibility of reopening the shop but it had to be theirs and done their way, not the old Nicolis' Fish and Chips. There were several places people could buy fish and chips in the bay. If they were to open the place it would need a point of difference. They'd already tossed around a few ideas.

"First you have to decide what kind of business you want," Lucy said.

"We want."

"If you go down the engineering path I won't be able to help you much."

"I'd need someone to run the office."

"And I'd be happy to do that if you were happy."

"Or we could pay someone and you could finally go back to nursing. Do some study if you want."

Lucy turned away from his excited gaze and stared at the old building.

"Do you think she's calling us?" Alec said.

"Maybe." Lucy poked him. "How often do you hear buildings calling you?"

He laughed and they turned back to their fish and chips.

"In the meantime, this job with Mrs Monk would be a foot in the door for you, Lou. I don't remember her all that well but Mum says she's a nice woman. She's worked hard all her life and for the community. And she hasn't got family here. She needs someone dedicated like you to help her. I don't imagine she'll be hard work and once it's finished you can bet there'll be others."

Hearing the name Monk again, Lucy remembered the afternoon she'd bought the wine and the woman she met at the bottle shop. She'd been chatty and a bit nosy but there'd been something else about her, a resoluteness, Lucy recalled now. "I think I've met her," she said.

"Then you'll do it?" Alec leaned back as the waitress came to clear their table.

Lucy stood up. "Time to go."

Alec remained seated. "Lucy?"

She locked her gaze with his imploring one.

"I want to find out about it first, exactly what care she needs and the hours."

"We can call in on our way home."

"We will not, Alec," Lucy snapped. "I'm not going to find out about a prospective client in my grotty cleaning clothes. We'll go home. I'll have a shower and change ... and think about it."

nine

Eve stared at her phone then at the notepad she'd scribbled the details on. Her arm hurt even to write, and using her left hand made it hard to decipher her scrawl. The bottom line was she could wait three weeks until the next visiting orthopaedic surgeon visited Wallaby Bay or she could go to Adelaide on Thursday and have tests and see the specialist in the late afternoon. She slumped against her chair and slid her arm back into the sling. It was the only way to ease the pain in her shoulder. It was already Tuesday. She'd spent Monday prevaricating, but the pain had finally been her undoing.

If she was a woman who gave in to tears she'd be sobbing right about now, but tears wouldn't quell the pain or transport her to Adelaide. She had to book the Thursday appointments but with Lisa's warning and the pain combined, driving herself was not an option. Gert would have taken her but she was still in Adelaide herself and even if she was back by Thursday it wouldn't be fair to ask her to turn around and make the over three-hundred-kilometre round trip again so soon.

She could ask Spiro but she knew he was busy getting things ready for the last run of the prawn season. He'd suggest Mary did it and Eve knew that would mean a terrible day for both of them. There was always the community car. She'd driven other people to Adelaide for medical appointments many times in the past. Only problem was there was often a lot of waiting around for others to finish their appointments.

Perhaps she should take up her sons' suggestion of buying another car. There'd always been a four-wheel drive in the shed until she'd sold off the last one and not replaced it. She could get one of the automatic SUVs they made these days. She tutted to herself. There was no way she'd part with her Torana, and buying a second car was a ridiculous outlay for something that would sit in the shed most of the time. Besides, she needed transport by Thursday.

Her phone began to ring again. Startled, she lifted her left hand and stared at the screen. It wasn't a number she knew. She accepted the call and listened.

"Mrs Monk?"

"Yes."

"My name is Lucy Ryan. You might remember we met briefly last week buying wine at the drive-through."

Eve immediately pictured the pretty young woman she'd met over a bottle of tempranillo and her aloof manner. "Yes."

"I had a call from Jess who works at the doctors' surgery. She said you might need some home nursing assistance."

"Are you a nurse?"

There was a brief pause. "Yes."

"Don't you work for Fred Howard?"

Once more there was a pause. "I fill in when he needs someone."

"I see."

"Look, Mrs Monk, I don't want to bother you. Jess told me you might need some help but if that's not the case …"

Eve shifted in her chair and the pain radiated sharply down her arm. She pursed her lips, waiting for it to ease.

"Mrs Monk?"

"I am in need just at the moment. When can you start?"

"Oh … I … I thought I should visit you first."

"Why?"

"We should make sure we're clear about your requirements before we decide anything. I've worked in aged-care support before."

Eve bristled. Aged care indeed. "Quite right. You might not be suitable to my needs. Can you come today?"

This time the silence dragged out so long Eve glanced at her phone to see she was still connected. "Hello?"

"Yes. Would two o'clock suit? I have some errands to run this morning."

"Two o'clock will be fine. Do you know where I live?"

"Alec can give me directions."

"Very well. I'll see you at two." Eve ended the call before the surly young woman could say any more. "Don't bust yourself," she said as she placed the phone back on the table. The only reason she'd agreed to Lucy's visit was because at this point in time there was no-one else.

"What jobs do you have on this morning?"

Lucy spun at the sound of Alec's voice. "I thought you were outside."

"I was. Came in for a coffee." He raised one eyebrow. "So, what's happening?"

"I told you yesterday, Alec, I won't be pushed into anything I don't feel comfortable with. Eve Monk sounded rather abrupt for someone who needed a favour."

"She's a tough cookie from what I remember. But didn't Jess say she had a shoulder injury? Pain can affect the way people respond."

"I am aware of that." Lucy folded her arms across her chest and leaned against the kitchen bench while Alec made coffee. "I'm not sure we'll get on. I wanted to give myself some time to prepare."

"What's to prepare?"

She moved away from his intense look and sat at the table. "I'm not rushing into anything before I'm ready and I'm satisfied this will work."

"Fair enough, but if you're driving out to Eve's at two do you want me to ask Mum to pick up the kids? You might not be back in time for school pick-up."

"I'll make sure I am." That had been her reason for choosing that time. If it took too long at Eve's place she had the excuse to leave to pick up the children.

Alec gave her a probing look as he set a mug of coffee on the table in front of her but didn't say another word about it. Instead he sat down beside her and opened the tin of biscuits his mum had sent home with him the previous day. "Mum wondered if you might be interested in helping her on the prawn festival committee. It's not till early next year but they've started the planning."

"She didn't mention it on the weekend."

"I don't think they've had a proper meeting yet."

"What would it involve?" Lucy was pleased to be talking about something else.

"I don't know much. I think they're planning it for March, after the first fish of the year. It'll be over a weekend and the early autumn weather should still be good. There'll be all kinds of food and drink stalls and some entertainment but that's all still to be organised. They're looking for some younger people to go on the committee and Mum thought of you."

It was a far cry from nursing and so totally different to anything she'd done before, Lucy felt a prick of interest. "I'll give Helen a call."

"I thought we'd drop in after we pick up the kids. Mum will want to know how you got on at Mrs Monk's."

Lucy's shoulders drooped. There was no avoiding it. She had to go and visit Eve Monk. She wished she'd said she'd go before lunch now, get it over and done with.

"Let's go for a walk," she said.

"Is this one of those jobs you mentioned you had to do?"

Lucy grimaced. "Are you coming or not?"

"The wind's like ice out there."

"Rug up then," Lucy said and unhooked her spray jacket from behind the back door. A good long walk in the fresh air was what she needed, with Alec or without him.

It was exactly two o'clock when Lucy pulled into the yard outside the rusting wire fence that surrounded Eve Monk's house. She'd sucked in a breath as she'd caught her first glimpse of the house close up. From this distance, everything about it reminded her of Charlie's; the walls made of stone blocks in sand and grey tones, the rendered corners painted cream and the turned wood posts supporting the return verandah. The only difference was Eve's house was bigger and looked cared for whereas Charlie's had been all peeling paint and sagging roof lines.

She got out of the car. A stiff wind with salt spray on its breath whipped her hair across her face. She approached the gate cautiously as if it might fly from its hinges and strike her. Even the garden was cement and gravel like Charlie's with only a couple of roses along the fence line, some succulents in pots beside the verandah and a few shrubs and windblown trees down either side of the house.

Lucy hesitated at the gate, half expecting Charlie's old dog, Bruce, to ease onto his arthritic legs and wobble down the path to meet her. There was a doghouse on the verandah but no sign of a dog in Eve's yard. Lucy squared her shoulders and drew herself up. This was not Charlie's place, Bruce was not here and all that was in the past. She hadn't thought of Charlie in a while but seeing this house …

Lucy shivered both from the memory and from the cold. She drew in a deep breath as she opened the gate, closing it behind her just in case there was a dog, and made her way to the back door. She was glad to reach the shelter of the verandah. The screen door was modern and the wooden door beyond it also freshly painted. She lifted her hand to knock and was surprised as the door jerked open.

"Thought I heard a car."

Eve Monk stood just inside. Framed by the solid wood doorway, she looked smaller than Lucy remembered but maybe that was because she was stooped a little in favour of her right arm, which was in a sling.

"You're punctual. That's good." Eve stepped back. "Come in."

Lucy braced herself but instead of the stale, fusty odour she'd expected, the house smelled fresh, almost salty, like the sea wind outside.

"How are you feeling?" she said as she followed the older woman down a wide passage towards the front of the house.

"I've been better but I'm getting by." Eve led the way into a large open-plan kitchen. There was a dining table in one half, and a desk with a computer tucked in a nook. A huge window above a long bench framed a panoramic view along the bay towards the town.

"Wow," Lucy couldn't help but exclaim.

Eve frowned and turned to look. "Oh, the view is good, isn't it? Sometimes I'm so focused on checking the weather I forget to take in the rest. My husband and I renovated the house early on and changed the floor plan. This used to be the main bedroom but it was ridiculously huge. We made it into kitchen and dining, and still have a separate living room across the hall which also appreciates the view. I've got a telescope in there. My sons gave me it for my sixtieth. I can almost wave to the trawler crews as they come in."

Lucy could find little comparison in the airy modern interior of Eve's house, except perhaps the piles of clutter, to the decaying gloom of Charlie's house. Some of the tension that had been building since she'd first agreed to come left her.

"Would you like a cup of something?" Eve rounded the large free-standing kitchen bench. It was strewn with dishes, packets and papers, but there were glimpses of the golden wood surface, which glowed in the afternoon sun streaming through the window.

"Yes, thank you."

"Tea?"

In the bright light of the kitchen Lucy could see dark shadows under Eve's eyes. She took a step forward. "Let me make it."

"We haven't agreed on anything yet." Eve nodded at a chair. "You're my guest. Sit. It's only a matter of chucking bags into a mug. I'm not totally useless."

Lucy pulled out a chair piled with newspapers. The next was clear so she sat. Eve set out two mugs and added the bags as she waited for the kettle to boil. She crossed the kitchen to the fridge, took out the milk and tapped the door closed with her foot. Lucy noted the wince she made. Eve had used her right foot and it was her right shoulder that was injured. It was obviously bad enough that any use of the right side of her body jagged the pain.

Lucy jumped up and moved to the bench as Eve struggled with the spout of the cardboard milk container. "Let me." She took the milk and opened it before Eve could complain. "I only have a splash of milk, no sugar. People often add too much." She eyeballed Eve across the divide of the bench. "Do you take milk?"

Eve glared back then nodded. "Just a dash, same as you."

Lucy dripped some milk into both mugs and let Eve remove the bags before she carried them to the table. She set Eve's beside a notepad and pen and took the seat opposite. Eve eased herself carefully onto her chair.

"Are you taking pain medication?" Lucy asked.

"Yes … sometimes … mainly at night so I can sleep."

"It would be better if you took it more regularly."

Eve's eyebrows shot up.

"It's the best way to manage the pain."

"Perhaps we should get down to what I require before you start dishing out nursing advice."

Lucy picked up her mug and blew gently across the surface, cooling her mounting annoyance as much as the tea. She'd had an exemplary – almost exemplary – career working with seniors. Perhaps she was out of practice or perhaps it was simply that she didn't want to be here but she was finding Eve difficult. Lucy searched her bag of soothing tricks and found it empty. She had no desire to win Eve over.

"Sure. Did you want to see my resume before you start?" She pulled out the pages she'd printed at Helen and Kon's before she'd come.

"No need." Eve gave a dismissive wave of her hand. "Beggars can't be choosers. You're Helen's daughter-in-law and I trust her good sense."

"I'm not."

"Not what?"

"I'm not married to Alec so I'm not Helen's daughter-in-law."

"You live with him, don't you? Have his kids? It's just semantics."

They stared at each other across the table, Eve's sharp gaze daring her to say more.

Lucy looked down at her mug. Took a sip and placed it carefully back on the table. Occupying herself so that she didn't just stand up and leave the grumpy old bat. "What is it you want me to do for you, Eve?"

Eve pushed back in her chair. Her face contorted in pain and a groan escaped her lips.

Lucy was instantly by her side. "What happened?"

"All I did was shift in my chair … the pain." Her head slumped forward.

"There is truly no point in trying to put up with it. Where do you keep your pain medication?"

Eve nodded towards the mess on the bench. Lucy found the tablets. She took them with a glass of water to the table. "Can you manage the glass?"

"My left arm's not injured."

"I know but you're obviously not feeling the best."

Eve took the tablets from Lucy and managed to lift the glass to her lips and take two big swallows.

"That sling needs adjusting," Lucy said. "You should have a pillow for support and it's worth trying an ice pack as well." She knew Eve was in a lot of pain as there were no more arguments, simply directions as to where she'd find all she needed. In a short time, Lucy had Eve re-settled and sipping her tea.

"How are you feeling now?"

Eve placed her mug back on the table. The pursed shape of her lips softened. "Better ... thank you. I think perhaps ... perhaps we got off to the wrong start. I'm not usually such a difficult person to get on with."

"Pain can make you irritable."

"But there's no excuse for rudeness. I'm sorry, Lucy."

The wall Lucy had built to protect herself after Charlie's death crumbled just a little. "I'm sorry too. I was probably a bit short with you. I haven't worked in nursing care since ... for quite a while and I must admit I hadn't planned to go back to it. But you're a friend of Helen's and Jess at the surgery said—"

"There's no-one else."

"Evidently not."

"So you're stuck with me."

"I'm not sure stuck is the right word."

They stared at each other across the table.

"I do appreciate you coming out of retirement for me," Eve conceded. "I'm feeling a lot better already."

"Good. Shall we come up with a plan then? How often I should come and what jobs you might need doing?"

"I've been managing."

"I know, but surely I can help make things easier for you. When do you see the doctor next?"

"Ah ... yes ... that's something I will need help with. My appointment with the specialist is on Thursday ... in Adelaide."

ten

Three things happened as Julia finished cleaning up the kitchen and gave the bench a final wipe down. She knocked over the vase of flowers she'd just topped up with water, her phone rang and there was a knock on her door. She threw a tea towel over the surge of water as it swept across the bench, plucked her phone out of the way of the advancing puddle but couldn't catch the crystal vase as it rolled to the floor and smashed, sending glass, flowers and water across the tiles of the small kitchen space.

She felt a pang of regret at the loss of her mother's vase and was still swearing as she put the phone to her ear.

"Things that bad, are they?" Margaret's voice had a bemused tone.

"Sorry, just broke a vase. Can you hang on a minute? There's someone at my door."

Julia pressed the phone to her ear with her shoulder and wiped her hands down her jeans as a second knock sounded. She tugged the door open and cursed again for not checking the peephole first. Glen was standing there with another bunch of flowers in his hand.

She stepped back to let him in. "You're just in time to clean up the last lot. I have to take this call." She grabbed her phone, turned her back on him and the disaster in the kitchen, and flopped on the couch.

"Sorry, Margaret." Then she remembered the meeting with Bill. "Actually, I'm not sorry. What were you thinking, sending me to work for Bill Russell?"

"What were you thinking turning him down?"

"The man's an idiot."

"And head of the biggest department at the institute with a track record for getting funding and results."

"You want me to sell my soul to the devil?"

"No, I hoped you might get a job in your field of expertise and not have to hunt for something further away. I know how happy you were to get that apartment so close to the institute."

"I can commute easily to somewhere else once I find something."

"You could keep an eye out for something else while you worked for Bill. The research is right up your alley."

"Not if it was the last job in the world, Margaret."

"How will you pay the rent on that place you love so much?"

"I do have some reserves and I'll find something. I'm not so desperate yet that I have to work for Bill." Behind Julia came the sound of glass tinkling into the bin. She put a hand to her forehead. "I've decided to take a few weeks off and go home to Wallaby Bay."

"Remote South Australia! How will you find a job from there?"

"Wallaby Bay is hardly remote and they've moved on from string-can phones, Margaret. They even have NBN."

"I don't want you committing career suicide."

Julia felt a small tug of remorse. Margaret had been her mentor as well as a long-time friend. She understood the vagaries of life in the research world as well as anyone. If she was worried about job prospects perhaps Julia should be more concerned. "I can send out some feelers before I go. I think I've earned a holiday."

There was a loud yelp – that was from Glen – and a solid thud and tinkling – that was the bucket he'd been putting the glass in, hitting the floor. Julia looked around to see him ashen-faced, clutching one hand to his chest.

"I have to go, Margaret. Thanks for the call. I'll be in touch." She tossed the phone aside and leaped to her feet. "What's the matter?"

Glen swayed and she reached him just in time to support his weight as he slumped precariously onto a bar stool. Beads of sweat formed on his brow and above his top lip.

"What is it, Glen? Speak to me." Her weight held him upright. She wondered how she could leave him to get her phone to call an ambulance. "Are you having a heart attack?"

His eyes widened and he gave a slight shake of his head. "Cut myself." His voice was a weak croak.

"Where?" She eased herself away so she could look at him. Her stomach roiled at the sight of the drops of crimson splattered down the front of his pale blue shirt.

"Hand." He wiggled the fingers of his left hand, which was pressing his right hand to his chest, and then she saw the blood oozing between his fingers. He swayed again. "Feel a bit light-headed."

Julia's heart hammered in her chest and her mouth went dry. She could deal with anything in a test tube but the sight of blood on a living human was a different thing altogether.

"I want you to slide off the stool and lower yourself to the floor." Julia kept one hand under his arm, pulled a cushion from the couch behind her and shoved it under his butt as he slithered down the kitchen bench. His head flopped back, his eyes closed.

"Is it bad, do you think?" she asked.

He nodded. Her stomach churned tighter.

"Probably only a scratch, you big wuss." She took in Glen's ashen complexion. He had a very low pain threshold. He worried about getting his flu injection, a teeth clean at the dentist, complained for weeks after stubbing his toe on the leg of the bed. It had turned out it was broken but truly you'd think he could have shut up about it. "I'm going to have a look."

He made a face. "You don't like blood either."

"Getting mangled in an accident can do that to you." She could make light of it now. Twenty years between her and the event that nearly killed her meant she could walk and run with barely a limp and most days she was pain-free. The nightmares had ceased but the image that never left her was waking on the road in a mess of her own blood, bone and shredded skin. She drew in a breath. "We can sit here and wait for you to bleed to death if you want."

His eyes widened and he pressed his hand tighter to his chest.

"I'm joking. It's probably just a surface cut that's bled a lot." She gripped his good hand in hers and began to prise his fingers back. "Turn away while I take a look."

She clenched her teeth together.

"I've got a bad feeling about this." When she still hesitated he said, "Use the force, Julia."

"You use the force, Glen." She prised his hand away from his blood-soaked shirt. Immediately she could see the jagged slash across his palm was deep and would require stitches. She grabbed the only fabric on hand, the scarf she'd left over the back of the stool, and pressed a wad of it against the cut.

Glen yelped.

"Curl your fingers over the scarf and hold your hand back to your chest. You'll need to get that looked at." She was careful not to mention the word stitches. She sat next to him on the floor, beads of perspiration on her brow. She had to do something.

"Did you drive over?"

"Yes."

"Give me your keys. I'll take you to Emergency."

His eyes widened in horror. He owned an old yellow MG convertible. It was his pride and joy and he'd never allowed her to drive it.

"Please yourself." She clambered up and tossed him a clean tea towel. "You should wrap it tightly. Not sure how you'll hold the wheel though." She'd rather not spend her evening at the hospital anyway.

His ashen face paled further. "Can you call me an Uber?"

"I guess." She thought of the smart MG. "It'd be quicker to take your car." Julia was already imagining herself behind the wheel. She loved their weekend drives out of the city, zipping along with the top down and the wind in her hair. Now was her chance to take the wheel.

"All right," he said and tugged the keys from his pocket.

She helped him up before he could change his mind, leaned him against the bench while she grabbed her bag and phone.

"Maybe I should take a towel," he said. "Don't want to get blood on the upholstery."

Julia glanced at him. There was a greenish tinge to his complexion now. She found a plastic shopping bag and slipped his bound hand inside it. Now neither of them could see it. With a towel and a vomit bag for good measure, she bundled him down the stairs and into his car.

He leaned his head against the seat and closed his eyes. She could see he was panting. Hell, he was such a baby. The cut was definitely deep but it wasn't as if he'd severed a finger.

"Long slow breaths," she said. If he vomited she'd join him. Blood was bad enough but someone heaving set her off too.

"Do you know how to drive a manual?" he croaked.

"I grew up on a farm. I can drive a truck if I need to."

"But do you even have a licence?"

"Of course I do." Her last car had been a shared purchase and was another thing that had sailed off into the sunset with Tim. She'd never bothered to get another.

Glen gave her a pained look as she bunny hopped away from the footpath.

"It's been a while since I drove a manual, that's all." She manoeuvred carefully around the local streets until she made it to the main road, then she put her foot down. Beside her Glen let out a soft moan.

It was dark by the time they'd worked their way through the emergency medical system and made it back to Julia's flat. Glen had needed five stitches in his hand, a tetanus shot and anti-biotics – her scarf hadn't been the cleanest option. He was far more alert on the way home though and full of driving directions; release the clutch slowly, give cyclists plenty of room, not so close to the car in front. She'd noticed him pushing his foot to the floor several times as they'd approached stop lights.

They pulled up outside her place and she handed back his keys with a grin. "See, I'm completely trustworthy with your precious car."

He took the keys and gave her a weak smile.

"Thank you, Julia, should be your response," she said.

"Thank you, Julia," he echoed with a hint of sarcasm.

"Are you staying?"

"I'd planned to before I sliced my hand on your bloody vase."

"My mother's crystal vase that was full of your bloody flowers."

"I thought you liked flowers."

She groaned. "I do. Let's go up. We'll order in food and there's still a bottle of red left. That'll cheer you up," she said as they made their way up to her apartment.

"I don't need cheering up and I probably shouldn't drink."

"Why not?" she asked as she unlocked the door.

"After all I've been through and the antibiotics." He flopped onto the couch as Julia side-stepped the mess in her tiny kitchen and took out the wine and two glasses.

"I think you deserve a drink after all that." She gave him a kiss on the forehead. "You were very brave."

"Humph!"

She kissed him again, on the cheek this time, and gave him a little nudge with her elbow. Once he'd realised he wasn't going to bleed to death, Glen had recovered his composure. He'd actually been quite chirpy in the end. Probably something to do with the young doctor who did the stitches being an MG fan.

"Sure you don't want a glass?" She couldn't believe she was encouraging him. He was prone to over-indulging these days but she felt a bit sorry for him. She poured some for herself and waved the bottle in his direction.

"I suppose one won't hurt."

Julia handed him a wine and settled back on the couch beside him.

Glen slipped his arm around her shoulders. "I'm sorry I made a fuss over a cut and a few stitches," he said. "I'll get you a new vase."

"There's no need."

"It was your mum's."

"So it's irreplaceable."

"I can look online—"

"Truly, Glen, it was only a vase. It doesn't matter." Julia sipped her wine. There was no point in being sentimental. "My parents are both dead. It's their memory I cherish, not their things." Although she had liked the vase. It was one of the few items of her mother's she'd kept.

"You're an amazing woman, Julia Paterson." He clinked his glass against hers.

"I know." She deflected his praise.

He squeezed her tighter. "You make light of it but to lose both your parents when you were young and to recover from your accident the way you did, it took guts."

Julia spun and pulled away from him. "How do you know what it took?" She told few people the story of her long and gruelling recovery.

"Eve. We had some good yarns over that brandy she drinks."

"Rakija! Don't let her hear you calling it brandy. And she shouldn't be blabbing."

"It's a part of your life I knew little about but it explains so much about you."

"Does it?" Julia flopped back and took a slug of her wine.

"To be told you might not walk again … when was it?"

"Twenty years ago." Almost to the day. The grim-faced doctor had made her determined to prove him wrong.

"A lot of people would be in a wheelchair. And now look at you, a few scars and barely a limp and you not only walk but you run."

"It was a tough time of my life I'd rather forget."

He pulled her back towards him and she let herself be tucked against his warm body. Glen kissed her forehead. "People get war medals for less. I think you deserve an award."

"Are you sure you didn't bang your head when you cut your hand?"

He chuckled and kissed her again. "I'm allowed to be proud of my lady."

Perhaps it was the wine or the soft warmth of his body – he was being overly possessive but she let it go.

"Giving up work's been good for you," Glen said.

"How?"

"You're in a much better mood today than you have been for ages."

She frowned. "Am I?"

"Or perhaps it was the fun of watching me at the mercy of the ED staff?"

"Or being allowed to drive your car?"

He winced.

Julia pondered Glen's words from the comfort of his embrace. He was right. In spite of their crazy afternoon in Emergency, there was a surge of optimism inside her she hadn't felt in a while. The pressure of her research work had been all-consuming and now that she'd let it go it was as if she saw the world with fresh eyes, full of possibilities and yet with no great responsibilities. Research was her life but she had to admit to feeling a bit lacklustre about returning to what they'd been doing before the pandemic. If she was temporarily out of employment, she was going to let her hair down for a while.

"I've booked to go home," she blurted.

"This is your home."

"Back to my family in SA."

"Really? I didn't think you liked spending time with your brother."

"I won't be with Heath all the time. He's always busy. I'll catch up with him and the family but I plan to stay with Eve."

"I'd like to see her again myself. Why don't you ask her to come here?"

"I want to get away from Melbourne."

"It's short notice. What about me ... us?"

She smiled to cover the relief she knew she'd feel to be away from Glen, to take a break, no matter how comfortable she felt in his arms right now. "It's only for a couple of weeks. I'm not going forever."

"Work's tricky and ... the girls might be coming to stay."

She lurched around. "You haven't mentioned that."

Glen had two daughters, now in their late teens. They'd come to stay during a school holiday when Julia and Glen hadn't been going out all that long. It had been an awful few days. They'd made their displeasure at Julia's existence quite clear and Julia hadn't been too keen on them either. Little bitches, replicas of their mother from what Glen had told her about his ex, not that he saw that in them. He had rose-coloured glasses where his daughters were concerned. Anyway, they'd never stayed since. He always had to go to Sydney to see them. They were his flesh and blood and Julia understood his fatherly bond but she'd been glad not to have to see them again.

"That'll be nice for the three of you and I won't be here as a fourth wheel."

"They're older now, Julia. And they've come to terms with the divorce. I'd like you all to try again. Can't you go home another time?"

"I want to go now, Glen."

"I can't get away at the moment."

Once more she hid her relief. "You don't need to come. It'll be too quiet for you. I plan to do little but sleep, eat and walk on the beach. Oh, and maybe drive a tractor." And enjoy some one-on-one girl time with Eve. As the only female child in their circle of friends, Julia had become a daughter to Eve, a position with attention she relished and suddenly realised how much she missed.

He shook his head, his expression pained. "If you'd given me some warning, I could have booked us something closer for a break. Still could once I know what date the girls are coming. There're always good deals going on weekend retreats."

"I need longer than a weekend, Glen. I've booked my flight. I leave on Thursday." She put her glass on the coffee table and jumped up, a spring in her movements now. "You order us in something for dinner while I clean up the mess you made in the kitchen."

eleven

"What have you done to yourself?" Spiro exclaimed as Eve opened the door.

"Torn rotator cuff." She avoided the bear hug he usually gave her and offered her cheek for a kiss instead.

"That bad, hey?" He followed her to the kitchen. "How'd you do it?"

"I think I jagged it a few times but last week the boatshed door flew open in that big wind we had. Took my shoulder out with it."

"It's always been a bastard to close, that door. Maybe I didn't hook it back properly last time I was there. Hell, a woman your age shouldn't be grappling with it."

"My age!"

Spiro laughed his deep throaty laugh. "Thought I'd get a bite." He stopped and looked at the loaded tray on her clear kitchen bench. It was set for afternoon tea with a plate of dainty cheese scones and another of banana cake. "What's going on here?"

"Just a bite to eat. You're always hungry."

"And you usually offer me bought biscuits, from a packet that you dig out from the clutter on the bench."

"I've got some home help while I'm laid up with this." Eve was careful not to waggle her arm. She'd done as Lucy had suggested and was taking the pain relief regularly. It certainly helped her get through the day and sleep better at night but any movement of her right arm was still harrowing. "I told her you were a big eater."

Spiro laughed again, sat, then leaped up. "Do you want me to make the coffee?"

"It's ready to go. I got Lucy to put a heaped teaspoonful in the mug. We just have to add the water. Would you carry the tray? I thought we'd sit out the front. There's not much of a breeze today."

She poured water from the recently boiled kettle into his mug and then the teapot.

Spiro lifted the tray. He was a nuggety man, with strong arms and callused hands from years of work on the prawn trawler. He nodded at the teapot. "Is your home help joining us?"

"No. She's left for the day. I asked her to use the teapot in case …"

"Sorry, Eve, I should have said, Mary's not coming."

Eve had guessed as much when she hadn't arrived with Spiro but sometimes they came out in separate vehicles, depending on who was busy with what. Although Mary had retired from her job as a part-time legal secretary so Eve wasn't sure what she did to fill her time these days.

She led the way outside. Sunshine streamed onto the verandah. There were still some small pools of water on the uneven cement from yesterday's scudding showers. Without the breeze that stirred Wallaby Bay most afternoons, it was almost warm for a winter's day. Eve loved to sit out here when she could. Spiro set down the tray then made himself at home putting food on his plate while Eve poured her tea.

They'd been friends a long time. Rex and Eve had married at the same time he and Spiro bought their first trawler. The three of them had started together in the fledgling days of prawning in the gulf. After Rex had died, Spiro's guilt over the accident, her need for help to raise her sons and their equal share in the prawn fishing licence had thrown them closer together. That was until Mary came along. Spiro's first wife hadn't settled to the long absences of a prawn fisherman's life. She'd left Spiro for a travelling salesman. Spiro had been heartbroken and had thrown himself even deeper into work. For years he'd avoided any suggestion of a longterm relationship. Eve had provided a feminine touch to his life. He'd provided some stable male influence for her teenage sons and they'd been happy enough. It was easy when it was just the two of them without Mary. No need for small talk, they were comfortable together. Almost like a married couple.

Now as she watched him fiddle with the handle of his coffee mug and line up his plate with the edge of the table, she sensed his discomfort, and she had a fair idea what was coming.

"Everything ready for the last fish of the season?" she asked.

Spiro stopped fiddling. "Yes. The *Mary Gee* is ready and Harvey has everything under control on the *Evie 3*."

"He's a good skipper."

"Others haven't been so lucky. Pero wants to get rid of both his skippers. Reckons they cut corners."

"Perhaps that's to do with Pero's management. He often cut corners himself back in the day."

They both looked in the direction of the bay where several prawn trawlers bobbed at anchor, dark specks on a deep green sea. Soon there'd be almost forty trawlers out there making up the

Spencer Gulf prawn fleet. Rex and Spiro had bought their first trawler and licence in the early seventies. Prawning had been like the wild west in those days: squabbles had led to threats, ill feelings to sabotage and gung-ho attitudes to huge risk-taking.

"We've seen some changes over the years."

"For the better mostly," Spiro said.

Eve smiled. These days tempers could still flare over perceived slights but in the main, the trawlers were well equipped and the fishing regulated to keep it a fair and sustainable industry.

She took a bite of one of Lucy's scones. "These taste all right." Eve could make a decent lasagne or a stew but baking had never been her forte. She'd given up once she no longer had to fill school lunch boxes, and Mary had taken over supplying most of the sweet food for the two sets of crew.

"Yes." Spiro broke his scone into small bits.

"The forecast looks good."

"Yes," he said again and put another piece of scone in his mouth. Normally he'd swallow something so dainty in one go but he chewed slowly, studying his coffee intently as if some kind of message was about to issue forth from it.

Spiro had something to say. Probably Mary had been at him again. She'd been wanting him to get out of prawn fishing since he'd broken his leg ten years ago. Her niggling at him had come to a head every year or so since. Eve had always been able to talk him round. Spiro was several years younger than her and last time he'd promised to wait until he turned seventy.

He shuffled his feet and cleared his throat but didn't say anything, just continued to stare at the bay. He was worried but determined; she could tell from his movements, the look in his eyes and the set of his jaw. Funny she knew the details of this man better than she'd ever known her own husband. Spiro she could read like a book. Rex had successfully hidden so much from her.

Spiro shifted his feet again and stood, went to one of the puddles on the edge of the verandah and looked up. "That gutter needs replacing."

Eve nodded. It was about the only thing that still needed attention and wasn't a job she could do herself. "I'm sure you haven't called out to tell me something I already know."

He studied her, his brow creased and mouth turned down. "I'm selling my share of the business, Eve."

She felt the small thud in her chest like a quick punch. They owned two trawlers between them these days but ran the business as one. Even though she'd expected it, this discussion was always fraught with emotion. "You're not seventy yet. Last time you promised to wait until—"

"Mary has cancer."

The breath left her chest altogether then. The case she would put forward for staying in business dried on her lips. She couldn't compete with cancer.

"That's tough, Spiro. What kind is it?"

"Lung. Contained, they think. She'll need an op and maybe some follow-up treatment but the doctors seem positive."

"That's good."

"We want some time to do our own thing. Not worry about the business. You can buy me out if you want but I think we should sell the licences, the boats, the lot. We're both getting too old for it. I've got a couple of interested buyers."

"This is a lot to take in." The ache in Eve's chest spread to her shoulders and had nothing to do with a torn rotator cuff. She knew the day had to come but she'd hoped to stretch it a little further.

"You don't need the worry of it, Eve."

"It's not a worry to me." She felt a small spark of anger at Spiro for not having the gumption to stick it out. "It's my life."

"To be fair, managing the books isn't quite the same workload as managing the trawlers."

She glared at him but he didn't look away, his resolve outweighing his concern.

"We can't go on working forever, Eve."

"Why not?" Her anger ebbed and a small wiggle of fear replaced it. What else was there for her to do?

"You should get involved in the local community again."

"You know I can't."

"There's nothing you can't do if you put your mind to it." He turned away from her, looking back towards the town. "I heard about your meeting with Audrey."

Eve snorted. "I don't think I'd call it a meeting."

"Sylvie was having coffee at the Cinnamon Bark."

"I knew it wouldn't take long for the gossips to spread a good story."

"Sylvie's not a gossip but she saw Mary just after and mentioned it."

"Of course she did." Sylvie was the mother of Trent, one of the museum volunteers. Trent was a sensible young bloke but Sylvie was also a close friend of Mary's so Eve was never sure where she stood with her.

"I think she'd been hoping you'd re-join the committee. I don't think she's a fan of Audrey's ideas."

"I can't go back after what happened."

"You could spend more time with your family?"

"You know that's not easy." Arlo lived in Singapore and she hadn't seen him other than via Skype for almost two years, and Zac was in Darwin, which was more than a quick visit away.

"Travel then. Take up a new hobby."

She glared at him.

He shrugged. "There's more in life I want to do, Eve. Mary's cancer is a wake-up call."

Eve looked yearningly at the boats on the bay. "Where are the buyers based?"

"Adelaide."

She sighed. Took another sip of her tea. "We're the last of the Wallaby Bay owners."

"I know."

"Our partnership's worked well for fifty years."

"Longer than a marriage." His lips twitched and one eyebrow arched.

She grinned. Spiro wasn't a man you could be angry with for long. "Better than a marriage."

He picked up his mug, took a slurp of coffee then set the mug down with a thud. "We should be having a real drink."

Before Eve could object, he'd disappeared inside, returning a few minutes later with a bottle of rakija and two small glasses. She watched as he poured the golden liquid then took the glass he offered and tapped it against his before taking a sip.

She recalled the first time she'd tasted the drink Spiro had learned to make from his Croatian parents. It had a plum base and was almost forty per cent alcohol. He and Rex had watched her with grins on their faces as she'd taken that first sip. The burning sensation in her mouth had been so intense she'd had to use all her strength to not show her shock and then it had spread down her throat leaving a soothing warmth and she'd wanted more. Rex had laughed when she'd held out her glass and Spiro had warned her against having too much. She'd only had two small glasses that night and a mighty hangover the next day but the next night she'd put her hand up to try again and now it was an almost daily ritual. Every summer, she and Spiro brewed a fresh batch using the plums from the trees in his yard.

Spiro took another sip and stared back at the bay. "You don't have to decide what you want to do about the business today but I'll need to know soon if it's a whole business we're selling or a half. Mary and I are going to Darwin as soon as her treatment's finished. We'll catch up with Zac then go on to Broome. I've promised her one of those Kimberley cruises. Neither of us have seen much of Australia. We're both keen to relax and do some sightseeing."

Eve turned away from the hope that sparked in his eyes. She'd done her share of travel in the past but it didn't appeal to her any more, and her community involvement was minimal now thanks to Audrey. The prawn business was her life. Without it she wasn't sure she'd have a life. She put her lips to the rim of the glass and sipped, hoping the rakija would work its wonderful healing powers on her heartache.

twelve

The pain in Eve's shoulder was all-consuming. After spending the day in the city, being contorted into every angle for scans and the late-afternoon visit to Jock Campbell, she was exhausted in a way that a hard day's work didn't match. She glanced around the all-but-empty waiting room again but Lucy still wasn't back. She'd told Eve she might have to shift the car if her appointment went too long. Jock had been running late and when Eve had finally been called in, he'd taken a lot of time looking at her scans, checking her shoulder and finally recommending surgery. By then Eve would have walked over hot coals if it meant she'd get some relief from the pain. She lowered herself to one of the waiting-room chairs.

"Sorry, Eve." Lucy rushed through the door. "Have you been waiting long?"

"Just come out."

"You look done in. I had to drive around looking for another park but I'm not too far away."

Eve went to stand but her knees didn't want to support her.

"Sit a moment," Lucy said. "It's time you had more pain medication. Do you have some water left?"

Eve shook her head. She'd drained the last of her bottle before she'd entered the surgeon's office.

"I bought more." Lucy extracted a bottle of water from her backpack while Eve withdrew the packet of pills from her bag. Once she'd swallowed them she leaned back and closed her eyes.

"We can sit a while until you feel up to moving."

Eve's eyes flew open. "I'm all right. I'd like to get on the road. We'll be late home as it is. Your children will—"

"Will be fine with their father. I'm not worried about them."

Lucy offered her arm and Eve took it with her left hand and raised herself to a standing position. She took some steadying breaths and they set off. Lucy was putting on a brave front but Eve had seen the concern register when she'd first explained they'd be all day in Adelaide.

They'd talked about all sorts on the way down – Eve's life in Wallaby Bay and her connection with the prawn industry, a brief mention of her dead husband and a bit more about her sons and grandchildren. Lucy had talked about her children, how they managed while Alec was away, her enjoyment of living close to the beach, even though it was a rented beach shack. Eve had gleaned Lucy was protective of her children and had a reluctance to rely too much on Alec's parents for childcare. They'd eaten lunch at a cafe out of the city and Lucy had checked her phone regularly.

She did it again as they reached her car.

"I'm sorry we're so late," Eve said as Lucy opened the passenger door for her. "I didn't want this to be a bother for you."

"This is not about being a bother, Eve." Lucy fixed her with that look Eve was learning was as determined as her own.

"You're paying for a service and I'm providing it." She bent in to help Eve with her seatbelt, made sure she was settled and shut the door.

They didn't talk while Lucy navigated the peak-hour traffic, but once they reached the edge of the city she turned into one of the large service stations that dotted the highway. "I'd like a coffee," she said. "What about you?"

"I'd much prefer a rakija but I'm guessing that's not on the menu."

"Another time." Lucy manoeuvred into one of the parking spaces. "What about a hot chocolate?" Her eyes gleamed as she stopped the car and turned to Eve. "I've got a special treat to go with it if you're feeling up to it."

Eve frowned. "I don't need treats."

"Everyone needs a treat after a day like you've had." Lucy reached in the back and brought out two small brown paper bags. "One for you and one for me."

Eve took the bag Lucy offered and sat it in her lap.

"Aren't you going to look inside?"

"I assume it's something to eat but I'm not in the slightest bit hungry."

"Maybe for later then."

The young woman's face was so lit up with expectancy Eve felt compelled to look. She couldn't help but chuckle as soon as she saw the green icing. "You found a frog cake."

"When I shifted the car there was a deli nearby. They were just as you'd described them. And they had them in pink and chocolate as well but you said you liked the green ones."

Eve nodded and pressed her lips firmly together – Lucy's kindness and her aching arm conspiring to overwhelm her.

Lucy opened her door. "I'll get the drinks."

She was gone and Eve realised she hadn't said thank you. She peeled back a bit more of the bag to reveal the cake covered in green fondant icing, with its two black dots for eyes and its open mouth displaying its creamy filling. They were very sweet treats but she and her sons had loved them. The last time she'd bought them had probably been a few years ago when her Singapore grandchildren had come for a holiday. They and their Queensland-born mother had turned their noses up at the treats. Eve and Arlo had eaten the lot.

She'd told Lucy about them the first day she'd started working for Eve. Lucy had offered to bake and they'd settled on scones and banana cake. Lucy had said banana cake was her favourite sweet treat and they'd got on to Eve's love of Balfours' frog cakes. They were a South Australian icon but Lucy had grown up in New South Wales and had never heard of them. Once upon a time Rex would bring Eve one every time he returned from Adelaide. Arlo and Zac had learned to eat them at her knee. Now they were men with children of their own and she rarely saw them.

"Here we are."

Eve startled as Lucy called through the window.

Once they were settled with their drinks Lucy offered to help her get the cake from the bag but Eve declined.

"I should have bought you something plain," Lucy said. "Your tummy's probably not up to sugary treats."

"It was a very kind thought, thank you. I will eat it as a special morning tea tomorrow. We'll need to make some new plans. The specialist can fit me in for the op next Tuesday."

"Oh. In the rush to get away I forgot to ask what he said."

"I've made a right royal mess of my shoulder, evidently. He seemed to think an op was my best option. I've got private health so I might as well get it done as soon as I can."

"Good plan. And yes, we'll need to rejig things." Lucy drove back onto the highway. "You'll need more help for a while. Alec is home for another week so it won't be a problem to begin with. School holidays will make it tricky but they're a few weeks away."

"Weeks! I'm sure I'll be back on my feet before then."

"Back on your feet, yes, but there'll be lots you can't do for months. No driving for at least six weeks, or lifting. You'll need physio appointments and an exercise regime."

Eve sat back and stared off at the darkening skyline. She'd been so focused on the operation she hadn't paid much attention to the recovery period. She'd be totally stuck if she couldn't drive. A knot of annoyance built in her chest and turned to anger.

"Thunderation!"

"What's the matter?" Lucy glanced briefly her way. "Do you need me to stop?"

"No. I'm all right. It's just that this shoulder is being a blasted nuisance."

Lucy said no more. Eve wanted to scream her frustration but that wasn't a good option here. Distracting the driver wasn't wise and no doubt Lucy already thought her kooky enough. Instead Eve juggled her hot chocolate with her left hand and concentrated on drinking it without spilling it down the front of her.

The headlights of Julia's hire car swept the empty yard outside Eve's garden fence.

"Damn!" She was fairly sure no-one was home. The driveway wound in from the main road and gave a good view of the house, which was in darkness. It was too early for Eve to have gone to bed but on the off-chance she was home and had turned in,

Julia thought it best to retrace her tracks and go to her brother's. Heath's place, the farm where Julia had grown up, was several kilometres across country from Eve's.

"Damn!" she muttered again and turned the car around. She should have thought this through. A surprise visit only works if the person you're trying to surprise is at home. Julia had based her plans on staying with Eve. Then she could call in for the odd visit to Heath. He and his wife, Verity, were always so busy, she'd hardly see them even if she stayed with them. It was better to pin them down to a set time to catch up.

At the end of Eve's drive she paused. There was plenty of accommodation in Wallaby Bay. Instead of turning left she turned right and headed back towards the town. One night in a motel wouldn't break her.

It was almost nine by the time Lucy pulled up outside the beach house. The wind had come up, and there was only a quarter moon and it was hidden by cloud. The only glimmer of light came from the one over her back door. Alec must have left it on for her. Thank goodness she had him to come home to. She'd made sure that Eve was settled at home again before she left but the house had felt so big and empty. She wondered why Eve continued to live in the isolated home when there were so many better options in the town.

Lucy took a deep breath and stretched her arms. It had been a long day. Driving Eve to Adelaide and back was a four-hour round trip and then there were the appointments to get to, the parking spots to find. She didn't know Adelaide all that well but it hadn't been too difficult. Eve had been an easy travel companion, chatty on the way down and quiet on the way home. Both situations had been fine with Lucy. The idea of the operation was obviously bothering the older woman. Lucy had tried to talk about it after she'd bought drinks for the journey home but Eve had been evasive and they'd lapsed into silence for most of the way. Hopefully they'd both sleep well and discuss what needed to be arranged with fresh eyes tomorrow.

The TV was on when she let herself inside but Alec was stretched out on the couch, sound asleep. He stirred as she slipped out of her shoes.

"You made it." He blinked at her then swung his legs to the floor. "How did it go?"

"We didn't have any problems getting to the appointments. Eve has to have an operation next week."

"So she'll need your help a bit longer?"

"Quite a bit longer, I should think, but she's very stoic. How were the kids?"

"Fine. Poppy seems to think you were bringing her something special from Adelaide."

"I brought them a sweet treat each." She'd bought two more of the frog cakes, pink for Poppy and chocolate for Noah, and a couple of coloured meringues just in case.

"I'm sure that will do." Alec yawned.

"You should go to bed."

"What about you?"

"I feel wide awake now. I think I'll have a cup of tea and veg out here for a while."

"I'll make it." He leaped up and waved her to the couch.

She was happy to let him do it. It was strange how sitting in a car half the day could leave you feeling so physically drained.

He brought tea for her and a glass of water for himself and eased in next to her on the couch. She left the tea to cool and snuggled closer. She could manage the children and the house and life in general when he wasn't here but it was the intimacy that she missed the most. Not just their sex life, but evenings like this once the kids were in bed and they simply hung out together.

He slipped an arm around her shoulders and rested his chin on her head. "I had a phone call today about work."

"You don't have to go back early?" she groaned.

"No. But instead of going back to my old job they want me to move on to the new one when I get back."

"The one out of Port Headland?"

"Yeah."

Lucy felt sorry he had to travel so far but they'd decided he'd only do it for another year or so. While the money was there it was a great chance to build their future.

"Are you sure you won't move up there, Lou? The rental agreement on this place is very flexible."

"If it was just me, maybe." She shifted away, turned back to his serious gaze. "I don't want to move the kids again so soon. They're just starting to settle here."

"The roster will be different. Shorter. I'll only be two weeks on, one week off. By the time I fly back to Adelaide then come up here I'd only get a couple of days at home."

She sighed, suddenly feeling the weight of fatigue. "Do you have to take this job?"

"No. But the money's extra good and it's only for five months, six at the most. I should be done by Christmas. Remember why we're doing this?"

"I do but I also remember some of your previous jobs and the men you worked and lived with day in, day out, their disrespectful talk about women and families, the mundane food and the awful dog-box accommodation. How you hated it."

"I shouldn't have told you." He screwed up his face. "Anyway, it's not all like that. And this is a different company to the last one. It's short-term pain for long-term gain."

"And then what?"

"We'll have enough for me to give up FIFO work. We'll buy a house and start our business. Or I could just stay at home and you could work full-time."

She snorted but a small knot of hope unfurled in her chest. Was the end of his time away really in sight? Could they truly turn their dream of a local business into a proper plan?

"We've done the hard yards, Lou. We stuck to our plan—"

"With a few arguments." She raised her eyebrows.

"I was never going to buy a motorbike."

"You came home with all the info and spent a week of your leave checking them out." Alec had owned an old motorbike when she'd first met him. That and his Commodore had been his prize possessions. He'd written off the bike in an accident that had thankfully done little damage to him and he'd never replaced it until he'd arrived home after one stint away full of plans to do so.

"And after we talked it through I realised how much time it would add to my FIFO work. You made me see sense. What about the fight we had over your bloody magical blender? At least that turned out all right. Going back to work to pay for something useful made sense in the end." He chuckled. "Remember how adamant you were about taking the aged care job and how worried I was about how you'd manage the kids in Melbourne where we had no family support. Now that we're here and you've got childcare laid on you don't want to work."

"It's not that I don't want to work, it's—"

"You don't want to be a burden to my parents, I know. Let's not go over old ground. We're so close to our goal now. This job pays extra and then I can kiss the fly-in, fly-out life goodbye."

It seemed hard to comprehend. They'd been living this life for six years now. They'd stuck to their plan, except Lucy going back to work to pay for the Thermomix and the dryer. Alex had no idea what a disaster that had been, and by the time he'd been allowed to come home to them it had all been over.

Lucy thought of Noah. The sunshine left him when Alec wasn't home. "Five months feels like a long stretch."

"I won't stay away all that time. We'll work something out. Maybe I can just come back once every six weeks."

"Six weeks!"

"We've done longer than that in the past."

Lucy pulled back her hands and lurched up straight. "Don't talk about it." It was still painful to recall what they went through the year before. Between Alec being trapped interstate and her … Lucy's stomach churned. She reached for the tea and took a calming sip.

"When do you have to let them know?" she asked.

"I've said I'll go."

She studied him over her mug. "We always discuss your job offers first."

"They weren't giving me a choice of jobs, Lucy. It was that or none at all."

"But you could get something with someone else?"

"Probably, but they really made this worth my while."

He placed a gentle hand on her shoulder. "It's only a few months in the scheme of things. We can do it and then we won't ever have to live like this again."

She stared into his dark brown eyes, begging her to trust him. He'd never purposely let them down but sometimes circumstances happened beyond their control. She'd never meant to let her kids down either. "Five months only. You promise."

"You know I can't, Lou. Sometimes these things don't go to plan. It could stretch out to six or seven. But I can promise I'll do my very best to make it as short as I can. Deal?"

She held his gaze a moment. The thought that he'd be permanently home with them in the near future was tantalising. She put her hand over his. "Deal," she said.

thirteen

Eve was pleased to hear Lucy call through the screen door at eight thirty the next morning.

"Come in." She turned down the radio then returned to making a list. She'd had a restless night between her aching shoulder and thinking of all the things that needed to be done and then of the surgery itself. She'd been looking forward to Lucy's arrival. Already Eve realised how lucky she'd been to find someone like Lucy. The young woman was sensible and practical and her presence reassuring. Eve didn't want to give herself over to the control of the medical profession but as she had no choice, she was glad to have Lucy in her corner.

"Hello." Lucy strode into the kitchen, a bright smile on her face. She hooked her small shoulder bag on the back of a chair and plugged her phone into the spare charger she kept on the now clear-from-clutter bench. "I hope I'm not too early. Alec dropped me here first. He'll take the kids to school and come back for me when I'm ready."

"You should have brought them in. I'd like to meet your family."

"Perhaps another time." Lucy gave her an appraising look. "How are you this morning? I bet you didn't sleep well last night."

"You win the bet."

"Did you try the pillow behind you?"

"Yes. It helped."

"Good. What about a shower?"

"I'm skipping today. I took some meat from the freezer last night. I thought I'd get you to make something in the slow cooker and perhaps change the sheets and towels while you're here."

"Right, I'll get the sheets going first."

"Then I've started to make a list of what needs to be done before I go and what I still have to organise."

"Okay. Won't be long."

Eve had shown Lucy her bedroom, bathroom and the laundry on her first day and, true to her word, the young woman was back in no time at all. Eve hadn't moved from her place at the table, still pondering over her list.

"You're sure you're okay to take me to Adelaide and bring me back?" She tapped her pen on her notebook. "It's an overnight stay."

"Of course. Try not to worry about anything. I'll be your gofer. You just concentrate on a positive attitude. And once you've had the op you'll feel so much better in the long run."

"I've never had surgery before."

"Never?" Lucy had her head in the fridge but she turned back to look at Eve. "That's pretty amazing."

"The beef's on a plate, middle shelf." Eve twirled the pen in her fingers. "My only stay in hospital was when I had my babies. And back then they made you stay for several days. Not like now when they kick you out the minute the baby's born. I've been to hospital plenty of times with Rex or my boys over the years and

Rex's parents when they were alive but I've managed to avoid any need for a stay myself."

"As you say, they're pretty slick these days. Unless you're very unwell the best place to recover is in your own home."

Lucy busied herself in the kitchen preparing the food, carefully explaining what Eve could expect from her admission, surgery prep and recovery. By the time she had the slow cooker on and left to hang out the sheets, Eve was feeling less anxious about the coming surgery and recovery. At least Lucy was confident in the kitchen. Eve would need help getting the meals ready for the boat crew. She always sent enough meals out to last them the first few days. She glanced at the list of cooking that needed to be done and hoped Lucy wouldn't mind.

It was already after ten when once more Julia drove into Eve's yard. By the time she'd checked into her motel room the previous night, she'd been tired from travelling all day and had fallen eagerly into the soft bed. She'd slept deeply, only waking to the sound of a car roaring past outside. She was surprised to see bright daylight streaming around the blind and had discovered she only had time for a quick shower before check-out. She'd called in at one of the many cafes that now dotted the main street and bought herself a takeaway coffee then headed back to Eve's.

A stiff south-westerly tossed everything in its path, kept the air chilly and twirled the sheets on Eve's clothesline as Julia pulled up at the back gate. She stepped out of the car and paused to take in a lungful of fresh salty air, then let herself in the gate with an eye out for Eve's dog, Merc, until she remembered he'd died. It was nearly two years since she'd last been here. Besides the dog dying, a few things had changed, if the fresh paint on the woodwork, the tidy garden and the neatly mowed patch of lawn were anything to go by. Maybe Eve employed a handyperson these days.

Julia opened the screen door, gave a light rat-a-tat on the wooden door and let herself in. "Hello? Eve?"

The delicious savoury smell of meat cooking wafted in the air. The washing machine rattled and whirred from the laundry. Music was playing somewhere; Eve was always one to have the radio on. The sound of chatty voices drifted from deeper in the house.

"Hello, Eve!" she called again.

"Did you hear someone?" It wasn't a voice Julia recognised. Too young for Eve. A head poked into the passage from the kitchen. A young woman stepped out, her arms folded across her chest. "Who are you?"

"A friend of Eve's. Who are you?"

"Oh my giddy aunt, is that Julia?" Eve appeared in the passage behind the woman guarding the space. "It is Julia! Where did you spring from?" Eve stepped around the young guard, who relaxed her stance a little.

"I thought I'd surprise you." Julia hurried forward then stopped as she took in the sling around Eve's arm. "What have you done to yourself?"

"Shoulder. Long story." Eve held out the arm that wasn't tied up. "It's so good to see you."

Julia stepped into her embrace, careful to hold her coffee out and not bump Eve. She inhaled the fresh citrusy smell of the clothes freshener Eve must still add to her washing and felt like she'd come home. That was until she saw the displeased look from the woman behind Eve. She stepped back, meeting the woman's stare with an equally assessing look.

"This is Lucy," Eve said. "She's been such a help to me, I can't begin to tell you how much. Lucy, this is my goddaughter, Julia." Eve flapped a hand at her. "But what are you doing here? Can you stay for a while?"

Julia nodded in the home help's direction then slipped her arm through Eve's. "I'm here for two weeks, if you have a bed?"

"If I have a bed!" Eve turned to Lucy and laughed. "She's a real joker, this one." She nudged Julia. "You know how many bedrooms there are here. You can take your pick." Eve laughed. It was a sound Julia loved and realised she'd missed for a long time.

"Where have you come from?" Lucy hadn't moved from her position at the door.

"Melbourne." Julia frowned. Lucy stared at her as if she was a bug to be got rid of. "We are allowed to cross the border without isolating these days," Julia said.

"You're just in time." Eve was oblivious to the tension. "Lucy's almost finished the washing and we were going to have a cuppa. Where are your bags?"

"In the car. I'll get them later."

"Can you put the kettle on please, Lucy?" Eve tugged Julia towards the kitchen. "Let's get you a cup and you can put your coffee in it and join us."

"Take it easy, Eve," Lucy said. "You don't want to stir up that shoulder."

Julia turned her back on Lucy, having taken an instant dislike to the young bossy-britches, and let Eve guide her into the kitchen.

"Why didn't you warn me you were coming?" Eve said.

"I decided to surprise you."

"What about Heath? Have you been to the farm?"

"Not yet. I wanted to see you first. Find out all the goss."

"You know I don't listen to gossip."

"I wish you weren't so goody-two-shoes."

They both laughed.

Lucy had followed them but hung in the doorway, still glaring at Julia.

"Can you take out one of those floral mugs from the back of the cupboard, please, Lucy. They're the ones Julia likes."

"And you've got frog cakes." Julia ignored the stiff-faced young woman and focused on the table instead. Her mouth watered at the sight of the green treats. "I haven't had one of them for years."

"Lucy bought them yesterday but we didn't feel like them then." Eve smiled at her. "We've only got two though. You can have mine."

"Oh no. You two eat them." Lucy flicked the switch on the kettle. "Alec cooked me a huge breakfast this morning and I'm not in the slightest bit hungry."

"Come and sit down, Eve." Julia sat and patted the chair next to her. "I want to hear all about this arm. What have you done?"

Lucy slipped away as soon as she'd poured Eve's tea. The load of towels she'd put in the machine would be finished by now. The two women were talking so intently they probably wouldn't even notice she was gone. Their effusive tones followed her down the passage, a joyful reunion she wasn't a part of.

The ridiculous anger she'd first felt at Julia for simply turning up from across the border had been replaced by a pang of envy. Making friends had never been easy for Lucy. Not that she'd call

Eve a friend, but they were already familiar with each other. Even though Lucy had sworn she'd never get too close to a client again, Eve at least made her feel as if she was a helpful visitor rather than someone paid to provide support. Julia's arrival was a timely reminder that Lucy was Eve's employee, not her friend.

She hefted Eve's large cane basket to her hip and carried it out to the line. It was heavy on its own without the burden of the few wet towels. It was no wonder Eve had shoulder trouble if she lugged things like this about. Lucy mentally added plastic washing basket to the shopping list they'd started this morning. There were a few things to organise and purchase before Eve's op.

The surgeon had said she'd need to stay in hospital overnight. Lucy wondered if Julia would want to go with Eve instead. She'd be disappointed not to make the trip now that she'd organised it. Alec would still be home and could stay with the kids. She didn't like giving up any time she had with him but she'd allowed herself to imagine some time alone in Adelaide. Perhaps she'd do a bit of shopping, wander in bookshops and maybe even visit the art gallery. There was an exhibition she'd seen advertised – the paintings and films of the Marek brothers. Alec would hate it. It was surrealism, not the kind of art she usually enjoyed either but the advertising for it had been intriguing and it was something she'd normally never do.

She hung the towels then untwisted the sheets, which had already blown dry, and bundled them into the basket. Not in a rush to go back inside, she dawdled around the backyard. It wasn't much of a garden considering the grandeur of the house. Eve was obviously not a green thumb. It was basic, almost barren but tidy except for the roses along the fence where several large weeds flourished. She squatted and began to pull them out. There was something quite therapeutic about pulling weeds. She had no garden at the beach shack. Her only bit of greenery was Zig, her fiddle-leaf fig. Alec had given it to her last birthday. It was her companion when he wasn't there.

"Are you the one who's been doing Eve's garden?"

Lucy jumped up as Julia marched along the path towards the back gate.

"I thought she must have had someone in. She's never been a gardener before. The backyard was always a jungle of weeds."

Lucy opened her mouth to say she wasn't responsible but Julia kept talking.

"Eve wondered where you'd got to. She's worried you haven't had your cup of tea yet. I told her workers did that on their own time, not hers, but she insists you go in and have it."

Julia strode on. From behind, Lucy noticed a slight roll to her stride as if one leg was shorter than the other. Julia opened the boot of her car. Lucy turned away and lugged the heavy basket inside. In the laundry she stopped to fold the sheets and put them back in the huge linen press that ran almost the length of one wall. One corner of the room, behind the door, was taken up by a large chest freezer and there was a washing machine under the window beside a stand of cement troughs. Like the rest of the house, or at least as much as she'd seen, the laundry had been given a more modern makeover and included a second toilet and shower.

By the time Lucy had finished, Julia was back inside and towing a case into the bedroom opposite Eve's. Lucy hoped the other woman might stop in there to unpack, give Lucy time to make her excuses to Eve and leave.

Eve was at the slow cooker, stirring the contents. "Luckily there's enough here for a few meals. There'll be plenty to share with Julia. I'm so glad she's here. I feel better about the operation already."

"So Julia will take you to Adelaide?"

Eve put down the spoon she'd been using to stir the meat and turned a puzzled expression to Lucy. "I don't presume so. I mean she might want to come but—"

"Of course I can take you." Julia was back.

"You can come with us if you like, Julia, but Lucy will be my carer."

"You don't need her now that I'm here."

Lucy felt as if she were the net in a tennis match.

"Yes, I do. I realise it must seem as if Lucy is here in a home-help capacity but she's far more than that. She's a nurse. She understands the gibberish that doctors speak sometimes, she knows about medications and … well, medical stuff. It would be lovely to have your support too, Julia, but I want Lucy to be with me when I have the operation and for as long afterwards as she has time to spare." Eve looked from Julia to Lucy, the determination on her face just as it had been the first day Lucy visited her. "As per our agreement."

"Of course," Lucy said, feeling the full brunt of Eve's piercing look and that of Julia's just to the edge of her vision.

"I think you've done as much as I need today though," Eve said. "And with Julia here I can manage over the weekend, but I do have a large amount of cooking to do for the trawler crews."

"You're not still doing their meals," Julia said. "I thought Spiro and Mary took that over."

"We share it. I make lasagnes and curries and slabs of savoury slices. It's a big job, feeding everyone." Eve's tone was defensive.

Julia shook her head.

"Could you come out Sunday or Monday to help me with the cooking, Lucy?"

"Yes, of course. I'll see what plans Alec has and let you know which day suits."

"Good," Eve said. "You get to have a bit more family time with that lovely man of yours and I'll have Julia to keep me company. Unless you have other plans, Julia?"

"Of course not," Julia said. "I'll catch Heath and Verity at some stage but I came back to visit you, and I'll be staying while you need help." She folded her arms across her chest and glared at Lucy.

"Well, aren't I lucky." Eve smiled. "Last week I could find no help and now I have two guardian angels."

Lucy nodded, avoiding Julia's penetrating look. Perhaps angel wasn't quite the right word but she was reassured Eve wanted her to stay.

***

Later that evening, Julia dropped her phone back to the couch, her ear warm from the long conversation she'd just had with her brother.

Eve stuck her head into the lounge. "Do you want a cup of tea?"

Julia groaned. "Not for me." She was full to bursting after sharing the slow-cooked beef and the sticky date pudding Lucy had prepared. Not only was Lucy a nurse and home help but she could cook as well. Julia jumped to her feet. "I'll make you one if you like."

"No, I'm good too. Thanks for clearing up in the kitchen. Let's just sit for a while."

Julia flopped back to the couch but Eve went to the big bay window and began to draw the curtains.

"I can do that." Julia started to get up again.

"I'm quite capable of pulling a curtain across with my good arm." She gave Julia a defiant look. "Was that Heath you were talking to?"

"Yes. He's somewhere in the south-east and Verity's in Adelaide. They'll be home by late Monday then Heath's off to the mid-north for some meeting or other."

"They're as busy as fleas, those two."

"Honestly, I don't know how he manages to run the farm; he's never home. I think the boys do it all. Anyway, he's asked me for dinner Tuesday night. I said I couldn't go."

"Why not?"

"Your operation. I'll be in Adelaide with you."

"Lucy will be with me. If it's the only chance you can catch up with your family you should do it."

"There'll be time later."

"You're staying a while?"

"I told you two weeks at least. I can extend it if you still need help longer."

"That's lovely. I'll be pleased for your company but you don't need to come for my op."

"You were there for me through several operations and months of rehab."

"Only when your mother or brother couldn't be."

Her mother had been her rock but Julia didn't remember Heath helping her that much during the long months of recovery. She frowned, stirring through the memories of a time she'd rather forget. Heath had been there sometimes while she'd been in hospital during the night. When her mum became too exhausted to stay on he would come and sleep on the lumpy recliner by her bed.

"You should relax," Eve said. "I'll be out to it most of Tuesday and then home again Wednesday. It will be wonderful to think that you'll be here waiting for me. Something to look forward to. I don't need you to be in Adelaide."

Julia felt the pang of dismissal. It was ridiculous that at forty-five she still craved Eve's attention. It had come easily in her growing years. Julia's mum, Pam, Eve and their other friend Gert had remained great pals through marriage and children. Gert had two sons, Eve had two sons, and with Heath and Julia the children made a gang of six with Julia the only girl. The Bellings lived in town and Gert had been strict about what children could and couldn't do, but when they were home on the Patersons' farm or at the Monks' place surrounded by space, there were very few rules. Eve had taken her godmother role seriously and had been like a second mum to Julia. Now it was as if Eve was keeping her at arm's length.

One of the support cushions fell to the floor as Eve lowered herself carefully onto her chair. Julia leaped up to get it. Eve winced as she settled back.

"I can't stand seeing you in so much pain." Julia eased the cushion under Eve's arm as she'd seen Lucy do earlier in the day.

"I'm managing, and things will get better after the op. That's what I'm telling myself. I'm so glad you're here."

Eve's smile washed away Julia's dissonant thoughts. Instead she felt guilty she hadn't kept in better touch with Eve of late. Arlo and Zac were so far away. Julia hadn't seen them in years and she wondered how close their relationship with Eve was these days.

Her phone rang again. Glen's name flashed on the screen. She ignored the call.

"Don't worry about me," Eve said. "Take your call."

"I'll talk to him later."

"Him?"

"Glen."

"Oh. You haven't mentioned him since you arrived. I wondered if you were still an item."

Julia laughed. "I haven't been called an item before."

"I thought him such good company when I came to stay with you for the tennis."

"Hmmm."

"You got on so well. Surely that wasn't an act each time I visited. I thought you were great together. What's happened?"

"Nothing really, that's the trouble."

Eve's mouth twitched but she didn't speak.

"We've become a bit …" Julia shrugged. "I should break it off with him but somehow we seem to stay together."

"There could be another reason for that."

"For what?"

"For not breaking it off. It's sometimes called love, Julia."

Julia snorted. To her love meant commitment and she was never going down the commitment path again. Tim had not only been insensitive in the timing of their break-up but he'd hurt her financially too.

"Glen's a much better man than any of your others."

"You make it sound as if I've had a string of lovers."

"I've no idea. I can only go on the couple I've met and I can tell Glen runs rings around them all. He's good for you. He's kind, reliable, makes you laugh."

"Did," Julia huffed. "Anyway I'll ring him back later. What shall we do for the weekend?"

Eve held her gaze a moment. When she was in inquisition mode she was difficult to deflect.

"I'd love to try some of the new eateries," Julia said.

"It's a long weekend so the town will probably be busy."

"We should kick our heels up before your op."

"Give the dying woman a last hurrah."

"Eve, don't say that," Julia snapped. "Not even as a joke. You're the only parent I have left."

Eve held her good hand towards Julia. "I'm not dropping off my perch yet, my girl."

Julia slid from her chair, sat at Eve's feet as if she were a child and gripped her hand. "I know you're not."

"So, weekend plans?"

"We can go for a drive. I see there're a few changes around Wallaby Bay since I was here last."

"The whole peninsula is changing. We have several breweries and distilleries these days. The tourists have always loved our beaches but there's even more on offer now."

"We could do a booze crawl."

"I'm not drinking much." Eve recalled Lisa's gentle warning. "And I can't drive, so perhaps another time."

"We could go out for dinner tomorrow night."

"Yes, or ... we could have dinner here. Ask Gert if she's home and Pete from across the paddock."

"Is he still alive?"

"Don't be cheeky. He's only got a few years on me."

"I'd like to see Gert."

"And perhaps we could ask Lucy and her husband to come. Someone more your age."

"I don't mind it being just Gert and Pete."

"It's a good chance to invite Lucy and Alec while you're here to help. He works a FIFO job and heads back to WA at the end of next week. You remember Kon and Helen Nicoli? They used to have the fish and chip shop? He's their son."

"They had two boys, didn't they? Younger than me but I don't remember an Alec."

"He's the third son; there's quite an age gap between him and his brothers. I haven't seen him for years. I'd like to catch up with him again." Eve's face shone with excitement and Julia swallowed her annoyance at the thought of Lucy being here again so soon.

"What about Spiro and Mary, if we're going all out," she said. "I haven't seen them for an age either." She'd always had a soft spot for Eve's business partner although his wife she could take or leave.

"I haven't told you, Mary's got lung cancer."

"Hell, that's no good."

"I think the doctors are very confident. She's having an op soon and maybe follow-up treatment."

"Then this weekend is perfect timing. Let's make it a pizza night and order in."

"I'm not inviting people for dinner to give them pizza."

"What then? You know my cooking skills aren't gourmet."

"Neither are mine. We could make some casseroles and a cheesecake, do it together."

"By together, you mean I'll do the work under your direction."

"Exactly. There'd be eight of us. A good number for dinner."

Julia was so pleased to see the joy on Eve's face she'd have agreed to anything at that point.

fourteen

Eve looked around her dinner table and smiled. She couldn't remember the last time her home had been filled with so many voices. There were only seven of them in the end – Pete had declined her invitation. He came over for the odd meal of fish when it was just the two of them but he wasn't one for socialising in bigger groups.

Eve had taken an extra painkiller just before the guests arrived and made sure she moved around as little as possible, determined not to let her dodgy shoulder spoil her evening. Julia had been a wonderful help with the food and Lucy had made a hot potato salad. Spiro and Mary brought a prawn entree, Gert some chocolates and all of them had brought drinks. They'd started with shots of rakija, of course, and with the exception of Eve, Mary and Gert, they were all well-oiled by the time Julia brought the cheesecake to the table.

"Your usual strawberry." Mary sat back from the table. "Not for me, thanks."

"I made it," Julia said.

Eve was glad once again Julia was here. There'd been a couple of times over dinner when Mary had said something annoying. Eve bit her tongue, as usual, but Julia had been quick to rebuff her or change the subject as if they were a team.

"It has strawberries on top but the base is a chocolate brownie crumb." Julia winked at Spiro. "I know what a sweet tooth you are."

He grinned. "Count me in."

"You know you shouldn't." Mary patted his rounded tummy gently.

"Just a small piece won't hurt."

In the end, coffee and tea were handed out and everyone but Mary had a serve of Julia's cheesecake.

"Oops!" Julia laughed as a piece of the base shot off her plate. "May have made it a bit hard. Watch out for your teeth."

She cut up Eve's serve with difficulty while the others tackled theirs with bursts of laughter as little pieces shattered and zipped off their plates. Everyone assured her it was delicious despite the crisp base.

"You cook like your mother," Gert said. "I loved Pam dearly but her food was often well done."

"That's why I cook as little as possible," Julia said. "I learned to hate it at my mother's knee."

"Best you stick to research. What are you working on now? Anything exciting?"

Julia frowned.

This time Eve jumped in. "She's between projects at the moment, Gert." During the entree when they'd been enjoying the margarita prawn skewers, Spiro had quizzed Julia about her research and she'd said her current job was finished. Gert had obviously missed that part of the discussion.

"I like the taste of your downy base," Gert said.

Once again Julia frowned.

"I think the crunchy base makes it," Eve said quickly.

There were more murmurs of agreement and smiles all round, except for Mary who remained stony-faced and silent while everyone enjoyed their dessert.

"Alec's looking for some storage space." Spiro put the spoon on his empty plate. "I wondered about the boatshed, Eve. There's hardly anything in it these days."

"What do we need storage for?" Lucy asked.

"Mum and Dad are selling the block of land they had with the shed on it."

"Oh."

"We've got furniture and boxes of gear we can't fit at the shack," Alec said. "It takes up about half a normal car garage space. They've had a couple of nibbles for the block so we'll need to find an alternative soon."

"Aren't there self-storage places here?" Julia asked.

"There are," Spiro said. "But as I was telling Alec, it seems silly to pay when there's an empty shed doing nothing."

"You're most welcome to the boatshed," Eve said. "As Spiro says, there's not much in it. It's solid and has a cement floor."

"Shall I gather the plates?" Mary said. "Spiro and I can't stay late."

He looked surprised.

"I'm feeling rather tired." Mary gave him a hangdog look.

"Alec and I can do the dishes." Lucy began to stack plates.

Mary had succeeded in bringing the evening to a close and suddenly Eve was feeling it herself. It was probably time to take more painkillers.

"Can you hang on a few more minutes?" Spiro put a gentle hand on Mary's shoulder. "I thought I'd whip out now and show Alec the shed while we're both here. Save worrying Eve."

Gert rose to her feet. "I'll help with the dishes."

"Everyone relax, there's a dishwasher." Julia flicked her hand at Spiro. "You go and do your shed business. I can clear the table."

Spiro and Alec headed out and Lucy helped Julia gather plates.

"Perhaps I'll go then," Gert said. "You have enough helpers. You young ones will make sure Eve looks after herself, won't you?"

"Of course." Julia came to hug her goodbye but Gert flinched away like she had when Julia had tried to hug her when she'd first arrived. Julia tugged her arms to her sides. She'd never been as close to Gert as she was to Eve. "It's been good to see you, Gert. Once Eve's up to visitors we'll let you know."

"I'll walk you to the door," Eve said. "I need to stretch my legs." And she didn't want to be left alone at the table with Mary while the younger women were busy cleaning up.

They stepped out into the cold air of the passage. Eve hadn't even had a chance to shut the door behind her before Gert spoke in a loud voice.

"Mary's her usual miserable self. I don't know how Spiro puts up with her."

Eve gasped. She had often unloaded her frustrations about Mary to her friend but always privately.

"I don't think she's feeling all that well tonight," Eve said in a low voice as she shepherded Gert down the passage.

"That's as may be but there's no need to be rude."

Eve hoped to hell Mary hadn't heard.

Gert stopped before they reached the back door. "I wanted to tell you something but not in front of the others." Her look was grave.

"Don't tell me you're not well either?" Eve had been concerned there was something going on with Gert but she wasn't ready to deal with more bad news at the moment.

"I'm healthy enough but … the boys suggested I move to Adelaide."

"And what do you think?"

Gert had always allowed her husband to make the big decisions in her life and now that he was gone she looked to her sons for that support. They were good boys, men now, but Eve wasn't a hundred per cent sure they weren't using Gert as a cash cow and babysitter.

"They showed me this lovely unit while I was in Adelaide last. It's in a nice suburb, about halfway between their two homes, a block of three new units with people my age either side."

"And what do you think?" Eve repeated.

"It's a nice layout, two bedrooms, light and airy. I can walk to a little shopping centre nearby. I'd like to be closer to the family. The house here feels so big and empty now. There's nothing for me in Wallaby Bay any more."

Eve felt a stab of hurt at that. "So you'll sell up and go?"

"Don't be like that, Eve."

"Like what?"

"You always question my decisions these days."

"No, I don't. But moving to Adelaide is a big change. I want you to be sure it's right for you."

"They help me and I'm not so old I can't still help a bit with childcare. You're not close to your sons like I am, Eve. You don't need your family near but I do."

Eve felt as if Gert had twisted the knife. "Arlo and Zac live too far away for us to be in each other's pockets."

"And why is that, Eve?"

"What?"

"They wanted to get as far away as possible."

Eve gasped.

"I'm sorry, Eve, but it's the truth. It wasn't your fault but it's what happened. I don't want to be so far away from my family."

"As long as they're not using you," Eve muttered.

"You know, you mumble more and more these days, Eve. I find it most annoying."

Eve's head snapped back and she flinched as the sudden movement jarred her shoulder.

"You should go back and sit down." Gert's tone softened. "I can see myself out. I'll be in touch after you've had the op. I doubt you'll be feeling like visitors on Thursday but I could pop out here for our coffee catch-up. Let me know how you're feeling then."

She was gone and the door shut so swiftly behind her, Eve had barely caught her breath.

"Eve, are you all right?"

"Yes," she hissed.

Lucy moved along the passage, slipping her arms into her jacket. "We've finished in the kitchen. I was just coming to see what was keeping Alec."

On cue, male voices echoed from beyond the door.

"That sounds like them," Lucy said as the door opened. "Thanks for a lovely dinner, Eve."

"We're off, are we?" Alec said as Lucy handed him the car keys.

"You won't stay for another coffee?" Eve asked, trying to gather back some of the fun from earlier in the evening.

"It's getting late," Lucy said.

"They've got a child-free night." Spiro stepped inside rubbing his hands against the cold. "You remember those, Eve." He was going to nudge her but stopped himself as he noticed her sling.

"Thanks for dinner," Alec said. "And the shed would be perfect. If you're okay with it, I'll get in touch later next week."

"Eve will be recovering from her op," Lucy said.

"I'm sure I'll be up to talking by then," Eve said. "Perhaps you could come out for a cuppa and another look in daylight."

Spiro stood beside her as they waved the young couple off then ducked to the bathroom. Eve trailed back along the passage to the kitchen. Once again, Gert, her best friend, had been sharp with her. And to say Arlo and Zac wanted to get away from their home had hurt. It was the truth, but it had hurt.

"There you are." Julia leaped up from her chair as Eve entered the room. "You look worn out. Perhaps we overdid it tonight. Sit down and I'll make you a cup of tea. The kettle's just boiled."

"Oh for goodness sake, Julia, stop fussing over her," Mary snapped.

Eve was halfway to the chair Julia was guiding her towards. They both stopped and stared at Mary. Her face was pinched with anger.

"I'm not fussing, Mary," Julia said sternly.

Mary gave a soft snort. "There's no doubt about you, Eve. You always seem to make yourself the centre of attention."

Eve lowered herself to the chair, determined not to let the other woman see how much pain she was in.

"That's a bit harsh," Julia snapped.

"She's got a sore shoulder. She'll have an op and recover. Whereas I'm accused of being miserable. Well, maybe I've got a good reason."

Eve's heart sank. Mary had definitely heard Gert's comment. How could she not have? Gert had been so loud.

"At least you won't have to put up with me much longer." Mary sniffed.

"You'll beat this cancer," Eve said.

"I plan to but I'm not talking about the cancer. I mean the end of this bloody partnership. Spiro says you've agreed to sell."

"You're selling the prawn boat?" Julia plonked onto a chair beside Eve.

"You'll no longer be pulling all the strings." Mary's eyes glittered, her red lips were pulled back over her teeth in a triumphant smile. "After all these years I can have my husband to myself."

"I can't believe you didn't mention it." Julia looked at Eve in surprise.

"I didn't because ..." She glanced back at Mary, gave the slightest nod of her head. "I haven't agreed to anything yet."

Mary's smile dropped away. "But Spiro said ..."

"I told him I'd think about it."

"The sale will be difficult unless you agree. The keenest buyer wants the whole business, not a share. Spiro said—"

"I was sure Eve would agree this time."

They all turned to the man framed in the doorway. Eve noted the slight stoop of his shoulders, the sadness in his eyes. Spiro had always been so strong but like her he was ageing and tonight it showed.

"It's time to let it go, Eve," he murmured.

For a moment there was silence except for the gentle hum of the fridge and the rattle of something outside in the wind.

Julia reached out a hand and placed it over Eve's. "You can't gang up on her when she's not feeling her best."

Once again Eve thought how wonderful it was to have someone in her corner. It could be so wearing having to always face difficulties alone.

"You said your buyer would take a half share." Eve no more wanted a stranger in her business than she wanted to sell, but it was a stalling point.

"He will but he's keen to take the lot."

"I haven't even seen this offer."

"Would you really be persuaded by the amount of money he's offering?"

He was right. Eve wanted for nothing. The money she got for the sale of the business would make her an even wealthier woman, but it wasn't about the money. She sighed. "I said I'd think about it."

"It's like everything you have a hand in, Eve. It's your way or no way," Mary said.

"Take it easy, love," Spiro said.

"It's a big decision Eve has to make," Julia said. "You can't rush her."

"She's had a year to think about the display for the museum. If we have to wait that long to sell the business we'll lose the offer."

"You know as well as I do the proposal put to the committee is ludicrous," Eve said. "It's not a factual representation of the prawn fishing industry."

"Have you come up with an alternative? Have you even met with them to discuss it?"

Eve stiffened then tried to relax as pain radiated through her shoulder.

"No." Mary gave a sharp nod of her head. "Spiro and I have contributed, but many other fishing families are following your lead. Nothing can go ahead now that you've pulled your donation."

"I won't make a donation for a badly thought-out plan. And I wouldn't expect others to."

"Is it the actual plan or is it because Audrey suggested it? You know I'm beginning to wonder if Audrey's version of events when she fell isn't the right one."

Eve didn't care what many people thought about her, but Spiro's opinion mattered. She glanced at her dear friend but he was studying his wife.

"Mary." His tone was soft, almost a rebuke.

"What's this about Audrey?" Julia asked.

Mary ignored them both. "Your dislike of Audrey is such a petty reason not to get things done."

"What is to be done then, Mary?" Eve was tired and her shoulder ached. "You seem to have all the ideas."

"There should be a hall of fame, for starters. Spiro and Rex and the other pioneers of the industry should have their names on display."

"Eve's one of the pioneers," Julia said.

Mary snorted.

"It's getting late," Spiro said. "This is not the time—"

Mary's face crumpled and her head fell forward. Spiro strode to her side and threw his arms around her as huge sobs racked her body. Julia stood, moved from foot to foot, but Eve stayed where she was. Mary blamed her for pulling Spiro's strings but she was wrong. He came to her as a friend and business partner. It was always Mary who played the emotional blackmail card. Eve had seen enough of her histrionics over the years to know what a good actress she was but Spiro was always fooled by it.

"Let's get you home," he soothed.

Julia dashed to get Mary's bag and jacket from the other room.

At the door, Spiro turned back while Julia helped Mary into her jacket. "I need an answer about the sale, Eve."

"I haven't even seen a copy of the offer." She lifted her chin and met his gaze.

"I'll email the details tomorrow."

"Then I'll let you know my decision on Monday."

He nodded.

Eve stayed where she was, listening to Spiro's soothing tones as Julia showed them out.

In quick time she was back. "I hope you're not truly too tired," she said. "I want to know what the hell all that carry-on was about."

"I'll need a tea and some painkillers." Eve had felt pleasantly lethargic during dessert but now she suspected it would be a long time before sleep would claim her.

fifteen

Julia rolled the hire car to a stop in the marina carpark. The wind from the day before had blown itself out, and at eight o'clock in the morning the air was still with barely a ripple on the water. Even though they'd been late to bed the previous night Eve had insisted on an early start.

"This is a nice little car," Eve said.

"Very easy to drive." Julia ran her hands around the steering wheel. "You should get something like this."

"I don't want to part with the Torana."

"You don't have to, Eve. Let's face it, you could buy yourself a car for each day of the week and not put a dent in your finances."

"You don't know what my situation is."

"I have a fair idea. And when you sell—"

"If I sell."

Julia pursed her lips. The previous evening, after the blow-up with Mary, they'd sat at the kitchen table late into the night talking about the prawn business. Julia got that it was Eve's life but she'd tried to convince her that selling was the best option all the same. She and Spiro both deserved some retirement years.

Eve got out and Julia followed, tugging her coat tighter around her. After being in the warm car, the crisp air slipped in around any gaps in clothing. She followed Eve down the path towards several boats moored along the marina, a mixture of masts and rigging stretching above them, a mish-mash of metal and rope and the bright orange of nets against the blue, cloudless sky of the fresh winter morning. Moored at one end was the *Evie 3*, her blue-and-white hull gleaming in the sunshine. The modern prawn trawler was vastly different to Rex and Spiro's first two boats, also named *Evie* after Eve. Not that she allowed anyone to call her Evie, but she had allowed it for their boats.

A man stepped out from under the cover of the cabin and lifted his arm in a wave.

Eve waved back. "Hello, Harvey."

Julia followed her along the floating walkway, watching her closely in case she lost her balance, but Eve moved with the sure-footedness of a seasoned seafarer. She stopped at the edge of the boat.

"You've been in the wars, Mrs M." Harvey looked her up and down.

"A temporary nuisance. I'm getting it fixed next week."

Eve allowed Harvey to help her carefully onto the boat then glanced back over her shoulder. "This is my dear friend, Julia. My daughter almost." Eve chuckled. "Julia, this is our skipper, Harvey. The best in the business, but neither of you are to tell Spiro I said that."

"Hello, Harvey." Julia smiled up at the tall man who offered a hand to help her aboard. His grasp was warm and strong. His skin was weathered and long locks of faded blonde hair hung below the thick woollen beanie on his head. She'd imagined someone called Harvey to be older like Spiro but he was probably several years her junior.

"The forecast looks good," Eve said.

"Smooth as a baby's bum, Mrs M."

"Perfect."

"So we're going out?" Harvey reached for one of the ropes that attached the boat to the pontoon.

"What?" Julia gaped at him then at Eve.

"Just a quick trip out into the bay," Eve said. "I won't be here next week when they head out for the last run of the season."

"You know I get seasick."

"We won't be out long," Eve said.

"You didn't say you wanted to go for a ride."

"Would you have come if I did?"

Harvey had folded his arms and was studying them. "What's it to be, ladies?"

"All right," she huffed to hide her fluster. "I guess I can survive a quick trip."

"With me at the wheel you're in safe hands."

Julia stared at his back as he moved away. Had he winked at her? She flinched as a whistle pierced the air.

"We're ready to go, Tony," Harvey called, then scooted up the steps.

A minute later another man stepped out onto the deck.

"This is our engineer, Tony." Eve introduced Julia. "We need the skipper and the engineer to take her out and we'll be crew."

Julia gave Eve an incredulous look as Tony headed to the front of the boat.

The giant motor thrummed to life.

Julia gripped the rail tighter. "We can't just stand here."

"Let's go and sit inside."

Julia gaped at the steep ladder-like stairs. Harvey had shot up them with ease but a one-armed Eve was a different thing. "Hell, Eve, don't you dare knock that arm."

"I'll be fine."

"It's not you I'm worried about. It's the wrath of your guard dog I fear."

"You shouldn't be so tough on Lucy. She's been a godsend for me."

Eve gripped the rail with one hand and made her way up to the cabin but Harvey stuck his head out the door before Julia could follow.

"Can you cast off that last one?" He pointed to the rope in the back corner of the boat.

"What do I do?" Julia had to raise her voice above the motor.

"It's all ready. Take off the last loop once I get back inside."

She crossed warily to the rope he'd indicated. Harvey went back inside then there was a yell, "Righto!"

She let go of the rope and they slowly moved away from the pontoon towards the marina mouth leading them out to the bay. Tony made his way back towards her. He wound up the rope then gave her a nod.

"I've got some things to keep an eye on in the engine room," he said and ducked inside.

Julia shivered at the cold air swirling past her. She climbed the steps and entered the cabin where she joined Eve on the leather seat that ran along one end and side of the table. Immediately she felt warmer. She took in the myriad of screens and dials that lined the console where Harvey stood focused on the view through the large windows. One of the screens showed Tony moving about in what must be the engine room.

Her gaze shifted to the window as the giant rocky arms of the marina were left behind and they picked up a little more speed and headed out into the bay. When Julia glanced back, Eve was resting her head against the seat, her eyes closed, one hand lying on the table in front of her.

Last night Eve had paced the floor as she'd explained her reluctance to sell. At seventy, she'd said, there was nothing in her life to look forward to. She'd done her share of overseas travel and hadn't been planning more, except to visit Arlo and his family in Singapore. She could visit her Darwin family but her trips there weren't for long. Everyone was busy with work and school, and to top it off Eve wasn't keen on the humidity.

"Dolphins ahead." Harvey broke into her thoughts.

"Go and stand at the front," Eve said. "They'll probably dive in and out of the wash."

Julia made her way forward. She was rewarded with several dolphins diving and cutting the water beside the boat. She gripped the rail tighter as they swam in front, playing chicken with the giant vessel, but relaxed again as they appeared further ahead and off to the side, unharmed.

"They're wonderful creatures."

Julia reeled around at the sound of Eve's voice.

"What are you doing here? Don't you dare lose your balance." Julia could feel her own legs moving up and down with the motion of the boat. One wrong lurch and Eve could easily fall.

"I'll be fine. Stop fussing." Eve gripped the rail with her left arm, turned her face to the wind and closed her eyes. "This is as close to freedom as one can get." She peeked from one eye. "You should try it."

Julia gripped the rail with both hands and faced into the wind.

"Let yourself meld with the movement."

Julia closed her eyes, forgot about the tonnes of steel beneath her feet and the huge motor propelling them forward and let her body move with the motion of the boat. She took long slow breaths of the fresh salty air then, buoyed with confidence, she pressed herself against the rail and held out her arms. It was almost like flying. "Now I know how Kate Winslet felt on the *Titanic*," she called.

Eve laughed and Julia gripped the rail again as the boat slowed a little and began to veer north so that they were travelling parallel to the shoreline.

"I don't know if I can do it," Eve said. Her voice was so quiet Julia barely heard her over the sound of the motor and the sea splashing against the hull.

"You'll feel better once you've had the op."

"I don't mean that. I mean sell."

"It's a difficult decision to make on your own. I'd like to see you take it easy in your—"

Eve glared at her.

"In your mature years. Spiro's obviously made his decision. Is there someone else you could talk to? Gert?"

Eve snorted.

"Your accountant?"

She shook her head. "It's as you said last night. I have three options. I can sell my share when Spiro does, I could buy him out or I can stay put and work with the new partner." Eve stared out over the bay. "None of them are palatable."

Unease stirred in Julia's stomach. It could be the early signs of seasickness or it could be her concern for Eve. Either way the ride had lost its sparkle.

As the town petered out, in the distance on the hill she could make out the structure that was Eve's house. Sorrow mingled with the sinking feeling inside her. If Eve didn't have the business and nothing else to do, it would be a rather lonely existence out there.

"Whatever you decide about the business, perhaps you should sell your house," Julia said. "Make a change." She didn't add "while you're fit".

Eve frowned. "Where would I live?"

"What about one of those townhouses with the fabulous views." Julia had been amazed at the new developments going up on what had once been industrial land in the centre of Wallaby Bay.

"No thanks."

Julia shrugged. That would be her choice. She loved apartment living. Eve's house was way too big for one person.

"Don't you get lonely out here by yourself?"

Eve looked towards land. They were almost level with her place now.

"I can't imagine living anywhere else but here and there's nothing to entice me into town these days."

Julia recalled Mary's reference to a bust-up with Audrey. They'd talked late about the business and Julia had forgotten to ask. She wondered if now might be the right time.

The boat slowed and they glanced back at the glass-fronted wheelhouse. Harvey waved then he pointed back the way they'd come.

"I think Harvey wants to go back," Eve said. "It's time."

Julia gave him the thumbs-up and Harvey steered the boat in a gradual about-turn so they were heading back towards the marina. Julia's hands felt like ice and she imagined Eve must be cold too. There was hardly any meat on her bones these days.

"Let's go back inside," she said and let Eve lead the way. Julia stayed right behind her, ready to grab her at the first sign of unsteadiness but Eve stepped into the warmth of the cabin without a problem.

"Forecast is looking good for the first half of next week," Harvey said. "Should be all systems go for the last fish of the season."

"I'm sorry I'll miss it. It will be the first time I haven't been here to wave you all off."

"Times change, hey?" Harvey said softly.

Julia felt another wave of sorrow for Eve.

"You want to take her back?" Harvey said.

Eve shook her head. "I've only got one arm."

"You only need one."

Julia felt the boat veer slightly right as he turned a dial on the bench.

"I'm old-fashioned, I know, but I prefer the proper wheel." Eve patted the polished wood wheel. "Why don't you have a turn, Julia?"

"Hell, no. I might run us aground."

"Nothing for you to hit out here." Harvey grinned.

Something about his look challenged her.

"Why don't we do it together, Eve?" she said. "We'll have your good arm and use mine as your spare."

Eve nodded and they both stepped up to the wheel.

Harvey moved to one side. "Eve, you've got this side and—"

"Yep, I get it," Julia said. She planted her feet like Harvey had and gripped the gleaming wheel with her right hand. A surge of adrenaline shot through her as she realised she was guiding this huge machine through the water, or at least she and Eve were doing it together.

"Isn't this bloody fantastic," Eve said.

"Woohoo!" Julia couldn't help the yell of delight. It made Eve laugh and Julia wanted to hear more of that.

Once they got close to the marina, Harvey took over again, guiding them safely back to the pontoon. Under his direction she helped tie up the boat. Eve watched them from the door of the cabin.

"You didn't have a look around the trawler before we put out to sea," she called. "This one's very different to our earlier two. Show her the bells and whistles before we go ashore, Harvey."

"Happy to."

"Sure." Julia moved back towards the cabin. By the time he'd shown her the state-of-the-art sorting machine, the huge prawn cookers and the freezers to store the boxed product, the kitchen and the crew's quarters that could have been from a show home, Julia was suitably impressed.

"This is a long way from the first boat Spiro and Rex had."

"I didn't ever meet Rex but they were the pioneers of prawn fishing in this region. I'm only a newcomer to prawning here but I've heard the sustainability of the industry is due to their efforts."

"And the other stalwarts who were determined to keep it viable." Julia remembered many a time at Eve's when the prawn fishermen would meet around her kitchen table. "Eve was a part of it all too."

They made their way back to the deck. Tony was there talking to Eve who was already on the pontoon.

"She's a remarkable woman, Mrs M," Harvey said. "I'll miss her and Spiro. They've been the best employers I've ever had."

"She's still not made up her mind to sell."

"It's a good offer." Harvey scratched his scalp under his beanie. "At her age she'd be crazy not to accept it."

Julia agreed with Harvey but no-one could make that decision but Eve.

"I'd better go," Julia said. "Thanks for the tour."

"Come back for another visit if you're staying a while." Once more his face cracked with that lazy grin and he lifted his arm in a wave. "Good luck with the op, Mrs M."

Julia glanced at the woman who'd been a mother and a friend to her for all of her life. Eve was tall but today she was dwarfed by the boat and hunched into herself, perhaps from the pain of her arm or against the strengthening sea breeze – either way it made her look frail. Harvey's words repeated in her head. *At her age she'd be crazy not to accept it.*

It made sense but Eve would make up her own mind, sense or no sense.

sixteen

There were two cars parked at Eve's back gate when Lucy pulled in on Monday afternoon. One was the small white hire car Julia was driving but she didn't recognise the other. Lucy would have turned around and gone home again except Eve had said to come out straight after lunch to tackle the cooking and to touch base about their plans for the next few days. Lucy hadn't thought it necessary – Eve was ultra-organised – but if it made her feel better about the operation ahead Lucy was happy to go along with it.

She'd only just let herself in the gate when the back door opened and Spiro and Julia walked out. They were so deep in conversation they didn't notice her at first.

Spiro smiled when he saw her. "Hello, Lucy."

She smiled back. Julia's face was set in a grimace.

"Eve's waiting for you," she said and the two of them continued on and out the gate.

Lucy let herself in and made her way up the long passage to the front of the house. She went to turn into the kitchen doorway when she noticed a figure standing in front of the huge window in the lounge.

"Hello, Eve."

Eve straightened and turned to her, one hand on the large tele-scope that stood tall in front of the window. "Good weather. It should hold for the next few days." She sucked in a breath. With the light behind her it was hard for Lucy to read her face but she had a defeated stance.

"Are you in pain?" Lucy asked.

"Yes." Eve's hand dropped to her side. "But not my shoulder. This is a different kind of ache. No pill for it."

"Oh."

"I'm all right. I'm feeling sorry for myself, that's all."

"Oh, Eve." Lucy took a step towards her.

Eve shook her head. "I'll be fine. I'll just go to the bathroom. Would you put the kettle on, please? We had a coffee earlier with Spiro but I fancy a tea now. Won't be long."

Lucy went into the kitchen and did as she asked, then leaned her back on the bench and stared out the window. Like Eve she was drawn to the view. Something about watching water was soothing. Now that Eve's op was almost upon them, Lucy was feeling anxious about it. She no sooner wanted to step inside a hospital again than chop off her head.

She wished she was back in the cosy little shack with Alec and the kids. They'd spent the morning walking on the beach and building sandcastles, had a sausage on the BBQ for lunch and then settled in to play board games. A perfect way to end their long weekend. Tomorrow the kids would go back to school and Thursday Alec left for his new job. Who knew how long it would be before they saw him next?

"Where's Eve?"

Lucy spun. Julia was at the table, tidying a stack of papers.

"Bathroom."

"I really don't know why she needs you out here again today. Eve's had me prepping food for you all morning. I could have cooked it but evidently you're better at it."

Lucy remained silent. The kettle flicked off and she got out more cups.

"Don't get one for me." Julia stood on the other side of the wide kitchen bench and watched Lucy prepare tea for two. "We've had so many cups of tea and coffee today I don't know how Eve can stand to drink more either."

"It's a comforting ritual and she doesn't always finish them."

"Listen to you, who's known her for five minutes."

Julia's words were as sharp as if she'd given Lucy a slap. Lucy looked away, poured the water into the cups then wiped down the bench while she waited for it to brew.

"That disinfectant spray gets a workout when you're here."

"Eve's at a low ebb. She's about to have major surgery. I'm trying to keep her safe from any outside—"

"From me, you mean." Julia glared across the bench. "I didn't know Eve was facing surgery when I came."

"Yet you turned up, with no thought to what you might bring with you." Lucy was speaking out of turn but she couldn't help it. She'd been bottling that mix of fear and anger ever since Julia had arrived.

"Oh, for goodness sake, I know all the precautions and I follow them. I'm no more a risk to Eve than you are." Julia's hands went to her hips. "In fact you've got kids and a FIFO husband so you're probably far more exposed to bugs than I am."

Lucy gripped the spray bottle tighter. Julia was right but old habits were hard to break.

"I'm going to stay on, you know," Julia said. "At least while Eve still needs help. So after this week she won't need you any longer."

Lucy met Julia's defiant gaze. She felt a mix of disappointment and relief. She'd grown to enjoy Eve's company but experience had taught her it wasn't good to become too close to the people she cared for.

"You know, Lucy, I've changed my mind." Eve strode into the room a much stronger-looking woman than the one Lucy had met when she'd first arrived. She stopped, glanced from Lucy to Julia. "Everything all right?"

"Of course," Julia said. "Lucy and I were just discussing the merits of Pine O Cleen."

Eve raised her eyebrows. "Exciting stuff." She went on to the fridge. "I've decided to open the bottle of bubbles Spiro brought."

"Thank goodness."

"Is that a good idea?"

Julia and Lucy spoke at the same time.

"I want to toast new beginnings and I doubt I'll be feeling like alcohol for a while after tomorrow. Mary likes quality champagne and he only ever buys the best stuff." She plucked a bottle from the fridge and brought it to the bench. "Who can open this?"

Julia whipped the bottle from Eve's hand before Lucy had time to shake her head.

"The champagne glasses are in that cupboard, Lucy." Eve waggled a finger. "I'll only have one glass. You girls can have the rest."

The top popped from the bottle and Lucy hurried to set out the glasses before Julia fizzed bubbles everywhere.

When they each had a glass, Eve raised hers in the air. "To the *Evie 3*, the *Mary Gee* and all those who sail in them."

Eve's voice wavered, giving the toast a melancholy ring.

"To new beginnings," Julia said.

There was a tension in the air Lucy didn't understand. She took a gulp of the champagne. The bubbles went up her nose as the liquid hit her throat. She savoured the tingles on her taste buds. She hadn't had champagne for a long time but this tasted extra good.

"You might as well know I've agreed to sell my prawn business, Lucy. It will be all over town before long."

Lucy nodded, ducked her head and took another sip from her glass. Somehow, she didn't think saying congratulations was quite the right thing. They were all quiet a moment, then Eve stood up.

"Come on everyone, buck up," she said. "There's cooking to do then we can put our feet up. Lucy, can you put on that playlist you made the other day?"

"Not seventies music," Julia groaned.

"It was good," Lucy said.

"Once again you and I will have to agree to disagree on what's good."

"Don't be a wet blanket, Julia," Eve said and positioned herself on a bar stool where she could keep an eye on the kitchen and give directions.

Julia reluctantly acted as kitchen help and Lucy soon had the bulk of the cooking in the oven or simmering on the stove top.

"Right, let's sit in the lounge while we wait for the timer," Eve said. "Have you left any champagne, Julia?"

"Of course."

Lucy and Eve had sipped their glasses while Lucy had finished the food prep but Julia had poured herself a second glass.

"There's still some of that nice cheese you bought," Eve said. "Can you organise some crackers and bring that in too, please?"

Elton John belted out "Rocket Man" as Lucy settled on Eve's couch. The second glass of champagne slipped down easily as she basked in a pool of late-afternoon sun streaming through the huge window. Julia curled herself into a chair on Eve's other side, chatting to her as if Lucy wasn't there, a subtle reminder to Lucy that she was the hired help. She sipped her drink and relished the thought that she wouldn't see the snooty bitch for two days and after that Eve would only need Lucy's services for a short while.

It was after five when Lucy arrived home again. Her content dissipated at the sight of Helen's car – she just wanted her family to herself. Then she remembered Alec was borrowing the car while Lucy was with Eve in Adelaide so perhaps they'd simply dropped it off.

The second glass of bubbles had gone straight to her head. She'd immediately sent Alec a text to say she'd be a bit longer, then she'd made sure she ate the cheese and crackers and knocked back Eve's offer of a top-up. When Lucy had left, Julia was well into her third glass, the speaker volume was up and both she and Eve were singing "I Am Woman" along with Helen Reddy.

The wind off the sea buffeted her and tugged at her coat as she made for the back door. From somewhere above came the sound of metal flapping. Lucy had forgotten to put "check roof" on Alec's list. A prick of angst jabbed as she remembered his time at home was nearly over again. She let herself in the back door and washed her hands, savouring the sound of laughter and the hearty aroma of spaghetti bolognaise. She'd left the ingredients ready to put together as soon as she got home but Alec must have already got it going. Such a relief not to have to do more cooking after all she'd done at Eve's.

The three of them were around the table, their heads bent forward over a stack of cards, the children in their pyjamas and dressing gowns and Alec in clean trackpants and a jumper.

"Mummy!" Poppy squealed. "I beat Daddy and Noah at Uno." She flew off her chair and into Lucy's arms. The flowery scent of freshly washed hair wafted with her.

"That's fantastic." She met Alec's smile across Poppy's head. "This is fantastic."

"Everything's under control," he said.

"Yiayia made spag bol," Noah said.

Lucy frowned at Alec, who threw up his hands.

"Mum insisted on getting the dinner started when I said you were staying at Eve's for a drink, even though I assured her I could do it."

"Yiayia made honey donuts for dessert too," Poppy said and ran to the cupboard where a baking dish sat ready to be reheated.

"And there are cheese and spinach triangles for our lunch tomorrow," Noah said.

"Alec, your mum shouldn't be—"

He held his hands up higher. "Her idea, not mine."

Helen obviously thought Lucy not capable of working and feeding her family. This is what would happen more if Lucy went back to nursing. "It's good you had some time off," Alec said. "When was the last time you went out for drinks with the girls?"

"I did a pile of cooking for Eve first so I wouldn't exactly call it drinks with the girls, but it was fun." She slipped out of her jacket.

"Can't Julia cook?"

"Not well, from what I gather. Eve sends a pile of meals to the prawn boats to feed the crew for the first few days. I helped get that done. Drinking champagne while I did it probably wasn't the best idea."

"So you won't be wanting a glass of red then?"

"I didn't have that much. I had to drive home." She smiled. "Some red would be nice."

The evening was busy after that. They played more cards, ate dinner, Lucy cleaned up the kitchen while Alec read the kids several stories. She flopped to the couch just as he shut the door on the kids' bedroom.

"Both out to it," he said.

Lucy tucked up her feet. She was pleasantly tired and a little sorry that their last weekend together as a family was over for another stretch.

"Shall we finish the red?" Alec said.

"I have to pick Eve up by five thirty in the morning."

"It's only eight. Another glass will help you sleep."

Lucy didn't need her arm twisted. She was more than happy to cuddle up with Alec on the couch. "Tomorrow night I'll be in a motel room on my own, then we've only got Wednesday night together before you head back to Adelaide."

"Mum and Dad are going to drive me to the airport."

"I thought you were getting the bus."

"The timetable was wrong for my flight and they said they were happy to. Mum's got an appointment in Adelaide on Monday and she was going to come home in between. I convinced them to stay down for the weekend, catch up with some friends."

"That'll be good for them. They rarely go away except to visit your brothers."

"Mum was worried they wouldn't be here for you and the kids."

"Doesn't she trust me to manage?"

"Don't get antsy. She was thinking Eve might need you to stay on a bit longer."

"She has Julia."

"Would you want her as your nurse?" Alec made a wry grin. "That woman hasn't got a gentle bone in her body. I think Eve needs you more than ever."

"We'll see." Lucy took the glass he offered and snuggled up to his warm chest. She was in two minds about Julia after this afternoon. She was brash and loud and she'd certainly spoken her mind, but once they'd settled in the lounge with their drinks she'd mellowed a little. Even though she'd all but ignored Lucy, it was obvious she cared a great deal for Eve. Initially Lucy had seen Julia as a threat to Eve's safety. Now she realised she'd jumped to that conclusion too quickly. Julia could take over once Eve was settled back at home and Lucy could go back to being mum and part-time cleaner for Fred. There was just one little corner of her heart that would be sad to no longer have a reason to visit Eve.

seventeen

Julia drove into the marina carpark, ignoring the sign that said *private access*. She'd been given a job to do and that gave her permission to proceed beyond the barrier. The early afternoon sun shone on the activity going on around her. There were vehicles everywhere and people coming and going from the boats moored along the pontoons. Everyone was preparing for the last fishing trip of the season. She recognised Spiro's four-wheel drive close to where the *Evie 3* and the *Mary Gee* were being loaded.

Julia found a space to park and opened the boot. Next to the foam boxes of food she'd helped Eve and Lucy cook, there were containers of freshly baked cake she'd collected from Lenore's Garden Cafe. Evidently Lenore made a bulk supply of cake which Eve purchased and delivered to the boats before each prawn run. When Julia had reminded Eve it was supposed to be Mary's job to do the sweets, she'd been told in no uncertain terms what the crew thought of Mary's healthy alternatives to cake.

Lenore had been welcoming, with a smile as wide as her ample hips. Julia hadn't met her before; the cafe hadn't been there the last time Julia had been home. It was out the other side of town in an old stone shed, converted now into the cafe with plants inside and out. Wallaby Bay certainly had a great selection of cafes and each made good coffee. Julia had tried every one since she'd been back.

Lenore had asked after Eve and sent her best wishes. Then she'd spent ages telling Julia how Eve had been such a support to her business when she'd first started and how her regular orders for the prawn boat crew were much appreciated. It was only when a large group came for coffee that Julia could prise herself away.

Loaded up now with Lenore's containers, she set off along the pontoon.

"Need help?" Harvey appeared on the deck of the *Evie 3*.

"Eve asked me to deliver these."

"Our cake supplies. Good old Mrs M. She's a treasure."

"I wouldn't let her hear you call her old if I was you." Julia smiled as she passed the containers across the rails into Harvey's strong grip.

"Don't know why I even said it. She's a doer. How did the op go?"

"Haven't heard anything so far. She might not even be out of theatre yet."

"Julia, hello." Spiro appeared on the deck of the *Mary Gee*, moored on the other side of the pontoon.

Julia waved.

"I'll get these stowed or they might not last," Harvey said. "Don't forget to come for the prawns when we get back."

"Any word on Eve?" Spiro asked.

"Not yet. Are you going out? I thought Mary was having her op soon."

"Next week." His shoulders drooped. "I couldn't skip going out on the last run."

"You'll miss it, like Eve."

"Not as much as Eve." Spiro walked back to the car to help her with the rest of the food. He hefted a box into his arms then paused. "It's good you're here for a while, Julia. She needs someone. She's changed. I guess we all have but she's ... she won't bend."

"I am a bit concerned she's avoiding anything much to do with the town. She used to be involved in half the things that went on there. Is this self-imposed exile something to do with Audrey?" Julia had tried to bring up the topic of Audrey before Eve left for Adelaide but the conversation had been diverted.

"Pretty much the whole thing is to do with Audrey. Has Eve talked to you about it?"

Julia shook her head.

"It's a bit of a story." Spiro put the box back in the boot. "It was always going to be tricky with the two of them on the same committee. Two strong-minded women with opposing ideas on things. The museum has been given a grant by the council to do some upgrades and there's also an opportunity for a government grant if the upgrade reflects the contribution of the prawn industry to the region. Audrey was bubbling over with suggestions for what could be done and very vocal about them too."

"No surprises there."

"Eve was all for getting the fishing families onside, asking them to donate money so that, along with the grant money, they could make a decent job of it. I jumped in with my donation to give it a kickstart." Spiro screwed up his nose. "It wasn't till later that I found out Audrey's proposition lacked substance. An expensive folly. And anyway, nothing had been finalised, so I didn't withdraw my donation."

"What about the other fishing families?"

"Eve suggested a fundraising dinner to get them along and see what could be done and for once Audrey agreed. It was to be held the day after Eve got back from a month's holiday, you know, about eighteen months ago – the last time she went to visit Arlo and then she came home via Zac's."

"I remember that holiday. She hasn't been able to go back to Singapore since."

"Yes, so much has changed since then. Anyway, there was a committee that included Audrey and Eve. A lot of planning was done before Eve left for her holiday but a few things had to be changed last minute while she was away. The venue for one. Originally the dinner was going to be at a hotel and then it got changed to the sporting club. It was meant to be a dress-up affair." Spiro cleared his throat. "It was a dress-up affair. We were told to dress for our 'A Game'." He used his fingers to put quotes around the words. "It was to be all glitz and glamour and we were warned to come ready to dig deep in our wallets. The men wore black tie, the women glamorous dresses and jewellery. Mary loved it. There's not often a chance to dress up like that these days. A few of the Port Lincoln fishermen and their wives came over as well. There was quite a stir when Eve walked in wearing a bowls outfit."

"What? Why would she do that? She doesn't play, does she?"

Spiro shifted his feet and shook his head. "Somehow, with the changes … Audrey had … well, the way Eve tells it, Audrey told her the dress code for the night had been changed to 'dress up ready for a game'. Eve had assumed as it was to be held at the sporting club she should come in a sports outfit. She popped in at the op shop and collected a bowls dress and hat. One of Audrey's friends works there and had conveniently put it aside for her."

"She was set up?" Julia gasped. Eve had never mentioned a word of this. "What a mean thing to do."

"Audrey said Eve had misheard and then it was all about who was supposed to have said what."

"Bloody hell, it sounds like kids' stuff."

"To add insult to injury there were plenty of photos sent to the local paper for their social pages and Eve featured in several. She stood out like a sore thumb in her white bowling outfit among the ladies in their finery. A few of her detractors had a field day on that."

"Like who?"

"Norma and several of Audrey's other friends plus a few people who haven't always seen eye to eye with Eve. You can't live in a place most of your life and get on with everyone."

"Poor Eve." Julia's lips twitched. "Still, I can't believe that would be enough to stop her continued involvement in her beloved committees."

"That was just the start."

"Spiro!"

They both turned at a shout from behind. One of the crew on the *Mary Gee* was beckoning him.

"I have to go." Spiro collected the box of cakes again and Julia picked up the other. They started back towards the boats.

"Like I said, it's good you're here." Spiro smiled. "You should get Eve to talk to you about what happened. There's more to it. She needs to get it off her chest and put it behind her."

"She's got a bit on her plate at the moment, with her shoulder and selling the business."

He shrugged. "I was surprised she agreed to sell."

"You of all people should know what a wrench that is for her."

"I do, of course, but none of us can go on forever. Mary's cancer was the final straw for me. We want to do other things. Not be tied down by the business."

Spiro handed his box to one of the crew and turned back for Julia's.

"I hope Mary's op goes well," she said. "You'll keep in touch, won't you?"

"Of course. Eve's my oldest friend, but Mary ..." He screwed up his face. "She's always found it difficult to understand our friendship but she's my wife and my first priority. She's going to need me close over the next few months."

Julia nodded. She understood, but it was as if Spiro was making a decision to not only cut ties with the business, but with Eve as well.

Spiro glanced towards a couple of crew with their heads bent over a cable.

"I'd better let you get back to it," Julia said.

"Bye, Julia."

He looked so sad. She resisted the urge to lunge forward and throw her arms around him. Instead, she smiled. "Safe fishing."

Then she strode away without looking back.

eighteen

Later that evening Julia was ready to head to her brother's for dinner when her phone rang. It was Lucy. After worrying all day, Julia was relieved to hear Eve's op had gone well.

"Eve wants to talk to you."

There was a pause and some rustling then Eve's voice slurred from the phone as if she was talking underwater. After a minute of gabble, Julia gave up.

"Eve, you're not making any sense. Can you put Lucy back on?" There was a clunk and a bang from Julia's phone followed by silence. She looked at the screen. The call had ended.

Then her phone rang again.

"Hi, Julia, it's Lucy again. Sorry about that. Eve badly wanted to talk to you but she's still groggy."

"Is that normal?" Julia worried the anaesthetic may have done some permanent damage. "She sounds terrible."

"She's doing well but I'm glad they're keeping her in tonight."

"So you're still planning to be home again tomorrow?"

"At this stage, yes. The surgeon did a bit more work than he'd thought would be needed so she was longer in surgery than first planned. By tomorrow morning she should be much brighter."

189

"Okay. Make sure you ring me if anything changes."

"I will."

"What's the care like? You hear some horror stories."

"She's being well looked after but ..."

Julia stood up straight. "But what? Are you worried about something? Should I come?"

"No ... it's just that Eve ... I don't think she likes one of the nurses and she keeps going on about it ... loudly!" Lucy lowered her voice. "It's probably just the drugs playing havoc but she seems to be calmer when I'm here. I think I'll stay with her."

"All night?"

"For as long as I can. The best thing at the moment is rest."

"Keep me posted."

"Yes. Eve wanted me to remind you about the food and the cake—"

"For the boats. I delivered it. I couldn't have forgotten if I tried. She's left notes everywhere."

"Okay then. I have to go. They're here to do more meds. All being well, we'll see you tomorrow."

"Ring when you're ready to leave the hospital and, Lucy ..."

"Yes."

"Give Eve my love."

"I will."

Julia slipped her phone into her bag. Eve's op was nothing too serious but any op was a risk.

They'd both been up early. Julia had got out of bed as soon as she'd heard Eve moving around. She'd helped her shower and dress. Lucy had arrived promptly thirty minutes later. Julia had waved them off and gone back to bed but hadn't been able to sleep again. She'd done all the jobs Eve had left for her including the cake delivery. While she'd been in town she'd bought a few things at the supermarket and bottle shop. Back at Eve's, she'd drifted from room to room, gone for a run until the icy wind had driven her home and tried to read a book. By the time she got Lucy's call she'd been pacing the floor and glaring at the clock.

Now the clock was telling her if she didn't leave she'd be late to the farm for dinner and that would start the evening off on the wrong foot. She hadn't seen her brother and his family face to face for eighteen months. They lived such different lives these days. They called each other on the odd occasion and sent text messages but they'd drifted apart since their mother had died.

Julia picked up the bag with the two bottles of wine she'd bought in town earlier. Verity preferred chardonnay and Heath cab sauv so she'd got them a bottle each. She also had a box of chocolates for good measure. At least she wouldn't be on her own for dinner. Eve's place echoed when there was no-one else in it.

Outside the wind had picked up. The hill where Eve's house perched was exposed to the weather. A prickle bush bounced from somewhere across Julia's bonnet and on out into the dark night beyond the headlights. There was hardly any moon. Perfect for the start of the prawn fishing.

Only ten minutes later she turned off the dirt road she'd been following and onto the farm driveway. On her left the familiar stand of gums towered beside her all the way to the house yard but she did a double take when she reached the end of the drive. In the glow of her headlights there was now a modern home where there once had been an old shed and, beyond that, what should have been the familiar shape of her childhood home had taken on new proportions. Light blazed from several places where there shouldn't be windows.

Julia swung past the smaller new house and pulled up at the side gate to the farmhouse. She gaped in amazement. She vaguely remembered Heath telling her about a new house for their oldest son, Oliver, and renovations to the original place but she hadn't imagined the enormity of it. New lights shone at intervals along the verandah and as she approached the house, she could see some of the windows on this side had been replaced by larger expanses of glass. She felt like a stranger as she knocked on the door.

Heath flung it open. "Julia, you made it."

"It's only a short way from Eve's." Had he thought she'd get lost?

They hugged. It was awkward and brief.

"Come in. We've got the ducted heating on and the fire roaring. The place gets cold when we've been away."

Julia followed Heath along what was now a grand hall with subtle ceiling lights and artwork on the crisp white walls and into what could only be described as a kitchen from *House & Garden*. Solid wood benchtops, white colonial-style doors and panelled glass replaced the mismatch of cupboards that had once been their family kitchen.

"Hello, Julia. Isn't it cold? Although I guess you're used to it, coming from Melbourne." Verity was at the sink peeling vegetables, her hair immaculate as always and an apron protecting her smart dress. Julia always felt like the poor relation next to Verity and now in this grand home she felt the difference even more.

"Something smells good," Julia said and produced the bag of wine and the chocolates. "I hope this will match it."

Verity leaned in as Julia brushed a kiss over her cheek. "It's just beef bourguignon thrown together in the slow cooker, I'm afraid. I had a mountain of washing to do and meals to make for the boys as soon as we got home. They've been doing most of the tractor work while we've been away and Heath's got to head off again later in the week. Oliver's on the tractor tonight and Hamish has gone back to uni for a few days while we're home."

"Sorry it's all such a rush," Heath said. "But you said you might be here for another week? Perhaps we can catch up again when I get back."

"I might stay even longer. Eve's had a shoulder op today. I want to help while she recovers."

"What about your work?" Heath said.

"I didn't know Eve was having an op." Verity came round the bench, wiping her hands on her apron. "Perhaps I could do something to help."

"You've got a full schedule," Heath said.

"I know but it's Eve."

"I don't know anyone as tough as Eve."

"People can be tough but that doesn't mean they don't feel the barbs and hurt on the inside."

"Small town gossip," Heath said.

Julia thought he was referring to the scandal that had ricocheted around town when Eve's husband had an affair. There'd been so much gossip and speculation at the time. Heath and Arlo had just started high school. There'd been lots of teasing and bullying. They'd used their fists to silence the perpetrators and the two of them had spent more of their first year in the principal's office than in the classroom. At Wallaby Bay Primary School, Julia had stood up for Zac, who had retreated into a world of his own. It had been a terrible time for everyone but long ago now.

"Eve's dealt with it before."

Julia frowned as she took in Heath's expression. "Wait, has something happened?"

"There was a bit of a blow-up last year," Heath said.

"Oh, the falling out with Audrey Owens." Verity's nose wrinkled.

"There's never been much love lost there," Julia said. "Spiro told me a bit of it, stuff about the fundraiser and Eve turning up in bowls gear and a few people making fun of her."

"It's done and dusted now," Heath said. "People forget."

"I'm not sure either of them have." A timer went off and Verity went back to the bench. "A while back I asked Eve to join the committee we're forming to look into running a prawn festival again. She wanted to know who else was on the committee. There are a few of us but I'm sure it was Audrey being on it that made her say no."

Julia was dying to hear more, but somehow asking Heath and Verity about it seemed disloyal to Eve. "She was seventy last birthday," Julia said. "Maybe she's had enough of committees."

"Maybe."

"As I said, Eve is tough but she will need some help," Heath said. "I believe shoulders take time to heal."

"I can stay," Julia said.

"What about your work?" Heath said again.

"It's fine," Julia said. "I'm between jobs at the moment."

"Well, that's turned out well." Verity rubbed her hands together, no doubt happy she could tick that task off as taken care of.

"You've certainly done some renovating since I was here last." Julia wanted to know more about whatever had caused the blow-up last year but she also wanted to steer the subject away from her work, or lack of it. She'd noticed the wall that had once separated the kitchen from the dining room was now gone and an elegant table was set for dinner with a large slow-combustion fire commanding the corner of the expanded area. Heath and Verity had made a few changes since they'd taken over the house but nothing on this scale before.

"We've been wanting to do it for years," Verity said.

"The government was handing out grants for renovations and new homes. We decided to make the most of it. Did these renos and built the house for Oliver."

"Great." Julia forced a smile. As if Heath needed a grant to do renovations, but no doubt he'd made it work in his favour. He always did.

"Why don't you take Julia on a tour while I finish the vegetables," Verity said. "Then we can all sit down and relax with a wine."

Heath took the lead and strode around explaining features, opening doors, pointing out fittings and new artwork. Walls had been knocked down, extensions added, wet areas remodelled. Her old bedroom was now a glitzy bathroom with a waterfall shower and a free-standing bath. By the time they got back to the kitchen Julia realised there was little left of the home she'd grown up in.

"What do you think?" Verity handed her a glass of chardonnay and Heath a glass of cab sauv.

Julia would have preferred the red. "It's amazing."

Heath took a seat in the padded cream carver chair at the head of the table. Julia couldn't imagine he'd be allowed to sit there if he was in his work clothes. There was another smaller table in the corner of the kitchen with modular chairs. No doubt that was their day-to-day eating area.

"It was the unprecedented times that started us off."

She nearly choked on the sip of wine she'd just taken. "Unprecedented times" had been bandied about every time a politician or a reporter opened their mouths during the early stages of the pandemic. She never wanted to hear those words again. It made Heath sound pompous. He seemed oblivious as she dabbed at the wine on her chin with a tissue.

"We had a family discussion," he said. "About where we'd all live when the boys get married."

"They're getting married!" Julia was horrified. Her nephews were still young – Oliver was twenty-one and Hamish only nineteen.

"Well, not yet, of course, but in the future," Verity said.

"Last year, during the height of the …"

Julia braced herself.

"Difficult times."

She blew out a breath.

"We were looking to pivot."

Julia swallowed her groan with a sip of wine.

"We decided it was a good opportunity to revisit our succession plan. Verity and I agree we're so close to town we want to continue living here for as long as we can."

"We don't want to move out if both the boys marry."

"Oliver's moved into the new house," Heath said. "It's a simple modern design. You'll have to come back another day and have a look."

"Hamish is still with us when he's not at uni." Verity directed Julia to a seat at the table then sat opposite.

Julia thought about the grand house Heath had just shown her and tried to imagine just Heath and Verity and sometimes Hamish in it. They'd rattle around like Eve did in her place.

"Heath said you've got a new apartment in Melbourne. Hopefully we can see it later in the year. He's got some business meetings in Victoria and we thought we'd come on to Melbourne and visit you."

"Oh … yes … my place is only one bedroom though."

"I thought you said you moved because you had more room and a view," Heath said.

"I did. It is bigger than my previous one-bedroom." Her whole apartment would fit into this kitchen and dining space. "I'm right on the edge of the city overlooking a park. You could stay close. There're some lovely hotels nearby." Julia took a swig of the wine. Why was it her brother always made her feel as if she wasn't quite up to scratch?

"And we'd love to meet Glen," Verity said.

"Hope he's better than the last bloke," Heath said. "We only met Tim a couple of times but we could see he was sponging off you and it's not as if you earn a fortune."

"Heath, that's not kind. Julia went through enough without you making her feel worse."

"Sorry, Jules." Heath went all floppy like a giant teddy bear. "I just want you to be looked after."

"I don't need looking after." Thank goodness she'd never told Heath how much Tim had ended up with after their break-up. Somehow it had been far more in his favour than hers. Heath would have urged her to fight back but she simply wanted to cut all ties before Tim found out what she'd inherited from her mother.

"Mum worried for you."

"Why?"

Heath looked positively hangdog now. "She didn't like Tim either."

Their mother had never said. Julia sucked in a breath. Hell, had she been the only one who hadn't been able to see him for the deceitful, money-grubbing bastard he was?

"That's all in the past now." Verity smiled sympathetically.

"I don't know why you don't sell the unit in Adelaide and buy yourself a place in Melbourne," Heath said. "It would make much better sense."

"I don't like to have all my eggs in one basket." When their mum had died, Heath got the farm and Julia her mum's super and the unit in Adelaide that her parents had bought when Heath had started uni. These days she had a long-term tenant who looked after it well and always paid on time. "You know the Melbourne market isn't the same."

"But it seems crazy to me that you pay rent," Heath huffed.

"And what's your new job?" Verity skilfully changed the subject. "The research you were doing sounded so fascinating. Such important work saving the world from that wretched virus."

"Something similar." Julia kept her response vague. All she needed now was for Heath to discover she had no new job and he'd bang on about it all night. "How are my nephews?"

Bringing up Oliver and Hamish was always a good tactic. Julia heard all about how well Oliver had done at uni and how happy he was back on the farm. Hamish was also doing well with his studies and wanted to go on and do a management course. Then they got on to Heath's commitments beyond the farm – he was chair or a member of so many committees it all became a blur to Julia. Especially after the third glass of wine. She'd planned to stick to two but she'd needed the buffer. There was still Verity's dessert to go. Julia was sure she'd be fine by the time she could escape and drive back to Eve's.

"You should have brought your things and stayed the night while Eve's away," Verity said, as if she'd read Julia's mind. "I could lend you pyjamas. It's so lovely catching up. I feel as if we haven't had a good talk for ages."

"I need to go back. I've got a few jobs to do for Eve first thing in the morning." Julia preferred Eve's cavernous spare bedroom to the sterile guest wing that had been added at the farmhouse.

Verity collected their plates. "Well, if you're staying in Wallaby Bay a while perhaps you can come another time. The boys would love to see you."

"I will, of course, but it depends on how much Eve needs me," Julia said quickly. "I don't think she realises what a tricky recovery she'll have."

To Julia's surprise, Heath reached across and gave her hand a squeeze. "It's good you're here for her, Jules. And we're glad to see you too."

Julia smiled and jumped up to help Verity. She wasn't used to sentimentality from her brother.

nineteen

Eve opened her eyes and blinked against the bright light shining through the window. Morning at last. She felt as if she'd hardly slept and yet she must have because the last time the nurses had given her medication it had been dark. There was movement on her left side. Lucy was stirring in the chair beside her.

"Have you been here all night?" She had vague recollections of the young woman's reassuring murmurs each time she woke.

Lucy yawned, sat forward and stretched. "Not all of it. I came back at seven."

"What time is it now?"

"Eight thirty. You were sleeping very peacefully. Do you feel a bit better?"

"Looking forward to going home."

"They'll be back in soon. The nurse said she'd wait until you either woke or your meds were due before she gave you a wash."

"Is it that grumpy woman from yesterday?"

"She wasn't grumpy, just …"

"Disagreeable."

"I was going to say efficient. Anyway, I didn't see her when I arrived so you might be safe."

Eve thought the woman more a little Hitler than just "disagreeable". Usually she'd give back as good as she got but the pain and lack of sleep were wearing her down. "Do you think I'll get out of here before lunch? They don't feed you in here."

"You weren't up to eating yesterday but your breakfast tray's here." Lucy wheeled the trolley forward from the end of the bed.

Eve glared at it. "What's in there?"

Lucy lifted lids on toast and eggs; there was cereal and tea and fruit. She went ahead and poured the tea. Eve's stomach roiled at the thought of the stone-cold food. She closed her eyes as the pain built again in her shoulder but opened them at the sound of bright voices. Two nurses entered, both carrying flowers. One was a young man and the other an older woman, neither of them the dictator nurse from yesterday.

"Hello, Eve. I'm Trudy and this is Kyle. You're looking a lot brighter. How's the pain level?"

"Rising."

"We'll get you some meds for that. These beautiful flowers are a nice distraction."

The nurses sat the flowers on a shelf opposite Eve's bed.

"Who are they from?" Eve asked.

"A good-looking admirer, I reckon," Trudy chuckled. "Now some meds for you before we do anything else."

Lucy removed the cards and Eve waved her hand at them.

"What do they say?" she asked.

"The bright oranges and purples are from Zac and the pretty pinks are from Arlo." Lucy slipped the cards back into their envelopes. "There's a message on each. I'll put them with your things to read later."

"We'll give you a wash next," Trudy said. "That always makes you feel a bit better."

"Do I have to? I just want to get out of here."

"Don't you like us?" Kyle quipped.

"Nothing personal," Eve muttered.

"The physio and the doctor will be here soon. You won't be going anywhere before they say so," Trudy said. "Let's get you freshened up."

"I'll go and get a coffee," Lucy said. "Back in a while."

"Can you bring me something decent to eat?"

"We can organise that for you," Trudy said. "What would you like?"

Eve sagged back against the pillows. The ache in her shoulder was becoming all-consuming and her empty stomach churned. She didn't know what she wanted.

"How about a toasted sandwich?" Lucy suggested. "Cheese and tomato?"

Eve did her best to smile. "And a hot cup of tea?"

"We'll get on to it as soon as we've finished here," Trudy said.

Lucy gave a wave and a smile and let herself out. Eve's small bit of optimism went with her. She told herself she was being ridiculous, but she felt like she was a child being left alone with strangers. Kind strangers who were doing their very best but inflicting a world of pain nonetheless. If she could just get out of their clutches and go home she knew she'd feel better.

Julia had whipped round the house to make sure everything was ready for Eve's return. Not that there was much to do. Eve's place used to be messy but there was little out of place these days. Lucy encouraged clear spaces. With everything done, she decided to pop into town for a coffee, much preferring the cafe coffee to Eve's instant.

The man behind the counter at the Cinnamon Bark was very chatty as she placed her order. When he realised she was connected to Eve, he introduced himself as Dale and asked after her.

"Eve's such a stalwart of Wallaby Bay. After all she's done for this town, some people should be more grateful."

Julia was about to ask him who when her phone vibrated in her pocket. Eve's name lit up the screen. Julia moved away from the counter.

"We're on our way," Eve said as soon as Julia answered.

"You sound brighter."

Lucy's voice rumbled in the background. "I know," Eve muttered. Then, louder, "Julia, we can't leave until we've got my medication from the pharmacy. They promised by two o'clock so they should be here any minute."

"So you're still at the hospital?"

"Yes."

Julia checked the time. It was almost two thirty. "I'll be waiting for you. I bought a chicken pie from Lenore yesterday when I collected the cake. Thought we'd have that for dinner if you're up for it."

"I will be. I'm paying all this money to stay in this fancy hospital and they've hardly fed me. I finally got some food at lunchtime that was palatable."

"Look forward to seeing you soon." She ended the call before Eve could make any more complaints. She didn't envy Lucy right now.

Julia had just settled in a corner of the cafe when her phone rang again. It was Glen. Feeling a little guilty, she accepted his call. Julia had sent a text to say she'd arrived safely and another about Eve having her op but they hadn't spoken since she'd arrived.

"Hi, honey," he crooned. "I was beginning to wonder if you'd dropped off the planet."

She ignored his dig at her lack of communication. Even though they didn't see each other every day back in Melbourne, he often rang her as he was going to bed. Sometimes she answered, sometimes she didn't. "Eve's had her op. It went well, I gather, and she's on her way home."

"Aren't you with her?"

"She's hired a young woman as nurse and home help."

"So you won't need to stay on for too long."

"Lucy's hired help. Eve won't keep her on once she's recovered from the surgery but she'll still need help."

"Oh."

"How come you're calling at this time of day? Aren't you working?"

"I've been in meetings all day. Just grabbing a late lunch and thought I'd ring to see how you are." There was a pause. "I miss you."

A few more seconds passed before she answered. "I miss you too." Once again she felt guilty. She didn't really miss him but it didn't seem fair to say it. "Have you heard any more from the girls? When are they coming to stay?"

"That's been put on hold."

"Why?"

"Their mother has organised a surprise party for her partner the weekend we'd planned."

"Oh, I'm sorry."

"I've got work in Sydney in a month or so. I'll see them then."

He sounded so glum Julia felt her heart break for him. His daughters were his Achilles heel and his ex knew how to use that to her advantage.

"Any word on work offers for you?" he asked.

"Not yet." Julia had actually spent the morning scrolling through possibilities but nothing had intrigued her enough to ask for more information.

Glen started telling her about the latest project he was working on. She sat back with her phone propped to her ear, soaking in the warmth coming through the glass and sipping her coffee. Wallaby Bay was such a relaxing world away from Melbourne. She wasn't ready to face reality just yet.

~

Lucy made sure Eve was as comfortable as possible before she carefully closed the door and climbed into the car beside her.

"Ready?" She smiled at the older woman, who was staring resolutely ahead.

"I thought they'd never let me go. Drive quick before they change their minds."

Eve was silent while Lucy navigated through the late-afternoon traffic and onto the highway away from the city. Finally they passed a huge sign listing the destinations along the highway and the tension in Lucy's shoulders eased a little.

Eve made a soft groaning sound.

Lucy glanced across. Eve's eyes were closed. "Are you okay? Do you want to stop?"

"Good heavens, no." Eve pulled her weary face into a smile. "I'm just glad it's over and I'm going home."

"You let me know if you need a break. We can stop any time."

They drove on in silence. Lucy thought Eve had gone to sleep so it startled her when she spoke.

"Thank you, Lucy," she said. "I don't know how I would have done this without you."

"I'm glad I could help but you would have managed. You have Julia—"

Eve made a scoffing sound. "I love Julia dearly but she's not nursing material. She's never been good with vomit. If anyone puked she'd disappear quick smart or she'd start heaving too. And then after her accident … well, she's not too good with blood either."

Lucy was surprised. She'd imagined nothing would faze Julia.

"You've the right temperament for nursing. Is it something you always wanted to do?"

"Since I was twelve."

Eve was silent for a moment but Lucy could feel her piercing gaze.

"Was there someone who influenced you then?"

"My mum, or at least my foster mum, Rita. She had cancer and had home nursing towards the end. There was one woman in particular who was wonderful." Lucy could picture Mrs Redmond's face more clearly than she could Rita's these days. "I'd already been doing lots for Rita and one of the visiting nurses, Mrs Redmond, always encouraged me to help when she was there. The others shooed me away as if I was a nuisance but not Mrs Redmond."

"That must have been a comfort to you and Rita."

Lucy nodded. "It was." She'd found some solace in at least being able to help with Rita's care. It had given her purpose, and in some way she felt she was repaying the love that Rita and Burt had given her. Dear Burt with his crooked smile and his sparkling eyes. He'd not been much help at all but he'd loved them both and that had been enough.

"Had you been in their care long?"

Eve's question pulled Lucy from her thoughts.

"Rita had been in her fifties and Burt in his sixties when they took me in. They'd fostered before but had decided not to take in any more kids. Someone persuaded them." Lucy smiled. "I was only a baby. Rita always said she thanked her lucky stars the day they put me in her arms."

"Sounds like they were wonderful people."

"They were."

"What happened after Rita died?"

"I was thirteen by then and Burt couldn't look after me. He was older than Rita and had been showing signs of dementia even before her cancer diagnosis."

"Oh dear."

"Burt cried when I left. Both our hearts were broken all over again." Lucy ached now with the memory of their parting. She'd been determined not to break down for Burt's sake. "I went to another family in another town. They were nice enough but it was a busy household and they could only have me short-term. I had a succession of foster homes until I was old enough to start nursing." She'd made sure she never relied on anyone ever again. Until she met Alec. His quirky sense of humour had attracted her first, then she'd discovered his intuitive, thoughtful side and finally his love had gradually crumbled the wall she'd built to protect herself from heartache.

"And Burt?"

"Mrs Redmond organised a few visits for me but he went downhill fast after Rita died." Lucy pursed her lips and inhaled deeply. "He didn't know who I was."

"Oh, Lucy, I'm so sorry."

"Don't be. My birth parents were druggies who both died young. I never knew them. Rita and Burt loved and cared for me and for that I'll always be grateful."

"And their influence has remained with you, obviously. No wonder you're such a good nurse."

Was she? So far it was working out with Eve but she was determined this was a temporary thing.

"Can we stop?"

Lucy glanced across. Eve was squirming in her seat. "Are you in pain?"

"Not my shoulder. I need the toilet."

"Right." Lucy peered ahead. It was dark outside now but they weren't far from the next town. "Won't be long."

Lucy's arms ached from gripping the wheel and her eyes were heavy by the time she pulled up outside Eve's house. It was dark but the verandah light was on and Julia hurried out as soon as they arrived. She tugged open the door, filling the car with light. Eve had been dozing for the last twenty minutes or so and blinked unsteadily in the sudden brightness.

"Are we home?" she croaked.

"Yes." Julia's voice was loud. "I've been watching out for you for the last hour."

"The traffic was heavy when we left Adelaide," Lucy said. "And we stopped a couple of times for the toilet."

"They've filled me so full of fluids I pee every five minutes," Eve grumbled. "I have to go again now."

"How are you feeling?"

"Bloody hunky-dory, what do you think?"

Lucy gave Julia an encouraging smile over Eve's head. "I'll come round and help you out."

"Julia's right here."

Julia was looking like she'd rather be anywhere but right here.

Lucy took a deep breath. "Let me show her how to best support you."

"I just want the bathroom then bed," Eve said as Lucy eased her from the car.

"What about dinner?" Julia asked.

"I'm not hungry."

"You should try to eat something," Lucy said. "It's time for your next lot of meds."

"They're not helping."

Once again Lucy met Julia's worried look over Eve's shoulder. "I think you'd be feeling much worse without them. I'll get you an ice pack as well."

Lucy walked Eve inside and up to the bathroom beside her bedroom. "Will you be okay?"

"Of course." Eve stepped into the bathroom then stopped. "What the hell's this for?"

"It's a toilet chair."

"I know what it is, but why is it here?"

"So you've got something to hang on to with your good arm."

"I'm not a bloody invalid. Did you get this, Julia?"

"I ordered it and Julia picked it up," Lucy said. "Luckily you have a removable shower head down in your other bathroom so the shower chair's in there. It will make life easier while you recover."

"Bloody hell, Eve, don't be so obnoxious," Julia snapped. "Lucy's trying to help you."

Eve shut the door on them.

"Hell, she's grumpy. Should she have come home?"

"I can hear you," Eve called.

Lucy moved out to the passage and kept her voice low. "The next few days will be tough but she's doing well so far."

"You're sure?" Julia gave her a sceptical look. "What did the doctors say?"

"They were happy to discharge her."

Julia snorted. "Get her out so the bed's ready for the next victim, more likely."

"Eve will be fine." Lucy kept her tone neutral. "You wait here. In case she needs help. I'll get her things from the car."

"Leave me to face the music alone, you mean."

Lucy simply walked away. She was paid to look after Eve but that didn't include putting up with Julia.

⁂

Alec opened his arms to her as soon as Lucy let herself inside. She held up her hand. "I'm showering first. Goodness knows what I've been in contact with in the hospital."

Ten minutes later she stepped into the kitchen, fresh from the shower, dressed in her pjs and dressing gown. Alec wrapped her in a hug. It was almost her undoing. She was so weary. The last two days had been long and busy. She'd spent a bit of time in the shops while Eve had been in theatre but other than that she'd been with Eve or in the little hotel room nearby. So much for some time to herself. It had been a long drive home and then Eve had been difficult to settle. She was in bed and dozing when Lucy finally left her to Julia's care.

"It's your last night and I'm so tired," she moaned into his chest.

"Have you eaten?"

She shook her head.

"Mum made a chicken casserole and there's plenty left."

"I thought you were cooking sausages."

Alec held her at arm's length. "You can have them tomorrow night."

Lucy reached for him again before he could see the tears brimming in her eyes. She didn't want him to go but she could never let him see it. Putting extra pressure on him was not fair when they'd agreed together he should do this work. "The kids okay?" she asked, steeling herself against her rising melancholy.

"Poppy's fine but Noah said he wasn't feeling well."

Lucy lurched back. "Again? When?"

"At bedtime so I reckon it was put on."

"You always say that. Did you check his temperature?"

"He's fine, Lou."

Lucy shrugged him off and let herself into the children's bedroom. She felt Poppy's head and kissed her cheek then did the same with Noah. No abnormal heat radiated from either nor did they stir at her touch.

Alec was at the stove when she came out.

"They seem okay."

"I told you. Come and sit down." He put a plate of steaming casserole in front of her and her stomach gurgled in anticipation. She'd been so busy with Eve she'd hardly eaten since her very early breakfast.

"Eve okay?"

"The op went well but it was more work than the surgeon had first thought." Lucy had called Alec several times while she'd been away. Each time she'd reported on Eve's progress but not in great detail. "She's off her food a bit though."

"She'll be fine now she's home."

"I tried to coax her to eat tonight before I left but she didn't have much. She used all her energy getting to the lounge. Reckoned she wanted to watch TV but then was too miserable. Julia and I had to put her to bed after that."

"Your own bed's the best place. I'm an expert on that."

"I just hope she sleeps."

"You said it was a pretty painful procedure."

"These first few days are tough."

"Eve's tough."

"Hmmm."

"But?"

"It's early days but I'm a bit worried she's not coping mentally. I'm glad Julia's there. At least Eve has someone when I'm not with her."

"Stop worrying and eat your dinner." Alec grinned. "There's honey ice cream for dessert if you're a good girl."

Lucy groaned. She was always a sucker for honey ice cream.

twenty

Lucy startled as Eve's back door flung open before she even reached for the handle.

"Thank God you're here," Julia hissed. Her eyes blazed and the tight auburn curls she normally pulled back in a ponytail frizzed out around her face, giving her a rather mad, dishevelled look. "There's something wrong with Eve."

"What's happened?" Lucy stepped inside, peering ahead along the gloomy passage. It was eight o'clock but the cloudy day meant little light reached the central part of the house.

"She didn't sleep. Moaned and groaned all night and now she won't eat or drink."

"Does she have a temperature?"

"How the hell would I know?"

"Has she been taking her meds?"

"Yes. I gave her the last lot an hour ago. At least when she swallows them I get a bit of water into her."

Lucy strode forward but Julia put a restraining hand on her arm. "She's just dozed off. Perhaps we should let her sleep."

Lucy ignored Julia, set down the bags she'd been carrying and went into the bathroom to wash her hands. The face she saw in the mirror didn't look much better than Julia's. At least her hair was tidy, but the grey smudges under her eyes highlighted her lack of sleep. In spite of Alec saying your own bed was best, she'd lain awake long after his breathing had fallen into the steady rhythm of sleep. The kids had woken them early and Alec had cooked crumpets. They'd eaten them in bed. She'd overlooked the sticky fingers and the crumbs, savouring the enjoyment of their last family time together for who knew how long?

Lucy glanced at her watch. Soon Alec's parents would come to collect them. The kids would be dropped at school and the adults would leave for Adelaide. Alec would begin the long journey to his new job. She wasn't usually quite so bothered by his trips away, but this time it was the added factor of not knowing exactly how long he'd be gone. Last year the pandemic had prevented him from coming home for almost five months. Now each time he left she felt anxious, worrying they'd be trapped in separate states again. She gripped the hand basin, took a deep breath, then walked past Julia, who'd been hovering outside the door, and into Eve's bedroom.

Eve was rolled slightly to one side, the pillows that supported her shoulder an extra bulk below the doona. She was snoring gently, her face pale but relaxed. She looked peaceful. There were no outward signs of fever. Lucy held her digital thermometer over Eve's forehead. Her temp was up a bit but Lucy decided to let her sleep.

She left the room and almost bumped into Julia who was still outside the door.

"I think she's okay."

"You think!"

"Let's get some food ready for when she wakes up." Lucy collected the bags and made for the kitchen.

"You've brought a lot of stuff," Julia said as Lucy placed the bags on the bench.

"I've got the ingredients for my special chicken soup and I bought some lemonade Icy Poles."

"Kid food!"

"You never know what might tempt a finicky tummy. I also got more of those frog cakes while we were in Adelaide." Lucy placed the little white box on the benchtop.

"You bought a box full?"

"They're the small ones and there're two missing. I left them home. My kids will need a treat tonight. The first night their dad's gone is always a tough one."

Julia eyed the box. "I guess it's a bit early to eat cake." Her tone softened. "Would you like a coffee?"

Lucy took it as an olive branch. "Thanks."

Julia flicked on the kettle and slumped onto one of the stools on the other side of the bench. She put her elbows on the shiny wooden top and dropped her head to her hands. "Eve didn't get much sleep and neither did I."

Lucy took pity on her. "You should go back to bed now, while I'm here."

"I wouldn't sleep." Julia sighed. "But maybe later before you go I'll have a doze ... thanks."

The kettle flicked off and Lucy made them coffee. Julia's phone rang. She glanced at the screen then took her coffee and phone to the lounge. Lucy could hear the tone of her conversation but not the words. She sounded annoyed. Lucy plugged in her phone and turned on the radio. She pitied the person on the other end of Julia's phone.

By the time Julia returned, Lucy had the soup simmering and bread sitting in the toaster ready to go.

"It smells good in here." Julia dropped her phone to the bench and swept her hair back into a ponytail, twisting a band around it to hold it in place.

"Would you like something?"

"It's okay. I can make myself some toast." She did a double take at the bread in the toaster. "Hell, who eats white bread any more?"

"My kids. I brought it from home. I didn't know if there'd be any bread left here."

Julia rounded the bench and opened a cupboard. "I bought some rye at the bakery yesterday."

Lucy thought that meant simply swapping brown cardboard for white but she said nothing. Instead, she slipped the slices of white bread back in the plastic bag and went to check on Eve.

A groan came from beyond the bedroom door then muttered swearing. Lucy stuck her head in just in time to see Eve struggling to get up.

"Hang on, I'll help you."

"Lucy, at last. I need to go to the toilet and I can't get up. I called out but no-one came."

"You should have rung the bell."

"What bell?"

Lucy looked around for the brass bell Julia had taken from the shelf in Eve's kitchen. Evidently it was a Buddhist prayer bell Eve had brought home from one of her trips overseas. It was lying on the floor beside a box of tissues that had also toppled from the small table beside Eve's bed.

Lucy picked it up and it tinkled softly. "We put it by your bed last night. It must have fallen."

Eve groaned again as she lay back on the pillows.

"Roll to your left side." Lucy eased back the covers. "Hang onto my arm and sit yourself up."

Once more Eve groaned.

"The pain's bad, I take it."

"Only when I move," Eve said through gritted teeth.

Lucy checked her bandage. "That all looks tidy. I can give you some extra pain medication and we can try the ice pack again. That helped yesterday."

Eve swung her feet to the floor. "Just get me to the toilet."

"You're awake." Julia strode to the other side of the bed.

"So it appears," Eve snapped.

"Should she be getting up?"

"She needs to use the bathroom."

"I can take her."

"Thunderation, if you two don't stop talking and get me to the toilet you'll be cleaning up a mess."

Lucy took Eve's good arm and Julia hovered behind as they shuffled with her to the bathroom.

"I can take it from here," Eve said and shut the door on them.

Julia blew out a breath. "She hasn't woken up any happier."

"I'll wait for her," Lucy said. "Can you take some pillows into the kitchen and crank the heat up in there? It's cold in the house today."

Julia went off without her usual debate. Lucy made the bed while she waited. When Eve eventually opened the door it was to say she wanted to have a shower.

"Okay, but we'll need to use the other bathroom. You can sit in the chair and direct the shower head with your good arm."

"Is that really necessary?"

"Unless you want Julia or I to stand in the shower with you, yes."

Eve glared at her but said no more. Everything took a long time; finding her slippers, selecting the clothes she wanted to wear, helping her down to the other bathroom, getting the water to the right temperature. And then when Eve eventually came out of the shower her dressing was wet and Lucy had to replace it. Then she managed to get Eve to do a few simple arm movements before she refused to do another thing. With every mutter from Eve, Lucy reminded herself that the older woman wasn't feeling her best.

By the time they settled her in a chair with cushions, it was morning tea time.

"You must be starving, Eve," Julia said.

"No."

"A cup of tea might help." Lucy put a small mug in front of her. Julia watched from across the table.

"Damn it, do you both have to stare at me as if I'm about to grow another head."

"Perhaps a second head would be more civil," Julia said. "I'm going to have a shower." She turned on her heel and marched out of the room.

Lucy closed the door she'd left ajar and checked the soup. It was ready except for the lemon juice she would add just before she served it. From the corner of her eye she saw Eve take a sip of the tea.

"Would you like something to eat with that? A small piece of toast perhaps?"

"Thank you, Lucy. With marmalade please."

Lucy used the rye bread Julia had left out. Just one piece and cut in half. Sometimes the amount of food could be off-putting when a stomach was being fussy.

"What the hell is that?" Eve said when Lucy set the plate in front of her.

"Toast and marmalade. It's from the jar you said you liked."

"I mean what's it spread on."

"Oh. That's Julia's rye bread. I assumed you liked it."

"Don't we have any ordinary bread?"

"I have some white sandwich bread."

"That will do."

By the time Lucy had made the swap, Eve had drunk most of her tea. She took a bite of the toast and screwed up her nose. "I don't feel like it now."

Lucy counted to five. There was no point in losing her cool but she was tired and Eve was testing her patience.

"What about plain toast, or a sandwich like you had yesterday?"

Eve shook her head. "What are you cooking in the pot?"

"Some of my special chicken soup for your lunch."

"Is it ready?"

"Would you like some now?"

"Yes … thank you."

By the time Julia returned looking refreshed, Eve had swallowed a small amount of soup and half a slice of plain buttered toast.

"You look brighter," Julia said.

"I've had some decent food at last."

Julia glanced at Lucy. "That's good."

"I'm tired now. I think I'll go back to bed."

"You should do your exercises first," Lucy said.

"Thunderation! My shoulder has settled at last and you want me to move it around. I need to rest." She eased up from the chair.

Julia took a step forward.

"I can manage," Eve snapped.

Julia and Lucy both remained statue-like in the kitchen until Eve's footsteps receded down the passage. Julia shut the kitchen door, turned to Lucy and folded her arms.

"So, how do you think the patient is faring, nurse?"

"It's a painful surgery. It's only day two." Lucy cleared Eve's things from the table, glad to be away from Julia's piercing look.

The rest of the day and the next continued on in much the same way. Eve slept in small snatches and was a mix of irritability and gloom when she was awake. Julia got tetchier and tetchier. By the next afternoon Lucy was glad when it was almost time for her to leave and pick up the children from school. The three women were seated around the kitchen table, having an after-lunch cuppa. Outside the wind was whipping the branches of the trees and the sky was a dark grey, matching the atmosphere inside.

"Surely those prawn boats won't stay out in this weather." Julia's worried gaze was turned to the window.

"No. They'd have called it off. They'll be sheltering somewhere," Eve said. "If not here, on the other side of the gulf."

"I should leave soon," Lucy said. "There're meals in the fridge if you need them." Her smile was as bright as she could muster.

"I can cook, you know," Julia said.

Eve snorted.

"They're easy meals that can be frozen for later if you don't use them over the weekend." Lucy carried her cup to the sink.

Julia sat up. "What day is it?"

"Friday. Alec and his parents are away so I don't have anyone to look after my kids over the weekend. I did explain that."

"I remember but … the days seem to just disappear."

"Who will help me with my exercises?" Eve croaked.

Lucy twisted her lips in a wry smile. Eve had done minimal exercise so far.

"I can help," Julia said.

Once again Eve snorted.

"Would you rather I wasn't here?" Julia's words fell on the room like a soggy sponge.

Lucy turned away from them and rinsed her cup.

"Of course I want you here," Eve said. "But I'm paying Lucy for her nursing ability as well as her home help. Last I checked you didn't have a nursing degree, Julia."

"I hardly need a degree to help you in and out of the shower and dish out a few pills."

Lucy rubbed the cup hard with a tea towel. She'd be glad to see the back end of both women for a couple of days.

"Could you come out over the weekend, Lucy?" Eve asked. "Just for an hour or so each day. You can bring the children."

"Let Lucy be, Eve. The kids won't want to come here," Julia sniped.

"There's a hardly used playroom to keep them entertained."

"You're being far too demanding of her time."

"Which I'm paying her well for."

"You don't need her."

"I like it when she comes."

Lucy shoved the cup into the cupboard with a clunk and shut the self-closing door with force. It made a soft, not very satisfying thud. She turned back to find both women staring at her.

"I'll ring in the morning," she said. "If you need me, I can pop out for a quick visit." Eve had Netflix. Lucy could bribe Noah and Poppy with a program they liked if she had to. "Now, I have ten minutes before I have to leave. Is there anything else you need me to do before I go?"

Eve opened her mouth, caught a glare from Julia and closed it again.

"We're fine, thanks, Lucy." Julia followed her to the door. "I'll walk you out."

Lucy felt as if she was under escort, but before they reached the back door Julia stopped her and opened another door opposite the laundry. The door to that section of the house was always closed and Lucy had never been inside.

"This is the playroom Eve was talking about." Julia walked into the room and Lucy followed. The blinds were closed and the air was freezing compared to the rest of the house. Julia flicked on the lights and illuminated the equivalent of a giant toyshop. The top half of one entire wall was windows and the bottom half was lined with shelves full of books and toys, jigsaw puzzles, dolls and prams, tubs containing who knew what. Opposite, mounted on the internal stone wall, there was a television. Cables dropped down to a low cupboard with a PlayStation and controllers. Two other doors were set in the wall on either side of the TV but they were both closed.

"We had lots of great times here."

Lucy glanced at Julia, who had picked up a child's microscope from one of the shelves. The room held a mix of toys. Some Lucy remembered from her own childhood and others that were closer to her children's era, like the boxes of *Frozen* and *Ninjago* Lego, and a large Mack Hauler truck and Lightning McQueen vehicle set. She knew Poppy and Noah would think this room was heaven.

Julia put the microscope back and ran her hands over a couple of well-worn teddy bears. "Eve's two sons are around the same age as my brother and me. Our parents were friends." She tapped the keys of a mini piano. It made a tinny plunking sound. "It's a pity Eve's grandchildren don't get back here often. They're probably a bit old for all this now. Except the PlayStation, that never goes out of fashion." She strode back to the door. "Anyway, if you do come tomorrow there'd be something for your kids to do."

"I'm sure you can manage."

"I'm sure I can too." Julia flicked off the light and they were returned to the gloom of the grey day.

"I'll call tomorrow then," Lucy said and stepped out into the wild weather.

twenty-one

Julia paced the floor of Eve's lounge room. Outside the wind howled and rain lashed the windows. Eve had gone to bed not long after they'd eaten their evening meal and Julia had been watching TV when the power had flickered. The noise of the weather was suddenly loud without it. The movie she'd been watching hadn't quite finished and it had taken a while for the screen to come back to life.

She hoped the prawn boats were safe somewhere as Eve had said. Julia pictured the *Evie 3*. It had seemed so big and steady when Harvey had taken them out on the calm bay but she couldn't imagine how awful it would be in this weather, even if the boat was moored in the marina.

The power flicked again and this time it stayed off.

"Damn!"

Eve's house was so dark. No streetlights, no moon, and now not even the glow of an appliance to help her. Julia waited for her eyes to adjust, wondering where she'd left her phone then turned towards the couch. She'd been looking at Twitter earlier.

She moved carefully, remembering Eve's solid wood coffee table was in front of the couch. Suddenly her phone lit up and began to ring. Julia pressed a hand to her chest. It had given her a start but at least she could find it now. She gave the table a wide berth and sunk to the couch, scooping up her phone as she did.

It was Glen's name on the screen.

"Hi, Julia."

"You're up late."

"All on my own on a Friday night. Did I wake you?"

"No." She snuggled back against the couch. "The fellas busy elsewhere?" He had several mates who often got together on a Friday night.

"Kids or wives, and in one case a mother, all demanding their attention."

"Thoughtless of them." He was feeling lonely, that's why he was calling at this hour.

"You sound so far away."

"I am."

"No, I mean your voice sounds faint. Are you okay?"

"Yes. There's a big storm here and the power's gone off so maybe it's affecting the mobile signals too."

"How's Eve?"

"Not much progress."

"I was hoping you'd be back soon."

"I told you I'd be at least two weeks, Glen. It's barely been one."

"Next Thursday is two weeks."

Julia had lost track of the days. "I can't see me leaving Eve for a while yet."

"I thought you said she'd hired someone."

"She has, but that's not the same as family."

"She's not your mother, Jules."

His voice was gentle but his words annoyed her. "She's just as important to me." Even if right now Eve was being so difficult Julia could cheerfully throttle her.

"Of course she is, but I miss you too."

Julia frowned. If he had a mates' weekend, two weeks could easily go by without them seeing each other.

"How's work?" she asked.

Glen launched into a long explanation of his latest commercial. The sound of the storm outside was loud and her thoughts wandered back to the prawn boats.

"What about your work?"

She'd only been half listening and she nearly missed his question.

"Nothing yet." She'd had another half-hearted look online that morning but still there'd been nothing to pique her interest. Research had been her life since she left uni, but once she'd arrived in Wallaby Bay it was as if she'd shed that part of herself. Maybe she had needed a break, or maybe a total change of direction.

Glen was talking again. He'd had the stitches removed from his hand but he was worried he'd have a scar.

"It's your palm, Glen. I'm sure it'll be fine."

He told her about his plans to see his girls the following month and she told him about her ride in the prawn boat then after more comments from Glen about how much he missed her, they'd ended the call.

Julia watched his photo as the light faded from the screen. She blinked. Without the glow from the phone, all around her was pitch-black once more.

From somewhere beyond the lounge came a thump and then a thud.

"Eve!" She leaped up, cracking her shins on the coffee table. "Ffffuu—!" Her yelp was cut off as the breath left her. She sagged back to the couch gripping her shins with her hands.

"Julia?" Eve called.

Julia sucked in a breath and chomped on her lip.

"Julia!"

"Yes," she gasped. "I'm in the lounge."

Light wavered up the passage then into the room. Julia flinched as it met her eyes then flicked away.

"There you are," Eve said. "The power's gone off."

"Yep." Julia rubbed her hands briskly up and down her legs.

"The wind woke me then I couldn't go back to sleep. You don't have to sit in the dark, you know, there are battery lights."

Julia sighed. "I might as well go to bed. The room will get cold without the air-conditioning."

Eve's light was already flashing around the kitchen and then there was a second steady glow.

"Come and get this lamp," she called. "You'll need it to find your bed."

Julia stood and moved carefully around the coffee table. On the kitchen bench a light designed to look like an old lamp glowed with the bright white of LED light.

A match flared. Eve was silhouetted in its glow.

"What are you doing?" Julia asked.

"Boiling some water."

"Why? Are you okay?"

"I feel like a cup of tea." Eve sat an old kettle under the tap. "I don't think I'll be able to go back to sleep for a while."

"I'll do it," Julia said. "You come and sit down."

"Thanks."

Eve settled at the table and Julia turned on the tap to fill the kettle.

"What were you doing sitting in the dark?" Eve asked.

"Glen rang. I was talking to him."

"He must be missing you."

"His mates were all busy doing other things."

"I like Glen. We've had some good times when I've stayed with you in Melbourne."

"He told me you'd been gossiping about me."

"When?" Eve gave her best impression of being affronted. "I never gossip."

"Hmm. He seemed to know all about my recovery from the accident and I've never filled him in on that."

"Then you should have. It's what makes you who you are, Julia. Glen's a good bloke. He's just the right person for you."

"Things change, as you well know." Julia clenched her teeth. She'd been with Tim for eight years, had thought they were happy and he'd left her just like that. She no longer imagined a constant partner in her life. Glen had been an easy stopgap – a fun guy with a sense of humour, and neither of them looking for permanency.

"Has something happened between you?"

"No."

"He found out what a terrible snorer you were."

"I don't snore." Julia sniffed. Snoring had been the least of their worries but she wasn't getting into a discussion about her relationship issues.

"Can you fix whatever's happened?"

"I told you, nothing has happened." And that was it really. Nothing happened.

"Me thinks she doth protest too much." Eve chuckled. A strong gust of wind hit the front of the house with a thud. They both looked towards the window as everything rattled.

"You're sure the prawnies will be all right in this?" Julia asked.

"Safe as houses."

Lucy peered at her phone. It was midnight, a long time to wait until the first rays of the sun would light the sky but with the rattling and banging outside, she couldn't imagine she'd be able to sleep. She pulled the blanket in tighter around herself and snuggled deeper into the couch. The power had gone off while she'd been watching TV an hour ago and in the absence of the noise from the show she'd been watching, she could hear clattering and banging overhead. She had no torch to go outside and check. She swallowed the rising panic. She'd already used her phone to peek at Poppy and Noah a couple of times. They remained deep in sleep, oblivious to the storm battering their little house. She mustn't keep using her phone. Who knew how long it would be until power was restored?

She hunched down as another strong burst of wind shook the house. Over her head there was a screaming, wrenching noise and then something hit the outside wall with an almighty clang. Wind surged inside. Terrified, she flicked on her phone torch. The bright beam reflected bits floating in the air around her; seaweed, sand and little particles of who knew what else. In the corner over the kitchen a piece of the ceiling had come away from the front wall and was flapping upwards. Lucy gripped her hand over her nose and mouth, dashed into the kids' bedroom and shut the door on the chaos.

The children didn't stir. The noise of the storm raged all around and the banging hadn't stopped but the room felt secure. Lucy lowered herself to the floor between the two beds and pressed her back to the wall. Her heart pounded in her chest. Would the shack hold together until morning?

"Alec," she whispered into the dark. "I wish you were here."

He'd rung at dinnertime to say he'd arrived in Port Headland. They'd all taken turns to talk with him. The storm had been building then, but was nothing like the ferocious beast it was now.

Lucy gripped her ankles without letting go of the phone and put her head on her knees. Why did the crises always happen when he was away? She managed FIFO life well most of the time. It was the curve balls that threw her. Like the week Alec had flown out on his very first job away. They'd still been living in Melbourne and someone had gone along their street smashing car windows and slashing tyres. She'd been without a car for weeks. Then there was the time Noah had tripped and put his teeth through his tongue, biting it half off. Poppy was only eighteen months and Lucy had juggled first the hospital ED then the emotion of watching her son wheeled into surgery with no-one to support her. There were many other times, not always so major but not easy to manage alone. Last year had been the worst. Alec had been stuck in Western Australia for months, her car had been stolen, there'd been her own work catastrophe and then the children.

Another strong gust hit the house. The rending sound intensified and then was drowned out by a groaning noise that vibrated through her like a living thing. She held her breath as the groaning got louder and then ducked her head at a resounding crash. The house shook, accompanied by the sound of breaking glass. The bedroom door burst open and cold air flooded in.

Lucy screamed.

"Mummy!" Poppy and Noah both cried out.

She flicked on the precious torch. "I'm here. Stay in your beds." She swept the light around the room. Except for the door blowing open, everything in here was holding together and they still had a roof over their heads.

"Mum?" Noah's voice wavered as Poppy began to cry.

"Hop in with Poppy." She helped Noah slip into the other bed and pulled the doona up around the two children.

Poppy's cries were getting louder. Lucy wrapped them both in a hug. "You're okay. Noah's going to hold you tight while I check what's happened."

"It's too dark," Poppy whimpered.

"Poppy, switch on Bluey," Noah said. His little voice sounded so grown up.

"Bluey!" Poppy's voice brightened.

"Good idea, Noah." Lucy flashed her light to the table on the other side of the bed. She'd forgotten all about the battery-operated night-light.

Poppy reached out and picked up the toy dog. Immediately they were illuminated in its welcome blue glow.

Lucy took tentative steps towards the door. Her torch high-lighted slices of the chaos beyond. More of the ceiling had pulled away over the kitchen, and beyond it there was no roof. She shone the torch on the table area and gasped. The window was smashed and a branch from the pine tree was covering the bench seat and part of the table. Glass and debris were spread across the room. They'd been lucky it hadn't happened earlier when they'd been eating their dinner. Or that the branch hadn't come down a few metres further along the verandah and crashed through the children's bedroom window.

The wind wailed through the jagged empty spaces and beyond it the sound of the ocean was like a roaring wild animal. Something wet slapped Lucy's face. She batted at it and stepped back into the relative safety of the bedroom. She had no idea what to do but she knew they couldn't stay here.

"Mummy!" Poppy cried again.

"We're going to leave," she said.

"Where will we go?" Noah was still trying to be brave but she could hear the fear in his voice.

"Put on your dressing gowns." Lucy thought about the glass-strewn living room. "And your sneakers."

Poppy sobbed. "I'll help you, Popsicle, don't worry. Mummy's here." Lucy shoved her daughter's warm feet into her shoes. "You hang onto Bluey."

"Where's Bingo!"

Lucy searched the bed for the stuffed toy. "Here," she said. "Now switch on Bluey's torch." She wrapped the doona around Poppy. "I'm going to carry you and you're going to be the light to show us the way."

"Like a lighthouse?" Poppy had been fascinated by lighthouses since Alec had explained what they were when they'd visited the local museum. Last time he'd been home they'd taken a drive one night after dark to see the light that flashed further down the coast.

"Yes, strong and bright like a lighthouse. Ready, Noah?"

"Yes." His wide eyes searched her face in the glow of Poppy's torch. He slid his hand into hers.

They stepped out into the living room. And then everything went black.

"What are you doing, Poppy?" Lucy snapped.

"I'm being a lighthouse. Daddy said you count to three between flashes."

Lucy took a breath. "I need you to be a stay-on lighthouse to get us to the car. No more flashing, okay?"

"Okay."

"Now shine your torch towards the laundry."

Lucy was relieved to see the back part of the house looked intact.

"I have to get my bag, Noah. You hold my jumper." Lucy took her bag and keys from the washing machine and reached for the door handle. "We're going to run for the car as soon as I open the door, okay?"

"Yes," they replied, their little voices barely more than whispers.

"Poppy, you keep the torch shining on the car."

Lucy took a deep breath. She hoped she was doing the right thing. Behind her came the screeching sound of metal.

"Let's go." She opened the door and a huge whoosh of air swept them outside. They hurried towards the dark shape of the car. Poppy's torch illuminated the seaweed and leaves splattered across the bonnet and roof. Lucy was relieved to see it was all small stuff. She bundled the children inside, jumped into the driver's seat and started the car.

She glanced behind her. Poppy was crying, Noah silently wide-eyed beside his sister.

"It's all right, Popsicle," Lucy said and forced herself to smile. "We're okay."

She drove out onto the road and caught her breath as she glimpsed the dark shape of the branch that had come down. It filled the space between the road and the house. She turned the car and drove away from the chaos.

"Where are we going, Mum?" Noah asked.

"We'll be fine, Noah." Lucy's response was a little sharp but now that they'd escaped the house, she had no idea where to go.

Along the street there were branches down and anything loose flapped. A cardboard box blew across the road in front of her. She kept driving, wanting to get further inland but the tree-lined road was littered with branches.

"Let's go to Papou's," Noah said.

Lucy's spirits lifted then tumbled again. "They're not home." She didn't have a key to their house, which they kept locked up tight.

She stopped at the T-junction. Bits of bush and paper blew along the road. Perhaps parking in Kon and Helen's driveway surrounded by big solid homes might be a better option than simply driving around. Then in the morning she would work out what to do.

"I'm thirsty," Poppy whined.

Lucy put a hand to her head. She'd brought no water or food with her. She hadn't been thinking about what would happen when they left the house, just that they had to leave before it fell down around them. What should she do? Who else did she know well enough to lob at their house in the middle of the night? Eve? Lucy abandoned that idea as soon as she'd thought it.

"I want Daddy," Poppy said in a wavering voice.

"Don't worry, Poppy, Mummy will keep us safe."

The certainty in Noah's voice compelled Lucy into action. She'd run out of options. Instead of turning towards town she took the road up the hill towards Eve's place.

"Where are we going?" Noah asked.

"On an adventure."

As she drove, Lucy convinced herself Eve's house was her best option. They'd be safe until morning. She knew where the spare key was kept. Eve and Julia's bedrooms were in the middle of the house. Lucy could sneak the children into the playroom without disturbing the two women and there was a bathroom opposite if they needed.

A few minutes later Lucy didn't know whether to laugh or cry as she turned into Eve's yard. There were lights shining from several windows and over the back door. Not sure what was going on, she told the children to wait in the car. Poppy immediately burst into big loud tears, so it was the three of them bundled together who arrived at Eve's back door. Even though the house was exposed on the hill, the wind didn't seem as bad here and it was immediately calmer under the verandah.

"Who lives here?" Noah asked.

"The lady I've been helping. Her name's Mrs Monk."

"With the hurting shoulder?" Poppy said.

"Yes. And she has a friend staying. Julia's not used to children so be on your best behaviour." Lucy hugged Poppy to her hip and opened the screen door. "Be very quiet and do as I ask. Remember Eve is old and she's not feeling the best." Lucy didn't mention Julia again. Goodness knows what she'd say when she saw them.

The light over the back door went out just as Lucy knocked.

"Who the hell's that?" a voice bellowed and the light flicked back on.

"Um!" Poppy said. "The lady swore."

"Shh!" Lucy's spirits sagged further. She hadn't expected Eve would be the one to let them in but she'd hoped. "It's Lucy," she called.

The door opened a crack. "What?" The door opened further. "What are you doing here?" Julia's gaze swept down to the children. "What's happened?"

"Our roof ... it's blowing off." Suddenly all the adrenaline that had got Lucy through the events of the night and as far as Eve's

door left her. "I couldn't think where else to go." A giant sob
hiccupped from deep in her chest. Noah squeezed her hand
tightly and Poppy buried her head into Lucy's neck.

"What're you doing, Julia?" Eve called from the other end of
the house.

Julia stepped back. "Come in, come in."

"Julia?"

Lucy shepherded the children inside.

"It's Lucy," Julia called as she shut the door behind them and
for a brief moment there was peace.

"Who?"

"Go up to the kitchen." Julia shooed them forward. "The
power's been off here. It's just come back on and we've got the
aircon going to warm the place up. I was going around switching
off lights that were left on when the power went out."

"Lucy!" Eve met them at the kitchen door. "And these are your
children. What on earth's happened?"

The concern on Eve's face was Lucy's final undoing. She began
to cry and then Poppy started again.

"Come and sit down," Eve said. Julia pushed a chair in close for
each of the children so they could sit by Lucy.

Noah sat on one but Poppy couldn't be persuaded to the chair.
She remained clamped like a limpet to Lucy's chest as Lucy told
the two women what had happened.

"I'm glad you thought to come here," Eve said after Lucy had
finished her story and dried her tears.

"I can't see how someone could rent a place out that was so
flimsy," Julia said.

"Some of those old shacks have been there a long time," Eve
said. "And sometimes we've had mini cyclones that tear through
leaving a trail of destruction, no matter how strong the structure."

BIRDS OF A FEATHER

Eve sat on the chair Julia had pushed close for Poppy. She patted Lucy's hand. "There's nothing more you can do tonight and we've got plenty of beds."

"Thank you," Lucy said.

"Mummy, I'm still thirsty," Poppy whispered in Lucy's ear.

"Julia and I were just about to have a hot chocolate," Eve said. "Would you like to have one too?"

Poppy peeled herself back far enough to stare at Eve. She nodded.

"Manners, Poppy," Lucy murmured.

"Yes, please," Poppy whispered then tucked her face back to Lucy's chest.

"Hot chocolate all round then," Julia said, and got busy in the kitchen.

twenty-two

Lucy woke to pitch-black. Her brain reeled as she tried to work out where she was and then it all came flooding back. She was in one of the spare rooms at Eve's house. After they'd had their hot chocolate and the sounds of the storm had abated, they'd all gone to bed. It turned out the two doors that opened off the playroom were bedrooms. One had twin single beds in it and the other a queen. The children wouldn't sleep alone so the three of them had snuggled into the queen bed together. The room had no window. Julia had explained there was a skylight but the cover was closed.

Lucy felt around the bed but she was alone now. She sat up and reached for her phone. Her heart thumped as she realised there was barely any charge and that it was already nine o'clock. She flicked on the bedside light and pulled on the outer layer of clothes she'd taken off before she'd climbed into the bed.

Bright morning sunlight almost blinded her as she opened the door onto the playroom.

"Mummy! Look at all these toys." Poppy sat at a small table surrounded by dolls and teddys with her own soft Bingo toy among them. A tea set was arranged on the table and at Poppy's feet there were several small tubs of toys upended on the floor.

"You shouldn't get so much out all at once." Lucy bent to toss some blocks back in a tub.

"I told you, Poppy." Noah was at the other end of the playroom with a box of toys she couldn't make out. He lifted one into the air. "Look at this Transformer, Mum."

"Wow!" Lucy put the lid on the tub of blocks and started putting an assortment of small dolls into a basket. "How long have you two been up?"

"A while," Noah said.

"Noah said we had to be quiet and let you sleep." Poppy got up from her chair. "But I'm hungry."

"I'll get you something to eat. First I have to ring the man who owns the shack."

It was a quick conversation. Mr Flavel had already had a call and was on his way to the property to assess the damage. He hadn't asked where Lucy was but had been relieved to hear she and the children were okay. She said she'd come once they'd had some breakfast.

"Can we eat now, Mummy?" Poppy moaned.

Lucy stuck her head out into the passage. At first she thought all was quiet but then she heard the faint sound of a radio coming from deeper in the house. She hoped that meant Eve was at least awake, if not out of bed. Lucy took a child in each hand and walked them quietly up the passage. Eve was at the table reading a book. She looked up and her weary face changed to a smile.

"You're awake. Come in. Oh, and the children too. I hope you all managed to get some sleep after your terrible night."

"We did, thank you, Eve."

"We're hungry," Poppy said.

"Well, your mum knows where everything is here." Once more Eve smiled. "Please treat this like home, Lucy."

Lucy made scrambled eggs and was happy that Eve also ate some of it. Her appetite hadn't picked up much since her op. Eve had an easy manner with Poppy and Noah and they were soon all chatting like good friends.

They'd finished eating and had started discussing what Lucy was going to do about her house when Julia stuck her head round the kitchen door.

"What's that smell?" She lifted her nose in the air. "Have you had eggs?"

"Mummy made eggs scramble," Poppy said. "It's our favourite."

"Ugh! I can't abide eggs."

Poppy's bright smile evaporated.

"She doesn't know what she's missing, does she?" Eve winked at Poppy.

"Did anyone sleep at all last night?" Julia sank to a chair and put her head in her hands. "I feel like the morning after a boozy night."

"Would you like a coffee?" Lucy gathered the plates and took them to the sink.

"Yes." Julia got up. "I'll get it though. I'm sure you're anxious to get back to your house."

"We were just talking about that," Eve said. "I've suggested the children stay here while Lucy goes to assess the damage."

Julia paused, the mug she'd been about to place on the bench suspended mid-air. "Who's going to look after them?"

It would have been easier not to take them with her but Lucy could see Julia's attitude had unsettled them. Poppy's lip wobbled and Noah's eyes were getting rounder by the minute. "It was kind of you to offer, Eve, but I'll take them with me."

"There's the playroom and a TV and a huge yard to explore," Eve said. "I'm sure they can amuse themselves with an adult nearby."

"Yes, but what if they need something?" Julia persisted.

"Come on, kids," Lucy said. She'd had quite enough of Julia's negativity. "We'll go back to the house together."

"I don't want to," Poppy whimpered. "It's all broken."

"Come on, Poppy." Noah was already standing beside Lucy at the door. "We have to help Mum."

"Poppy can stay here with me," Eve said. She smiled at the little girl. "I can sit in that comfy chair in the playroom and keep you company while your mum's away. You too, Noah, if you'd like."

"I'll go with Mum."

A short while later Julia was scowling over a cup of coffee in the kitchen and Lucy had settled Poppy and Eve in the playroom with strict instructions to Poppy not to ask Eve for anything. Noah sat silently in the car beside Lucy as they drove back to town. She wondered if they'd find anything left of their little beachside house.

Eve leaned back in the recliner chair and closed her eyes, delighting in the sound of Poppy playing an imaginary game with the toys around the little table she sat at. It had been a long time since her grandchildren had been in this room. While she'd been laid up with this wretched arm she'd thought about her family a lot and how much she missed them. Gert had been wrong when she'd said Eve didn't need her family close. She wished with all her heart they weren't so far apart, but this was the way life had worked out.

She hadn't driven her sons away as Gert had suggested. She'd set them free. They'd grown up in a town where their father's infidelity was common knowledge. They'd both been marked by it. Arlo had fought his way through the taunts and teasing, and Zac had become so withdrawn. If it wasn't for Julia making him join in with life, Eve would have considered counselling for him.

When Arlo got into uni, Zac had wanted to join the fishing crew. Eve let him when it didn't interfere with his schoolwork, but he fought her on staying at school. He'd never been one for books, instead he was always hands-on. Finally, Eve had said he could leave school if he worked for someone else in the fishing industry for a while. He'd got a job on a boat out of Darwin. It was his calling. In the six months between when he left home and Eve went up to visit him he'd changed from a sullen teenager into a confident young man. He met his future wife up there and eventually there'd come the chance to buy in to the business. Eve had loaned him the money, rather than needing a bank, and he'd long since paid it back. In the meantime, Arlo had done well in finance, working his way up the ladder of international banking. He and his wife lived in Singapore with their two kids and it was unlikely he'd come back to Australia to live any time soon.

Eve did miss her sons but they were both happy and living good lives, and she couldn't ask for any more for them.

"You don't look old."

Her eyes flew open. Poppy stood right in front of her, inspecting her closely.

"I'm glad."

"Mummy said you were old and you're not feeling well."

"Did she?" In Eve's head she was still forty, but to a thirty-something like Lucy she supposed she was old.

"Is your shoulder hurting?"

"Only a little bit." While Eve had been daydreaming in the old recliner, she'd actually felt quite comfortable.

"You were frowning?"

"I was thinking."

"That you were hungry?" The little girl's smile was both hopeful and beguiling.

"No." Eve smiled. "Are you hungry, Poppy?"

"A little bit."

"I see you've got morning tea ready for the toys. Perhaps we could have some too."

"I like sweet things for morning tea."

"Do you? I'm sure we've got some biscuits somewhere."

"What kind of biscuits?"

Eve tilted the chair forward and braced herself for the pain that usually accompanied getting up out of chairs. Once she'd regained her composure and her balance, she offered her left hand to Poppy. "Shall we go and see what's in the kitchen?"

Lucy drove away from the destruction that had been their home. For Noah's sake she was holding herself together, trying not to let him see how worried she was.

Mr Flavel had been there when they'd arrived. The main part of the house was a wreck. In the daylight, the sight of the huge branch that had crushed the verandah and smashed the window made her realise how lucky they'd been. The living area was a shambles. Between the tree through it and half the roof missing, the whole place was beyond repair. Miraculously, her precious Thermomix, while splattered with leaves and seaweed, appeared relatively dry and unharmed.

Noah had helped her load it and what they could of their personal belongings into the car. Mr Flavel said he'd store the rest of her stuff in the shed at the back of the house until she could shift it. The bottom line was Lucy and her children were homeless.

Noah had taken it all in and said little. Now, as they headed back to Eve's, he was staring ahead, his young face so serious.

"We might need to buy a tent," Lucy said, trying to lighten the mood.

His frown deepened. "It would blow away."

"I'm kidding." She reached across and ruffled his hair. "We'll find somewhere safe."

"We can live with Yiayia and Papou. Their house is new and big and strong."

"We might have to." Lucy imagined how smothering that would be. "Until we find another place."

"Not by the beach."

She glanced at his worried face. "Okay."

She'd been the one who'd wanted them to live in the old shack. Apart from the cheap rent, living so close to the beach had seemed a good idea. And it had been, until now. Once again her choices had traumatised her children.

She called out hello as they let themselves in Eve's back door.

"In the playroom," Julia called.

Lucy and Noah both pulled up short. Poppy had set up what looked like a tea party beside Eve's recliner and Julia was perched on one of the small chairs between Poppy and Bingo, who had her own seat. Instead of the child's tea set Poppy had been playing with earlier, there was a real teapot and cups and saucers.

"Mummy, we're having frog cake for morning tea."

"They thought they were going to eat all the cake without me." Julia laughed.

It was the last sound Lucy had expected to hear and, along with the total absurdity of the scene in front of her, she was suddenly overwhelmed by tears. She blinked them back.

"It's all right, Mummy, we saved you some," Poppy said.

"Come and join us," Eve said. "The tea's still hot."

Noah darted forward. He loved the little frog cakes.

"It is okay for children to drink tea, isn't it?" Julia said and shifted Bingo to her lap so Lucy could have the last chair. "Poppy said you made it for her sometimes."

"Once." Lucy raised her eyebrows at her daughter. "A weak cup with lots of milk."

"That's what we gave her." Eve chuckled.

Lucy still hadn't tried a frog cake. She'd given hers to Julia the day she turned up. She inspected the strange-looking cake, peeled off the paper and took a bite. "Ugh! That's so sweet." She screwed up her nose against the sugar hit. "How can you eat them?" She looked at the remaining cakes, horrified she'd been buying them for her children.

"They're delicious, Mummy." Poppy slipped one into her mouth.

Julia winked at the little girl and leaned in. "That's good she doesn't like them. All the more for us."

Poppy giggled.

Lucy glanced around, taking a more careful look at their little group. Poppy placed more of the little cakes on plates and offered one to Noah, who removed the paper in a flash and popped the cake into his mouth. Eve's sling had been decorated with animal stickers and she nursed an assortment of colourful unicorns on her lap. Julia was laughing and pouring a cup of tea with Bingo tucked under her arm. Lucy blinked, not to hide tears this time but to check her eyesight. She felt for all the world like Alice must have, down the rabbit hole.

twenty-three

Julia walked away from the lounge and the sound of the TV and the children's giggles. Eve's bedroom door was still closed. After their crazy morning she'd decided to try to get some sleep. Lucy was back at her house getting the last of their things. Poppy and Noah had gone with her before lunch but had complained when she'd said she had to return for one last load. To everyone's surprise, including her own, Julia had offered the television in the main house. Eve's lounge was big and the TV huge. Evidently it was something Zac had talked her into when he was home last. It was almost like being at the movies, and for a while Julia had been sucked in by the show the kids had chosen, then her phone rang.

"Hello, Margaret," she said as she shut herself in her bedroom.

"Have you got a moment?"

"Of course." Julia sat on the bed she hadn't yet made. "What's up?"

"We've had a few interesting conversations with the head of the uni research team."

"We?"

"Bill and I."

"I hope you're not still trying to get me to work for Bill. I'm not—"

"Julia, just listen!" Margaret's voice was sharp. "This is something worth your while pursuing."

Julia flinched. Margaret rarely raised her voice let alone snapped. "All right. I'm listening."

By the time Margaret had filled her in and answered several questions Julia was more than a little intrigued. The uni in Queensland was sharing their research with a couple of other universities and, while Julia's team had become defunct, the uni's was expanding. There was to be a meeting with the group leaders soon and they wanted to meet Julia. The work was something she could get her teeth into, a little different to what she'd been doing, and the backing was strong. The only downside was being based in Brisbane. She didn't like heat, especially humid heat. She told Margaret she'd think on it and get back to her on Monday.

She let herself out of the bedroom. The TV was still going in the lounge and from outside she heard a car. Probably Lucy; she'd said she wouldn't be long. On her way outside Julia stopped at the open playroom door. The tea party had been tidied away and tucked in a corner was a mounting stack of bags, toys and clothing. Considering Lucy had said they didn't have much, it was quite a pile.

Lucy's car door and boot were open and she was draping bedding over the clothesline.

"I found something on the TV the kids seem to like," Julia said. "A family of cartoon dogs talking in Aussie accents."

"Thanks." Lucy nodded. "It'll be *Bluey*."

"It's actually quite good."

"Noah will probably get sick of it after a while but Poppy would watch it all day if I let her." Lucy tossed a doona over the line. "It's so sunny now I thought I'd air the bedding I brought from the shack. Everything felt damp."

Julia tugged the other end of a doona out straight and the breeze caught it. "Hard to believe we had such a wild storm last night."

"Here, yes. There're a lot of trees down around where we lived, a few fences and sheds worse for wear, and the damage to the shack, of course."

"Is it fixable, do you think?"

Lucy shook her head as she tossed another doona over the line. "The owner wants to build something new one day. He says the storm's done him a favour."

"That's all right for him," Julia huffed. "What about all your things?"

"Most of it's his stuff. The rental was fully furnished. It even had crockery and some kitchen appliances. A lot of our things are in storage. We only had our bedding and clothes, the kids' toys and a few other personal items. And most of that was in the bedrooms so it's okay. The living area is the part where the roof came off."

"Sounds awful."

"I salvaged what I could but some things ... my poor Zig ..."

"Who's Zig?"

Lucy sunk to her haunches and her words were muffled in sobs. "It ... only ... pla ..."

Julia took a step forward, clenched her fingers shut then open. She leaned down and placed a hand on Lucy's shuddering shoulders. She was confused by the reference to Zig. "There's no-one else in your family, is there?"

Lucy straightened immediately, wiping at her eyes. Julia's hand dropped back to her side.

"It's a plant. A fiddle-leaf fig."

"Oh."

"The tree branch snapped it off at the base." She blew her nose on a tissue and put it carefully back in her pocket. "It was only a plant. At least my children aren't hurt."

"What's wrong?"

They both turned at Eve's call.

"Nothing." Julia strode back towards Eve. "I thought you were resting."

"Spiro rang. They've been in the marina since Friday morning, safe and sound. They're heading out again this afternoon." Eve glanced around. "Where are the children?"

"Watching TV," Julia said.

"TV's playing to an empty room," Eve said. "And they're not in the playroom. I thought you must have brought them out for some fresh air."

"They must be in their bedroom," Julia said.

Lucy dashed past her into the house. "Poppy! Noah!"

Julia met her as she came out of the playroom. Her face was drained of colour. She hurried up the passage, calling the kids' names as she went.

"I thought you were watching them," Eve said from behind her.

"I was. They were glued to the TV."

"They're not in the kitchen." Lucy's voice had taken on a desperate tone. "Can I look in your rooms?"

"Of course," Eve said.

"They won't be in there," Julia said. "Perhaps they've gone outside."

Lucy came back. "Weren't you with them? You said you watched *Bluey* with them."

"I was but … I took a phone call …" Julia put a hand to her head. Her call with Margaret hadn't been that long.

"Can they get to the beach from here?" Lucy asked.

"Yes," Eve said. "But it's quite a walk. Let's check the sheds and yard first. I'm sure they're just playing somewhere."

Eve stayed on the verandah while Lucy and Julia did a circuit of the house yard. They went in opposite directions and met in the front. Julia averted her gaze from Lucy's desperate look as she sped off at a jog back around the house, calling the children as she went.

"I'll check the car shed," Julia called after her.

She took the side gate, a sick feeling swirling in her stomach. Julia had never liked children much. She'd had some fun with her nephews when they were little but she'd been younger then too and she hadn't seen them that often. Verity had certainly never left her alone with them. Once they'd become young men, they were much more entertaining. They'd visited her in Melbourne a few times and they'd gone to the tennis, the footy or a concert together. She had to admit she was awkward with children the age of Lucy's two. Surely they couldn't have gone far.

***

"Take a deep breath, Lucy," Eve said. "There's no need to panic."

Lucy glared at the older woman.

Julia came round the side of the house, shaking her head. "They're not in the car shed."

A sob fought its way up Lucy's constricted throat. She ran out of the gate, around her car and scanned the barren space between her and the huge stone shed. "Poppy! Noah!" she yelled, but the breeze blew her words away.

"Take Lucy to the boatshed," Eve said. "The walls are solid stone and you can't hear much beyond them once you're inside. I don't think they could open any of the doors, they're so stiff, but maybe …"

Lucy was already jogging across the yard towards the huge doors in the side of the shed.

"This way." Julia had headed in the opposite direction.

Lucy followed her to a smaller door, partly obscured by some straggly gum trees. It was firmly shut. "I want to go in."

"I'm sure they couldn't get in," Julia said. "Look, it's got a sliding bolt on the outside."

Lucy called the children while Julia wiggled the stiff bolt until it finally slid back. The door swung inwards.

"Noah! Poppy!" Lucy's voice echoed around the cavernous shed. She went further inside. There was only a small window and the open door to let in light. She could see the boxes and furniture that Alec and his dad had brought, stacked in one corner, but it was obvious the children weren't inside. "Where are they?"

"Lucy!"

She hurried back outside. Eve was halfway across the empty yard.

"I told them about the boat," she called. "Maybe they've gone there."

Lucy's heart thundered in her chest. "What boat?"

"Of course. The first *Evie*. Round the back of the shed." Julia led the way. "We used to love playing on her."

As Lucy followed Julia around the shed, she thought she'd ended up in a junkyard. Stacked against the outside back wall were planks of wood, rolls of wire, posts, drums, all kinds of scrap and, looming out of it as high as the shed, was a boat. Paint peeled from the hull, a tangle of cables and ropes hung from towering metal arms and a couple of windows were missing from the cabin. There was no sign of the children.

"Noah! Poppy!" Lucy yelled.

A muffled response came from above. Lucy's heart thudded harder, then Noah's head bobbed up. "Mum. Come up."

"Where's Poppy?"

"Driving the boat. It's cool."

"How did you get up there?"

"There's a ladder." He pointed and Lucy noticed the old ladder propped against the side of the boat.

Her relief at finding her children turned to anger. "Get Poppy and come down now!"

"They'll be okay." Julia had come to stand beside her.

"Says the woman who lost them," Lucy snapped.

"Mummy! Mummy!" Poppy appeared above the side of the boat, jumping up and down. "We're playing a game. We're being pirates."

Lucy went to the bottom of the ladder. It was wooden and, like the boat, had seen better days. "Come down."

"Why are you cross?"

"I didn't know where you were." Lucy started up the ladder as Poppy's little leg waved over the side searching for the top rung. She reached up and guided her daughter's foot then together they came down, followed by Noah.

When they were all at the bottom, Lucy checked them over for any sign of injury, admonishing them for not telling anyone where they were going.

"You told us not to bother Eve," Noah said stubbornly. "And we couldn't find Julia."

Lucy sent the woman a withering look.

"For goodness sake, stop fussing," Julia said. "This boat's been a kids' playground for years."

"I don't care about that. You said you'd watch them."

"They weren't out of my sight for long."

Lucy put a hand on each child's shoulder. "Back to the house."

"Ohh!" Poppy wailed.

"You know not to go off without telling someone where you are."

"We're at Eve's place, Mum," Noah said.

"I'm hungry," Poppy said.

They rounded the shed and almost ran into Eve.

"You found them." She smiled at the children. "Were you on the boat?"

"Yes, but Mummy said we had to get off." Poppy pouted.

Lucy ignored Eve's questioning look. "Inside and wash your hands," she said. "I'll get you some lunch."

She was aware of the two women murmuring behind her as she marched the children back across the yard and into the house. It was stupid of her to have left Noah and Poppy in Julia's care. She'd let her guard down since they'd moved to Wallaby Bay. She'd been getting used to leaving the children in Kon and Helen's care. The storm and then the house almost caving in had been a distraction. When Julia had offered to watch the kids while Lucy went back and collected the last load it had been a relief. She'd known she wouldn't be gone long.

Now as she supervised her grumbling children washing their hands, she berated herself. She'd vowed she'd never leave them with anyone else again. How could she have been so careless?

twenty-four

Eve lay on her bed staring at the ceiling. The joy of having four extra people in her house had soured and turned rotten, and her with it. This morning's tea party had lifted her spirits only to have them come crashing down when the children went missing for a brief time.

Eve didn't blame Lucy for being upset. She understood a mother's fear. Her sons had given her many chances to experience it, but Lucy's reaction had been intense. Both Julia and Eve had quietly agreed on that as they ate their lunch in the kitchen. Lucy had fed the children in the playroom. She had the contents of her fridge in an esky. Eve had offered for her to transfer everything to her fridge but Lucy had declined, politely and firmly.

After lunch Julia and Eve had spent a restless afternoon, expecting Lucy to emerge, but she and the children had remained at the other end of the house until late in the day. Julia had begun to prepare dinner and Eve had gone quietly down the passage and knocked gently on the playroom door. Lucy had opened it to reveal the children dressed snugly. They were going out for a meal. That'd been two hours ago and they still hadn't returned.

There was a tap on her door. She turned as it opened and Julia poked her head in.

"Would you like a cup of tea and something to eat? You hardly ate any dinner."

"No, thanks."

"Are you all right?" Julia came further into the room. "Do you need pain medication?"

"I've taken it and I'm fine."

"You're not still worrying over Lucy, are you?"

"I enjoyed having the children here."

"She's probably just tired. They'll be fine in the morning. You can't do anything about an overprotective mother."

Eve rolled to her side and sat up. Her shoulder was aching a little but her heart more. "She's often on her own. I remember what that was like. If you leave your children with someone you expect that they will be supervised."

"Are you saying it's my fault she's having a tanty?"

Eve took a breath. Julia had no idea of the weight or responsibility of being a sole parent. "When you say you'll watch someone's kids you must do it."

"They snuck off."

"They're kids, not stuffed toys, Julia. They don't always stay where you put them."

"I apologised."

Eve sighed. "I know."

Julia sat on the bed beside her.

"I know you've got a lot to deal with at the moment but ... I've been wanting to ask you about something?"

"What?"

Julia twisted her fingers in her lap.

"Spit it out. It's not like you to be backwards at coming forwards."

"I heard about the bowls outfit debacle."

"Who told you about that?"

"Spiro."

"Humph!"

"There was more though, wasn't there?" Julia said.

Eve waggled her head and pulled a face. "Spiro again?"

"He didn't tell me what. Just that there was more."

"It's a wonder you haven't heard from someone by now," Eve said. "I'm such a vicious person you need to beware of me."

"Ha!" Julia blurted.

Eve shook her head. "The dinner was nothing, and a few people had a laugh over the photos in the paper at my expense. I was annoyed at Audrey for setting me up but not as annoyed as I was over her ideas for the museum upgrade. We were promised a lot of money that night and the next week we had a committee meeting. Audrey wanted to spend the money on a ridiculous white elephant – there'd be no structural improvements, it would give minimal reference to the prawn industry and would further expand the smelting history exhibits, which had only recently been upgraded."

"Surely you put forward some better ideas," Julia said.

"I was still pondering my opinion. The meeting was only meant to be a tidy-up of the fundraiser paperwork and to plan the next steps, not to decide there and then what we'd do with the money."

"Didn't anyone else have a suggestion? Tom? He was on the committee, wasn't he?"

"He was too unwell to attend by then, a few others were away – we barely had a quorum. With the large amount of funds possibly at our disposal, I suggested we all think on it further and get it right. The majority agreed. Audrey wasn't pleased."

"When is she ever?" Julia said.

"A few days later she caught me as I left the supermarket and bailed me up about it. She was blowing off steam but I'd run out of patience with her. We had heated words and Audrey went for me."

"What? … Hit you?"

"Tried to. I saw her arm come up and I lifted my bag of shopping to deflect her. It was an automatic reflex. She overbalanced, I tried to grab her but she fell. She landed across the gutter and broke her wrist."

"Oh, hell."

"You can imagine her scream. I can still hear it. I felt terrible." Eve rested a hand on her sling. She had a fair idea of how Audrey would have suffered.

"It was an accident," Julia said. "Which she caused."

"People came running from everywhere, Norma among them. She said she'd seen me push Audrey."

"What?"

"A few people gave me the evil eye. I was mortified but we were all so focused on getting Audrey sorted. Someone came over from the surgery, others blocked off that section of the carpark, the ambulance arrived – so much was happening. It wasn't until a few days later when people were looking at me oddly in the street that I thought something might be up. And then Spiro told me he'd heard I'd had a blazing row with Audrey, shoved her over and broken her wrist."

"Oh, Eve." Julia slid a hand carefully around her waist. "How awful. Surely you told him what really happened."

"Of course, and Gert and a couple of other good friends – the rest could please themselves. I felt bad enough about what had happened without taking the blame for it. I overheard a few snide remarks and then one day Norma made a show of giving me a wide berth outside the supermarket, telling people to watch out. It was around the time when everyone was in a frenzy, buying toilet paper and flour. The place was going mad. That was it for me. I came home and washed my hands of the lot of them."

"And you've been holed up here ever since."

"Not holed up. I go into town to get what I need, visit with the people who matter to me, manage the business ... at least I did."

"Oh, Eve," Julia said again and rested her head gently on her good shoulder.

They sat there a moment, the two of them, mother and daughter almost.

"How about I make us a cuppa?" Julia said.

Eve sighed. "All right."

The back door rattled. They glanced at each other then both rose and went to the passage.

"Hello." Poppy waved at them.

"Go and put your pyjamas on," Lucy said and directed both children towards the playroom.

"Did you enjoy dinner?" Eve called. The long passage emphasised the distance between them.

"We had pasta," Noah said.

"It was good," Poppy added, her little face bright with a smile.

Lucy ushered them through the door.

"Julia and I were going to have a cuppa." Eve took a step along the passage. "Would you like to join us once you have the children settled?"

"No, thanks." Lucy's face remained sombre. "I'm going to turn in as well. We didn't get much sleep last night."

Eve's heart sank even further. "Good night, then. We'll see you for breakfast."

Lucy gave a noncommittal shrug and went into the playroom. The door closed firmly behind her.

"I'll put the kettle on," Julia said.

"Don't worry for me," Eve said. "I think I'll turn in too."

"But you just said—"

"I've changed my mind. Goodnight, Julia."

Eve shut her bedroom door and began to undress. The sadness that had almost been her undoing a year ago was building again, and coupled with the queasy feeling that churned inside her from time to time, she was totally out of sorts.

After the blow-up with Audrey and the museum committee, and then the accident and having people she'd called friends turn on her, she'd shut herself away. And it was then that her poor old Merc had taken his last breath. Poor Gert had been consumed with grief over Tom's death and Eve hadn't wanted to add to her burden. Eve had never felt so alone.

Her neighbour, Pete, lived a hermit-like existence but at least he'd kept in touch. And eventually it was Pete who'd helped give her a new focus. She'd been lamenting some cracked woodwork one day when he'd called past and he'd shown her how to putty it so she could paint it. That had been the start of her home maintenance project that had lasted almost a year. She'd spent her time giving the house a makeover, painting and fixing what she could.

Julia, Arlo and Zac had rung and skyped regularly and Zac had visited a couple of times. She hadn't told them about the gossip though. Without her committee and charity work, it had been communicating with her family, keeping busy with home projects and the prawn business that had kept her going.

But soon there'd be no business to keep her occupied, her shoulder would heal and she wouldn't need help. Lucy would stop coming and Julia would return to Melbourne. Eve slid her arm out of her sleeve, moving it a little further than she should have and caught her breath as pain ricocheted around her shoulder. She remained rigidly still except for long slow breaths. The pain faded and she crawled into bed. Sleep wouldn't come easily but she longed for the nothingness it would bring.

Julia paced the lounge. In spite of their lack of sleep the previous night, it was too early for her to go to bed. During the afternoon, while Eve had been resting and Lucy and her kids were shut away in the playroom, Julia had gone for a long run. Now, after Eve's story, she felt both helpless and restless.

A noise came from further down the house. She paused to listen – a door closed. Probably Eve or Lucy using the bathroom. How weird it was. Five people in this house and suddenly they were all in separate corners. Not that she cared if Lucy kept out of the way but Julia was sorry Eve had adopted a similar attitude. The weekend had held such promise on Friday. Then the storm had driven Lucy and her children to them and everything had changed.

Julia regretted suggesting she watch the kids. What a kerfuffle that had caused. How was she to know they'd sneak off outside? And after their brief disappearance, they'd turned up perfectly fine. The *Evie 1* was a kids' playground. Had been for years. Julia, Heath and the boys had played wonderful imaginative games on the old boat many times, and then Eve's grandchildren. From Lucy's reaction you would have thought Julia had left them to play in the middle of a freeway.

And Eve had followed her lead. To start with she and Julia had both been puzzled by Lucy's overreaction but then tonight Eve had taken Lucy's side. It was so unlike Eve to fuss. Granted she'd had shoulder surgery but Julia was sure she wasn't coping with the sale of the business, and now that she'd heard the Audrey story it was no wonder she was feeling low. No matter how much Eve said she didn't care, Julia was sure she must miss her involvement with the town.

Julia's pacing led her to the kitchen and she decided she'd have the cup of tea no-one else wanted. She had plenty of things on her own plate to work through. Glen had rung while she'd been out jogging. He'd said again how much he was missing her. When she'd left Melbourne she'd thought it a good opportunity to put some extra space between them. It had been fun with Glen, when their relationship had been more casual. Before the cruise. Then they'd had those weeks together on the boat and ... well, she'd never been so glad to get back to her apartment and her own space. But then today something about the sound of his voice had ... She shivered. Maybe it was because she'd been all alone on a windy clifftop path a long way from anywhere, but she'd felt a longing for him she hadn't mustered in ages.

The uni research offer had been turning over in her mind as well. There was a lot to sort out there if she was going to take the job. What would it mean for her and Glen if she moved to Queensland? It truly would be the end of their relationship then. She felt a small tug of regret. How things had changed. Two weeks ago she was ready to give Glen the flick for good. It wasn't only Eve who was acting strangely. Maybe it was this house. Living out here was affecting them both.

twenty-five

Lucy sank onto one of the playroom bean bag chairs. Thank goodness the weekend was nearly over. She was exhausted. She'd finally got the kids to sleep after another long day of avoiding Eve and Julia as best she could. Tomorrow Noah and Poppy would be safely at school all day and then, by Tuesday, Kon and Helen would be home again. She couldn't believe she was actually looking forward to moving in with Alec's parents. After the debacle of the weekend it was her only option until she was able to find new accommodation for her family. At least if she was at Kon and Helen's she'd be back to simply working for Eve, keeping her at arm's distance and her family life separate.

She put on the TV, kept the sound low and flicked through the channels. Nothing caught her eye but earlier it had kept Poppy and Noah amused for some of the time. Today she'd tried to keep them busy but being confined to the playroom had lost its glow. All they'd wanted to do was go back and play on that damned boat. After lunch she'd taken them to the beach even though the wind had come up and it had been chilly. After they'd run their

263

sillies out she'd brought them home, showered them and rugged them up, and taken them out for a meal again, this time fish and chips.

Alec had rung this morning. It was their first talk since the house had almost blown away. She was glad there'd been twenty-four hours since it had happened and she could tell him about it with some calmness. He was ready to pack up and come home but she'd assured him they were okay. The kids had spoken about it with excitement now that the danger was past. Poppy had related her lighthouse role with great importance. The boat at Eve's hadn't been mentioned so she hadn't told him how she'd totally lost her cool. He'd have said she was overreacting, and in hindsight she knew he would have been right.

There was a tap on the playroom door.

"Hello?" Eve called softly.

Lucy opened the door.

"Are the children asleep already?"

"Yes, they've got school tomorrow."

"I'd forgotten it was Sunday." Eve looked disappointed. "Won't you come and join me in the kitchen? The kettle's on."

Lucy suddenly felt like a petulant child. Her own children were safely in their beds. After Eve's kindness taking them in Lucy should at least be civil. "Okay, thanks," she said and followed her host along the passage.

Julia was getting cups out when they reached the kitchen. Lucy paused in the doorway. If it was just Eve she'd have no problem, but Julia …

"Tea for three?" Julia asked brightly.

Lucy hesitated. Eve turned back and smiled.

"Thanks," Lucy said.

She'd barely taken another step when her phone rang. Helen's name lit up the screen.

"Sorry, I have to take this," Lucy said. "Back in a minute." She went into the passage as she answered.

"Lucy! Alec's just told us about the house. You poor things. Are you all okay?"

"We're fine, Helen."

"Truly? I know you wouldn't want to worry Alec but you can tell me."

"Truly. We got a fright, that's all."

"You should have rung us."

"I would have but it was the middle of the night. Eve Monk has given us rooms at her place."

"That was good of her. I said to Kon we should have made sure you had a key to our place in case of emergency. Anyway, we're changing our plans. We'll come straight home after my appointment tomorrow."

"Wait, Helen, what plans?"

"We were going to go to Goolwa for a couple of days. Kon's brother's not been well but—"

"Don't change your plans for us, Helen."

"Of course we will. We can't have you and our grandchildren without a roof over your heads."

"But we have one. The kids will be at school each day and I'd be coming out to Eve's anyway." Lucy couldn't believe she was putting Helen off. She'd been looking forward to being able to move out of Eve's as soon as she could.

Helen wavered. "Are you sure?"

"Of course," Lucy lied.

"We'll only make it a quick trip."

"Don't hurry back for us, truly."

Helen asked a few more questions then the call ended. Lucy's phone beeped. Low battery.

When she re-entered the kitchen, Julia switched on the kettle again.

"We thought we'd wait for you to come back," Eve said.

"That was Helen." Lucy chewed her lip. "She and Kon are going to Goolwa for a few days. I hope it's okay for us to stay a little longer."

"Of course it is," Eve said. "You can stay as long as you need."

Julia made a snorting sound but her back was to Lucy so she couldn't see her face.

"I'm sorry … it's just that I … with Alec away and then … well, it's …"

"Sit down, Lucy," Eve said. "There's no need to apologise. You've had an awful shock, we understand."

Lucy went to sit then remembered she was still clutching her phone. She plugged it in with the cord she kept on the kitchen bench as Julia poured the tea.

"You can leave that phone sometimes, you know," Julia said.

Lucy followed the jabbing point of Julia's finger and unease wormed its way from her stomach to her chest. "I like to make sure it's fully charged."

"It doesn't have to be with you every minute though. It's not as if you're totally isolated here."

"Don't preach to me about what I can and can't do with my phone, Julia. You know nothing about me or what I've been through." Lucy gasped in a breath, surprised at her sharp retort and the rush of terror that engulfed her.

Both women studied her closely, Julia with surprise, but Eve with a look of understanding. Lucy's fingers trembled and tears brimmed in her eyes. Since Rita died, she'd spent her life keeping a guard around her emotions. Alec and then her children were the only ones to see the real Lucy. Now Eve seemed to be able to look inside her and understand her need to keep her only family close, to be the best mother she could be.

Lucy had never known her biological parents. While her life with Rita and Burt had been loving, it had been short. She did her best to make up for not giving Noah and Poppy grandparents and cousins on her side. She never wanted them to feel like they were outsiders, not truly belonging.

Julia didn't get the importance of the phone. Up until last year Lucy hadn't thought about it much either, but then it had become the lifeline to her children, to Alec, the only thing that kept them all together as a family.

Lucy had worked hard to keep her emotions in check and now her insides felt like molten lava. The thought of the tea Julia had poured made her want to vomit. She jumped as a gentle hand rested on her shoulder.

"Come and sit." Eve guided her to a chair.

Her knees gave out and she slumped to the seat as large hot tears rolled down her cheeks.

Eve's hand remained, gently patting her shoulder. The lava exploded up and out and Lucy sobbed harder, aware of Julia moving around beyond her tear-blurred vision. A box of tissues appeared in front of Lucy and then the cup of tea. She tugged several tissues out and mopped her face. Gradually the tears subsided, her shuddering shoulders relaxed and her distress was replaced by embarrassment.

"Try to drink some tea now," Eve said.

The kindness in her voice sent another series of sobs hiccupping from Lucy's throat. Eve had reminded her of Rita.

Lucy blew her nose hard and raised her gaze. Eve was watching her closely and Julia had sat opposite, clutching her own cup and staring into it. Lucy wrapped her still-trembling fingers around the cup and lifted it carefully to her lips.

"I know it's been a difficult few days," Eve said gently. "But is something else bothering you?"

A shudder vibrated through Lucy's body but no more tears came. She put the cup back on the table.

"I don't suppose you'd look on us as close friends but we're good listeners," Eve said. "Would it help to talk?"

Would it? She'd never told anyone the full story ... not even Alec.

"I let everyone down, my kids, Alec, my patients, Charlie ..." She hiccupped another sob.

"Who's Charlie?" Eve asked.

Lucy sniffed and blew her nose again. "Last year I did in-home aged care as well as working part-time at an aged-care facility. It was my first job since Poppy was born, and then the pandemic started. Charlie was one of my at-home patients. He was a funny bloke – clever, wise and yet often politically incorrect." She recalled his cheeky grin, the thinning grey hair he liked to keep long, the old army hat he insisted on wearing even to the end. She drew in a deep shuddering breath, stopped herself. "It's done now." Lucy pressed her lips together. She wouldn't talk about it, couldn't without it consuming her and if that happened she'd be lost.

"So many mistakes were made," Julia said. "People had no idea of the danger."

"And your holiday – lucky you got home when you did," Eve said.

"Our attempt at one. I'm not sure I'd describe it as a holiday."

"What happened?" Lucy was relieved to shift the topic away from her.

"My part— friend, Glen, talked me into a cruise."

"Not one of those that made the news?"

"No, we were back before that, in February, but I shouldn't have gone. Margaret, the head of our department, called just before we left on the cruise. The news wasn't good even then. Many of those in research could see what was coming."

"You didn't tell me that," Eve said.

Julia shrugged. "I didn't want to be an alarmist."

"Pfft."

"And now I know about the upset bloody Audrey Owens caused I'm glad I didn't tell you."

"It blew over."

"Still, it wasn't a great time to have the town turn on you."

"I'm quite used to the vagaries of this town."

"You're an amazing woman, Eve."

Julia's look held such adoration Eve had to turn away. Amazing was not a word she'd use to describe herself. Determined, resolute, robust maybe, even stubborn, but not amazing. She'd done what she'd had to do to survive; there was nothing special about that.

"What happened?" Lucy asked.

"Misunderstandings that led to some nonsense. All water under the bridge now."

"Total rubbish," Julia snapped.

"Things settled down, eventually."

"Have you heard about Eve and the bowls outfit, Lucy?"

Lucy looked at Eve in surprise. "I didn't know you played bowls."

"I don't," Eve said and Julia laughed.

"It's all right for you, laughing at my expense." Eve's tone was snappish but there was a sparkle in her eyes.

"We have to tell Lucy now," Julia said.

Eve looked from Julia to Lucy. While they'd been talking, Lucy's face had lost the terrified look she'd had earlier. Perhaps if Eve shared her story ... but could she be bothered?

"You tell her."

Julia didn't need a second invitation. She quickly gave Lucy an account of Eve's debacle with Audrey, the carpark injury and the fallout it had caused. It felt strange to listen to Julia tell it. Eve could almost believe it had happened to someone else.

"That's awful, Eve," Lucy said, once Julia finished.

"There're worse things in life than wearing the wrong outfit."

"Like being the victim of a smear campaign," Julia said.

"Surely Audrey corrected the story," Lucy said.

Eve shook her head.

"Audrey has a lot to answer for," Julia said.

Eve pursed her lips. Much more than Julia knew but there was no point in raking up the past.

"What about Spiro or your friend Gert. Didn't they defend you?" Lucy asked.

"Yes, of course," Eve said. "But Spiro's attitude was to let it all blow over and poor Gert was with Tom at the hospital by then and when he died she was so consumed by grief she hardly took in anything. And who could blame her? She and Tom were a very close couple. Did everything together. Losing him was like chopping off her arm. Then there were restrictions on funeral numbers so only Gert and a few close family members were able to attend."

Lucy gripped the mug of tea tightly. "Poor Charlie had no-one. I don't even know where they buried him." Once more her face contorted.

"Sounds like you cared." Eve smiled. "At least he had that in his final days."

"I suppose."

"Hell," Julia said. "Did you get sick too?"

"No."

"Was Alec working away?" Eve asked.

Lucy chewed her lip and gave the slightest nod.

"And Poppy and Noah?"

Tears brimmed in Lucy's eyes again. Eve reached out and put her hand over Lucy's.

"With a neighbour. It was awful."

Eve felt Lucy's hand tremble under hers. "You don't have to tell us."

Lucy looked up, a haunted look replacing her tears. "I ..." Once more Lucy chewed her lip.

"Sometimes it helps to talk, but only if you want to," Eve said.

"I haven't even told Alec all of it."

"A trouble shared ..." Eve gave Lucy's hand a squeeze.

"We haven't got anything else to do," Julia said.

"Well, if you're sure." Lucy blew her nose and wiped her eyes. "It's a long story."

twenty-six

Lucy shrugged her backpack over her shoulders and picked up the bag containing her PPE. Charlie was her last home-visit patient for the day. He lived in a narrow street and, as he no longer drove, she usually parked in his driveway. This afternoon someone had parked part way across it and she'd had to drive into the next street before she found somewhere to leave her car.

The previous week, on her Thursday visit, there'd been a hire car parked right in the driveway. Some distant relatives of Charlie's had called in. She'd been pleased to begin with. Charlie didn't have family and got few visitors other than Meals on Wheels a few times a week, a fortnightly cleaner and Lucy's twice-weekly call. The couple had been seated either side of the old bloke and had obviously spent some time with him. His usual kitchen clutter had been cleared and every surface cleaned. Even the lounge had been tidied – Charlie's newspapers, magazines and books were in orderly piles or put back on the bookshelves.

It was only after a while that Lucy realised the couple had recently flown in from overseas. They explained they were on a long-planned trip touring the east coast of Australia and had decided to look up their distant relative, Charlie.

Alarm bells had rung. Even though she was very particular about her own sanitising and protection, she was extra careful when it came to Charlie. His emphysema made him an easy infection risk. She'd asked how long the couple had been in Australia. Only a week, the man had said, and when she'd mentioned requests for tourists to self-isolate he'd ridiculed her and the Australian Government's stance regarding the coronavirus, saying they were being far too fussy.

Lucy had showered Charlie, changed the dressing on his ulcerated leg and cleaned his oxygen equipment, checked his medication and reluctantly left. The visitors were making a coffee and looked as if they planned to stay longer. She was glad they hadn't been there the following Monday when she'd called, but the evidence of their visit had remained with the neatness of Charlie's house.

Today there was no sign of anyone else, not even Charlie. Lucy collected two newspapers from his front yard, hefted her backpack higher on her shoulders and trudged down the drive. In between her home visits she worked two days a week at a local aged-care facility. She was glad tomorrow was Friday, and her day off. The tension caused by the pandemic was wearing everyone down. It all seemed too hard to believe, as if they'd all suddenly wake up and it would have been a bad dream.

Charlie's back door was locked when she tried it. That wasn't unusual. Sometimes when she arrived he hadn't got out of bed, even though it was afternoon. She glanced at the two newspapers, today's and yesterday's. Charlie nearly always managed to get the paper in and make himself a coffee, but his dear old dog Bruce had died a few weeks prior and Charlie's get-up-and-go had gone with him. She donned her PPE and took down the key he hid near the back door.

"Charlie?" she called as she went in. "It's Lucy."

The kitchen was empty and still relatively tidy.

"Charlie?" she called up the passage to announce her arrival and continued on. The rear bedroom he'd recently moved into for easier bathroom access was empty. A small worm of concern wiggled in her stomach.

"Charlie? Are you in the lounge?"

She stuck her head into the gloomy room and was instantly relieved to see the old man propped up in his recliner.

"Hello, Lucy," he wheezed. "Is it that time again already?"

"Yes, I'm here again, ready to administer your twice-weekly torture," she chirped as she crossed the room.

He chuckled and it turned into a long wheezy cough. He was struggling for air even though his nasal tube was in place. She checked the canister behind him. Still half full.

"You sound a bit chesty today," she said.

"Not one of my better days," he rasped.

"What's up?"

"Struggling to get the air in," he told her in gasps.

He was still in his pyjamas, surrounded by a clutter of empty cups and dishes. Not a strange occurrence for Charlie but his face was flushed. Outside it was a pleasant March day. Charlie always had a window open and the house was cool. His pyjamas were made of light cotton. Only the bottom few buttons of his shirt were done up. Perspiration glistened on his chest.

"Do you feel warm, Charlie?"

"Hot. Must be a hot day outside." He glanced towards the window and coughed again.

Under her PPE Lucy was wearing long pants and a jumper. She took a thermometer from her kit, pointed it at Charlie's forehead and was alarmed at the result.

"Do you feel up to a shower?" she asked.

"Not sure I can make it today, Lucy," he wheezed.

He was showing all the signs of an infection. Without a test there was no way of confirming what was wrong with him but she was concerned enough to ring Charlie's doctor.

While she was on hold, she glanced at her watch. It was already after three. She was glad she'd asked her neighbour, Beryl, to collect Noah from school and Poppy from kindy. Beryl's granddaughter went to the same school and Beryl always offered to collect all three children when Lucy had an afternoon shift. The kids loved going to Beryl's.

Lucy paced the worn carpet runner in the dark passage as she spoke with the doctor.

There'd been several local Covid-19 cases and after discussing Charlie's visitors and his symptoms, the doctor had suggested she call an ambulance.

"What did old misery guts say?" Charlie gasped as she came back to him.

"He wants you to go to hospital."

"No." That had come out loud and clear.

Lucy had been Charlie's nurse for nearly two months and in that time his health had slowly declined. There'd been a couple of times when he should have gone to hospital – the leg ulcer had been the latest – but he'd insisted on remaining at home.

"I can't do anything more for you here, Charlie."

He succumbed to another coughing fit; short, sharp hacks that left him breathless. His face was still glowing and there were more beads of perspiration on his forehead and chest. She adjusted his oxygen tube and made him as comfortable as she could. Keeping herself busy kept the creeping worry from her mind. Charlie was always at high risk when it came to infection, but if he did have Covid-19 that put her at risk too.

"You think I've got that bug, don't you?" His words came out in short raspy breaths. "The corona thing that's been spreading overseas."

"You have some kind of infection, Charlie." She tried hard to keep her voice matter-of-fact. "You need hospital care. They have drugs and equipment that would make you much more comfortable."

"I'm dying, Lucy. We knew my time … was short … anyway." He lifted his hand but was too weak to reach her. "Please … let me … stay … here." His eyes implored her even when he no longer had the breath or the energy for words.

She was torn between wanting to help him and wanting to be as far away from him as possible. She couldn't risk taking this infection home to her kids. At least they were safe with Beryl for the moment. She'd even had them overnight on a couple of occasions when Lucy had agreed to the odd night shift at the aged-care home.

Lucy's thoughts raced. Even if she sent Charlie to hospital now, she'd still have to isolate until they found out what he had. Alec was away for another two weeks. What the hell was she going to do? There was another friend of hers who sometimes had the kids sleep over so that Lucy and Alec could have the odd date night. Other than that, there was no-one she could rely on to look after her kids for long.

Charlie had another coughing fit then sank back against the recliner, looking tired and frail. She didn't have a crystal ball but without access to more help than she could provide, he wasn't going to last much longer. Regardless of whether he went to hospital, she'd need to be tested and self-isolate. There was no point trying to get another nurse involved. She'd see Charlie through the night. If she needed help she could ask for it in the morning.

"Are you sure, Charlie?"

He gave a slight nod of his head.

Lucy squeezed her eyes shut and thought. She knew her kids would be okay with Beryl for the time being. She rolled her shoulders and opened her eyes to meet Charlie's beseeching look. "Okay. No hospital." She'd make it up to Beryl later.

His look changed to one of gratitude then he winced and closed his eyes. He'd always known the emphysema was a death sentence. Lucy steeled herself for what lay ahead.

Her phone beeped, the low sound of her battery going flat. Damn! There was a charger in the car. She'd have to go out for that later. She left a message for Charlie's doctor then called Beryl. She explained the situation but left out the possible Covid connection. Beryl was already panicking about that. She'd spent her fortnight's pension on extras from the supermarket, worrying they'd close. Lucy spoke briefly to Noah and Poppy. Poppy had been excited to stay at Beryl's because her granddaughter was there as well. Noah stoically informed Lucy he'd look out for Poppy. She smiled. He acted so grown up sometimes she wondered where her little boy had gone.

Her last call was to her boss, at the nursing agency. Mina offered to send someone to replace her but Lucy already knew how short-staffed they were. She'd reassured her boss that she was prepared to see Charlie through the night and check in again in the morning.

Her phone rang again as soon as she hung up. It was Charlie's doctor. He was outside. They spoke through the screen door. He'd brought Covid-19 test kits, more PPE and drugs to keep Charlie more comfortable. Even though he wouldn't come inside, it was reassuring to discuss Charlie's symptoms and care.

"You're fairly sure it's Covid-19, aren't you?" she said as she put the test kits, hers and Charlie's, into the container he'd placed by the door.

"From what you've told me, it's quite possible Charlie's visitors brought him more than their presence." His look was serious as she closed the screen door between them again. "You know a positive result will mean you'll have to quarantine yourself."

Lucy's spirits sank again. She'd tried to put that out of her mind.

"I'll text you my personal number. Call me if there's anything ..." He shrugged, gave her a sympathetic smile and walked away.

It was awful watching him go. He felt like her one connection to the world. She'd nursed plenty of dying people but always in a hospital or aged-care home, never on her own. She wanted to run after him, beg him to stay. She berated herself – she'd chosen to remain and she was more than capable of looking after Charlie on her own.

"Was there someone at the door?" he whispered between breaths.

"Just the doctor checking on you."

"Too scared to come in, was he?"

"I gave him his marching orders. I knew you wouldn't want to see him."

Charlie's laugh came out in wheezy gurgles. She adjusted his pillows.

"How about I move you back to your bed? You'd be more comfortable."

He shook his head. "Staying here," he wheezed. "Like the view." He half turned towards the window.

Lucy let out a small sigh. The rush of breath was warm beneath her mask. She knew he was too weak now – she wouldn't be able to move him on her own.

He drifted off to sleep, the only sound the rasping of his breaths. She put the TV on low and searched for a channel that wasn't regurgitating Covid news. With the comfort of the background noise, she tidied around Charlie and settled herself in a chair nearby.

Over the time she'd been his nurse, he'd slowly revealed bits of his personal story. He hadn't had an easy life but she admired his quick wit, his knowledge of world affairs, his determination to do things his way.

Charlie had told her he'd done two tours in Vietnam but had said little about his service. His dad had died not long after his return and then Charlie had lost his wife and child in a house fire. He'd worked in mining, only returning to Melbourne permanently to care for his mother who'd had dementia in her final years and had died here in this house. After that he'd done any work he could find until he'd retired, living a hermit-like existence in his family home.

Lucy dozed, stirring when Charlie did, doing her best to keep him comfortable. Her phone died just before midnight. Charlie seemed to be sleeping better so she took the opportunity to dash out to her car. She had to strip off her precious PPE but it couldn't be helped. Outside the night was cold and the yellow glow of the streetlights weren't much help. She hesitated at the end of Charlie's drive and peered down the street. The car that had blocked her access was gone. She could drive hers back and at least have it near.

She started to jog, reached the end of the street and came to an abrupt halt. The light wasn't much better in this street but it was enough for her to see the space where she'd left her car was empty. She blinked and looked around, not believing what her eyes were telling her. She jogged on a little further. There were only two cars left in the street and they were both on the other side. Neither of them were the old Commodore that had been Alec's pride and joy.

She cursed and the sound was loud in the still night. Her bag with her charger, her coin purse and a few other personal items had been in her car. Normally she'd bring it inside but today in her rush to check on Charlie, she'd forgotten.

A door slammed further down the street. A female voice yelled and a man swore. She turned tail and dashed back around the corner. Charlie didn't have a landline or internet connection but he had a basic mobile phone. It was a flip phone with buttons and a large screen, perfect for someone with gnarled fingers and poor eyesight, but sadly it didn't have internet connectivity. She would have to use that to report her car stolen and to keep in touch with Beryl and the doctor.

No sooner had she gowned up again and let herself inside than she heard Charlie groaning. She strode to the living room where he was doubled over, part on, part off his makeshift recliner bed. She settled him back and did her best to make him comfortable with the drugs the doctor had left. He calmed a little and the creases across his brow softened. His eyes fluttered open and his gaze focused on her.

"Thanks, Lucy," he whispered. "You're a gem."

His hat had slipped off and she sat it back on his head. "You're welcome, Charlie."

In the end Charlie went downhill so quickly she could hardly believe it. He didn't speak again but it was a mercy when he lost consciousness in the early hours. After that, all she could do was sit beside him, hold his hand and listen to his struggling breaths until finally they stopped. She checked his signs, made a note of the time then sat for a moment contemplating his life.

"I'll miss you, Charlie," she whispered as warm tears rolled down her cheeks. "You can rest now. See you again one day on the other side."

Preparing Charlie's body made her think of her foster mum. They hadn't wanted to let her help with Rita. Even though Lucy had been the one to bathe her in her final months, the adults who came to take Rita away had deemed her too young to be involved in the rituals of death. She'd dug in her heels, and Burt and Mrs Redmond had supported her. In the end she'd been a part of it. Helping prepare Rita's body had been the final loving thing Lucy could do for her on this earth, just as it was for Charlie now.

Once she was done she sat back in a chair, exhaustion leaching her energy. She dozed for a while then startled awake as the soft pre-dawn light crept around the edge of the curtains. Charlie was lying just as she'd left him, serene and at peace.

Her stomach growled. She'd made herself several cups of coffee during the night but hadn't eaten anything since lunch the previous day. She closed the window, picked up Charlie's phone and shut the door on the lounge. As soon as it was late enough she'd also use his phone to check in with her children and let them know she was all right.

She hurried to the bathroom, scrubbed her hands and washed her face, then rubbed herself vigorously with a fresh towel. The house was freezing.

In his kitchen she put on the small blow heater and found a loaf of stale bread. She toasted it and added some cheese. Once she'd eaten, she used Charlie's phone to report her car stolen. It was still too early to ring the doctor's rooms, and his personal number was on her phone so she'd have to wait until the practice opened to get in touch.

Lucy's heart thudded in her chest as another thought struck her. Beryl's number was on her phone. She didn't know it off by heart. Usually they spoke face to face. She didn't know her own work number either. Alec's was the only number she'd committed to memory. She glanced at her watch. There were still several hours before his shift finished. Her heart beat faster. It was a possibility she could have caught Covid from Charlie, if that's what he had, so she couldn't go home, and now she couldn't even phone her children.

She needed to charge her phone, but how? She gripped the kitchen bench and swallowed down the crazy thoughts tumbling around in her head. "Deep breaths, Lucy," she murmured. There was no need to panic. Directory assistance would help. Beryl wasn't listed in the white pages but Lucy's work was. She resisted the urge to snatch up Charlie's phone and start dialling. She'd be able to call as soon as the office opened.

Feeling calmer, she stared from the window and watched the soft light of the new day creep across the garden. Of course she'd been crazy to think it would all be sorted easily.

Lucy rang the surgery as soon as it was open. Charlie's doctor wasn't in and when she explained the situation the receptionist said she'd put her through to a nurse. The phone rang and rang and finally went silent. Lucy called again, got the same receptionist and repeated her story.

"Didn't I put you through to the nurse?"

"I was disconnected."

"Oh, I'm sorry, the nurse must be busy. I can get her to call you back."

"Don't hang up," Lucy said quickly and tried to explain the help she needed.

The young woman was more worried about Lucy than Charlie. Then Lucy realised the receptionist's concern was all about getting her tested for Covid.

"I've had a Covid test already," Lucy said. "The problem is I'm stuck here without a vehicle, my phone has gone flat and there's a body that needs taking away."

"Oh, that's good."

Lucy rolled her eyes. What was good about anything she'd just told the woman? "I won't be able to get the results. My phone's flat. This is Charlie's phone I'm on."

"When did you have the test?"

"Yesterday."

"Oh, you've got plenty of time to recharge your phone then. The results have been taking a couple of days."

A mixture of anger and fear surged inside Lucy. She couldn't wait that long. The doctor had said he'd put a priority on her test. She took a breath and tried to keep her voice calm. "I have children to care for. I can't leave here until I know my results, and I can't charge my phone. Can you arrange to ring Charlie's number with my results?"

"I'm not sure if we can do that. I'll have to find out."

"Thank you."

A phone began ringing in the background.

"I'll have to call you back," the young woman said.

There was silence followed by a soft beep. Lucy looked at the phone she gripped tightly in her hand and realised it was low on battery.

Her heart thudded. Where did Charlie keep his charger? She scurried from room to room, looking in all the obvious places. In the end she found it hiding in plain sight. Charlie had a cobble of cords plugged into a power board near his TV and the phone charger was one of them.

She took it out, plugged the phone in by the hall table and blew out a sigh of relief as she watched the battery icon begin to flash. She thought of her kids. They'd be expecting to hear from her by now. Beryl had probably tried to ring her. She would take Noah to school but Poppy didn't have kindy today.

Lucy paced the passage, racking her brains for some way of getting Beryl's number. Then it came to her. Noah's school. Beryl was listed as a second emergency contact number because Alec worked away. Lucy could get the school number from directory assistance.

She didn't go into too much detail with the school receptionist but finally she was punching Beryl's number into the phone. It went straight to voicemail. Deflated, she looked at her watch. Beryl was probably taking Noah to school. She always turned her phone off when she drove. Lucy left a message and Charlie's number then she rang her boss.

She gave an abbreviated version of what had happened.

"Poor old Charlie," Mina said when Lucy finished. "How are you? You had a Covid test as well, you said?"

"Yes. I feel fine though. Just tired."

"That's to be expected. I'll look up Charlie's information and contact whichever funeral place he listed. I'll get back to you as soon as I can. Is there anything else you need?"

"A charger for my phone."

They ended the call and Lucy sank to the old chair beside the hall table. All she wanted was to be home with her kids but she'd have to wait for the test result. She prayed it would come back negative. The implications of a positive result were too worrying. What would happen to her kids? It would take Alec time to get back. She'd have to impose on Beryl longer. She pulled herself up. There was no point worrying until she knew what she was dealing with. She tried Beryl's number once more, but once again it went straight to voicemail.

Over the course of the morning she tried several more times, in between calls from the funeral parlour, her boss, the doctor. Finally, it was all over. They took Charlie away and she was left alone. She'd agreed to wait at Charlie's until her test result came back.

Mina had arrived just as the funeral people had so there had only been time for a quick word through the door. She promised to keep in touch and left a paper shopping bag for Lucy. Just some things she thought might help pass the time, she'd said. Inside were some fresh sandwiches, milk and coffee and, Lucy groaned, a packet of Tim Tams. She took them all out then snatched the remaining item from the bottom of the bag. A phone charger. She raced to get her phone.

"Thank you, Mina," she said to the empty house.

twenty-seven

"I'm so sorry," Eve said. "For both you and Charlie."

Lucy looked down at her hands gripped tightly in her lap and forced herself to relax.

"What the hell did you do?" Julia exclaimed. "Obviously you made it through."

Lucy nodded. Her mouth felt dry despite the two cups of tea she'd drunk while she'd told her story.

"You look done in," Eve said.

Lucy lifted her gaze to the kind face studying her. "So do you." There were dark shadows under Eve's eyes again and she was holding herself stiffly upright. "Do you need some pain relief?"

"I'll get it." Julia jumped up.

"I'm all right," Eve said.

"Have you been doing any of your exercises over the weekend?" Lucy asked.

Eve's look was rebellious and Julia's surprised.

"They will help, you know," Lucy said.

"Hell, Eve, we haven't. Unless you've done some without me."

"I do the movements the doctor said."

"There are more than those you should be doing," Lucy said. "You have the sheet."

"It's lucky Lucy's back on patrol tomorrow," Julia said. "We've been a bit slack."

"I feel weary all of a sudden." Eve closed her eyes.

Lucy met Julia's raised-eyebrow look.

"We'll tackle the exercises when we're all fresh tomorrow," Lucy said.

"Good idea." Julia nodded and glanced at the kitchen clock. "No wonder we're all tired – it's nearly midnight."

Eve's eyes fluttered open.

Lucy rose to her feet. "I shouldn't have kept you up so long. Let me help you get ready for bed."

"I'll do it." Julia stood resolutely behind Eve's chair. "You take yourself off."

Lucy was too tired to argue. "Goodnight then." She started for the door then remembered her phone and went back for it.

"I guess that explains why your phone, its charger and you are joined at the hip," Julia said.

Lucy frowned, not sure if Julia was having a dig or being empathetic.

"Sometimes it's good to talk." Eve gave her a warm smile. "You sleep well."

Julia offered an arm to Eve, which she rejected, and the two of them shuffled out the door.

Lucy turned off the light and followed, staring at the phone she gripped in her hand. After her time at Charlie's she never went anywhere without it. And she'd bought extra chargers. She had one at home, one in the car and one in her bag. She'd never let it go flat again. To her it had become the equivalent of a life jacket in a boat.

She crept into the children's bedroom. Since the night of the storm when they'd shared her bed, they'd been happy to sleep in the other room in the two single beds. She tapped Poppy's night-light. The soft blue glow showed the little girl sprawled across her bed in an untidy jumble. Lucy tucked her back under the covers and kissed her soft cheek. Noah was on his back, one arm flung above his head. She kissed him too then she stood watching her children until the night-light turned itself off. Only then did she drag her tired body to her bed.

Eve fidgeted a while before she found a comfortable position. She'd left the bedside light on thinking she might read but she couldn't be bothered picking up the book. She was not used to feeling unwell and she was fed up. Eve hadn't let on but it had been harrowing listening to Lucy's story.

Beyond Eve's slightly ajar door, she could hear the muffled sounds of Julia whistling a tune from the bathroom. Eve's troubles with Audrey weren't as awful as what Lucy had been through, but even so it had been hard. She did her best to swallow the depth of the hurt she'd felt when the town turned on her.

Eve had always been different in the eyes of many locals. Once she married Rex, she'd become involved in the prawn business. Beyond doing the books and cooking for the crew, she'd learned all there was to know. She'd even crewed on the trawler before she had babies. In the eyes of some of the locals that made her unusual. Her friends, Gert and Pam, had followed the correct path for women; married, had children, stayed home for their baby days and then returned to teaching. Eve loved the prawn business, and at sea or at home she was happy to do her share. She and Rex, along with Spiro, had made a good partnership.

Rex hadn't helped her cause in the town's eyes though. He'd been a risk taker. That hadn't bothered Eve. It was one of the qualities she'd admired in him. But in business and in his personal life he'd made several enemies who'd included her in their dislike, and they had long memories.

Eve was no saint but she'd never done anything illegal or malicious. She'd done her best to toe the community line after Rex had died, not wanting any of his influence to taint her sons' lives. She'd still been a young woman then and had her share of male admirers, but she'd shunned them. Another cause for suspicion. A rumour had gone around that she was a lesbian. That had given her something to chuckle about. She'd kept her personal life quiet and remained celibate. At least until her sons had left home, and after that she'd only accepted invitations well away from Wallaby Bay and the gossips. Only Pam and Gert knew about her private life beyond the bay.

She loved Wallaby Bay and most of the people in it had recognised her commitment and forgiven her Rex's past, but bloody Audrey had stirred up a new form of distrust and Eve had been an easy target.

Julia stuck her head round the door, her body wrapped in a towel. "I thought you'd be out to it by now."

"I was just about to turn out the light."

"See you in the morning then. Sleep tight."

"You too."

Julia reminded Eve so much of Pam. Not in looks – Julia's height and red curls had come from her father – but she was matter-of-fact like Pam. And tougher than Pam. Eve had been at

Julia's side through the difficult times, losing her dad, the terrible accident and the months of rehab, then dear Pam dying before her time. And at the same time her rat of a boyfriend had not only deserted her but fleeced her as well. Julia appeared confident but Eve also knew her vulnerable side. Her determination to walk again against the odds had sometimes resulted in days of despair. While she'd been stoic when she'd lost her mother, she'd come to Eve for comfort. She acted tough but she bled the same as everyone else.

Eve eased over and flicked off the light. She stared into the dark and thought about Glen. He was a good influence on Julia and Eve had hoped he'd stick around. Not that she was one to believe a woman had to have a man in her life to be happy, but Eve had truly thought Glen completed Julia. They were a good match. Pam would have liked him.

"Wish you were here, dear friend," she whispered then forced her eyes shut and waited for sleep.

Julia pulled on her pyjamas and slipped quickly between the sheets. She was used to the chill of the big rooms and the darkness of the nights in Eve's house now. The only light in her room was a soft glow from beside her bed where she'd plugged in her phone.

Lucy's story had revealed so much about her. To have nursed a dying man was not a situation Julia could imagine, then the quarantine, the wait for test results and the worry about her kids. Nurse or not, Julia wasn't so devoid of empathy that she couldn't understand what a challenging experience that must have been for Lucy. And to have her car stolen and her phone go flat. Everything

Julia needed was in her phone. Hell, if it hadn't been for her phone she would have gone completely mad during the cruise Glen had taken her on.

She grinned. Instead of just slightly barmy. What a terrible time it had been. She'd lost a little bit of her sanity she'd never regained. Bloody Glen! What he'd said would be a relaxing twelve-day cruise had ended in a nightmare. If he hadn't booked the cruise, they'd have been on some Queensland island like she'd hoped for, or even in the South Pacific. Either way she wouldn't have been cooped up on a floating disaster.

How people enjoyed constantly stuffing themselves with way too much food, swimming in tiny pools with a zillion shrieking kids and attending endless singing and dancing shows was beyond her. And their room had been internal, dark and hardly big enough to swing the proverbial cat. Glen had bought a drinks package and thought that meant he had to consume his daily allowance. Their few attempts at sex had been futile and most nights he'd passed out and snored like a chainsaw. The shore days had been fun, at least, and the cruise had improved slightly once she'd discovered the gym and the spa for the sea days.

She should never have agreed to him surprising her when she'd arranged the time off. Thing was, his surprises had been one of the things that had attracted her to him in the first place. He'd been spontaneous and funny, turning up on her doorstep with an invitation to the footy in a corporate box, a weekend away at a couples' day spa, a mid-week bottle of wine and takeaway Mexican. And the sex had been amazing. They'd had a lot of fun together … until the cruise.

Glen had rung her earlier today asking her again when she was coming home. She'd been noncommittal, hadn't told him anything about the possibility of the job in Queensland. Bloody hell, Queensland. Julia wrenched her arms from under the doona and thumped them down on top of it. She didn't want to leave her lovely apartment in Melbourne and move to Brisbane, but she couldn't hide in Wallaby Bay forever.

twenty-eight

"Mummy, I can't find my school clothes."

Lucy blinked. Poppy's face was only a few centimetres from hers in the dark. "It's night-time, Poppy. Go back to bed."

"It's eight twenty, Mum," Noah's voice came from further away.

Lucy bolted upright and tried to focus her blurry eyes. He was in the doorway and light glowed behind him. She scrabbled for her phone.

"Shit!"

"Umm!" Poppy exclaimed.

"I'll get you some breakfast," Lucy said, brushing aside her daughter's scandalised look.

"We already had breakfast with Julia," Noah said.

Lucy stopped part way through pulling on her trackpants. "You did?"

"She made us toast with lots of yummy jam," Poppy called gleefully.

"Okay, well, you two go and clean your teeth while I get your uniforms."

Lucy finished dressing and went into the other bedroom. Thankfully she'd left the pile of clothes in readiness for this morning and, against her usual practice, she'd bought packaged supermarket items for their lunch boxes and packed most of it already.

Several minutes later they were dressed and Lucy knew she'd get them to school with a minute to spare. She was just brushing Poppy's hair when Julia tapped on the playroom door.

"All under control here?"

"Yes." Lucy smiled. "Thanks for making them breakfast."

"They did most of it themselves. I just pointed them in the right direction."

"How's Eve?"

"Still sleeping."

"Okay, well, I'll drop the kids at school and be right back." Lucy ushered Poppy and Noah past Julia and out the back door.

"No rush," Julia said, then she lowered her voice. "But when you get back I think we need to work on Eve and some kind of a routine. She's not keen on the exercises."

"It's probably a bit scary at first. She could be worrying about causing herself pain. Once she gets going with them, she'll realise the benefits."

"I hope that's all it is. She seems a bit down to me."

"It's probably the worry of the shoulder. It was a pretty big op in the end."

"Eve's always been so stoic."

"Let's see how today goes." Lucy stepped through the back door and was met by a rush of cool air. The children were hopping from foot to foot beside the car. She hurried out of the yard, zapping the doors unlocked as she went.

"Are we moving to Yiayia's house?" Noah asked as she checked Poppy's seatbelt.

"Not today. I told you Yiayia and Pappouli are still away for a few days."

"Yay!" Poppy shouted and Noah smiled.

It was such a rare thing to see his face light up lately that she paused to study them both. "Don't you want to go to Yiayia's?"

"Yes," Poppy said, more quietly.

"But we like it here too," Noah said.

Lucy jumped into the driver's seat and headed off towards town, flicking a glance at Noah in the rear-view mirror. "How come you had breakfast with Julia?"

"When we woke up you were still asleep so we played for a while. Julia was in the passage when we came back from the toilet."

"You mustn't bother Julia."

"We didn't bother her," Poppy said indignantly. "She heard my tummy was rungelling."

"She said we should let you sleep," Noah said. "And she'd help us get breakfast."

"That was nice of her." Lucy forced a civil tone. She still wasn't sure she could trust Julia but at least she couldn't muck up breakfast. Except giving Poppy jam, which they reserved for weekends but Julia wasn't to know that. Jam-lover Poppy wouldn't have apprised her of that rule.

"Julia said there might be some bikes we could ride," Noah said.

Once more Lucy glanced his way. Her heart melted at the wistful look on his face.

"She's going to look in Eve's shed," Poppy said.

Lucy grimaced. They'd both had tricycles but by the time Noah had been big enough for a two-wheeler they'd been living in small apartments. When they'd moved to Wallaby Bay he'd asked if he might get a bike for Christmas. Alec had been keen, Lucy not so. She was the one who'd be doing most of the supervising. Noah hadn't ever ridden a bike, and where they lived by the beach, the roads were all up and down. There was nowhere safe for him to learn. They'd put it off but Noah hadn't forgotten. He'd asked about one for his next birthday.

"Neither of you have ridden two wheelers," she said. "And Julia might have a busy day helping Eve. You mustn't nag her if she doesn't remember."

They went quiet then. Lucy glanced at them in the mirror. They were both staring glumly out their windows. Somehow she felt as if she'd failed them all over again.

Eve had kept her eyes shut each time she'd heard someone tiptoe to her door. It had meant she'd made it to nearly ten o'clock without Julia or Lucy bothering her. Now her full bladder was going to force her to get up. She'd already been twice during the night.

"Thunderation!" she muttered.

She'd just made it to the door when Julia appeared.

"I was coming to check you were still alive."

"I was tired."

"You've slept well then," Julia said. "That's good. It's a shower and then exercises for you."

Eve drew herself up as best she could. She'd never let anyone organise her and she wasn't going to let Julia do it now. "I'm going to eat something first." And with a nod of her head she stepped into the bathroom and shut the door firmly. Bloody exercises were a waste of time. She'd tried to do some when they'd left her alone but it had been painful and her shoulder weak. The damn specialist had lied. She could tell her shoulder would never be good again. She'd be forced to live life with a gimpy right arm. She thought of her beloved Torana. Perhaps she'd have to give that up or they'd never let her drive again either.

On her way to the kitchen she paused. The smell of food cooking wafted around her. No doubt Lucy had been busy. It was something savoury, but her stomach rejected the delight her head perceived. She'd felt queasy a lot since the op. In hospital the nurses had put it down to the anaesthetic, but it regularly returned to unsettle her still. She'd hardly taken any pain medication in the last day and it had made no difference to her woozy stomach.

She turned to go back to her room when Lucy popped her head out.

"Good morning," she said brightly. "Julia said you were hungry. I've got a few different things on the go."

"I'm not!" Eve was shocked by the sharpness of her own voice. "Thank you anyway," she said more demurely.

"I'm sorry I kept you up so late. I shouldn't have worried you with my problems."

Eve felt uncomfortable then. Poor Lucy had shown her nothing but kindness and she was taking her misery out on her.

"I haven't been sleeping well."

"Oh. Julia said you'd had a good sleep. Perhaps we need to look at your pain medication, readjust the way you lie in bed, or—"

"I'm managing fine." Eve wobbled slightly and put her left hand to the wall.

Lucy stepped up to her and slipped her hand into the crook of her arm. "You should be feeling much better by now."

"I am." Eve tried to escape Lucy's hold but her knees suddenly felt weak.

"Come and sit down." Lucy guided her to a kitchen chair and put a glass of water in front of her. "You might be dehydrated."

"Huh!" Eve snorted. "I've drunk so much tea since I've been home I should be floating, and water too."

"You might think you have, but you never finish the cup or the glass."

"Well, I keep having to pee all the time. It's driving me nuts."

Lucy bent closer. "You look a little flushed. Do you feel warm?"

"No. I feel perfectly fine."

"I'll take your temperature." Lucy got out her digital thermometer and placed it close to Eve's forehead.

"No need to make a fuss." Eve closed her eyes. "I'm fine," she muttered.

The thermometer beeped. "Your temp's up a bit. Let me check your shoulder."

Eve sighed but let Lucy slip the dressing gown from her arm then the sleeve of her pyjamas.

"That all looks good." Lucy helped her re-dress. "It's healing well."

"What's going on?" Julia strode into the room. "Is something wrong?"

"Thunderation! Nothing's wrong."

"I'd like to call your GP," Lucy said.

"What's the matter?" Julia said.

"What's she going to do for me?" Eve sniffed.

"I suspect you might have a UTI."

"What's that?" Julia asked.

"A urinary tract infection." Lucy bobbed down beside Eve. "With all you've been through it's a possibility we should check."

Eve huffed. "If you must."

The next few hours disappeared in a jumble of phone calls and fussing. Eve was exhausted by the time they'd finished with her and took to her bed. The only upside was she'd avoided those damnable exercises.

twenty-nine

Julia tiptoed away from Eve's door as Lucy walked up the passage. "She's sleeping," she hissed.

"That's good. It'll give the antibiotics a chance to kick in."

Julia went on into the kitchen and Lucy followed. She was both grateful and annoyed by the younger woman's presence. Eve's doctor had done tests and agreed with Lucy's diagnosis. She'd prescribed antibiotics. Julia had been the gofer, driving into town and back while Lucy had coaxed Eve to take fluids and eat. Thankfully, Eve already seemed more settled but, bloody hell, it wouldn't hurt Lucy to crack a smile once in a while. She did for Eve and for her kids, why not for Julia?

Lucy began to stack cooled sausage rolls into containers. She'd already put away a batch of small quiches and a container of apple muffins. She'd had her fancy blender working overtime. Julia had sampled one of each item for lunch after her trip into town. Now that Eve was settled and Lucy was busy, there was nothing for Julia to do.

"I think I'll go for a run while Eve's resting," she said.

"Didn't she want you to get some prawns?"

"Hell, I'd forgotten about that." Eve had received a call from Spiro. The prawn boats were back in and the season done. Julia glanced at the clock and snatched up her keys. "I guess they'll still be unloading."

There was a hive of activity around each boat as Julia pulled into the carpark. A couple of seafood trucks were being loaded from other boats. Aboard the *Evie 3* men moved about on the deck. One of them was Spiro, who looked up and waved as she approached.

"Hello, Julia. You're just in time. We've unloaded and done what we can for today. The boys are going home for an early night and we'll tackle the rest of the cleaning tomorrow." His smile changed to a look of concern. "How's Eve? She didn't sound too good on the phone."

"Her shoulder's healing okay but we've just found out she's got an infection. The nurse seems to think she'll pick up quickly once the antibiotics kick in."

"I'll try to get out there once we're finished but there'll be a bit of work to do on the trawlers before handover, and then I have to get Mary to Adelaide for her op on Thursday."

"Let me know if there's anything I can do." Julia glanced around. She had no idea what was needed in preparing the boat but she was capable of manual labour.

"Thanks. I'll email all the tallies to Eve once I get home. She'll have the pays to do and the rest of the paperwork to finalise. None of it should be a problem. I could help but with Mary's op ..."

Julia gave him a hug. "She's going to be fine, Spiro."

He nodded against her shoulder and stepped back. "Perhaps you could get Eve to reconnect with the community while you're here."

"You can't blame her for not wanting to after all that happened."

"She told you the whole story?"

"Yes."

"It wasn't good but time goes on. People forget. And now that we're selling the business ... I worry about her out in that big house, alone. What's going to keep her occupied?"

"Eve's never one to be idle for long."

"The museum committee want to get moving with the upgrade. She's the best person to oversee it. Maybe you could convince her to re-join."

"Have you ever known anyone to convince Eve to do anything she didn't want to?"

Spiro smiled. "It's good you're here, Julia. I'll get the prawns."

She huddled into her jacket. She had to agree with Spiro that the business had been Eve's life and if she didn't have that and her town committees, what would she do?

Julia stepped out of the way as one of the crew climbed on board. Several other blokes came and went, ferrying things to and fro, and then Spiro was back.

"Here you are." He held three boxes in his thick-rubber-gloved grasp. "There's one box of green and two of cooked. Put them straight into the freezer when you get home."

"I can take them."

"Your hands would be frozen before you made it to the car."

Julia led the way along the pontoon and across the carpark. Spiro stacked the boxes into the boot then paused and ran his gloved hand over them. The top of each box showed a picture of the *Evie 3* and the *Mary Gee* at sea and the writing on the side declared *King Prawns – wild caught from the pristine water of Spencer Gulf South Australia.* His lips turned down. "It's the last of our own prawns."

"You're doing the right thing, Spiro."

He nodded. "I know, but Eve doesn't see it that way."

"She's not feeling the best but she'll come round. Eve always bounces back." Julia spoke with a conviction she didn't truly feel. The Eve she'd spent the last two weeks with was so different to the confident woman she'd known all her life.

"Keep me posted, won't you," Spiro said and walked back down the slope towards the pontoons.

Just as she pulled up at Eve's back gate her phone rang. It wasn't a number she recognised and she was surprised by the curt officiousness of the person on the other end.

"Dr Julia Paterson?"

"Yes."

"I have Professor Terrence Nguyen on the line for you. Please hold."

Julia opened her mouth to speak but recorded music played in her ear. She sifted through her various contacts trying to think who the hell Terrence Nguyen was and couldn't make any connections.

"Dr Paterson?"

"Yes."

"Please excuse this call out of the blue but your information was passed on to me by Cecily Cooper."

"Yes." Cecily was the head of the team in Queensland who'd taken over their research.

"She said you're currently in Adelaide, is that correct?"

"Not quite. I'm in South Australia but a two-hour drive from the city."

"I'd like to arrange a time to talk about your research. We have an opening in our department for a group leader. We could have a meeting via Zoom but it's much better to be face to face when possible, don't you agree?"

"I'm looking after a friend at the moment. I'm not sure—"

"I understand that, Dr Paterson, but I wondered if it was possible for you to come to Adelaide?"

"Oh … you're in Adelaide. Yes, that's possible." Julia would prefer to talk to the professor while he was visiting South Australia than have to make a trip to Brisbane. "When would you like to meet?"

"One day this week?"

She thought about what she needed to do for Eve over the next few days. "What about Thursday?"

They made a time and a place and he ended the call, leaving Julia staring at her phone. She sighed. She couldn't stick her head in the sand forever and she'd been impressed by the information Margaret had passed on about Cecily.

Being here away from Melbourne had given her the breather she'd craved and needed. She'd almost convinced herself she could leave Melbourne. She'd have to suck it up and adapt. It saddened her to think she'd be so much further away from Eve though, and then there was Glen. Moving to Brisbane would be a strain on their already waning relationship. She told herself she could live without him but deep down—

Julia jumped at a tap on her window. Lucy was peering in at her. She opened her door.

"Is everything all right?"

"Yes. Eve's up again. It's nearly time for me to get my kids and there're a few things I need from the shop so I thought I'd head in now."

"How is Eve?"

"Feeling a bit better, I think. I got her to do a little bit of exercise but she didn't last long at it. She's watching TV now with a cuppa."

"Should I try her again with the exercises?"

"I think we can leave it for today and try again tomorrow. Just concentrate on getting fluids into her and coaxing her to eat a bit more."

"Right. You head off; we'll be fine."

Julia flicked her hand at Lucy, whose eyes flashed as she turned on her heel and strode to her car. She got in and drove away without a backward glance.

Julia shrugged. She knew Lucy was deeply upset with her over the boat incident with the kids, and after hearing her story last night she was beginning to understand why she clung so tightly to her kids but she'd hoped Lucy's feelings were thawing. What the hell had happened now?

Noah and Poppy certainly brightened Eve's day and that was all that mattered to Julia. Remembering they'd be home soon sent her hurrying inside. She'd better find out from Eve if the assortment of bikes she used to keep still existed before the kids got back. When Julia had told them there might be bikes, their little faces had lit up with so much excitement you'd have thought she'd offered them a year's supply of lollies.

"Did Julia find the bikes?" It was the first thing Noah said when he ran out of the classroom.

"Hello, you two." Lucy smiled as Poppy joined them.

"Mum?" Noah begged.

"I told you not to get your hopes up."

"Ohh!" Poppy's shoulders sagged and her school bag slipped to the ground.

"We've had a busy day with Eve."

"I thought you looked after her," Noah said. "Why couldn't Julia get out the bikes?"

"We both needed to help Eve today." Damn the bikes. Lucy was still smarting from the casual dismissal Julia had given her as she left. A flick of her hand as if she were the hired help. Which technically she was, but—

"Eve's being lazy," Poppy said.

"Poppy, that's not very kind." Lucy bobbed down so she could look both her children in the eye. "I told you Eve had a big operation and it will take her a while to feel better. It's very kind of her to let us stay at her place. We don't want to make more work for her. Today she wasn't feeling well and we had to get her some different medicine. I did some cooking so we've got things for all our lunches. Julia had other errands to run so there just hasn't been time to look for bikes." Thank goodness. Lucy wanted to talk to Julia about it first but there hadn't been a chance.

"We can't go on the boat and we can't ride bikes." Noah glared at her. "What can we do?"

"Noah, that's rude." Lucy stood up again. "There are plenty of other things to do where I can keep an eye on you and still help Eve."

"You don't have to watch us all the time, Mum." Noah strode ahead to the car.

Poppy slipped her hand into Lucy's. "Maybe Julia can look for the bikes tomorrow?"

"Maybe," Lucy said as they set off after Noah. He'd never been a moody child but lately she was seeing evidence of attitude that reminded her of a teenager. It was times like this she missed Alec's support.

⁂

"They're Lucy's children, Julia," Eve said.

"I'm offering bikes in the backyard, not cars on a highway." Julia folded her arms.

"All I'm saying is you need to check with her first before you go bringing out bikes. They might never have ridden before."

"Probably not, the way she keeps them wrapped in cotton wool."

"She's their mother and has every right to parent her children in her own way."

"So I can't get the bikes out?"

"There are several in the big shed. I'm happy for you to see if there's something their size, but only if Lucy's fine with it."

Julia's mouth twitched but she remained silent.

"Let's set out some afternoon tea for when they get home," Eve said. "Children are always ravenous after school and I wouldn't mind one of those apple muffins Lucy made this morning."

"That's good." Julia flew into action, getting out plates and cups and a knife to cut up the fruit. "You must be feeling better."

"A little." Eve pulled a smile. She'd felt refreshed after her sleep and not so out of sorts, but the exercises had been painful and she was still feeling a bit off.

Julia had everything ready by the time they heard voices from the other end of the house.

Eve's spirits lifted then dropped as it went quiet. Julia stuck her head out and glanced along the passage.

"Washing their hands," she said and ducked back into the kitchen as the voices grew louder again.

"Hello." Eve beamed as the children came into the room with Lucy close behind. She got the mildest of responses back. Lucy took some bags of shopping to the bench.

"Who's ready for something to eat?" Julia asked.

"Meeee!" Poppy's reserve dropped away but Noah slipped quietly onto a chair.

"How was your day?" Eve asked as Julia handed around a plate loaded with pieces of fruit.

"Good," Poppy said as she took a piece of banana.

Noah's look was grim, as if the weight of the world was on his shoulders.

"Are you feeling better, Mrs Monk?" Poppy asked.

"Yes, thank you, Poppy."

"So Julia can look for the bikes." Poppy bounced up and down in her chair.

Noah brightened momentarily then his earlier sombre look returned as Lucy reprimanded her daughter.

"I told you not to bother Julia about that," Lucy said and put glasses of milk in front of her children.

"Lucy, can I talk to you please?" Julia nodded her head towards the door. "There's something we need to discuss."

Lucy glanced at Eve, a frown on her forehead.

Eve shrugged her shoulders then remembered she shouldn't as pain rippled down her arm.

Lucy followed Julia into the passage and the door shut. There was silence around the table then Poppy said in a stage whisper, "I think they've gone to get the bikes."

The three of them ate for a moment in silence.

"I asked Mum and Dad if I could have a bike for my birthday," Noah said softly.

"I want a bike for my birthday too," Poppy said.

"No, you don't. You're just saying it 'cause I am."

"Can you ride a bike, Noah?" Eve asked.

"Not very well but I like doing it. Dad says he might get me one but Mum always says no."

"I have two sons. They're grown up now but I used to worry about them too. Mums do that because we love our kids."

The door opened and Lucy came back alone. They all stared at her as she leaned in and took a piece of apple from the plate.

She stared at each of them in turn. "Julia's gone to look for the bikes."

Poppy gave an ear-splitting shriek and bounced on her chair. Noah simply smiled.

Lucy turned to Eve, her face unreadable. "She said you'd mentioned there were helmets inside somewhere."

"In the wooden box in the corner of the playroom, I think, but don't get too excited yet." Eve looked at the children. "The bikes in my shed haven't been ridden for a long time. They've probably got flat tyres."

"Can we go outside and wait for Julia?" Noah asked.

"Pleeeze, Mummy," Poppy wheedled.

"Stay in the yard."

They were off before Lucy had finished her sentence.

"It's the perfect place to learn to ride. Plenty of space." Eve smiled encouragingly.

"I never had a bike as a kid. Didn't ever want one." Lucy lifted her chin, looked Eve in the eye. "During my stint in ED I had to patch up several broken bones and terrible scrapes on bike riders."

"They won't come to too much harm out here."

They stared at each other across the table a moment then Lucy's face softened. "I'd better go and see they're not driving Julia crazy."

"I'll come with you."

Outside, Poppy and Noah were hopping from foot to foot.

"She'll probably have trouble," Eve said. "I hooked them all up high on the wall of the shed."

"Can I go and help her, Mum?" Noah pleaded.

"I'll go," Lucy said.

"Me too." Poppy jumped up and down.

"Here she comes." Eve caught sight of Julia emerging from the trees that hid the shed door. She was guiding two bikes, one on either side.

"Yes!" Noah shot out the gate and across the yard, closely followed by Poppy.

Eve and Lucy trailed along behind.

"They're coated in dust," Julia said as she relinquished the bikes, one to each child. "And their tyres are flat but I can fix them."

"There should have been some trainer wheels there somewhere," Eve said.

"I don't need trainer wheels," Noah said. "I've ridden bikes before."

"I don't need them either," Poppy said as she tried to swing her leg over the bike.

"Hang on, Poppy," Julia said. "They're all dirty and we don't want to ride them while the wheels are flat."

"I want to ride now," Poppy wailed.

"They're not ready yet," Lucy said.

"They need a clean-up first." Julia brushed her hands down her jeans. "Tomorrow while you're at school I'll patch the tyres and they'll be ready for when you get home."

"Can we help clean them?" Noah asked.

Julia looked to Lucy, who only hesitated a brief moment before she nodded. "I think that's fair if you're going to ride them."

The children shouted happily and it was all go after that. Eve sat on the back verandah and watched as they worked to clean up the bikes. The excited chatter of the children and the sight of Lucy and Julia actually working together was just the panacea she needed.

Finally Lucy broke up the fun. "Time for a shower before dinner, kids."

"Let's put the bikes on the verandah, ready for me to fix them tomorrow," Julia said before the children had time to complain.

Poppy sidled up to Eve and leaned against her good arm. "Where's your dog?" she asked, her eyes wide with enquiry.

"I don't have a dog any more."

"Why do you have a doghouse then?" Poppy pointed towards the old kennel at the end of the verandah.

"I used to have a dog but he died."

"What was his name?"

"Merc. Do you like dogs?"

Poppy shook her head. "Not very much."

"Poppy and Noah, inside now and strip off in the laundry," Lucy said.

Eve wondered if dogs was another thing Lucy worried about when it came to her children.

Lucy paused at the door. "I'll whip in and put the casserole in the oven to reheat."

"Thanks." Eve was grateful for Lucy's cooking. She was being paid, of course, but she also made far more interesting food than Eve or Julia.

"We should have kept out some prawns for an entree," Eve said. "It's a bit late to—"

"The prawns!" Julia's mouth made a perfect O then another word began to form on her lips.

"Julia!" Eve cut her off. "You did put them in the freezer."

"No, I forgot!" Julia turned and fled along the path, shouting as she went. "They're still in the boot of my car!"

thirty

Lucy ripped another head from a prawn and tossed it in the middle with the rest of the shells. Thank goodness it had been a cool day. Most of the prawns were still frozen when they'd removed them from Julia's car. It was just the upper layers of the top box of cooked prawns that had started to defrost. Eve had said they'd have to eat prawns every day.

"What a hardship," Lucy and Julia had chorused. They'd both laughed then looked at each other with startled smiles.

Dinner had begun with a prawn cocktail. Noah and Poppy had never eaten prawns and to Lucy's surprise had loved them, minus the cocktail sauce.

"That's lucky," Julia had quipped. "We've got a lot to get through."

Once the children were in bed, Eve had suggested they peel the defrosted prawns and package them up to eat over the next few days. Lucy's brain was scrambling with possible recipes for cooking with them as she tossed another prawn in the bowl.

"Cack!" Julia flicked some prawn shell from her fingers to the scrap bowl. "I hate doing this."

"We wouldn't have so many to do if you hadn't forgotten them," Eve said.

"I had more important things on my mind."

They glared at each other across the table and Lucy giggled.

"You two are so alike, you could be mother and daughter."

"I've always thought of Julia as my daughter, even when her mother was alive."

"Eve! You didn't take the poo line out." Julia plucked up a prawn Eve had just shelled and tugged the grey stringy tube away from the flesh. "It's probably too fiddly with your sore arm."

"I never do."

"What? You mean I've been eating prawn poo all these years?"

"Hasn't done you any harm."

Lucy remained silent. She liked to remove the poo line herself. She might take a second look at the prawns Eve had shelled later. There weren't many to check. Eve had slipped her arm from her sling but was making slow work of the shelling.

"I think we're going to get sick of prawn cocktails," Julia said.

"How could you get sick of them." Eve popped a prawn in her mouth.

"You have to whistle while you work." Julia chuckled. "That's what you always told us."

Lucy looked at the mountain of prawns they still had to shell and popped the one she'd just stripped into her mouth. The sweet flesh melted on her tongue.

"I may as well join you." Julia waggled a large prawn in the air then bit into it. "Divine," she mumbled.

"After all these years I've never tired of them," Eve said.

Lucy was pleased Eve's appetite was returning. She'd eaten better tonight than she'd done since her op.

"Spiro was keen for you to go back to the museum committee," Julia said.

The smile left Eve's face. "Spiro can be as keen as he likes. In fact, he can join the committee once he's retired." She stood. "I don't think I can do any more." She washed her hands at the sink and slipped her sling back on.

"Would you like a cup of tea?" Julia asked.

"Yes, but I can make it. You two keep going so we can get these prawns packaged and back in the fridge."

"We'll have to come up with different ways to eat them," Julia said.

"I was thinking a creamy garlic prawn fettucine for tomorrow night," Lucy said.

"Oh stop," Julia groaned. "I didn't think I was hungry but that sounds good."

Eve's phone rang.

"Hello, Jess." Eve listened for a while then told Jess she was recovering well.

Julia gave a soft snort as she ripped another head from a prawn.

"Come whenever you like," Eve said into the phone. "That'd be great. See you then."

"Who's Jess?" Julia asked as Eve put her phone back on the bench.

"She works at the doctor's surgery."

"Oh yes, I think I met her the day I called in for your script," Julia said.

"You've met her, haven't you, Lucy?"

Lucy shook her head. "We've only spoken on the phone."

"She was checking in on me and she's coming out for a visit," Eve said. "I promised her a look through the house."

"Why?" Julia asked.

"Her husband's a builder and she loves old houses. She's trying to convince him to buy one they can renovate. She's interested to see the changes we made to this place."

"When's she coming?" Julia glanced around as if expecting Jess to arrive any minute.

"Later in the week." Eve glanced at Lucy. "I think you'll like her. She's closer to your age and you've nursing in common."

Lucy nodded and kept shelling the prawns. She didn't care about the nursing link but Jess had been warm and helpful when they'd spoken on the phone about Eve's care.

Eve fiddled around in the kitchen and one at a time ferried them each a cup of tea before she rejoined them at the table. She watched them as she sipped from her cup. Lucy could tell she wanted to say something and finally she did.

"I hope you don't think I'm prying, Lucy, but—"

"But you're going to anyway," Julia said.

"I've been thinking about what you told us last night and wondering what happened. Did Charlie have Covid? How did you get on?"

Lucy had been about to reach for another prawn to peel but she stopped, her hand hovering over the box. It had been such a relaxed evening, she'd let her guard down and now Eve wanted to stir up things she wasn't sure she wanted to admit.

"I'd like to know too," Julia said. Her voice was gentle, with a caring tone Lucy didn't recognise coming from her.

Lucy sighed and rested her hands on the table. "It turned into a series of mis ..." She shrugged. "It was ... nobody ... I guess I ..." She shrugged again. "I ended up in what you might call a perfect storm."

thirty-one

Melbourne, March 2020

With a huge wave of relief Lucy plugged her phone in, held her breath a few seconds and then smiled as the pings and chimes of text and voice messages flooded in. It was the message from Beryl she played first.

"I've woken up feeling terrible. I'm going to the doctor. The children are with Kylie. She'll take Noah to school." There was a wheezy pause. "I'll be in touch later." Another wheezy pause. "Hope your man's all right."

Lucy stared at her phone. The message had ended. Kylie was Beryl's daughter. Lucy didn't know her last name and only had a vague idea of where she lived. Once more she had no way to make contact.

"Arggh!" She stomped a foot on the floor. She felt so helpless. Until she got her test result back she had to stay put.

She flicked on the kettle and took a bite from one of the sandwiches Mina had provided. Her stomach growled its thanks. The sound made her realise how quiet it was in Charlie's house. And

316

how cold. She huddled closer to the blow heater. It wasn't big enough to warm the cavernous room. The kitchen was a mix of ancient appliances and modern, worn cupboards with new door handles, an antique dresser and much newer table and chairs. Charlie had never mentioned any close living family. She wondered who would come and deal with his house and contents. She hoped he hadn't left everything to his distant bloody overseas relatives.

The kettle boiled and she made a coffee with the fresh milk Mina had brought. On top of the fridge sat a radio. She turned it on and the detached voice of the newsreader announced that people who'd disembarked from a cruise ship in Sydney were testing positive for coronavirus. Then there was an announcement on physical distancing for people in public. She hoped Kylie was staying at home with Poppy and that Noah was safe at school.

School! She almost dropped her mug in her hurry to reach her phone. Beryl's granddaughter was at the same school as Noah. They'd have a number for Kylie.

She got someone different at reception this time and had to explain her predicament all over again. It took some time – the receptionist couldn't give out someone else's number, but she went to speak to her boss. Eventually, with the added surety that Beryl was on both children's emergency contact list, Lucy was allowed to have Kylie's number. She was also able to discover Noah was at school.

She rang Kylie. "I'm your mum's neighbour, Lucy," she said as soon as Kylie answered. "I had a message from your mum to say Poppy's with you. Thanks so much, Kylie, I—"

"She was but I've had to ask a friend to have her. I've been called to go in for an extra shift at the supermarket. You've just caught me. I'm about to start."

The bottom dropped out of Lucy's stomach. "Which friend?"

"Maz. She's got a young one at home. Poppy'll be fine with her and she'll pick up our kids from school when she gets hers and keep them till I get there. Or Mum. I'm sure she's fine. She's just feeling a bit panicky with all that's been going on with this vir—"

"Can you give me Maz's number? I might be able to get away soon." Lucy hoped the stars would align. "I'll get the kids and check on your mum."

"Oh, that'd be great. It's crazy here at work and I'm not sure when I'll get away. Just so you know, Maz has a big dog. It looks and sounds scary but it's a pussy cat."

Lucy rang Maz's number, hoping with all her might she'd get a negative test result and be able to collect Poppy. She hit her forehead with her palm as Maz's phone went to voicemail. She left a message to explain who she was and asked Maz to ring her back. Lucy hoped Poppy was okay. She was very timid when it came to dogs.

She put her phone down, then snatched it up again and scrolled through her messages. There was a voice message from Alec she'd overlooked before. She closed her eyes and played it, imagining he was close instead of thousands of kilometres away.

"Sorry I missed you guys. You must be out having fun. Be good for Mummy, Noah and Popsicle. Babe, I won't be able to call for a few days. Not looking like I'll be able to get home next break with all the coronavirus stuff. I'll talk to you Sunday when I know more. Love you all."

She longed for him and yet was glad she couldn't talk to him right now. The kids had been shunted around and she felt bad enough about that. He hadn't wanted her to go back to work until Poppy was at school. She thought about the gleaming new

Thermomix at home on her kitchen bench. She'd put something she wanted above the needs of her kids.

Lucy put the phone back on the bench and hugged herself close. The kitchen didn't seem to be getting any warmer. She moved back in front of the heater and held her hands towards it.

The radio kept repeating the news headlines over and over: cruise ship passengers testing positive to coronavirus, a health debacle, who was accountable, people flouting social distancing directives. Lucy turned it off. She longed for Alec, wondered what he was making of all this. They'd spoken only a few days before and, while the news had been worrying then, it had still seemed so distant. Now the world truly had gone mad.

Her phone pinged with an incoming message and her knees went to jelly as she read it. Her test was negative.

"Thank you, thank you, thank you." She clutched her phone to her chest then checked the time. If she ordered an Uber she could get to Maz's house, collect Poppy then go on to the school for Noah and Beryl's granddaughter.

She gathered her stuff, turned off the heater and checked to make sure everything was secure. While she waited on the front verandah for the Uber she tried Beryl again – no luck – and then Maz, who answered.

"I'm Poppy's mum, Lucy."

"Oh yeah, I was going to call you back but I've been busy."

"Thanks so much for having Poppy. I'm on my way to get her."

"Okay."

"How is she? Can I talk to her?"

"She's having a nap."

Lucy frowned. "She never has a daytime nap. Isn't she feeling well?"

"She's fine. My little one always sleeps at this time of the day so Poppy is too. If she wakes up before you get here I'll tell her you're coming."

Lucy waved to the driver as the Uber pulled up, then washed her hands with sanitiser and put on her mask. She still didn't know Charlie's result. She'd been very careful with her PPE but just in case.

"I'm being cautious," she explained. "I work in aged care."

The Uber driver shrugged. "Lots of people wear masks these days."

Lucy watched Charlie's house recede then disappear as the car turned out of the street. She flopped back against the seat. Her children were her priority now. She hoped Poppy was okay. She'd given up daytime sleeps when she was two, only succumbing if she was sick or maybe really tired. Perhaps she hadn't slept well at Beryl's.

The Uber driver wasn't chatty and that suited Lucy. She kept her window part way down in spite of the cold and watched as the suburban landscape slipped by. She'd only been at Charlie's for twenty-four hours but it felt like a lifetime.

Her phone rang.

"Beryl, thank goodness."

"Hello, love. I only just got your message. Forgot to turn my phone back on."

"How are you?" Lucy asked.

"They tell me I'm fine. Just my asthma playing up. I'll pick up the kids."

"Are you sure?"

"Yes, I'm feeling much better. Glad to get out of the doctor's. Sick people everywhere there."

"Thanks, Beryl. I'm on my way to pick up Poppy so I'll meet you at home."

"See you, love."

"This the right place?"

The driver had pulled up beside a high slatted fence. Lucy peered through the gaps. The garden was littered with assorted toys and bikes. The driveway had three cars in it, but none of them looked like they could move too far. One was up on bricks with its wheels missing.

She checked the number on the fence and noticed the 'Beware of the Dog' sign.

"I think so," she said and rummaged in the carry bag Mina had brought her. She slipped a sandwich into her jacket pocket, then climbed out of the car. "I shouldn't be long."

As soon as she approached the gate a large German Shepherd flew across the yard, barking ferociously.

"Are you sure you're going in there?" the Uber driver called.

"Yes," she nodded keeping her gaze on the dog, who was jumping at the gate.

"Hello," she said with as much calm as she could muster. "Kylie says you're harmless. I wonder what your name is. I used to know a dog just like you. His name was Bruce." She recalled her first visit to Charlie's when Bruce had met her at the door with a ferocious bark. Unlike this dog his legs weren't strong, but he'd still frightened the life out of her. Charlie had said his bark was worse than his bite and she'd soon had him eating out of her hand. Literally. He always gobbled up the remains from Charlie's meals.

She took out the sandwich and carefully dropped a piece in front of the dog. He hoovered it up and sat looking at her expectantly. She dropped another small piece beside him and opened the gate. Once more he ate and sat.

"Maybe your name is Bruce." She smiled at him, dropped one more piece and walked steadily along the path to the front door. The screen was all but non-existent, just a frame and a few shreds of mesh. She knocked firmly on the weathered door beyond it, the dog sitting expectantly at her feet.

The door opened a crack and a child of about Poppy's size peered through the gap.

"Hello," Lucy smiled. "I've come to collect Poppy."

The door opened further. The dog tried to push inside but a woman appeared blocking his way. "Stay, Brutus." The dog sat again. "You must be Lucy."

"Yes. I've got an Uber so I can't stay. Is Poppy ready?"

"She just woke up. I was going to change her." Maz lowered her voice. "She wet her pants."

Poppy appeared beside Maz. Her little face was blotchy and she began to cry. Lucy scooped her up and hugged her close, only then discovering the smell of urine and the damp seeping from Poppy's trousers.

"I wet the bed, Mummy," the little girl whispered in her ear.

"It doesn't matter, Popsicle," Lucy whispered back. "Thanks, Maz. We'd better go."

Ignoring Brutus, who walked beside her with his nose close to her jacket pocket, she walked quickly back across the yard.

"The big dog was scary," Poppy whispered.

"It's all right, sweetie." Lucy hugged Poppy to her. "Mummy's here now."

thirty-two

"And did Charlie have Covid?" Julia's question brought Lucy back to the present. She brushed at the moisture on her cheeks.

"Yes." Lucy nodded as the anger bubbled in her chest again. She still felt it after all this time. And pure luck she didn't get it. Her PPE wasn't to the standard they'd later discovered was necessary.

"Poor man," Eve said.

Lucy took in the kind blue eyes that were studying her. While she'd been pouring out her story neither woman had said too much. They'd just let her talk, and while she had they'd finished peeling the prawns. Julia had cleared away and they'd had a second cup of tea. Somehow these two women had opened the door on her failure as a mother and listened without judgement.

"I've never told anyone the full story until now," Lucy said. "Not even Alec, but that wasn't the end of it."

"There's more?" Julia said.

"The children were all right, weren't they?" Eve asked.

"Physically, yes. Poppy hadn't wanted to have a daytime sleep at Maz's, as I'd suspected, but Maz had insisted she lie down with her child. And she brought the dog inside. Poppy had been terrified and too scared to leave the bedroom, even when she wanted to go to the toilet. That's why she wet her pants. She was so embarrassed." Lucy plucked a tissue from the box and blew her nose. "She's been toilet trained since she was three, but she wet the bed that night and on and off for a while after. Noah didn't say much but he watched me like a hawk.

"Mina got someone to take over my other clients but the aged-care facility where I'd been doing two shifts a week asked me to do more hours. I didn't want to leave the kids again, especially as schools closed, but the facility was terribly short-staffed."

"It must have been difficult on your own," Julia said. "Why didn't you just say no to the aged-care work?"

Lucy took a deep breath as she thought of the people she worked with. "If any staff member had the slightest ailment they had to stay home. There weren't enough staff and the residents deserved good care. I couldn't turn my back on them. The kids didn't cope very well with me working though. They worried as soon as they knew I was going to work.

"Beryl offered to help but I didn't want her to be put out again. In the end we compromised. I did some extra shifts, and if the kids weren't at school and kindy they went to out of hours care, and Beryl was my last resort."

"What about Alec?" Eve asked.

"Stuck in WA. If he came home he would have had to quarantine, and then he wouldn't have been allowed back. We didn't think it would last for long so he stayed. In hindsight, perhaps he should have come home. We could have lived off our savings and my wage but we didn't know what to do, what was going to be for the best."

"No-one did," Eve said.

"Alec hated the idea of the kids being left in care. He was okay with Beryl having them though, so I played down how much they were in outside care. He was worried enough not being able to come home to us."

"Surely he'd be supportive," Julia said.

Lucy sighed. "You'll think it's crazy but that Thermomix," she nodded to the bench, "was the reason I badly wanted to go back to work early. And then there was the new washing machine and the dryer. I was locked into payments for them."

"Basic household appliances?" Julia looked bemused.

"We have this long-term plan, you see. We agreed Alec would take the FIFO job, I would stay home until the kids were both at school and all the extra money would go to our house and business fund. We agreed to live on the basics, no frills, except for birthdays and Christmas and even then we didn't go overboard. Then, about eighteen months ago, Alec came home with a plan to buy a motorbike. We argued. It was big, not something we do very often. We revisited our plan and goals and he backed down. Not long after that I went to a Thermomix demo. I only went to fill a space. I had no intention of getting one. They're pricey items. Anyway, I fell in love with the potential. This machine replaces most kitchen appliances. Not that I had that many. There was a payment scheme, and I thought if I worked a day a week while Poppy was at kindy I could pay it off and I wouldn't have to ask Alec for the money."

"That sounds fair," Julia said.

"It went well to start with. Alec didn't mind in the end. Beryl was there as backup when he wasn't home. It was tricky, but to begin with I managed my shifts at the residential home without needing her help. Then the washing machine broke down. We had a contingency fund, but when I went to buy a new one there was a great washer–dryer package going. I'd been offered some work by the nursing agency so I decided to take it and get the package. The agency was more flexible than the home for hours so once again it worked well … until the pandemic. I didn't want to let down the people I worked with but I was also locked into those payments."

"It was beyond your control," Eve said.

"Work was awful." Lucy ignored Eve, seeing herself back at the home. "I was working the day they found out one of the residents had Covid."

"Hell," Julia hissed.

"It was hell. Or like one of those old war movies Burt used to like. We felt like soldiers in the front row. When one of us went down, we closed ranks to fill the space and kept working. Each time I went home I worried I was bringing it to my kids. I'd strip in the laundry, wash myself and my clothes before I collected them. The next shift I'd go back worrying about who would be sick – another resident, another nurse or carer."

"It must have been terrible," Eve said.

"We got on top of it in the end but not before we lost a few residents. At work I was focused but at home with my kids I had to hide my fear. But they sensed it and they didn't want me to go. I kept leaving them when they needed me most. I'm no better than my druggie parents."

"My giddy aunt, Lucy!" Eve exclaimed. "You cannot for one minute compare yourself to your birth parents. Is that why you didn't confide in Alec?"

Lucy wiped tears from her cheeks. "He was right. I shouldn't have gone back to work when I did. I'm Noah and Poppy's mother and I let them down."

"Hell, Lucy, I reckon you're being tough on yourself," Julia said. "Think of all the people you helped."

"You were one of those frontline heroes," Eve said.

"At what cost?"

"Your children seem like happy, healthy, bright young human beings to me," Eve said. "Are you going to blame yourself for that too?"

Lucy frowned.

"When my boys were young, my husband, Rex, had an affair. I blamed myself for not being a good enough wife to keep their father from straying."

"Now you're being ridiculous!" Julia huffed.

"I know that now. I tried so hard to hide my own feelings of shame and distress from my sons but I couldn't protect them from the town, the rumours and snide remarks, the humiliation." Eve looked at Lucy again. "Most parents feel guilt at some stage. We have to learn how to stop being controlled by it. Things happen in life, good and bad; you chalk them up to experience and move on. It took me a long time to work through that. Once I opened up about how I was feeling, my boys did too. We had lots of deep and meaningfuls around this table."

"Is that what you called those all-night sessions?" Julia said.

Eve smiled. "My boys were lucky. We had some good close friends who were there for us during tough times. You've moved around a lot, Lucy, but perhaps Wallaby Bay will become home. A place to settle, make friends and connections ... feel safe."

Lucy thought about how happy the kids had been since moving here. She was too, and Alec. "We do like it here."

"There're a lot of good people in Wallaby Bay."

"That's rich coming from you, who's cut them all off," Julia said.

"Not all of them." Eve rose to her feet. "It's late."

"Yep, I should go to bed too." Julia waved. "I've got bikes to fix tomorrow."

Eve went to the sink and Lucy picked up a magazine that Poppy had left on the corner of the table. After dinner they'd been cutting out pictures of things starting with P. Julia had got quite involved finding all kinds of obscure items like a pill-box hat from a vintage photo, and calling a verandah a porch. Poppy had loved it and then when Julia had offered to take her photo and print it on Eve's printer, Poppy had been beside herself with excitement. "I can go on my 'P' page," she'd squealed.

Lucy put the magazine and the scissors on the desk in the kitchen and stopped to look at the photos on the wall above. They were a series of black-and-white shots taken from a prawn trawler at sea. Some were of men working, a few close-ups of rugged faces under woolly beanies, another of boats in a row on a calm sea, and a great shot of dolphins riding the waves at the front of a boat. She'd looked at them several times before, wondering if any of the men in the photos were Rex.

"They're good, aren't they?" Eve had come to stand beside her.

"Yes. And I really love that big one on your lounge wall with the whale breaching beyond the trawler and the sun peeping over the horizon. It's an amazing shot."

"The photographer was an acquaintance of Spiro's. He went out with them for several prawn runs over the period of a year. Poor bloke suffered from seasickness but he was so dedicated to his work he didn't let that stop him. His photos have been used in many settings – magazines, websites, et cetera. I bought these but it was so hard to pick from the many incredible shots. He captured the life of a prawn fisherman so well."

"Are any of them your husband?" Eve had several modern photos around her house of her sons and their families but Lucy hadn't seen any of their earlier years.

"Oh no. These were taken years after Rex died." Eve opened a drawer and took out a large, framed photograph. She handed it to Lucy. "This is Rex. I only get it out if my sons are coming home."

It was a standard family portrait – the parents seated and the two young boys standing between them. Eve was beaming at the camera, a bright confident smile. "Look at your gorgeous long hair," Lucy said.

"I had it cut short after Rex died," Eve said. "I was too busy to be fussing with hair."

Lucy turned her attention to the tall, fair man smiling brilliantly for the camera. There was a certain charisma about him even in an old photo. "He was very good looking."

"And didn't he know it. He could charm the birds from the trees when he wanted to." Eve took the photo back and studied it. "We all look so happy, don't we? We were then. Or at least I thought so. The boys were in upper primary and doing well at school, the business was booming. We worked hard and played hard. Life was pretty good." She returned the photograph to the drawer. "It was only a year after that photo was taken that I found out Rex was having an affair."

Lucy recalled Eve's earlier comments about guilt. "Which you surely can't blame yourself for."

Eve smiled. "Just as you can't blame yourself for what happened with your children back in Melbourne."

"Mothers are supposed to protect their children."

"After Rex died, I kept myself too busy to think about anything but work and trying to be the best parent I could for my boys. They started acting up and I was nearing burnout. A school counsellor ended up being the one to help me. I was there to talk about the boys and we ended up talking about me.

"He reminded me I wasn't perfect and neither was life, and it was okay for my boys to learn that. I wanted to protect them from all the hurt but living can hurt. We have to make adjustments and understand that we all have foibles and make mistakes. It's how we deal with the lumps and bumps of life that make us. By trying to protect my sons, I wasn't helping them. They needed my guidance and support but they had to find their own path."

"Like riding bikes and climbing on broken boats?"

"The *Evie 1* isn't broken. Nothing that a bit of TLC wouldn't fix anyway." Eve smiled. "Single parenting can be tough but you're not totally responsible for your children. I know Alec's away a lot but he seems level-headed."

"Are you saying I'm not?" Lucy surprised herself with her teasing tone.

"You're a fabulous mum and I've certainly appreciated your nursing skills, but you don't have to manage everything on your own. I'm the last person to give relationship advice." Eve gave a snort. "But a partnership is about sharing the load. Alec's a good bloke. I think he'd be more upset that you haven't shared your worries with him and I reckon you'd feel a hell of a lot better if you told him."

Lucy knew Eve was right. She'd felt some release just talking about her guilt and fear with Eve and Julia. How much better would she feel it she shared it with Alec?

"He's a man, Lucy. You can't tell me he's never made a mistake."

Lucy grinned. Eve was nothing if not forthright.

"Now come on. We all need our beauty sleep. Some more than others." Eve led them to the door. "I'm glad Julia's fixing the bikes," she said. "It will give her something to do, and Poppy and Noah will have a lot of fun on them."

"They've not ridden much and Poppy only ever on a tricycle."

"They'll be fine, and they've got the whole big space of the outer yard to ride in or they can just run around in it. That stand of trees over by the big shed is perfect for climbing. They won't come to too much harm out here."

"So you're saying I have to let them go."

Eve fixed her with a knowing look. "Not altogether, they're still young. Just far enough to test their fledgling wings."

To Lucy's surprise Eve leaned in and brushed a kiss across her cheek.

thirty-three

"Thank goodness that's over," Eve groaned as Lucy walked with her from the physiotherapist's room.

It was the afternoon of the following day and Lucy had driven Eve into town for her appointment. She'd been hopeful the sparky young woman who'd greeted Eve might have more luck with her but Eve had remained stubbornly resistant.

"You've a long way to go." Lucy opened the car door and made sure Eve was comfortable.

"It's too painful."

"Perhaps you should take the pain medication again."

"I don't need it."

Lucy climbed into the driver's seat and started the car. "It might help you with the exercises. You won't get proper use of your arm unless you persist."

Eve looked stubbornly out of the window, not speaking as they drove. Lucy sighed quietly to herself. It had been a hectic day. Eve had been demanding, asking for things she couldn't reach or tasks to be done that she couldn't do. Lucy had tried to get her to do a few exercises first thing that morning. Eve had refused and Lucy had let it go, knowing they had to see the physio later in the day. Julia had been no help. Every time something needed doing she'd disappear outside to the shed or into town on an errand.

It was already mid-afternoon and Lucy wouldn't have much time between returning Eve home and dashing back to pick up the kids.

"Julia hasn't brought in the washing and her car's not here," Eve said. "She must have gone off again. You'll need to bring it in before you collect the children, please, Lucy. The air gets damp much earlier these days."

Lucy gritted her teeth as she pulled the car in by the back gate. She didn't feel the slightest bit guilty about being paid by Eve while living rent-free in her house any more. She was on-call almost twenty-four seven and she was well and truly working off any debt she might owe.

Julia still wasn't back by the time Lucy went in to pick up the kids. Noah and Poppy talked of nothing but bikes all the way home and she had to be a wet blanket and tell them Julia might not have finished the bikes. They were all disappointed to discover Julia's car was not at the house when they arrived. The kids groaned and complained as she sent them inside to wash their hands. For Lucy it was a mix of hurt for her kids and relief as well. She still wasn't comfortable with the whole bike-riding thing.

She tried to cheer everyone up with fruit and cake. Eve at least pulled on a smile for the children and said she was sure Julia would be back soon.

They all stopped at the sound of a dog's bark and then a knock on the door.

"Oh that'll be Pete, my neighbour. I rang him and asked if he'd like some prawns. Would you mind getting out one of those packs we didn't peel, Lucy?"

Lucy went to Eve's freezer while the children followed Eve towards the back door. Earlier, on the way to the physio, they'd dropped off a small bag of peeled prawns to Gert; some of those they'd spent ages preparing the previous night. At least Lucy hadn't slaved over this pack of unpeeled prawns Eve was giving away to her neighbour.

The dog barked again and Poppy squealed. Lucy's heart sped up. She quickened her pace then paused mid-step as she caught a glimpse of a man through the screen door. Tall and lean, a hat on his head – he could have been Charlie.

She pushed open the door. Of course he wasn't anything like Charlie. She could see he looked much fitter for a start. Thick grey curls sprung from under his broad-brimmed hat and he held a long stick, like a staff, in one hand.

"Pete, this is Lucy."

The man gave a brief nod of his head. Beyond him Poppy squealed again. She was rolling on Eve's patch of lawn with a small brown kelpie licking her face. Noah was there too, trying to pat the excited animal.

Eve chuckled. "Not sure if you'll need to worm the child or the dog or both."

"Belle, that's enough. Come!" Pete commanded and the dog immediately ran to his side and sat, turning back for a quick look at the children. "She loves kids."

Eve sat on the bench and Belle immediately moved to sit at her feet.

"And she loves Eve."

"She stays with me sometimes when Pete's away." Eve patted the dog, who writhed in joy at the attention. "You're a beautiful girl, aren't you, Belle? Sit."

Belle immediately stilled and Eve slipped something from her pocket that the dog inhaled. Now Lucy knew why there was a packet of dog treats on the laundry shelf.

"Can I do that?" Noah asked.

"Me too?" Poppy was immediately in on the act.

Eve showed them how to make Belle sit and how to offer the treat. Lucy was pleased to see Poppy's easy interaction with Belle. She'd always been so fearful.

"These are for you." She handed over the small pack of frozen prawns and Pete put them in his backpack.

"Thanks. Good to see you're recovering well, Eve."

"It's only a shoulder patch-up," Eve said. "Not like having your knee replaced." She nodded at his leg.

Lucy swallowed a smile at Eve's making light of her op.

"Come on, Belle," Pete said. "Time to finish our walk." The dog got a barrage of pats and a hug from Poppy before Pete finally set off again.

"He's a bit of a recluse," Eve said as they watched him disappear over a rise. "He lives down closer to the beach in an old shack. One of the upsides of the pandemic was we got to know each other a little better. He usually calls past once a week or so when he's out for a walk and we've had the odd meal of fish and chips together. He catches them and I cook them."

In the distance the sound of a vehicle caught their attention.

"Maybe it's Julia," Noah said, his face bright with expectancy.

"That sounds like a bigger vehicle than Julia's hire car," Eve said.

A four-wheel drive ute came along the track and pulled up beside Lucy's car. "Stay in the yard," Lucy called.

"It's Julia," Eve said, as a woman jumped out and waved to the children. "What's she been up to?"

As they reached the gate Julia beckoned them over and began unstrapping a tarpaulin that covered the tray of the ute.

"Your bike's ready, Noah," she said.

"Thanks," he said, as they all tried to get a closer look.

"I couldn't fix yours yet, Poppy, so I've got something else you can ride while we work on the two-wheeler."

Finally she flung back the covering. Noah's bike was lying flat in the tray and tied to a rail beside it was a large three-wheeler bike. Its colours had faded and there was a bit of rust on its back step but there were some bright new ribbons attached to the handlebars.

Poppy squealed in delight and jumped up and down while Lucy helped Julia lift the bikes down. Poppy grabbed gleefully at the handles and Lucy flashed Julia a smile.

Noah hooked one leg over his bike.

"Helmets," Lucy said and both children dashed back inside to get the helmets they'd tried for size that morning.

"Great idea to bring the three-wheeler, Julia," Eve said, inspecting the old bike.

"I'd forgotten all about it. I'd fixed the tyres on both bikes but I was having trouble with the chain on the little one. I rang Verity to see if one of the boys might help me and she invited me out for a cuppa. It was Oliver who remembered my old three-wheeler was still in the shed. It's been well used over the years but they made them tough. Verity had some ribbon and they let me borrow the ute to bring it back. Oh, and I've got a frozen meal from Verity in the cab. Don't let me forget that!"

They all laughed. The kids came racing back and climbed onto the bikes. Lucy wasn't so worried about Poppy now but she kept a close eye on Noah as he swayed his way across the yard.

"I could have put trainer wheels on," Julia said. "But he wasn't keen."

Noah wobbled wildly and Lucy took a step forward. He put his foot to the ground then got himself started again, riding in a big arc around the yard and back towards her; the smile on his face so wide her heart was ready to burst.

"He'll be an expert before dinner," Eve said.

It was well after eight that evening before Lucy finally got her excited children to sleep. They'd had such a wonderful time riding. Eve had been right – before Lucy had dragged them inside to shower before dinner, Noah was riding the two-wheeler as if he'd been doing it forever. Now she felt a stab of guilt for not letting them have bikes before. She headed up the passage but the memory of the previous night's chat with Eve pulled her up. She had to stop feeling guilty every time something happened with her kids. Lucy continued on to find Julia and Eve settled in the lounge with a glass of wine each.

Julia jumped up. "Would you like one?"

"Thanks," Lucy said and nestled into one of Eve's comfy chairs.

"They're asleep?" Eve asked.

"At last. Luckily the bikes had to stay outside or I'm sure Poppy would have worked out a way to have hers right by her bed."

"They're great kids, Lucy."

Julia arrived back and handed her a glass of wine.

"Thanks again for the bikes," Lucy said. "You've made two little people so happy."

"And an older person not so." Julia jerked her head at Eve. "We were talking about the prawn festival and Eve's adamant she won't be involved. Did you say you were interested in helping with it?"

"Maybe," Lucy said. "I'm not sure what I can do but Helen said there was a meeting."

"It's in a couple of weeks. Perhaps you could go with Lucy, Eve. Introduce her."

"I suppose you'll be gone back to Melbourne by then," Eve said. "I've got so used to you being here, I forget you'll have to leave."

"I'll be here a little longer. I've got a meeting in Adelaide on Thursday with a professor from the uni in Queensland. They might offer me a job."

"In Queensland," Eve said. "That's a long way away."

"I know and it might not happen." Julia picked up her wine and settled back again. "I'm just exploring opportunities, as they say."

"Your appointment with Professor Campbell is on Thursday, Eve," Lucy said.

"In Adelaide?" Julia asked.

"No, here at the visiting specialist rooms."

"What do you think he's going to say about the patient?"

"Don't talk about me like I'm not here," Eve snapped.

"The wound is healing well." Lucy looked Eve squarely in the face. "But not a lot of progress has been made with the rehab."

"I'm going to have a bung arm forever."

"No, you're not," Julia scoffed.

Lucy thought Eve was joking but the sad look on her face said otherwise. "It's only been a week since your op."

"Feels like forever," Eve grumbled. "And I don't want to hear any more about that blasted prawn festival." She struggled up from the couch. Julia reached out but Eve waved her away. "I'm fine. Just tired. I'll leave you two to the wine."

Lucy glanced at Eve's glass. There hadn't been much in it to begin with and the level had barely dropped. She took a sip from her own glass feeling awkward, the silence between her and Julia growing until Julia broke it.

"Do you think the antibiotics are working?"

"Yes, but she's not finished the course yet. Her temp's normal, she's drinking plenty of water and not having to go to the toilet so urgently, and her appetite's picked up. She only left a little on her plate tonight."

"I ate the last of her pasta before I put the plates in the dishwasher." Julia groaned. "That creamy sauce was divine."

Lucy smiled. "I'm glad you enjoyed it. At least it used a few more prawns. I was thinking we could have a stir-fry tomorrow night and then some with steak the next, a surf and turf? That should just about finish them off."

Julia groaned again and clutched her stomach. "I'm going to put on weight if I keep eating like this."

"They're not big serves and it's all good healthy food."

"You're right. I shouldn't complain. I don't keep much food at home and I don't do much cooking."

Lucy couldn't imagine not making her own meals. "What do you eat?"

Julia's eyebrows raised.

"If you don't mind me asking. I've always loved cooking so I'm curious."

"I have a lot of pre-prepared meals, I order takeaway, or eat out; there are so many great places within easy distance of my apartment. My favourite is Mexican."

"But isn't that an expensive way to eat?"

"I've never done a comparison." Julia picked up her glass again. "But I used to waste a lot of food when I cooked at home. Glen, my partner, likes to cook but he makes such a mess I discourage him. Does Alec cook?"

"Sometimes. Spag bol and barbecues are his favourites." Lucy's phone pinged with an incoming message. She glanced at it. "Just one of the real estate agents. A house has come up for rent but it's not furnished. There don't seem to be any furnished places available at the moment. We've got all our gear in Eve's shed. I'm sure Kon would help me move but he's not long had a hip replacement and I don't know when Alec will be back next."

"It must be difficult with him away so much."

Julia always surprised Lucy with her intermittent bouts of empathy. "We manage. And it's not forever. He could be finished by next year."

"And then what will he do?"

"We've been planning to start a business here in Wallaby Bay."

"What kind?"

"Alec's a diesel mechanic so he'd like to have his own workshop. But since we've moved here and his parents' old fish and chip shop's empty, we've been thinking about reopening that."

"They're quite different choices."

"I know. Alec's drawn up business plans for both. It gives him something to do on his days off while he's away."

"Which would you prefer?"

"The fish shop." Lucy's response was so swift she surprised herself. "I'd like it to be something we could do together and it would get everyone off my back about returning to nursing." She paused. That had come out rather sharply.

"You don't want to go back to it?"

Lucy shook her head. "Not for now anyway. A fish shop would be a new beginning for both of us. Something we could build together."

"You could sell all kinds of prawn dishes."

"We certainly want to change the menu from the basic fish and chip shop it used to be, but it's still in the dreaming stage."

"Eve might give you her tempura prawn recipe. It's to die for. Like me, Eve's not the world's fanciest cook but she can produce jolly good prawn dishes."

"She should have said. We could have had that instead of what I made."

"Oh no, we had to use up the cooked prawns. Eve's special recipe works best when they're green. I'll see if she'll do it over the weekend. I can help her." Julia screwed up her nose. "I'll peel the prawns."

They both grimaced, remembering the huge number they'd peeled the previous night.

"A bit of praise about her cooking might brighten her up," Julia said. "She still seems so down in the dumps."

"Sometimes surgery can knock people. Shoulder surgery particularly has a long recovery period. If we can get her to tackle her exercises I'm sure she'll notice the improvement."

Julia sighed and drained her glass. "It won't be easy in her current mood."

"Tomorrow's a fresh day." Lucy sipped the last of her wine. "I'd better get to bed." She took her glass to the kitchen and waved goodnight to Julia, who was pouring herself a second.

"Lucy?"

She turned back.

"There's really no rush for you to leave. Eve's brighter when you're here … and the children. You're all good therapy for her now."

Lucy nodded. Another dose of Julia's empathy was an amazing thing. As she let herself into her bedroom her phone rang. She was surprised to see it was Alec, then she remembered it was only eight o'clock where he was.

"Hi, Lou, thought I'd check in and see how you're getting on. Have you shifted to Mum and Dad's yet?"

"They're staying longer with your uncle."

"Oh, so you're still stuck at Eve's."

"Not stuck exactly. We're settling in here." Lucy flopped onto the comfy bed. "I've tried to find us some other accommodation but everything's too expensive or totally unfurnished."

"I hate being away at times like this."

"We're fine, Alec." Often she said that when things weren't fine, wanting to protect him from the guilt of being so far away, but this time it was true. "Julia's found some old bikes for the kids and they're loving it."

"That's good." He paused and there was a tentative tone to his voice. "You weren't so keen on bikes."

"I know." She took a breath. "Alec, there's something I need to talk to you about."

"Has something else happened?"

"No. Not recently, anyway. It was last year." She swallowed to get some moisture in her mouth, thought of Eve saying what a good man Alec was and kept going. "I didn't ever tell you exactly what happened." Lucy continued on and Alec didn't interrupt even when she told him about her work, her fears for the kids and what she'd put them through – and all because she'd wanted a Thermomix and a dryer. When she finally stopped talking there was silence except for the sound of her heart thudding in her ears.

"Babe, you poor thing."

Lucy blew out a sigh and rolled over on the bed.

"I knew it had been bad for you but … I can't believe you felt guilty about household appliances. We don't have to be so stingy that we can't be comfortable. Why didn't you tell me back then?"

"We'd had that fight about the motorbike."

"I wish I'd never come up with that idea."

"And I don't like to worry you when you're away." She tried to picture his remote setting, and him all alone in his accommodation. He was helpless to do anything for them while he was there.

"But I've been home many times since then."

"I know. It's just that the more I distanced myself from it the less it bothered me."

"But it has affected you. You were always the carefree parent when the kids were little. I was the one to fuss if they fell over or had a temperature."

He was right. She'd always dusted the kids off. Told them they'd be okay. She'd seen far worse in hospitals than most of Noah and Poppy's minor bumps and scrapes.

"So is that why you don't want to nurse any more?" he asked.

"Partly. After last year I lost my mojo for it and I hate the thought of leaving the kids with anyone else."

"My parents aren't just anyone, Lou."

"I know. And they do have the kids sometimes. I don't think it's fair to lock them in to regular childcare, that's all."

Once more there was silence.

"I'm sorry," Lucy said.

"What for?"

"I should have waited till you came home. I know how hard it must be for you being so far away. And we made a deal. You'd be the main breadwinner and I'd take care of the kids. I let them down, and you."

"Lou, that's ridiculous. It was all out of your control. You're the best mum."

Tears rolled down Lucy's cheeks. The emotion that she'd bottled up until she'd told Eve and Julia hadn't run dry, it had simply simmered and now it had boiled over again. She sobbed.

"Don't cry, babe."

"I'm okay." She wiped the tears brusquely from her cheeks and blew her nose.

"I wish I was with you now."

"I'm fine, really. It's just the release of telling you about it. The kids are great. We're all good. I don't want you to worry about us. Tell me about your new job and the camp. Is it better than the last one?"

They talked a long time until both of them finally ran out of things to say. When Lucy ended the call the low battery signal beeped. Her nearest charger was out in the playroom. She gripped the phone, staring at the low charge icon, then turned it off and dropped it down beside the bed. Her body sunk deeper into the doona. She was still fully clothed except for her shoes. She rolled over, pulling the doona with her, and closed her eyes, knowing sleep wasn't far away.

thirty-four

Eve groaned and sat back against the chair. The small cushion that had been between her elbow and her body fell to the floor.

"Let's try that again," Lucy said and picked up the cushion.

Eve glared at her. She'd been up early that morning to see Julia off on her trip to Adelaide. Then she'd sat on the back verandah drinking her tea, watching Poppy and Noah ride around the outer yard. Noah was already riding like a pro. Poppy was a little more cautious. Julia had brought back the small two-wheeler from the farm the previous day, complete with trainer wheels. Poppy alternated between wobbling around on that and riding flat out on the three-wheeler. The melancholy that plagued Eve had lifted while she'd watched them but had settled back around her now. She had a useless arm and a desolate future ahead of her.

"I'm feeling tired," she said.

"Just a few more exercises and you can rest." Lucy slipped the cushion back in place.

"My whole arm hurts when I do that exercise."

"It's probably more stiffness from lack of use than anything wrong. The surgeon will check you over this afternoon and be able to tell what's going on."

345

"Bloody Jock. He said he could fix me and he's made it worse."

"Try squeezing your arm into your side again."

Eve glared at Lucy.

"If you won't do the exercises here you'll have to go to rehab."

"I will not."

"The specialist may send you if he thinks you're not making progress at home."

"Bloody Jock," Eve muttered again and pressed her arm against the cushion. There was no way they were sending her to any kind of rehab facility. She grudgingly continued.

Finally, Lucy stopped her torturous treatment. "Would you like to go and lie down now?"

"No."

Lucy turned away.

"What are you going to do?"

"Make your bed."

Eve felt a pang of remorse then. Lucy was a saint the way she ran the household and put up with Eve's bad humour.

"How about we sit and have a cup of tea instead?"

"Sure," Lucy said and switched on the kettle.

"Have you spoken to Helen lately?" Eve hated the thought of Lucy and the children leaving but she knew the Nicolis would want them to stay there once they returned.

"She rang last night. I haven't had a chance to tell you about it." Lucy pulled a face. "I hope you don't mind but I convinced them to stay at Goolwa a bit longer. Kon's brother has ended up in hospital and his wife needs some support."

"Oh no, I don't mind at all." Eve pursed her lips. That had gushed out very quickly. "At least it's good they can stay and help, and you know there's no need for you to rush to leave here. The children are very settled."

"A bit too much. I don't know how I'll get them away after all their bike riding."

"They can have the bikes."

"Oh no, Eve, we couldn't take the bikes." Lucy shook her head. "Goodness knows where we'll end up living but it'll be somewhere in town. It won't be safe for them to ride there." She had that panicked look she'd had when the children had been momentarily lost on the boat.

"Well then, they can come out here and ride them whenever you like."

"That's so kind." Lucy put mugs of tea on the table and sat down. "I don't know what I would have done without you."

"Nor I without you." Eve sagged as a wave of sorrow washed over her.

"What is it, Eve?" Lucy's voice was gentle. "Are you in pain again?"

"No, not physically anyway."

"I know your shoulder recovery seems daunting now but you should get the full use of your arm back."

Eve huffed out a breath and shook her head.

"You're a strong and determined woman. From what I know of you, you've faced tougher times than this and overcome them."

Eve sighed. "Sometimes you just get sick of fighting to keep your head above water."

"Is that what you're doing?"

"That's what it feels like." Eve picked up her mug. "Thanks for this, Lucy, I think I will go and lie down for a while." Eve walked as steadily as she could with the mug of hot tea. She'd been shocked to feel moisture pooling in her eyes and she didn't want Lucy to witness her weakness. What an old fool she'd become. She was burdened by a crook arm, her fishing business was gone and her fractured relationship with Audrey had severed her connection with activities in the town she loved – what did she have to look forward to? She was beginning to think that Julia was right. She wouldn't be any good out here on her own. Perhaps she should look at moving into somewhere smaller in town. Just thinking about that possibility made her feel miserable.

—✦—

Julia left the cafe and wandered out into the cavernous space of the Adelaide railway station. She was in such a daze she wasn't sure whether to hop and skip or hang her head and cry.

Professor Terrence Nguyen, or Terry as he'd asked her to call him, had just treated her to a delicious lunch and the most interesting job proposal. It had come totally out of left field. She walked up the long flight of steps to street level and paused, forcing the steady stream of people to flow around her.

Terry was based in Adelaide, not Brisbane. The job he'd offered was still connected to the university in Queensland so she'd have a few trips up there a year, but the bulk of her work would be here, in Adelaide. Julia had never imagined she'd live here again, possibly working at the university where she'd first studied science so many years earlier.

Someone bumped her. She started walking, blending in with the pedestrian current. The wind was chilly but the sun shone brightly, reflecting off the glass of the high-rise buildings. Thick traffic moved along North Terrace beside her and above the noise came the familiar ding of a tram bell. Adelaide's climate wasn't so different to Melbourne, there were lots of great eateries, housing was cheaper and getting around the city easier. And the job Terry had presented, well, if she'd been offered it in Melbourne she'd not have hesitated to accept, yet she'd just asked him to give her the weekend to think it over.

She stepped out across King William Street and strolled the broad tree-lined footpath towards her old uni. She did own a unit here but it was out in the burbs and she wasn't keen to evict her long-time tenant. He'd been a dream occupant, paying on time, able to do minor repairs and keeping everything tidy. Perhaps she could find something to rent close to the city, similar to her Melbourne apartment. She'd only been in that for eight months but she loved the light airiness and the easy access it gave her to the city one way and to work, her ex-work, the other. It would be a blow to let it go and a bother, since she'd signed a long-term lease.

Julia stopped in front of the art gallery and studied the banner announcing the current exhibition. It was the work of the Marek brothers. She smiled, recalling her teenage self despairing over their paintings and her art teacher doing his best to explain surrealism. Julia still didn't get it.

She wandered on. It was possible to settle herself back in Adelaide but did she want to? And finally, the thoughts she'd been pushing away. What about her relationship? Glen's work was in Melbourne. Long-distance relationships were tricky. Perhaps moving to Adelaide was the catalyst she needed to end it anyway. She stiffened against the discomfort that started as a prickle at the back of her neck, swept down and around her body and nestled in her gut. No matter how hard she tried to keep Glen compartmentalised he didn't stay neatly in his box.

She jumped as her phone vibrated in her pocket. It was Glen. She hesitated, her finger hovering over the screen. He knew she

had this meeting in Adelaide today. She couldn't decide whether
to talk to him now or wait.

—

Lucy glanced across at Eve as she stopped at the carpark exit and
waited for the road ahead to clear. Eve hadn't wanted Lucy to go
into her appointment with her. When she'd reappeared twenty
minutes later there was a deep scowl on her face. Lucy had asked
how she'd got on. Eve had said "fine" and walked swiftly from
the building. The scowl had remained. It was as if the wind had
changed and etched her face in a permanent grimace.

"Can you take me to the post office please?" Eve's voice cut the
silence, the gentle tone a sharp contrast to the rigid set of her jaw.

"Of course, then it'll nearly be time to pick up Poppy and
Noah," Lucy said. "Would you mind waiting till I get them before
we go home?"

Eve glanced at her watch. "Fine by me."

Lucy walked beside Eve to her post office box and bent to
retrieve the keys when Eve struggled with the lock and they
slipped to the ground.

"Thunderation!" Eve snarled. "Everything is so difficult."

"It's a stiff lock to turn left-handed," Lucy said. She stepped
back while Eve cleared the mail then locked the box again for her.

"Mostly junk," Eve muttered then her face changed to a smile.
"Hello."

A young couple were passing with a roly-poly puppy on a
lead. It was walking anywhere but in the direction they were trying to go.

"What a fine dog," Eve said. "What have you called him?"

"Goliath," the guy said proudly.

"He should grow into it," Eve chuckled. "May I pat him?"

"Of course."

Lucy smiled as Eve made a fuss of the puppy and soon had it eating out of her hand, literally.

"Have you thought about getting another dog?" Lucy asked as the couple walked away.

"I can't bear the thought of going through the puppy stage again."

"What about a rescue dog?"

"I loved my dear Merc but I don't want another dog," Eve said firmly. "I enjoy other people's though. It's a bit like what they say about grandchildren. They're fun to play with and then you can give them back."

"And do you keep those treats in your pocket all the time?"

Eve grinned. "You never know what might happen when you're out and about. You might meet a dog who needs a treat."

Lucy shook her head as they set off for the car. At least the puppy had improved Eve's mood.

"Hello, Eve."

They both stopped as a smartly dressed woman approached.

"Hello, Verity. Have you met Lucy?"

"No, but I feel as if I know you." Verity smiled.

"Verity is Julia's sister-in-law."

"Oh, yes, the bikes," Lucy said. "Thanks so much for your help with that. Poppy loves the three-wheeler."

"That was all Julia and my son Oliver's doing. I just found a bit of ribbon. I'm glad someone's using the old bike again. And I'm glad I've run into you, Eve. I was going to ring you later. I've just come from the museum. They've asked me to chair the next meeting to get a workable plan for the additions and upgrades. They have to move forward with it or they'll lose their grant money. The local council rep's going to be there. I know you've just had your surgery but I was hoping you'd come along. I feel a bit like a fish out of water and I'd value your input. Especially since you've offered a considerable donation towards it yourself."

Lucy glanced at Eve and wondered if her head was spinning too. Verity spoke so fast she barely took a breath between sentences.

Eve's frown returned. "Will Audrey be there?"

"The meeting is open to anyone."

"I'll think about it."

"Oh, that's good, Eve. I'm so glad, thank you."

"I didn't say yes."

"But I'm sure you will. The museum needs input from sensible people with local knowledge like you." Verity waved at someone else walking past then turned her beaming smile back to Eve and Lucy. "I must go. I've a million jobs to do before I finish in town. Nice to have met you, Lucy."

"She's running for council at the next election," Eve said as they watched Verity stride away. "I've no doubt she'll get in."

"Will you go to the meeting?" Lucy asked.

"Like I said. I'll think about it."

Lucy found them a park not too far from the school gate. The clouds had cleared and the sun warmed them nicely inside the car.

"You were right about Jock Campbell." Eve spoke quietly, staring at the view from the window. "So much for bedside manners. He didn't mince his words."

"It's not long since your surgery."

"Still, I have to do better."

"I know it doesn't seem like it now, Eve, but the pain will ease and eventually disappear. You will recover."

"That's what Jock said but he didn't phrase it as nicely." Eve grinned. "Perhaps I should have offered him one of my doggy treats. Might have improved his manners."

Julia's heartbeat sped up a little as a man stopped in the bar entrance and scanned the room. She didn't move, taking a moment to study him. He was tall, and his thick dark hair was tousled back from his forehead. It needed a cut. He was dressed in a business suit, smart but not too fancy, the jacket hanging open over a rounded stomach, his tie not quite straight. His gaze rested on her and he broke into a wide grin, striding towards her.

Julia braced herself as he approached.

"Julia." He bent down and hugged her, planting a warm kiss on her lips that made them tingle. "It's so good to see you."

"Aren't you a surprise?" Julia said. She'd answered Glen's call only to find out he'd been in Adelaide all day for meetings. "I haven't ordered anything yet."

"When I knew you were going to be in Adelaide today I decided to fly in for my meetings instead of doing them online." He put his wallet and phone on the table and sat down.

She breathed in the spicy scent of his favourite cologne. It was perplexing to realise she'd missed him.

"I haven't got too long before I have to get back to the airport," he said. "A drink would be good but let's talk first."

That was a surprise. Since their cruise, he'd become a drink first, talk later guy.

He adjusted his tie, a slightly worried look creasing his face. The splash of pleasure she'd felt at seeing him ebbed away.

"What do you want to talk about?" she asked.

"Us."

Unease wormed its way into her stomach. Julia had kept Glen at arm's length for so long he was probably fed up, had found someone else in her absence who was better company.

She gasped as he lurched forward and grabbed her hands. She felt the roughness of his palm on her skin and wondered how the cut was healing.

"I've missed you, Julia."

"I've only been gone a couple of weeks. Sometimes we don't see each other for that long even when we're both in Melbourne."

He grimaced.

It wasn't overly warm in their nook in the bar but small beads of perspiration broke out on his forehead and his skin felt clammy against hers.

She eased her hands from his grip. "Have you got a fever?"

"What?"

"You're warm. Do you feel unwell."

"I'm fine. Julia, what I'm trying to say, very badly, is I'd like us to be more permanent."

She frowned. That wasn't what she'd been expecting. "By permanent you mean …?"

"Live together."

"Oh."

He was obviously encouraged by her surprised response because he reached into his pocket and drew out a small red velvet box. "Julia, will you marry me?"

The pounding in her head nearly drowned out his words.

He opened the box to reveal a thin silver band, inlaid with diamonds. "I chose something plain and simple because you're already beautiful and smart."

"That's a bit corny for an advertising guru." She grinned to hide her shock.

"But it's come from my heart."

The smile dropped from her face when she saw the solemn look on his.

"You're serious?"

"Trust me, Julia, I wouldn't be exposing myself to a possible bout of your derision if I wasn't."

She felt bad then and took the little box from him. The ring caught the light from the table lamp and glittered up at her.

"I know you're quite particular," he said.

"Is that another word for fussy?"

"No. I respect that you know your own mind and aren't afraid to speak out. Do you like it?"

"It's beautiful but ... you always said you didn't like the married state."

"I liked being married, just not to my wife."

Julia's head was spinning. This was the last thing she'd expected from Glen. They'd always kept things casual. Hadn't even talked of moving in together. Maybe he did once, not long into their relationship, but she'd canned the idea quickly and he'd never mentioned it again.

He cleared his throat. "This isn't very romantic, I know, but ... I was going to ask you on the cruise and then that all went to shit."

"You'd planned it even back then?"

"Of course. That's why I wanted to take you on a holiday. Get away from our work commitments and take it easy and ..."

"So much for that."

"Exactly. It wasn't what we expected, was it? I didn't want our engagement to remind us of that so I thought I'd leave it for a while. Since then, well, I let life get in the way."

"People like us don't marry, Glen."

"What are we like?"

"You've been married before. You've got an ex and kids."

"I'm legally divorced and the kids are grown up."

"We're both committed to our work."

"We can balance it better."

"You've got your own private life, I've got mine."

"But we like the same things. Our private lives would blend if we let them."

"Your boozy mates?" She raised her eyebrows.

"I was thinking football, movies and Mexican food." He looked down at his hands. "I got into bad habits while we were on the cruise and I've continued to drink too much. I've cut right back since you left."

"You'll feel much better for it, I'm sure." They'd both over-done it on the cruise but she'd cleaned up her act as soon as she was home and back at work. Glen hadn't.

"I was going to break my no drinks on a week day rule and order us champagne but—"

"This has come as a surprise, Glen. I never expected you to be talking marriage when we arranged to meet."

"Does that mean you don't want to marry me?"

"I ... marriage is not something I've thought about." She had once, with Tim. She'd thought it a natural progression of their relationship. How wrong she'd been. She drew in a deep breath. "Things have changed for me work-wise. The job offer wasn't in Queensland, as I'd expected. It's based in Adelaide."

"I see." He looked even more crestfallen. "I did tell you when you were talking Queensland I could be flexible ... but Adelaide ..."

"What's wrong with Adelaide?" She felt suddenly defensive of the city she'd abandoned twenty-three years ago.

"Nothing. It's just that I thought you were going to Bris-bane and I'd been planning how to make that work." He sat up straighter. "Actually, Adelaide could work out better. It gives me easier access to Melbourne."

His phone began to vibrate across the table. He glanced at it. "Sorry, work. I've got to take this." He answered and strode away.

Julia sat the little box on the table. She stared at the ring, imagined it on her finger, tried to imagine life full-time with Glen. She closed the lid and sat back in the soft leather chair. Through the windows, she could see Glen, pacing back and forth along the footpath, his phone pressed to his ear. He enjoyed his work and she enjoyed hearing about it. He made her laugh. Or he used to. She didn't feel as if there'd been much to laugh about for a long time.

His marriage proposal staggered her. She'd assumed he never wanted to go down that path again. She sure as hell didn't. Not that she'd ever actually been married but almost. She cringed, remembering Tim's phone call ten years ago. She'd been back in Wallaby Bay helping Heath sort out their mum's financials and personal effects. She'd thought Tim had been ringing to see how she was and instead he was breaking up with her. When she'd been at her lowest point, the man she'd devoted herself to had broken her heart and her spirit. It had taken her a long time to date again. Glen had walked into her life just at the right moment. So different to Tim, he'd oozed confidence without being pushy. He'd shown genuine interest in her work, also unlike Tim who'd been threatened by her successes. Glen was funny and kind and he hadn't wanted too much from her, hadn't wanted strings. She looked back at the little box. That had obviously changed.

"Sorry, Julia. Time's got away." He rushed towards her and grabbed his wallet. "I've got an Uber coming. I've stuffed this up, I'm sorry. I should have waited until you were back in Melbourne." He pulled her into his warm embrace, kissed her cheek.

She wanted to rest her head on his shoulder but he was already stepping away. "I'll ring you." And then he was gone.

Julia sank to the seat and realised the red velvet box was still sitting on the table. She stared at it a moment then picked it up and slipped it into her bag.

"Would you like to order a drink?"

She looked up at the waiter. First a job offer then a marriage offer. "Yes, please. A scotch … on the rocks."

thirty-five

It was Friday night and they'd all just enjoyed a pub meal. Eve hadn't wanted to go out. She was tired and sore, but had tackled her exercises several times with more determination after Jock had given her a telling off the previous day. The blasted man had the nerve to say his skills as a surgeon had given her shoulder a perfect makeover. Any difficulty she was having now was due to her own lack of effort and she had to try harder.

Julia had been doing something outside most of the day. She'd been very secretive about it. And she'd said little about her trip to Adelaide, only that she had a lot to think about, and Eve hadn't pressed her. She'd joined them briefly for a cuppa when Jess had called in after lunch.

Eve had been pleased to see the young woman again, and happy that she and Lucy seemed to hit it off once they'd both got over a reticent start. Jess had been very interested in the house and they'd walked from room to room with Eve explaining the changes they'd made to the original.

By the time Jess left and Lucy had set off to get the children, Eve was weary. She'd wanted a quiet night in but Julia had said she wasn't in the mood to cook and they couldn't ask Lucy to cook for them every night. Eve had felt selfish then and agreed to go out, and they'd asked Gert to join them.

The four adults were sitting back now, relaxing with a final drink. The children were settled at the end of the table watching something on the iPad Lucy had brought with them. There were several other tables of diners spread around the large room and sometimes Eve's group had to lean in to hear each other over the noise.

Gert was leading the current conversation. She'd made up her mind to move to Adelaide and had been telling them all about her plans.

"When will you shift?" Julia asked.

"Not for a while yet. I've got a house to pack up and sell. Nearly forty years I've lived there." Gert's resolute look wavered.

Eve tried to imagine packing up her own place. She was momentarily overwhelmed by the thought.

"Since I started nursing, I've never lived in one place longer than a couple of years," Lucy said.

"Apart from the farm, I've never had all that long in one place either," Julia said.

"My sons want to hire me a skip," Gert went on. "But I'll be inviting the women from the op shop in before that."

"Good idea," Julia said. "You'll need to downsize big time if you're moving into a two-bedroom place."

"You know, Eve, I'd really like to see the museum upgrade started before I leave," Gert said. "Tom would have wanted it done. Are you going to the meeting next week?"

Raucous laughter echoed from the table behind them.

"About the museum?" Eve asked.

"Of course the museum. Most of the committee are sensible people. It's just that Audrey's loud and persuasive and she sways people to her way of thinking. In the past you always stood up to her when necessary."

"I'm fed up with being treated like a pariah," Eve muttered.

"A higher what?" Gert shook her head. "Sometimes you really don't make sense."

Eve noticed a look pass between Julia and Lucy.

"You used to be such a hard worker for this town," Gert went on. "And now that you've sold your business you've dropped your bundle."

"I didn't drop my bundle. People cut me off."

"Oh, that's old news." Gert batted the air with her hand. "There'd be plenty who'd support any decent proposal you put forward."

"What's so bad about Audrey's proposal?" Julia asked.

"You haven't heard?" Gert's eyebrows shot up.

"Bloody Audrey and her cohorts want to use the money to build a big prawn," Eve snapped.

Julia laughed. Then her eyes widened. "You're serious."

Eve nodded. "That's what they came up with."

"But isn't there already one of those in New South Wales?" Julia said.

"And another in Western Australia. And it's not just me who doesn't like the idea. None of the other fishermen I've spoken to want a big prawn as the only commemoration of the industry."

"Surely you've thought of alternatives," Julia said.

"Of course, but I haven't been to a meeting since ... for quite a while."

"Mummy, I need to go to the toilet."

Lucy stood and took Poppy's hand.

"I'll come with you." Julia followed them across the room.

"Audrey's a funny woman," Gert said once they were gone.

"Hmm. That's one way to describe her."

"You know, sometimes people act the way they do because it makes them feel better about their own choices." Gert lifted her chin, her gaze locked on Eve. "Or they're covering something."

Eve glanced down the table. Noah was still enthralled by the screen.

It was the old straightforward Gert staring at Eve now with a knowing look in her eye. But she couldn't know. The only person Eve had ever told about Rex's second deceit had been Pam.

Gert leaned in. "Pam told me about Audrey. I was sorry you hadn't felt you could share it with me but I understood how awful it must have been for you. To find out about Rex on the day he was killed."

For once Gert was speaking in a low voice but Eve glanced at Noah again. Even though Lucy had asked the children to keep the sound down, the noise of whatever was playing could still be heard from where Eve sat.

"I shouldn't have told Pam," Eve said. "It was one night when we were at my place, just the two of us. We had a few too many drinks. I got maudlin and before I knew it I was telling her. I swore her to secrecy."

"Pam told me after Audrey had made a fuss that time about the cakes at the local show. Said you'd influenced the judges against her. Everyone got hot under the collar about it."

"Oh yes, I remember. I never offered to judge again. I don't know why they asked me. I can't bake."

"You'd won that women in business award and they asked you as a celebrity judge."

Eve huffed out a breath. She'd done all sorts the year following her award. There'd been meetings, guest speaker roles, but judging the cakes at the local show hadn't been a highlight.

"Audrey and Norma were always a pair of bitches," Gert said. "But I think Audrey's spitefulness springs from jealousy."

"Of what?"

"You."

"Oh, for goodness sake, you come up with some ideas." Eve lowered her voice. "Why would Audrey be jealous? She was the one who had an affair."

"Who's Audrey had a fling with?"

"Shush, Julia!" Eve glanced around but no-one was paying them any attention. She'd been so intent on Gert she hadn't heard the girls return. Poppy was already cuddled up beside Noah, both of them glued to the screen. Julia was leaning across the table, an incredulous look on her face and Lucy had slipped onto the chair beside her with the expression of someone who wished they were anywhere but here.

The group behind Eve started a noisy rendition of "Happy Birthday".

"What's going on?" Julia hissed.

"Let it go, Gert," Eve pleaded.

"You might as well let her tell us now," Julia said as hip hoorays sounded behind them.

A puzzled look crossed Gert's face then she nodded sagely. "I'll tell you how. When Audrey had that affair she was engaged to Keith. Poor Keith. He's a good bloke but he's struggled to keep a decent paying job most of his life and Audrey's kept them poor. She's never worked but likes to spend money. Something you have plenty of."

Eve shook her head in despair. "It's not as if I haven't earned it."

"Of course you have, but often people who don't have much think that those who do get it easily. And, you have to wonder, if Rex hadn't died, would she have imagined he'd leave you and she'd be the one to have inherited his business?"

"Shush, Gert." A swell of heat surged up Eve's body. She fanned her face with a coaster.

"What's this about Rex?" Julia gasped.

"Mummy, I'm tired." Poppy slid up alongside Lucy, slung an arm around her neck and opened her mouth in a huge yawn.

"Gee, yes, it is late," Lucy said. "I'm sorry to break up the evening but is it okay if we go soon?"

"Of course. We should go now." Eve stood quickly. They'd all squeezed into Lucy's car for the drive in.

"Oh, I suppose it is late for the children," Gert said. "Thanks for inviting me. It's been lovely to catch up with you all again."

Eve said goodnight and walked off, hoping the others would follow behind.

"Will I see you at the meeting, Eve?" Gert called after her.

"I'll see how I'm feeling." Eve put her good hand over her sling.

Once they were all in the car she took some slow deep breaths.

"Well, that was interesting," Julia said.

"Not now, Julia," Eve warned.

"But when we get home," Julia crooned.

"What are we doing when we get home?" Poppy's sleepy voice wobbled from the back.

"We're going to bed," Lucy said swiftly.

"There's no school tomorrow," Noah said.

"It's late. If you want to ride bikes in the morning you need a good sleep."

Nobody spoke as Lucy drove out of town.

"Gert says some funny things sometimes." Julia broke the silence.

"I said no more, Julia," Eve snapped.

They were all quiet again until Lucy pulled the car in by the back gate. She opened her door and turned back to Eve.

"I wonder if Gert has hearing loss," she said. "I was watching her tonight and she struggled when there was extra noise around us or if one of us spoke and she wasn't looking at us."

Julia leaned in from the back seat. "Maybe that's it. I thought she was losing the plot."

Eve snorted. She could try to explain away Gert's story as losing the plot but she knew Julia wouldn't fall for it. "You might be right, Lucy. She's been getting the wrong end of the stick for a while now. I was worried she might be developing some kind of dementia."

"Do you know if she's ever had a hearing test?"

Julia raised her eyebrows at Eve and looked back at Lucy. "Good luck with finding out."

"I'm thirsty," Poppy said.

Everyone moved then, heading inside. Lucy went to help the children prepare for bed and Julia to the kitchen. Eve ducked into her bedroom. If she feigned tiredness they couldn't stop her from slipping off to bed. It'd been a big day for someone who'd only recently had major surgery.

She changed into her pyjamas and sat for a moment thinking back over what Gert had said. It was all so long ago, there was no point in stirring things up.

"What are you up to?" Julia leaned on the door frame, a glass of wine in her hand.

Eve turned back the covers. "I'm going to bed."

"No way. It's only eight thirty on a Friday night and I want to know all the juicy bits."

"It's real life, Julia, not some TV soap."

Julia crossed the room and stood in front of Eve, a repentant look on her face.

"I know. But now that I've heard some of it you might as well tell me the rest."

Eve pursed her lips.

"I could snuggle up next to you on the bed," Julia cajoled.

"No." Eve sighed. "I'll come out."

"Okay."

"On one condition."

Julia glanced back on her way to the door.

"You have to tell me what's bothering you."

"Nothing's bothering me ..."

Eve held her goddaughter's look.

Julia crumpled. "Okay."

"And you can pour me a small glass of that red," Eve said. "I've been on soda water all night."

By the time she'd got her sling back on and struggled into her dressing gown and slippers, Julia had set up in the lounge with the red wine.

Eve looked at the three glasses she'd put out. "I don't think Lucy will want to hear about my dirty linen."

"We can't leave her out. She's heard some of it now."

At that moment Lucy popped her head around the door. "I'll say goodnight."

"We thought you might join us," Julia said.

"Oh."

"Glass of red?" Julia waved the bottle. "And some juicy gossip. What more could you want on a Friday night?"

"Julia," Eve warned.

"I'm sorry, Eve, but I cannot for the life of me picture Audrey and Rex." She wrinkled her nose. "It has to be a joke."

"It isn't." Eve looked from Julia's grimace to Lucy's pained face. "Oh, for goodness sake. Everyone sit down and let's have a drink."

Julia poured the wine and Lucy perched at one end of the couch as if ready to run away again at any moment.

"No more excuses," Julia said. "Tell us the story about Audrey and Rex. I can't believe he'd be interested in her, with her bouffant hair and drawn-on eyebrows."

Eve took a sip of her wine. "Audrey was a looker in her day and it's no secret Rex had a wandering eye. I just didn't know how much more wandering he'd done until the day he died."

"That must have been awful for you," Lucy said gently.

"It was. Rex had an affair two years before and I stayed with him. We had two sons, this home and a business. I wasn't letting any of that go and Rex swore he'd never do it again." Eve closed her eyes at the memory of his earnest plea. "He was probably worried I'd cost him too much money."

"Eve!" Julia's face paled, her earlier bravado gone.

"I'm sorry, Julia. Of course you know what that's like but at least you didn't have children. I really don't know what Gert was on about though. Why would Audrey be jealous of me? Why would she even care about me?"

"Don't you think she would have worried her husband might find out?" Lucy's voice was little more than a whisper. "Gert said Audrey was engaged when she ..."

"Bonked Rex, yes, but so what?"

Eve shook her head at Julia. Sometimes she had no filter.

"Audrey must have wondered if you knew anything," Lucy said. "And perhaps she worried that if you did, you might spill the beans."

Eve placed her glass carefully back on the table so that it didn't wobble in her trembling fingers. Lucy's words had triggered a memory. She was transported back to that day in 1988 when she'd realised Rex had been unfaithful again. She'd dialled the number she'd found in his pocket. Audrey had answered and when Eve had spoken, Audrey had said her name.

"I'm pretty sure she knew that I knew."

"There you are then," Julia said. "Lucy's right. It must have been like waiting for a bomb to fall. She went on to marry Keith."

"So why be jealous of me? She still ended up with a husband. I ended up a widow to a disloyal man."

"Like Gert said, you're better off financially than Audrey," Julia said. "And you have a popularity around town she doesn't have."

"You're kidding."

"She's probably been plotting for years how to oust you as the queen of Wallaby Bay, and with the help of the museum committee debacle and you feeling sorry for yourself, she's done it."

"I don't feel sorry for myself."

Julia raised her eyebrows.

"And I'm hardly the queen of Wallaby Bay."

"People speak highly of you," Lucy said.

Eve snorted.

"They do. When they know I've been helping you here, several people have said what a great person you are and how hard you've worked for the town and how they hope I'm looking after you properly."

"Who?" Eve was amazed.

"The guy at the bottle shop."

Julia snorted.

"Fred Howard," Lucy said.

"Ha, ha," Julia blurted then covered her mouth.

"The man at the newsagent, Dr Sandeep and Professor Campbell."

"What would Jock Campbell know?" Eve snapped.

"He's been a visiting orthopaedic surgeon here for years," Lucy said. "He told me when he called in after your surgery how hard you worked in the community."

"All jokes aside, Eve, you are pretty special, and the vile Audrey isn't. If Verity and Heath were here they'd back me up." Julia shuffled along the couch and squeezed Eve's hand. "You're the most wonderful woman, mother and friend."

Warmth filled the cold spaces inside her and she was surprised to see tears brimming in Julia's eyes. She cupped her goddaughter's face with her hand.

"It's so kind of you to try to cheer me up." Eve glanced at Lucy. "Both of you. I have to admit I was flabbergasted when people believed I'd deliberately pushed Audrey."

"Not everyone believed it," Julia said.

"The loudest ones did." The hurt still sat heavily in Eve's chest. "I know I've been outspoken at times but I've always listened to other people's views before forming an opinion. I thought I'd at least be offered the same courtesy."

"It's done now, Eve," Julia said. "In the words of the song, let it go. I think you'll find most people around here already have."

Eve put a hand to her chest. "I should be used to it, but it hurt to have the town turn on me."

"I'm sure you're the only one thinking about it," Julia said. "No-one cares any more. They've moved on and you should too."

Eve thought about her trips into the bay since her self-imposed isolation. How she'd planned them carefully to avoid people like Audrey. How she flicked her gaze away from acquaintances if she saw them first. How she surreptitiously studied friends, wondering if they'd been among those who'd turned against her.

"And you mustn't hide yourself away because of Audrey," Lucy said.

"Remember what you used to tell us about forgiving?" Julia said. "Forgiveness isn't—"

"A sign of weakness." Eve finished the sentence with her.

"I don't agree with what you did but I forgive you anyway," Julia chanted in a singsong voice. "Hell, how many times did we hear that when we were growing up?"

"How many battles did you kids fight?" Eve said.

"Lots." Julia smiled. "But you were always there to heal the wounds."

"And now here you are trying to heal mine." Eve felt something warm roll down her cheek. She batted at it, horrified to realise it was tears.

"Oh, Eve." Julia gave her a one-sided hug.

Lucy dashed off and came back with a box of tissues.

Eve took one, wiped her eyes and blew her nose hard. "This is what I've come to. A useless old woman."

"You're not old and you're the least useless person I know," Julia said.

"I don't want to retire, you know. It's being forced on me. How will I adapt to life without the prawn business?" Eve recalled the feeling of her younger days when she thought she had forever to do anything she wanted. Now that she had time on her hands she had no idea what she wanted to do with it.

"Getting involved in the town again would be a start," Julia said. "Don't let Audrey and her cronies stop you. You need something to do and you're good at planning and organising and helping people."

"I agree," Lucy said. "It seems to me Wallaby Bay needs people like you, with a square head on their shoulders, someone with the ability to see the bigger picture and who has the best interests of everyone at heart."

Eve looked from one young woman to the other and blew her nose again. "Since when do I take advice from young ones?"

"You said you listened to people." Julia looked at her expectantly.

Eve felt a wiggle of unease she hadn't felt since the rumours about her had run rife. "I'm not sure I'm ready to face a room full of people."

"I'll come with you," Julia said.

"If Helen and Kon are back by then, I'll come too," Lucy said. "I'd like to know more about the project."

Eve looked from one to the other. "All right, I'll go to the damned meeting."

"You'll need a proposal with costing and logistics." Julia whipped a pen and paper out from under the couch.

Eve opened her mouth and closed it again and Lucy laughed.

thirty-six

The wind flicked a strand of Julia's hair across her face as she strode ahead of the others towards the shed. The kids were on their bikes and Eve and Lucy brought up the rear. She was ready to show them all what she'd been up to the last few days. Julia hoped Lucy would approve. She'd been a lot more relaxed since sharing her experience and fears from the year before. Perhaps there was something to be said for unburdening.

Over the last few days physical labour had been Julia's panacea. It had kept her busy yet given her time to think about the future. She hadn't made a decision but there was so much to consider: the job offer, packing her things if she moved ... Glen's proposal. That was the elephant in the room.

He'd rung her late on the night of their catch-up in Adelaide. She'd asked for time to think. He'd asked for more information about her job offer. She'd filled him in, said she hadn't decided. They hadn't spoken since but she knew she'd have to talk to him again soon. A marriage proposal was different to a job offer. Marriage involved far too much emotional baggage. The job was a clinical thing. She could compartmentalise it. Break it down into manageable parts, dissect it and put it back together again. Moving from her apartment was more subjective. If she did take the Adelaide job, she would have to say goodbye to it. She did love that apartment.

"Where are we going?" Poppy's big round eyes peered up at her from under the brim of her helmet.

"You'll need to leave your bikes here," Julia said. "We're going round behind the shed."

"We're not allowed to—"

"To the boat?" Noah's excited yell cut Poppy off.

Julia met Eve and Lucy's enquiring looks. "I've made some modifications."

"Modications?" Poppy looked at her expectantly.

"Close enough," Julia said.

"What are modications?" Poppy asked.

"Come and see."

Julia led the way past the stand of trees and around the shed to the back.

"There's a fairy path." Poppy squealed and ran ahead.

Julia looked at the path she'd cleared through the scrap heap to the boat. All she'd done was move some bits of pipe and wood aside and dig out some weeds to create a clear space for the children to access the boat. She'd found two old plastic whirligigs among the junk. They were faded but still spun and she'd stuck them in bottles either side of the path. She shrugged. "Fairy path works for me."

Noah reached the boat two steps behind Poppy. "You've fixed the ladder," he called.

"What have you been up to, Julia?" Eve said.

They caught up to the children and looked up at the ladder. Julia had reinforced a couple of the loose rungs and fixed the structure firmly to the side of the boat with some rope so it didn't wobble when they climbed it.

"The old girl needed a bit of TLC so the kids could have fun on her." She looked at Lucy. "If it's okay with you?"

"Can we go up, Mum?" Noah pleaded.

"Pleeeze!" Poppy said.

"I've removed anything that was loose and taken out the broken glass. There's nothing they can hurt themselves on."

"Unless they fall off," Lucy said.

"We won't fall," Noah groaned.

Lucy glanced from Julia to the boat. "I suppose it's okay."

"Yes!" Noah said and leaped for the ladder.

"Take it slowly," Lucy warned.

Poppy started up the ladder after him.

"I'll follow you, Poppy." Julia put one hand on a rung and turned back to look at the two women behind her. "You should come up too, Lucy, but I think you'd better stay on terra firma, Eve."

By the time Julia swung her leg over the boat rail at the top of the ladder, the children were already exploring, exclaiming at each new find. Noah climbed up onto the skipper's chair. It had been worn with springs exposed. She'd put one of Eve's outdoor cushions on the seat and covered the whole thing firmly with an old blanket.

Poppy stuck her head out of a door. "We can have a tea party in the cabin, Mummy. There's some cups and bowls. Come and see."

Lucy followed her daughter inside.

"What do you think, skipper?" Julia stood beside Noah. She'd removed any broken windows and washed those still holding together.

"It's great."

"Must be time to cast off then." She ducked down and called below. "First mate, time to pull up the anchor."

Poppy giggled and came out onto the deck. "Where's the anchor?"

"This way." Julia walked around the outside of the boat, which she'd also cleared of any loose rubbish. At the bow she showed Poppy the rope she'd attached to the rail. "Pull it up."

Poppy tugged on the rope, pulling hand over hand until the pipe Julia had attached to the other end came over the edge.

"Ready to go, Skipper," Julia called back towards the wheelhouse.

Poppy hung on to the rail and leaned forward like Julia had on the *Evie 3* the day she'd gone out on the bay with Eve. Julia grabbed the rail beside her and turned her face to the sun.

"What do you think of the modifications?" she asked.

Poppy turned her bright smile on Julia. "The best."

"You've done a great job, cleaning it up." Lucy had come to stand beside them.

"See, Mummy. It's good on the boat, isn't it?"

"Sure is, Popsicle." Lucy smiled at Julia.

"Great job, Julia."

"Eve!" Julia gasped. "How did you get up here?"

"Climbed. And the gallant young captain helped me over the rail. The step you've put on the deck side was most helpful. Where are we off to?"

"Broome to see Daddy," Poppy said.

"Perfect," Eve smiled. "Nice and warm there this time of year."

They all stared ahead at the paddock beyond Eve's boundary. Poppy left them to explore further.

"Spiro rang before I climbed up," Eve said. "Mary's op went well and she's making good progress."

"That's good," Julia said.

"Will she need follow-up treatment?" Lucy asked.

"They're as certain as they can be that they've got it all. Luckily, it was caught very early and Spiro was hopeful nothing further was needed."

"That's good news."

"Yes." Eve nodded and gazed forward again. "Spiro loves her dearly."

Julia slipped an arm around Eve. It wasn't easy to be generous when there was so little love lost between the two women.

Eve straightened. "Shall we abandon ship and leave the children to play?"

"I should keep an eye on them," Lucy said.

Julia raised her eyebrows. She'd thought Lucy would be reassured by her clean-up efforts.

"They're out of sight of the house," Lucy said. "I might just sit on one of those drums by the shed. So I can keep an eye on them."

"Good idea," Eve said.

Julia climbed down first and kept a wary eye on Eve as she took the ladder, closely followed by Lucy.

"It's too nice a day to be inside," Eve said.

The three women picked a small, upturned drum each to sit on, and with the huge bulk of the shed behind them they were out of the wind and being warmed by the morning sun.

"Thank you, Julia." Lucy's smile was a grateful one. "You've done so much. The bikes and now the boat. Poppy and Noah won't want to leave when Helen and Kon return."

"Do they have to?" Julia said.

"I think Helen will want us to stay with them."

"I'll have to go back to Melbourne soon. I'm sure Eve would enjoy your company." Julia glanced at Eve. She was looking towards the boat and didn't appear to be listening. "You'd be happy for Lucy and the children to stay, wouldn't you, Eve?"

The sounds of the children playing drifted down to them. A giggle from Poppy, a call from Noah in a funny voice – they had some game on the go. Eve continued to stare in their direction.

Julia and Lucy exchanged glances.

Finally, Eve spoke. "Lucy knows she and the children are welcome to stay as long as she wants." She turned, a questioning look on her face. "Is going back to Melbourne to do with your job offer … whatever it is?"

Julia felt a pang of guilt at not having said much to Eve about her meeting with Terry in Adelaide but she'd needed time to process it. The only other person she'd told about the job had been Glen and then not in great detail. "It's everything, work, life, Glen … you."

"Me? Why would I have anything to do with you returning to Melbourne?"

"I don't mean that. I've been thinking about you and living out here on your own."

"As I've done for a long time." Eve shook her head. "For an articulate person, you're not making a lot of sense."

Julia adjusted her butt on the drum. "The job the professor offered is a good one. A dream job for me. A combination of research, teaching and mentorship. And better remuneration than I've had before, and more stability."

"Why on earth are you dithering over accepting?" Eve asked.

"The job is in Adelaide."

"I see."

"I wouldn't mind coming back to South Australia. It's certainly more my cup of tea than Brisbane. I'd never survive the humidity up there."

"What's stopping you?" Lucy's question surprised Julia. She'd been keeping her gaze firmly in the direction of the children.

"I … I prefer Melbourne. I have a nice apartment. Friends …" She dwindled to a stop. She'd miss her friends, but in truth they were mainly work colleagues. She couldn't say they'd remain close now that the work connection had been severed. She'd miss Margaret, but she was more a mentor than the kind of friend you took to a movie or shared personal confidences with over a drink.

"You'll make new friends," Lucy said. "Find another nice apartment."

"You own a unit in Adelaide," Eve said.

Julia wrinkled her nose. "I prefer something a bit more modern with a view these days."

Eve pursed her lips.

"What about your partner?" Lucy asked. "Glen, was it? What does he do? Would he be able to move with you?"

"His work's in Melbourne but he does a lot more from home these days." Truth was he did almost eighty per cent of his work from home. "He says he could make Adelaide work for him."

"What's stopping you, Julia?" Eve's tone was sharp.

"Glen's asked me to marry him."

There was a heartbeat's pause then Lucy spoke. "Congratulations."

"That's wonderful." Eve's sharp look was replaced by one of maternal pride. "When did this happen?"

"Last Thursday. We met briefly while I was in Adelaide."

"And he proposed? Julia!" Eve chided. "Why didn't you tell us when you came home?"

"I didn't say yes."

"Oh."

"I was shocked when he asked me." Julia wriggled to find a more comfortable spot on the unforgiving drum. "I'm not the marrying kind. And I didn't think Glen was either, after his first marriage ended so badly."

"But you two are made for each other," Eve said.

Lucy's phone began to ring. "It's Helen," she said. "Excuse me." She moved away towards the boat as she took the call.

"I can't believe you didn't talk to me about Glen," Eve said.

"I was too confused and I have to decide about the job. I gave that my priority."

"Julia, Julia." Eve shook her head. "Don't compare Glen to Tim. They're chalk and cheese. I've always thought Glen a decent bloke. Perfect for you."

"You're not the best person to give marriage advice."

Eve frowned and Julia immediately lamented her sharp remark.

"My marriage to Rex was good for several years," Eve said. "I'll never regret that."

"I'm sorry, Eve. I didn't mean to—"

Eve batted a hand at her. "You're right. My track record isn't good but I've learned a few things about relationships since then, so allow this older and wiser woman a say, please. You and Glen have had other relationships. You're both set in your ways and yet you get along. That's testament in itself."

Julia supposed they got along. Glen's drinking had bothered her but he said he was turning that around.

"Search your heart instead of your head, Julia. You always hold people at arm's length. I know you lost your dear parents but not everyone's gone. You've got Heath and Verity and the boys, me, Gert, and if Glen's important to you, don't let him go. You don't want to end up a lonely old woman like me."

"Oh, Eve. Don't say that. You've got good friends here, and your family. I know they don't live close but they love you. I love you." Julia reached out and gripped the hand that rested on Eve's knee.

"I know." Eve nodded. "I've been feeling a bit sorry for myself, that's all. I'm fine really." Eve pulled her hand from under Julia's and patted her cheek.

"I don't really keep people at arm's length, do I? At least not any more than you have to these days."

"I'm talking metaphorically and not about strangers. I mean the people who want to be close to you: family, old friends."

Julia gave Eve a scornful look but deep down she knew Eve was right. People she loved had died or left her: her parents, Tim. It was too painful, too risky, to form close relationships. She'd let Glen into her circle because he hadn't asked too much of her in return, until now.

"I want you to be happy, Julia," Eve said. "I think Glen makes you happy, when you let him."

"I don't want marriage."

"Maybe Glen would accept that. It might be that he's sick of living alone and he wants to live with you. The woman he loves. Perhaps he thinks formalising your relationship is the way forward. There's nothing unusual about that."

"So you're saying we should live together?"

"Why not?" Eve gave an encouraging smile. "Give it a try. What's the worst that can happen?"

"He leaves with half my stuff."

"Humph! Glen would have far more to lose financially than you." Eve sighed. "Don't judge this relationship by that money-grubber, Tim."

Julia was suddenly aware Lucy had stopped talking on the phone and had moved back beside them.

"Sorry, I didn't mean to interrupt," she said.

"It's fine, Lucy," Eve said. "You're not interrupting. And I think after all we've shared the last few weeks, you're part of the family. Perhaps you could talk some sense into Julia. I'm not having any luck."

Lucy looked perplexed.

"I think it's time we changed the subject," Julia said. "Anyone feel like a cuppa?"

"Actually, I've got a favour to ask first," Lucy said. "Helen and Kon are coming back tomorrow morning."

"Oh."

Eve tried to hide her disappointment but Julia saw it in her downcast look.

"They're bringing Kon's brother and wife back with them. He needs to convalesce, and she still needs some support." Lucy grimaced. "It'd be a squeeze and not very restful with us all at their place so I told Helen we'd stay on here a bit longer. I hope that's okay."

"Of course it is." Eve beamed.

"And Helen's happy to have the children the night of the meeting. So I can come with you."

"Great," Julia said, pleased the subject was firmly diverted from her.

"And you know what," Eve said. "Being here with *Evie 1* and watching the children playing on her has given me another idea for the museum."

"You should keep it simple for the meeting presentation," Julia said.

Once she'd started jotting down Eve's ideas the other night, the three of them had talked it over for hours. It'd been late by the time they'd sorted everything into a concise plan, and Eve hadn't stopped there. She'd spent the next day talking on the phone and sending emails but she'd kept everything to herself. She'd said she didn't want to share any further until she had the final elements nutted out.

Eve stood up. "Do you girls fancy a coffee in town? I bet the children would love a smoothie. There's something I want to look at."

thirty-seven

It was late on Sunday afternoon when Lucy stepped out of the passenger seat of Kon's car. He'd pulled in at the back of the closed-up fish and chip shop, and even though he wouldn't tell her why they were here, there was a sparkle in his eye.

Lucy and the children had been invited for afternoon tea when Kon and Helen had returned home. No sooner had her cup of coffee been empty than Kon had asked her to go with him to look at something. Helen and her sister-in-law were teaching the children a new card game and suggested they stay back. Both Kon and Helen were acting mysteriously but wouldn't explain further so Lucy had agreed.

Now she looked at the old building and hoped Kon wasn't going to try to convince her to reopen the business before she and Alec had the money.

"What are we doing here?" she asked.

"There's something I want to show you." Kon pulled a set of keys from his pocket and unlocked a padlocked gate set in the high wooden fence. Lucy had driven past the old building many times, she'd bought fish and chips from the shop when the people who'd taken over from Kon and Helen still ran it, but she'd never been out the back.

He held it open for her. The wind was whipping cold air from the sea but inside the high fence it was suddenly calm. There was a small lawn area and a courtyard partly covered by a verandah. Kon led the way to the back door and once more took his bunch of keys and unlocked it.

"Let me switch on the power first," he said and stepped inside.

Lucy hunched her shoulders. Even though they were out of the wind the day was getting colder.

"In you come."

"You're being very mysterious," she said as she entered the building. She was in a small hall space. There was a door to one side with a sign that said *Private*. Ahead of her she knew must be the kitchen and beyond that the shop.

"This way." Kon pointed to her left. He flicked on a light and led the way up a narrow set of stairs. The building was warehouse-like in appearance from the outside and Lucy had never thought about what was above the shop. Kon flicked on another light and she stepped into a living area with a kitchen along the back wall. He strode to the window and pulled up the blind.

"Wow!" Even in the dull late-afternoon light she had a great view across the bay and north along the coast.

"We lived here when we first took over the shop. It was fine while we had the two boys but when Alec came along Helen wanted more space so we bought our first house. We used this for storage. Then when the shop didn't sell and we let the Whites rent it, they asked if they could live up here." Kon strode across the open living space and opened both doors leading off it.

Lucy followed him. The two rooms were empty but for the carpet on the floor and the window dressings. She imagined there'd be more great views from the windows.

"We used these two rooms as bedrooms and there's a bathroom-come-laundry down below opposite the stairs. Our tenants painted before they moved in, so the old place has had a minor facelift." Kon looked at her expectantly. "What do you think? It's nothing fancy but it's bigger than that shack you were in. Probably better fitted out too. And solid as a rock. This place has weathered many storms. It won't blow away. We wish it had been available when you first moved to the bay, although it was pretty shabby before the Whites worked on it."

She turned back to look at him. "Are you suggesting we live here?"

"It's got great views and I hear the landlord's a good bloke." Kon smiled.

Lucy blinked back tears and pressed a hand to her lips to stifle a sob.

"Don't be upset." Kon put a hand on her shoulder and peered closer, his face crestfallen. "I know it's not that wonderful but Helen and I thought it might do until you and Alec decide where you want to live permanently. But you don't have to move here ..."

Lucy dug in her pocket for a tissue. "It's great, Kon, truly. It's just a surprise." She glanced around again, already seeing the potential. It was close to everything, including the beach and ... She wiped her eyes and crossed to the living room window. "As you said, that view is pretty good."

"So you like it? Helen worried you're not very close to your neighbours. And it's a bit of a nuisance having the bathroom downstairs."

"We weren't close to neighbours when we were in the shack. Most of the places around us were holiday rentals. And I'm sure a downstairs bathroom won't matter."

"The stairs are a bit steep but Poppy and Noah are big enough to manage. And there's no furniture but I can help organise for all your things to come from Eve's shed."

"Oh, no. I don't want you to be worried by that."

"It's not a worry. If you like the place, we can work out what to do next." He studied her expectantly again.

"What if you get someone who wants to buy your business or rent again?"

"Our block has sold. That's helped with our financial situation so we've taken this place off the market. We want to give you and Alec time to decide whether you want to take it on or not." He held his hands in the air. "No pressure. Today is just about finding you somewhere to live … if you like it."

"I'd have to talk to Alec about it."

Kon looked down at his feet then back at her. "We rang him last night. He's keen if you are."

Lucy felt a load slide from her shoulders. "I love it."

Kon clapped his hands. "Let's go and tell Helen. She'll be so pleased."

Helen was at the door of the house as soon as they returned.

Lucy looked beyond her shoulder.

"The children are fine," Helen said. "They're watching TV. What do you think about the flat?"

"Let us get in out of the cold first," Kon said.

"I love it," Lucy said as she stepped into the warmth.

"Oh, I'm so glad." Helen wrapped her in a hug.

Lucy stiffened then willed herself to relax and hug Helen back. She'd never done that before. It was awkward but there were tears in Helen's eyes as she released her.

"You do know you're like a daughter to us," she said.

Lucy smiled. She knew how lucky she was to have them and her children were lucky too. "You're special to me too," Lucy said and Helen hugged her again.

"About time that son of ours made an honest woman of her."

"Kon!" Helen stepped back and clicked her tongue. "That's Alec and Lucy's business."

Kon shrugged. "How's my brother feeling? I think we should have a drink to celebrate their visit and Lucy's move to the flat."

"He's watching TV with the children but I don't know that he should be drinking," Helen said.

"A nip of ouzo will be just what the doctor ordered," Kon said.

Helen shook her head at him as he walked away, then slipped her arm through Lucy's as they followed.

"I made some keftedakia while you were gone."

Lucy smiled. Helen couldn't help herself. "I hope Poppy and Noah didn't eat them all." Lucy loved the little Greek meatballs as much as her kids did.

"I let them have two each but the rest are to take with you to help fill their lunch boxes."

Lucy stopped, pulling Helen up with her. "You don't need to cook for us, Helen."

"I know. You're a great cook and I'm not trying to interfere but you're much busier than me. And the day will come when Kon and I might be a burden for you and Alec."

Lucy opened her mouth to protest but Helen held up a finger to silence her. "Cooking for my family brings me great joy. Let me help you while I'm able."

Poppy and Noah loved the food Helen made. Lucy did too, but she'd always been so determined to do everything herself, to not be a burden to Alec's parents. Lucy's stiff shoulders drooped as she let go her resistance to Helen's help.

"Thanks," she said. "It will be good to have something savoury for their lunch boxes tomorrow."

"Good." Helen nodded.

From further in the house came the sound of the children giggling then the deeper laughs of the three adults.

"We'd better go and see what's happening before Kon gives the children some of his ouzo."

Lucy followed Helen to the living room where everyone had a small glass of clear liquid in their hands. And there were two spare glasses on the bench. Lucy could see the bubbles in the children's and knew Kon would have given them lemonade.

He gave Lucy a wicked wink and raised his glass. "Yamas!" he called and they all echoed the sentiment.

Later that night after baths and dinner and bedtime stories, Lucy and Alec talked on the phone about the flat above the shop.

"It would mean we could have a real good look at the shop too," Alec said. "Make a decision about whether we want to go ahead with our seafood business or not."

"I agree." Lucy had already told him about her lovely afternoon at his parents' place. It was so sad that he missed special family time. She knew he felt it keenly. "How are you?" she asked.

He told her about a couple of the blokes he'd got to know already – family men who missed their wives and kids like he did.

"The work environment has a good vibe," he said. "The food is good so far and there's a really well fitted-out gym."

"You won't want to come home," Lucy joked. She was glad to hear he was making friends and he was well fed and keeping busy. It helped her not to worry about him.

"How are you doing, Lou?"

"I'm fine."

"Truly? You're not bottling up anything else you need to tell me?"

"No, Alec. No more disasters. We're all good." She told him again about the bikes and the boat, even though Poppy and Noah had done that via their Skype session earlier. By the time they ended the call, Lucy was feeling happier than she had in a long time. Things were falling into place.

She had a spring in her step as she went in search of Julia and Eve.

"We're out here," Julia called.

The front door was open a crack. Lucy could see the two women sitting out under the verandah, an outdoor gas heater glowing red behind them.

"It's such a mild night now," Eve said. "We might not get the chance to be out here again for a while."

"There's a blanket on your chair." Julia waved at the spare seat. "And a glass of red."

Lucy settled in and stared out into the night. The light of the three-quarter moon shone across the bay. "It's so good when there's no wind."

"Doesn't happen often," Julia said. "The town should be called Windy Bay, not Wallaby Bay."

"How are you feeling, Eve?" Lucy asked.

"Perfectly fine, thank you." She raised a small glass of rakija. Just the smell of it wrinkled Lucy's nose.

"What about your shoulder," Lucy asked, "now that you've got a better routine with the exercises?"

"It's hard to describe. I'm not in pain as such but I get weary from it, if that makes sense."

"It does. When you were still in hospital, Professor Campbell described recovering from shoulder surgery as more a marathon than a race."

"Did he? I don't recall."

"You may have been asleep at the time." Lucy smiled.

"Or pretending to be." Julia raised her glass. "I want to propose a toast to Eve's recovery. And—" she looked from Eve to Lucy, "my new job."

"You're taking it?" Eve beamed.

"I made the decision earlier today when I went out for my run. I'll have to let the professor know officially but, yes, I'm moving to Adelaide."

"That's great news, Julia." Eve reached out and squeezed her arm. "I'm so pleased for you, and selfishly for myself. It will be good to have you closer."

Lucy took another sip of wine. The love between the two women was palpable. They were so lucky. Earlier today at Helen's she'd let herself relax and enjoy a developing closeness with Alec's mum but she couldn't imagine sharing with her in the way Julia and Eve did. It made her long for Rita and wonder what life would have been like if she were still alive.

"What did Glen say?" Eve asked.

"He's pleased for me."

"And what will he do?"

"We haven't talked about that yet."

"Have you ever told him about your previous relationship?"

"No."

"Perhaps you should. It might help you to put it into perspective."

Julia stared into her wine glass.

"You know, I really think if Glen had asked you to marry him a year ago, you might have said yes," Eve said.

The two women studied each other and fell silent. Lucy pressed back against her chair, once more feeling the odd one out.

—

Julia looked from Eve to the night sky and took another sip of wine. "Evidently he planned to but when it all went pear-shaped, he decided not to."

"What went wrong, Julia?" Eve asked. "I know you didn't exactly enjoy the cruise but Glen didn't do something, did he? Something terrible."

Julia snorted. "Let's just say being on a cruise wasn't a good test for our relationship."

"Perhaps you should tell us the full version instead of the comedy farce you portrayed for me," Eve said.

Julia's phone calls to Eve from various ports had helped keep her sane. She'd made light of being shut up in a small room, unable to open a window, and the heat if she spent too long out of the air-conditioning. She hadn't mentioned how morose Glen had become after his failure in bed. How he'd drunk far too much, the TV he'd kept on all day and night, or of his stubbing his toe on the end of the bed and his constant griping about it.

Julia glanced beyond Eve to Lucy. In the glow from the gas heater she could see the younger woman was staring straight ahead. "I don't think Lucy wants to hear my boring woes."

Lucy turned slowly and fixed her gaze on Julia. "You listened to mine."

"And mine," Eve said.

Julia shrugged. "All right, but it's no biggie. Not compared to Lucy's frontline work. And I wasn't ostracised like you, Eve. It was more that the relationship wheels fell off, big time." Julia took another sip of wine then remembered it wasn't just Glen who'd drunk too much when they'd been on the cruise. She put the glass down.

"The first few days of the cruise were okay. We ate, we drank, we read, we slept when we liked and made love often."

"Sounds like the perfect holiday." Eve chuckled.

"Then reality set in. I realised I was stuck in this floating hotel for sixteen days and nights. Alcohol became our daily ritual. We'd start at lunch and drink on and off all afternoon until dinner. And then … after a couple of nights … the sex failed."

"What do you mean it 'failed'?" Eve said.

Julia reached for her wine again and took a gulp. "Glen couldn't …" She flicked her finger up. "You know. I told him it didn't matter but he was devastated. He drank more, watched TV if we were in the room and partied until late. We stopped talking. I was so grateful to be able to ring you, Eve, but Glen hardly spoke to anyone and he was so down. I'd never seen him like that. He kicked his toe on the end of the bed halfway through the cruise and he whinged about it all the time. Turns out he'd broken it, but I was over his complaints. By the time we got off that ship in Melbourne we were barely communicating.

"Once we were home again we both threw ourselves into work and the lock-downs kicked in. I put in extra hours and had little energy for anything else, not friends, not you, Eve, not Glen. Then about three weeks after we'd returned home he turned up on my doorstep one Friday night, beaming like he'd won the lotto. He'd had a few drinks but he wasn't drunk, just very pleased with himself. Told me he'd got tablets and did I want to jump into bed with him?"

Julia emptied her glass and poured herself another without looking at Eve or Lucy. There was silence for a minute then Eve leaned forward. "Is that it?"

"What do you mean, is that it?" Julia snapped. "How do you think I felt to be told my partner has to take a pill to be able to make love to me?"

Once more there was silence and then a strange clucking sound. Julia stared hard at Eve. She was squirming in her chair with a hand covering her mouth.

"Eve? What is it?"

Eve's hand dropped away and the clucking sound became a laugh, a deep belly laugh. "Thunderation, Julia, what is your problem? I'd have hardly had sex at all in more recent years if it wasn't for those pills. Alleluia to them, I say."

"Eve!"

"What?"

"I'm sure I don't want to know the answer to this question, but who the hell have you been having sex with? Please tell me it's not Pete."

"Of course it's not Pete and sadly it's been a few years since my last ... encounter."

"You haven't been going to—"

"Julia! My husband died when I was thirty-seven. You surely don't imagine I've been celibate since then? Top up my glass, please." Eve held hers out. "And it looks like Lucy's is empty too."

Julia poured some more rakija for Eve and wine for her and Lucy, and sat back. "I can't believe you'd ..." She waved a hand in the air.

"Want the warmth and companionship and enjoyment of male company? My husband died, not me."

"But ... I don't remember you having any boyfriends."

"I didn't for a long time. I had plenty of offers from locals, I can tell you. You'd be gobsmacked by some of the men who paid me attention. Some of them when their wives weren't looking. But my boys had been through enough scandal and grief. I kept myself to myself until they'd both left home and then I sought companionship further afield. None of it ever amounted to anything more than a bit of fun but that was all I was after."

Julia shook her head. "I can't believe it."

"Anyway, as time went by and my partners got older, those pills kept a smile on our faces."

Julia groaned and put her hand to her forehead. Another awkward thought struck her. "Is there someone now?"

"No. Hasn't been for several years. The last chap was a bit intense. He was an opal miner and wanted me to move to Coober Pedy with him. He was fun, but not that much fun."

Julia wrinkled her nose. "Eve, I can't believe you're telling us this."

"I'm telling you because something went wrong physically for Glen and it's not necessarily about you. Maybe it was the situation, the drinking, the poor man's broken toe – who knows, but he loves you enough to go to a doctor and get help so he can keep that part of your relationship alive. You should be thankful for it."

"But we have to plan sex in advance. It's not very spontaneous. I certainly don't find it romantic."

Eve sighed. "It's not all about you, Julia. Have you talked to Glen? Asked him how he feels about it?"

Julia took another slug of her wine. "No." She'd been so mortified that first night when he'd come over and asked if she felt like sex she hadn't given his feelings a thought. Then she remembered their last time together before she'd left Melbourne. She shrugged, a smirk on her lips, still amazed she was having this conversation. "Our sex life improved."

"I'll drink to that." Eve raised her glass and turned in Lucy's direction. "You're too young to be worried about these kinds of things but I'm sure it will be useful knowledge to store away."

Julia wasn't sure if Lucy's cheeks were pink from the heat of the fire or powered by an internal glow.

"I hope you don't think I'm going to talk about Alec and me," Lucy spluttered.

"Of course not." Eve grinned. "Unless you have something interesting to add."

Lucy almost choked on her wine. "I can't believe I'm sitting here talking sex with ..."

"Old women."

"Hey!" Julia said.

Lucy giggled, Eve joined in with a chuckle and then all three of them were laughing.

thirty-eight

The evening of the museum committee meeting was bitterly cold. Eve had put on an extra layer beneath her clothes and Lucy had pinned a pashmina around Eve's shoulders so that she didn't have the bulk of a coat to worry about. The old church hall where they met was small and solid but had cavernous ceilings, and even though there were a couple of wall heaters they only raised the temperature in the room a little. To one side, Eve caught a glimpse of Audrey and Norma chatting to some others. She was glad she had Julia and Lucy by her side. It was all very well to put on a brave front, but now that she was here the meal she'd eaten sat like a rock in her stomach. Tonight's meeting had drawn quite a crowd for a Thursday.

Eve had been a member of the museum committee for almost fifteen years up until the previous year. Many people had come and gone over those years but for a few stalwarts. There was Gerald, an old bloke whose father had been a harbour master and whose knowledge of ships and boats was second to none. Trent was much younger and a fabulous historian who gathered social history like bees did honey. He loved nothing more than to hunt down anything to do with the history of the area. Audrey had become involved several years earlier when the smelting history exhibits had been given an overhaul. Her ancestors had been involved in the local smelters.

Eve had first volunteered when they'd needed help gathering anecdotal evidence from local fishermen. She'd become so involved in the museum she'd kept volunteering long after the project had been completed. Being here tonight brought home how much she'd missed it.

"Hello, Eve." Audrey stepped up in front of her. Eve had been so lost in her own thoughts she hadn't seen the damn woman coming. Julia was off talking to Trent, who she'd gone to school with, and Lucy was saving them seats together across the hall.

"How are you, Audrey?"

"I'll be better when this is all decided. The council want an end to the prevaricating."

"I'm sure something will be settled tonight." Eve smiled to hide her nerves. She truly hoped the people gathered here would think her plan much more entertaining and informative than a big prawn but she'd been out of touch for so long.

"You've sold your prawn business now so you won't have the sway you once had over the others." Audrey smiled at someone over Eve's shoulder. Eve glanced around. Audrey's daughter Chrissie was there with Nick Colston, his grandfather Ralph, and another owner from across the gulf. They were long-time fishing families. If Audrey had them onside it would make it difficult for Eve.

"They won't get a vote, of course," Audrey said. "But they have influence in the industry. In the past the other prawn fishermen agreed with you out of courtesy, your age and the fact that you're a woman."

Heat built deep inside Eve and radiated up. In the early days after Rex had died she'd had to work hard to be accepted by the all-male prawn boat owners. Many of them had had different views to hers about what a woman's place should be but she'd long since earned their respect. She opened her mouth but was stopped short by Julia.

"Hello, Audrey. Haven't seen you for ages. Gosh, your hair hasn't changed a bit over the years, has it?"

Audrey put a hand to her hair, teased and combed and lacquered in place as always. The look on her face suggested she wasn't sure whether Julia was paying her a compliment or not.

Lucy stepped in on Eve's other side. "Hello, I'm Lucy. You must be Audrey. I've heard so much about you." She smiled sweetly, a saccharine grin that was odd for Lucy.

"I've saved us three seats together, Eve. And the bag is under my seat." She slipped her hand through the crook of Eve's arm.

At that moment Verity tapped the microphone and asked everyone to be seated so the meeting could get underway. Gert arrived and found a seat right behind Eve. Verity introduced herself and the council rep, and clarified their role was to act in both a mediatory and advocacy capacity. She explained that the council wanted action on the project or their support would be withdrawn and that there were two proposals to be put forward tonight. She introduced Audrey and Eve, and then asked Audrey to present first.

Eve's stomach had begun to churn but irritation replaced nerves as Audrey made her way to the front of the room. She oozed confidence, smiling and nodding at people as if she were in control and the outcome a fait accompli. She stepped up onto the podium and approached the microphone.

"Good evening, everyone. It's wonderful to see such a large turnout tonight. I do hope some of you will stay on as committee members or volunteers at the museum. We always need more volunteers."

A gentle burble of throats clearing and feet shuffling rumbled around the hall. Audrey continued, telling everyone about her connection to the smelting history of the town, her work on committees and in particular the museum committee, at which point Verity very politely asked her to make her presentation.

"Of course," Audrey said. "I was just getting to that. Most of you know my proposal is twofold. The first part is that we incorporate a special display inside the existing museum with information on the prawn fishing industry and include the honour roll of long-serving industry members. The second part is to build a giant king prawn out the front of the museum."

That brought another rumble of voices.

Audrey paused and glanced in Verity's direction.

"Have you finished?" Verity asked.

"Yes. I didn't want to bore people going into too much detail."

"I have two questions then," Verity said. "I'm sure most people would like to know the proposed cost of the giant prawn and how long until it would be completed."

"I did talk to the engineering people about cost and time," Audrey said. "It was quite a while back now because the project was put on hold." She glanced at Eve. "So I'm not sure when they could go ahead and what the final cost would be but with the council grant ..." Audrey turned towards the rep on her other side. Eve leaned forward. Audrey was batting her eyelashes. Damn the woman, she was being flirtatious with the council rep.

"And with the money already promised," Audrey looked back at Eve again, "plus some extra donations, we could have the giant prawn erected near the door of the museum, ready by next year's prawn festival."

"Thank you, Audrey," Verity said. "Are there any other questions?"

Gerald, who'd been sitting in the front row, cleared his throat and stood.

"Good evening, Gerald." Verity smiled.

Gerald cleared his throat again. "Thank you, Verity, for chairing and making sure this meeting went ahead. Where would the display planned for inside the museum fit, Audrey? It would, I assume, need a significant amount of space and the museum is already at capacity with exhibits."

Audrey looked down her nose at Gerald from the podium. "We all know the museum needs a revamp. I'm sure an internal shuffle would find room."

"And who will do that work and make the decisions about which part of our history we remove to make space?"

"The committee, of course, Gerald," Audrey said in a pompous voice.

"That's a valid point, Gerald," Verity said. "Thank you. I'm sure those of you who are familiar with the museum will know Gerald's long-standing involvement and knowledge of all it contains. His question is something to think on. Are there any more questions for Audrey?"

Eve was startled as Julia's hand shot up.

Verity nodded at her. "Julia, could you stand please?"

"I wondered what materials would be used and the purpose the prawn would serve?"

"We're the heart of the Spencer Gulf prawn industry," Audrey sniffed. "It's simply a symbol of that, and also a drawcard for the museum. I believe the engineer spoke of a metal framework and moulded plastic coating."

"The museum already has a lighthouse to attract attention to its heritage building entrance. You don't think a plastic prawn might ..." Julia scrunched up her face. "Detract from that?"

People murmured and shifted in their seats.

"Not at all." Audrey lifted her shoulders. "As I said, it would be a drawcard to attract people's attention to the museum."

Eve was amazed as Lucy raised her hand.

"Yes, Lucy, isn't it?" Verity said.

Lucy rose slowly to her feet. "I wondered how safe the prawn would be. I imagine something like that would be a magnet for children who'd want to climb on it."

"Oh no." Audrey shook her head. "It would have to be roped off. Definitely out of bounds."

"And would there be anything interactive with your display? Children are very hands-on."

"It's a museum, not a playground," Audrey said.

Lucy sat. Julia reached across Eve and patted Lucy's hand. Eve looked from one to the other. She'd been surprised when Julia had asked her question but even more so when Lucy had one as well.

One of the younger prawn boat owners, Sven, stood up. "Given that our product is second to none and our fishery is world renowned for its best practice in environmentally sustainable fishing – we worked hard for our MFC certification – I wonder if a plastic prawn is the best way to highlight our industry."

There were a few murmurs of agreement.

"What's MFC?" Lucy whispered in Eve's ear.

"Some people might not understand the importance of what you just said, Sven," Verity said, taking the microphone again. "Can you explain MFC?"

"Sure." He glanced around. "The Marine Stewardship Council operates a certification program that assesses whether wild-capture fisheries are ecologically sustainable and well-managed. Our fishery meets this scientific and vigorous standard. You may have noticed the MFC blue tick logo on our boxes."

A general hum of voices followed as Sven sat again.

Someone pressed Audrey about the cost of the project, but she only gave a vague response, saying the final costs were still to be decided, and the conversation fizzled out.

"If everyone's happy, we'll move on to Eve's presentation," Verity said. "Thank you, Audrey."

Eve tensed as she stepped up to the microphone. The crowd had grown in number and were restless. Would they howl her down? Her plan was more ambitious and she assumed would cost a lot more than what Audrey had proposed. She glanced around at the sea of faces. So many people she knew, and a few she didn't, all watching expectantly. Spiro must have arrived late. He leaned against the back wall and lifted his hand in hello. Then Eve noticed Albie Brown beside him. Albie had started prawn fishing around the same time as Rex and Spiro but had been retired for many years now. Even so, he was still respected as one of the pioneers by the fishing community. She'd tried to get him involved in planning something for the museum but he'd always declined in the past. She had no idea what his thoughts would be on tonight's proposals.

"Good evening, everyone." She moved her head back a little – the sound of her voice was loud in her ears. "My proposal is also designed to attract people's attention to our museum but to complement the fine features that already exist, like the lighthouse and the heritage building. My proposal is to build a separate structure within the yard of the museum. From the road it would look like a prawn trawler and on its other side it would extend into a building that would match the style of the existing building and house an interpretive centre. I have some sketches and costings that you can look at."

She nodded at Julia and Lucy, who swept the sides of the room handing out the pages they'd photocopied earlier that day.

"You might need to share," Eve called over the rustle of pages and murmur of voices. "I wasn't expecting quite so many people." She grimaced at Verity, who gave her an encouraging smile.

"You will see the front page is an artist's sketch of the proposed structure. The second page is a draft plan and the third has inclusions and approximate costings."

There were more rustles and the murmurs got louder as people reached the last page.

"That's a ridiculous amount of money," Audrey called out and a few more voices echoed around her.

Verity tapped the glass of water on the table beside her. "Eve will take questions when she's finished her presentation." The crowd quietened and once more she smiled brightly at Eve.

Eve swallowed. It had been risky declaring the costs before she'd finished her presentation but prawn fishermen were business men in rubber boots. If she could explain her project, how it would showcase and benefit the industry, and get them onside, she knew many of them would contribute.

Eve cleared her throat. "The bow of the boat structure would point towards the existing lighthouse and the bay beyond. People would be able to climb up onto it and in it, to get a feel for what a prawn trawler looks like, physically and structurally. The other section, the shed part of it, would house the information: short movie clips of prawning trips, interviews with prawn fishermen talking about the various stages of operation over the years, information about the MFC and how our fishery achieves their standards." Eve paused to make eye contact with Sven. He nodded and she went on. "There would be active displays that people can touch, such as a working model of a trawler showing how the nets swing out and lower. A moving display showing the life cycle of the unique Spencer Gulf prawns. An interactive sorting table demonstrating how the prawns are sorted and what other kinds of creatures are found and how they're returned safely to their habitat."

Eve paused again. Her gaze swept the room. They were all listening now. Julia and Lucy were beaming at her. She went on.

"The interpretive centre would have a small kitchen and a bathroom, which would increase the existing bathroom facilities at the museum. There would also be a small meeting room which would house photos and names of the current fleet and the honour roll of people who have contributed to the development of the prawn fishing industry." She looked to Albie at the back of the room. He was smiling. "The prawn committee could hold their meetings there. I also envisage special open days that would see chefs from local restaurants demonstrating prawn dishes, local school children could visit to hear about the industry, training workshops could be held. I'd be happy to pass on my net mending skills." She smiled and there were a few chuckles. Then someone started to clap and soon the hall was loud with the sound of many joining in.

Verity stood beside Eve and waited for people to be quiet again. "Does anyone have any questions for Eve?"

There was more paper shuffling.

"I think all the information is here." The council rep indicated the papers Eve had prepared. "Very efficiently and succinctly, I might add."

"That's all well and good." Audrey stood and waved the rolled-up pages in the air. "According to your projected figures there's way more money needed than the council grant and what's already been offered. Where is all the extra money coming from?"

That was Eve's difficulty. She could put all the money up herself but she didn't want it to become the Eve Monk project.

"I'll contribute some more," Spiro announced from the back of the room.

"And me." Albie raised his hand, and before she knew it there were offers from other prawn fishing families including the Colstons and even some from people not involved in the industry.

"Well." Verity tapped on her glass again to call the room to attention and smiled at Audrey. "It seems the issue of money won't be a problem."

Audrey prodded Norma who leaped to her feet. "How long will it take? It's a big undertaking. The big prawn would have been ready for next year's prawn festival."

"It shouldn't take us long to finalise the plans and get them to council for approval. I've already spoken with the council building inspector and shown her the idea. She made some suggestions but can't see any reason for the plan to be held up. The builder will be available as soon as we have the go-ahead so it could even be finished well before the festival."

Norma sagged to her chair and the room was silent.

"If there are no other questions for Eve," Verity said, "I think it's time to put the two propositions forward for voting. I promised we wouldn't have a late night."

"Heath need you to drive the tractor?" a male voice called.

"Quite possibly," Verity chuckled. "Now I think a simple raise of hands will do."

Eve's proposal was accepted by an almost unanimous vote and a small working party formed with the council rep, some from the museum committee and a few representatives of the prawn fishing community. The meeting was adjourned and tea and coffee distributed.

People milled around and congratulated Eve on her foresight and planning. They were excited by the project. It was something positive for the town and Eve found herself feeling it was a positive for her too. Albie and Spiro quizzed her a while on some of the finer details then moved away and Gert arrived at her side.

"I'm so pleased for you," she said as she gave Eve a careful hug. "It's a great idea and the best outcome for everyone." Gert leaned in a little closer. "Not that I heard everything that was said. That microphone wasn't very good, was it? If I hadn't known Audrey was saying 'prawn' I'd have sworn it was 'porn'." Gert chuckled.

Eve thought about Albie at the back of the hall. He'd worn hearing aids for years and, from what he'd said, had clearly heard the proceedings.

"Gert," she said gently. "Have you ever had your hearing checked?"

"Good heavens, you're sounding just like my family," Gert laughed. "I hear just fine when people speak clearly."

"Hello, Gert." Verity stepped up to them. "Eve, that was an excellent presentation and a fabulous concept. Everyone's excited about it."

"Not quite everyone." Gert nodded her head towards the other side of the hall where Audrey and Norma and a couple of other women were in a huddle.

"They'll come round," Verity said brightly. "Now you must come out for dinner before Julia leaves. Isn't it marvellous about her new job? Such a feather in her cap and we'll see a lot more of her if she's living in Adelaide." Verity's gaze shifted around the hall as she spoke. "Excuse me, I need to have another word with the council rep before he leaves."

"And I'm going home," Gert said. "We must get back to our weekly coffees now that you're feeling a lot better."

With a wave of her hand, Gert left and Eve found herself alone for a moment. It was such a relief to have the presentation done, to have people enthusiastic and onside with her plans, to take on her vision as their own. It would mean a lot of work but Eve was looking forward to it, to meetings and planning and seeing the concept come to life.

"You've certainly used your magical charm." Audrey's voice came from over Eve's right shoulder. She went to turn but Lucy was suddenly between them.

"I got you some tea, Eve." She handed over a mug that was slopping its contents precariously from side to side. "You must be dry after all that talking."

"I'm sure she could keep talking till the cows come home." Audrey stepped around Lucy as Julia arrived on Eve's other side.

Eve glanced from Julia back to Lucy. She'd have to remind them she didn't really need carers any more.

"I hear you've all been living together," Audrey sniped. "Must be a cosy arrangement. Plenty of time to cook up schemes."

"No sour grapes, Audrey," Julia said. "Let's face it, a big prawn's been done before but Eve's idea is rather unique."

"And a lot more interesting and interactive," Lucy said.

"Hmph!" Audrey pursed her lips and glared between the three of them. "Well," she said. "You really are b ..." She harrumphed again. "You really are birds of a feather." Then she turned on her heel and left the hall. Norma scurried after her.

Lucy shook her head. "Was that meant as an insult?"

"Oh dear," Julia said, the sarcasm dripping from her voice. "I hope we haven't upset her."

"She's a hard worker," Eve said, feeling a little sorry for Audrey.

"She's a bitch," Julia snapped.

"That's a little harsh, Julia."

"I know I said you should let past hurts go but ..." Julia leaned in and lowered her voice. "You do remember she had an affair with your husband."

"Shush, Julia."

"I think she was going to bump your right arm, Eve," Lucy said.

"Is that why you stepped in so quickly?"

"I saw her from the refreshment table. She made a beeline for you and picked up speed."

"Good grief." Eve slid a protective hand over the sling under her pashmina.

"Horrible cow," Julia muttered.

Eve glanced at her watch. "Look at the time." She put down her mug, slipped her good arm through Julia's and gave Lucy a nod. "Come on then, birds. We need to get home to the nest."

thirty-nine

Julia glanced across at Eve as they turned onto the road that took them up the hill towards home. She was fiddling with the edge of her pashmina. She'd been fidgety ever since she'd hurried them away from the meeting. They'd dropped Lucy at her in-laws to collect her car and children, and Eve had barely contributed to the conversation Julia was trying to engage her in.

"You shouldn't be worrying about the museum," Julia said. "Your proposal was a resounding success. I wish some of the research projects I've had to find money for were so easily funded."

"I'm not worried now that it's in the bag. You were a wonderful help, and Lucy. When I think back over your time here and my behaviour … I'm not very proud of myself for some of it."

"Don't beat yourself up. We've all had some upheavals this last year. Between Lucy, you and me we could write a book on it."

"With the beauty of hindsight, I'm glad of my enforced isolation. It's made me rethink many things. To begin with I was looking backwards, wishing life was how it had been before, but now I think I need to focus on a future where I may need to do some things differently."

409

Julia slowed to turn into Eve's driveway. "And not build giant plastic prawns," she said. She expected a chuckle from Eve but when she glanced over, Eve was peering ahead towards the house, her face creased in a frown.

"Are you all right? Is your shoulder hurting."

"No."

The headlights lit up the house yard as Julia drove around the last bend. "What the hell?" There were lights on in the house and a car parked at the gate, a small yellow MG.

"Is that Glen's car?" Julia stopped several metres from the MG. With the engine idling, she turned to Eve, her heart thudding in her chest. "What's going on?"

"Take a breath, Julia." Eve glanced towards the house and back again.

"Glen's never been to your house. I didn't give him directions."

"I'm sure he's capable of using Google Maps."

"Eve!"

"Oh, all right, I gave him directions. Glen and I had a chat. He knew you were planning to drive the hire car back to Melbourne instead of flying. He wanted to come over and drive you instead."

"What on earth for?"

"So you could spend some time together, I assume."

Julia peered at Eve. "How did he even have your number? And don't tell me the white pages because you haven't had a landline for years."

"He rang your phone. You were out supervising the children on their bikes while Lucy was in town looking at the flat again. I answered and we had a chat."

Julia frowned. "That was Monday."

"Was it? Anyway, it doesn't matter."

"Glen and I have spoken since then. He didn't say anything."

"He wanted to surprise you so I gave him my number. We've had a couple of chats."

Julia looked back at the yellow MG. Glen was here and she didn't know whether to feel annoyed or pleased.

"He called this morning to say he was on his way," Eve said. "When I realised he'd arrive while we were at the meeting, I left the key under the mat for him and told him to make himself at home."

"You answered my phone and didn't tell me?"

"That's the idea of a surprise. The recipients are not supposed to know."

"I can't believe you've been organising this behind my back." Headlights from behind illuminated the interior of the car. "Was Lucy in on it?"

"No, but that'll be her behind us with the children. We should go in."

Julia rolled the car forward until she was level with Glen's and Lucy pulled in beside her.

Eve opened her door and Noah's excited voice carried across the yard. "Cool car."

"It belongs to Julia's friend," Eve said as they all gathered beside the little yellow car.

"Can we meet your friend, Julia?" Poppy asked.

"Perhaps tomorrow," Eve said quickly. "He's probably tired from his long drive. Julia will go ahead and see how he is. I'm going to come and help you get ready for bed."

Lucy gave Eve a puzzled look but didn't say anything.

Eve prodded Julia with her fingers. She moved forward slowly. Behind her Poppy's voice turned pleading.

"Can you read us a story, Eve?"

"It's a bit late for stories tonight," Lucy said.

"Perhaps one short one if they get ready for bed quickly," Eve said as Julia opened the back door and stepped tentatively inside.

Ahead of her, at the other end of the passage, Glen was silhouetted by the lights from the lounge and kitchen on either side of him. She strode forward. The reality of seeing him had shaken her from her stupor. She was ready to give him a piece of her mind.

"Hi, honey," he said and opened his arms wide.

Instead of the singsong voice, his tone was deep and caring. Her anger evaporated and she stepped into his embrace. "I'm home," she murmured into the soft fabric of his jumper.

"I've missed you," he murmured into her ear.

Goosebumps prickled down her neck.

"Is that Julia's boyfriend?" Poppy's voice came as a stage whisper from behind.

Julia walked Glen into the lounge and shut the door. "We need to talk," she said.

He bent down and kissed her. A long deep kiss that made her toes curl. She hadn't had that feeling in a long time.

"Right," she said as they finally pulled apart. "How about a red wine?"

"It's a weeknight."

"Oh, yes, good point. What about a coffee?"

"I've had so many on the drive over I could be a percolator."

"Tea then?"

He shook his head. "I don't need anything but you get whatever you want."

Julia opened the door. There was silence from the other end of the house. She wondered how long Eve was planning to stay locked away with Lucy. Julia got two glasses of water, went back to Glen and shut the door on the rest of the house again.

She waited for him to sit on the couch then chose a chair nearby.

He studied her closely across the space between them. "I asked you to marry me. You said you'd give me an answer."

"When I got back to Melbourne. You've surprised me, turning up here."

"That was my plan." He smiled, a slow wide smile, and his eyes sparkled. "You usually like my surprises."

She looked away, noticing for the first time a vase of flowers that hadn't been on the side table earlier in the day. The vase was cut crystal and looked familiar.

"I scoured second-hand shops and found a vase like your mum's. I know the sentiment's not the same but ... I hope you like it."

Julia couldn't believe he'd have given her mother's broken vase a thought. She took a sip of her water, remembering it was his thoughtfulness that had appealed to her when they'd first got together.

"It was very kind of you, thank you." Her hand trembled and she placed the glass back on the table. She was acting like she was a young girl again on her first date. Having grown up with a brother and four almost-brothers she knew most things about men but she'd had no idea as a teenager how to be with one who wasn't brotherly.

Her first date with a boy holidaying at Wallaby Bay had been a disaster. She'd already felt jittery when he'd slipped an arm around her waist as they'd walked along the beach. And she'd been a bundle of nerves when they'd attempted what had been a first kiss. Two teenagers with bands on their teeth – it hadn't gone well but he'd asked her out again and they'd perfected the kissing. She smiled at the memory.

"It's not all bad then," Glen said. "Or are you preparing me for the worst?"

She glanced up. "I know since the cruise … our relationship hasn't been the same but can't we go back to the way things were before that?" Pre-cruise Glen was the man she'd fallen for.

"You want to go back?" He scratched his chin.

His words echoed in her head with Eve's voice. What had she said in the car about looking to the future?

"I don't get it, Jules. Even before the cruise I felt as if we were drifting apart and I didn't want that. You wouldn't move to my place, I wouldn't fit at yours."

"It was a good arrangement."

"Was it?"

"We had each other but still enjoyed our own space."

He leaned across the coffee table between them. "I love you, Julia. I'd like to be with you full-time. I don't know what else I can say."

Once more Julia heard Eve's voice in her head. Perhaps it was time to tell Glen about her past relationship. Maybe then he'd understand why they couldn't live together.

"I need to tell you something."

He sat back. "Okay."

"Before I met you I'd been in a long-term relationship."

"You told me. That's got nothing to do with us."

"It has in a way." Julia wrinkled her nose. She was struggling to find the right words.

"Spit it out whatever it is."

"We lived together for several years. Tim asked me to marry him."

Glen nodded along with her words. She'd told him that much before. She drew in a breath. "We were planning our wedding and he left me the week I was back here helping to tidy up Mum's things after the funeral."

"Bastard."

"That was one of my milder names for him." Julia gripped her hands together tightly. "I admit I'd been caught up between finishing my studies and supporting Mum. She hadn't been well for a while before she died. I'd made several trips home in the months leading up to that time." Julia felt the familiar ache in her chest. Ten years on, the pain of losing her mum still caught her out. "He was a heavy drinker – not that I was teetotal, but I'd started to notice some not-so-nice things about him. He'd get sarcastic when he had a few drinks under his belt, try to put me down. He was in a similar research job to me but I was on a better salary and when I was made doctor the year Mum died, he got worse.

"Looking back, I think he had some weird inferiority complex. Anyway, we shared my apartment. He paid some of the bills and contributed to the loan payments. When he left he wanted half of everything. On top of Mum dying, I lost my partner, my home, my car and a hunk of my savings."

"That's worse than my divorce." Glen stood and started to pace. "Surely you could have fought it."

"I did. In the end I wanted it dealt with quickly before everything was settled from Mum's estate. She left me the family unit in Adelaide and her super. He didn't know about that or I would have lost that too."

Glen stopped beside her. He opened his mouth, closed it again and squatted down, taking her hands in his. "What can I say, Jules? I can't make any of that right but I hope you know I'm a better man than that."

Julia chewed her lip. How could she be sure?

Glen frowned, reading her face as if she'd said the words out loud. "I want to apologise."

"What for?"

"For my poor behaviour towards the end of our cruise, and then after ... the drinking—"

"I was guilty of overdoing it too."

"Yeah, but you got yourself back on track quicker than me. The failure of ... well, not being able to make love to you in the way that I wanted was a blow to my ego. I didn't like the idea of the pills when my GP prescribed them but I thought it would make you happy."

Julia looked down at his hands holding hers. "I'm sorry, Glen. I didn't handle all that very well."

"Neither did I. Drinking was my way of dealing with it. I've had a couple of good chats with my GP recently. He helped me to put things in perspective. You're the most important person in my life. I don't want to lose you."

Julia stared at him, unable to form words. Nearly all the important people in her life had left her – her parents, her ex. To let Glen fully into her heart would make her vulnerable again.

He let go of her hands and stood. "I get that past relationships can make you wary. My ex-wife turned me off commitment for a long time but when you meet the right person you have to trust that it's time to move on." He shrugged. "Otherwise, well ..." He shrugged again. "I don't know."

Tears pricked at the back of Julia's eyes. She sucked in her cheeks, gripping the skin between her teeth. She was not going to go all soppy in front of Glen and cry. Before she could stop him, he was back beside her, pulling her against his chest. "I think you're the right person, Julia. Life's no fun without you."

She could taste blood in her mouth and feel the damp of warm tears on her cheeks. No matter how hard she tried she couldn't hold them in. She hadn't cried when the car accident had left her mangled, she hadn't cried when her bastard ex had left, or when her beloved mum had died, but she was crying now. She slumped forward and two arms slipped around her.

Glen rocked her, whispered soothing words and held her tight. She clung to him like a drowning woman would a lifebuoy. Her tears soaked his jacket. He gave her a hanky with one hand but still kept her close with the other. She wept for a long time until at last her shuddering sobs eased, the tears dried up and the pain she locked deep inside her was replaced by a lighter, hopeful feeling.

She eased back from Glen's embrace and looked up at him through bleary eyes. "I'm sorry," she whispered.

"What for?"

"I'm not the blubbering type and I've soaked your jacket."

"The jacket will dry and everyone needs the release of a cry."

She looked at him sideways.

"I cried when we watched that movie about the Indian guy who was adopted by the Australian family," Glen said.

"*Lion*? You didn't!"

He grinned. "I didn't let you see me." His smile dropped away. "I cried when my grandparents died. It means you're normal, Jules."

Julia dragged damp strands of hair back from her face.

"I must look ghastly."

"Your cute little nose is almost the same shade as your beautiful hair."

"Glen."

"Okay." He let her go and put his hands in the air. "I know you don't like the flowery stuff." He tipped his head to one side. "If I promise no more soppy lines, will you marry me?"

"No."

Glen winced.

"It's not you. After Tim left I thought about it a lot. If we'd have been married the legalities and division of assets would have been the same, I know that, but it's changed how I feel personally about marriage. I just don't see the point of the piece of paper."

"Oh." Glen's expression deepened to a grimace.

She looked at the face of this funny, kind man, the one who had stayed by her side no matter how hard she'd tried to keep him at arm's length. She let go of the last rope grounding her to distrust and took a leap forward with faith. "I would however accept your proposal to live together."

"You would?"

She nodded. She knew she'd missed Glen too. The pre-cruise Glen, the same man who was emerging out the other side. "I love you too," she murmured.

"Pardon?" He put a finger to his ear. "What was that? I didn't catch it."

"I love you, Glen Walk—" Her words were lost as he dragged her to her feet and kissed her.

Then he spun her around. "Yes!" he yelled.

"Quiet," she said, glancing towards the door.

"You sure you don't want to get married?" he said in a softer voice. "I don't mind the idea of Mr and Mrs Walker again."

"Even if we married, I wouldn't be changing my name. I worked hard to become Doctor Paterson."

"Oh." His look was crestfallen.

"It's a piece of paper, Glen. I don't see the point."

His struggle with her response was open on his face.

Finally, he spoke. "Okay, but we will move in together, right?"

"We can give it a try."

"Do or do not. There is no try."

She rolled her eyes at Glen's Yoda impersonation.

"I can accept us having no legal marriage ceremony," he said. "But I do want your commitment that you'll give us your very best, Julia."

"I will," she said.

"There, that wasn't so hard, was it?"

"As long as I don't have to watch *Star Wars* movies."

"I'll save them for when you're out."

"But what about my new job? How will we—"

"I've looked into moving to Adelaide and I can make it work."

"You seem to have everything planned."

"You're not the only one who can organise things."

Julia thought of all the planning he'd done to get them to this moment. "You should take the ring back though."

"Don't you like it?"

"It's beautiful but if we're not going to get married ..."

He took her hands in his. "It's my gift to you. A sign of our commitment to each other."

"I'll have to find one for you then."

He hugged her. "I'd like that."

His lips were warm on her cheek. She almost purred as they moved on to her ear.

"We should tell Eve," he whispered. "She'll want to know we're officially a couple."

"Mmm," she murmured as his lips moved on to her neck in a sensuous trail that made her shiver. She pressed her body to his. "We'll tell her in the morning."

"Perhaps you're right." He pulled his head back and wiggled his eyebrows at her. "I think we should consummate our agreement."

"Won't we need some time?" She glanced down. "For the tablet to work?"

"There's plenty we can do to fill in the time." He winked and pulled her close. "The way I'm feeling right now we might not need to wait."

~~~

Eve let herself out of the children's bedroom to find Lucy sitting in the old rocker in the playroom looking at her phone.

"They're almost asleep."

"Thanks, Eve. A story always settles them but I wasn't in the mood."

"It's not easy being a single parent."

"It must have been harder for you. At least I have Alec home sometimes and we talk and Skype regularly."

"There were times when I cursed Rex for dying and leaving me to raise our sons alone. But then, given the kind of man he was, perhaps we would have disagreed about the best way to do it." Eve gave a soft snort. "And who knows how things would have been if he was still alive. Being more involved with the prawn business has been my life's work and I've loved every minute of it."

"Are you happy with tonight's result?"

"Yes. And grateful for your support and Julia's."

"You must be tired." Lucy rose from the recliner. "Why don't you sit here for a while?"

"Actually, I was thinking I'd like a cup of tea. I didn't end up drinking the one you made me. Do you think we could venture up to the kitchen?"

"I stuck my head out a while ago. The lounge door was still closed."

"Right, well, this is my house and I want a cuppa. Let's go." Eve reached the playroom door then stopped and turned back.

"I've been so lucky to have had you as my nurse and home help, Lucy. I might need your support a little longer if Julia leaves soon but I'm looking forward to the day when that won't be necessary."

"You'll be fit enough to do everything for yourself soon."

"I hope so. And that will be good. I don't like to rely on others but also, I hope it will mean you can come out for visits rather than for work. Bring the children so they can play on the boat, ride the bikes, use the toys." Eve waved a hand at the playroom then placed it on Lucy's arm. "I'd really appreciate the opportunity to have you visit as my friend, rather than my nurse."

Lucy smiled and the warmth of it bolstered Eve's courage.

"I know there's an age gap and of course you have Helen, but perhaps you'd think of me as you would an older relative."

Lucy's smile widened. "We'd love that," she said.

"Good." Eve felt as if she would burst with joy. "Yes, that's great. Let's go and get that cuppa." Like a pair of co-conspirators they trod quietly up the passage.

⟶

The lounge door was open and the room in darkness – only the kitchen light was on.

"They must have gone to bed," Lucy said.

Eve winked. "I hope they're making up for lost time."

Lucy's cheeks glowed as she busied herself in the kitchen making the tea. She tried not to think about what Julia and Glen might be doing in the bedroom. Instead she focused on Eve's suggestion that Lucy and the kids continue to visit. It had been a surprise. Lucy had thought Eve had been going to say she'd be glad to have her home back to herself but instead she'd made an open invitation to come anytime.

Lucy had found happiness here she'd not expected when she took the job, and there was the unforeseen bonus of Eve's friendship. Helen was a wonderful person and a special grandmother for Poppy and Noah. Perhaps Eve would become a kind of aunt, something Lucy had never been able to give her children.

Lucy put their mugs on the table.

"Have you spoken to Alec more about the move to the flat?" Eve asked. "Not that there's any hurry for you to leave."

"We spoke tonight, actually. While you were reading to the kids. He's going to come home on his week off after all."

"Is that soon?"

"He should get back to Adelaide on Saturday."

"You must be pleased."

"I am. We weren't sure how long he'd be away for this time. He only gets a week off and loses some of that travelling back and forth. With all that had happened since he left, he badly wanted to come home and be with us." Her excitement was tempered with sadness though. "If everything is sorted with the flat by the time he has to return to work, this might be our last weekend here. We'll miss it. The kids have adopted you and they love the freedom out here. Their confidence has returned and … I've learned to let them have some space."

Eve smiled. "You know you can come anytime for visits."

"I do."

"And if you get busy with building your new business, perhaps the children could come out here for a few hours. I know Helen and Kon will help out with them but sometimes it's nice for kids to run free for a while."

"Thank you, Eve. We will certainly take you up on that."

"So are you and Alec thinking you'll start the seafood business?"

"We're certainly leaning that way. Living in the flat will give us the opportunity to have a good look at the building and how it might work for us. We don't want a dine-in eating area. There are already plenty of those in town. We want to focus on quality takeaway seafood but with an outdoor area people can eat in if they want. And so many people have dogs with them these days so we want to make it dog-friendly."

"Oh, that reminds me. Pete's dropping Belle off tomorrow. Looks like he's going to get his other knee replaced so he's going down for a specialist appointment and staying overnight with his niece."

"Poppy and Noah will love that."

"I don't suppose you could get them a dog if you're going to live above the shop."

"No, thank goodness. They love Belle, but … what about you, Eve? Are you sure you won't get another dog to keep you company?"

"I've given it a lot of thought and I'm sure. They're a tie, and now without the prawn business I can come and go as I please. Once my shoulder's up to it I'll head to Darwin. I don't mind the winter up there and Zac's house has a granny flat underneath so I have my own space. I'd have to find someone to look after a dog if I got another. I think it's a good idea to make your outdoor eating area dog-friendly though."

Eve asked about the menu they might serve and that led them to the prawn festival and back to the museum meeting. They chatted till late and when Lucy finally fell into bed it was with the realisation that with Eve's help and, she had to admit, even Julia's, here in Wallaby Bay she'd found a home.

forty

Lucy carried the basket of washing out to the line. The stiff sea breeze whipped her hair across her face as soon as she stepped out from the protection of the verandah. It was icy but it couldn't cool her excitement. Alec would be back this afternoon. It was going to be a crazy week ahead. Julia and Glen were leaving tomorrow so Eve would still need Lucy's regular help. There'd be the flat to clean and furniture to move but Lucy was looking forward to it.

She put down the basket and paused to listen. The wind stirred the trees and beyond that she could hear the occasional squeal from Poppy and bark from Belle. Julia and the dog were with Poppy and Noah at the boat. Julia had been growling like a pirate when they'd set off so who knew what was going on but Lucy felt pleased with herself for not worrying. It was such a relief to let go of the responsibilities of parenting, just for a while.

Earlier Eve had gone off somewhere with Glen. They'd driven away in the MG. Eve had waved regally from the passenger seat with a huge smile on her face. Before they'd left, Eve had asked Glen to start her Torana and back it out of the shed. Lucy glanced at the bright orange car gleaming in the weak sunshine. Goodness knows what that woman was cooking up next.

The sound of a car coming closer was mixed with the sound of singing. Julia and the children emerged from the trees. Belle danced at their feet. Poppy was riding on Julia's shoulders, Noah was hopping along beside them and the three of them were singing "We All Live in a Yellow Submarine", which was drowned out by the burble of Glen's car as he pulled into the yard. Another car followed them and Lucy waved as Jess and her husband climbed out.

"I've bought a new car," Eve announced after they'd said their hellos.

"At last," Julia said as she lowered Poppy to the ground.

"Glen was a great help."

"I'm pretty sure you had that car salesman sorted without my help, Eve." He chuckled.

"Something sensible that's easy to drive, I hope," Julia said.

"Good grief, no," Eve said. "Except for the easy to drive part and that's where I had to rely on Glen's expertise."

"Please don't tell me you've bought an MG," Julia groaned.

"I was tempted but there's nowhere to buy one around here and I like to shop local."

"What did you get?" Julia said.

"No old lady car for Eve," Glen said. "She's bought herself a sporty little SUV."

"A red one," Eve added.

"Can we see it?" Noah asked.

"I can't have it for a few weeks," Eve said. "It's not ready yet but it should be here about the time I can drive again. I'll take you for a spin then."

"Yes." Noah fist-pumped the air.

"Did you trade in the Torana?" Julia asked.

"No," Eve said. "That's why Jess and Chris are here. Chris is interested."

"Very interested," Chris said.

"You've got the keys, Glen," Eve said. "Why don't you two take her for a run?"

"And me," Jess said. "If we're buying this car I have to see if it can fit a child seat." She patted her rounded tummy.

"Not in the Torana," Chris groaned. "The car seat will go in the four-wheel drive."

"We'll see," Jess said as she opened the back door.

Eve, Julia and Lucy wandered back to the verandah out of the wind as the Torana disappeared down the drive. Poppy and Noah got out their bikes and Belle ran along beside them.

"Look at the bling light up on that engagement ring," Eve said as Julia's hand flashed in the sunlight.

"It's a commitment ring." Julia fixed Eve with a stern look. "I've told you Glen and I are happy to be together without the official paperwork."

"It's very pretty," Lucy said. While she'd found quite a lot of common ground with Julia since she'd got to know her better, this was another point of difference. Lucy would be happy if the man she loved asked her to marry him. Over the moon in fact. It would be the icing on the cake. She and Alec had talked about marriage when she was pregnant with Noah but they'd put it off. Lucy had wanted to wait until she could party properly. Then Poppy had come along and life had got busy.

"I'm not anti-marriage, you know," Julia said, as if she'd read her thoughts. "It's just not what I want for me."

"As long as Glen is happy too," Eve said.

Julia opened her mouth, must have thought better of what she was going to say and licked her lips instead. "He is."

"Good."

"Although Verity is not happy being denied a wedding to organise," Julia said.

"Well, I for one was glad Verity was in charge at the meeting the other night," Eve said. "She kept a tight hold on proceedings. There were one or two there who liked the sound of their own voices."

"Like Audrey?" Julia said.

Eve turned to Lucy. "Do you really think she was trying to bump me?"

"It was just how it seemed from my perspective," Lucy said. "I may have been wrong."

"I doubt it," Julia said.

"I hope so." Eve sighed. "It took me a while but I forgave Audrey her fling with Rex a long time ago. Then last year when she broke her wrist and accused me of pushing her ... well, it made it difficult to keep turning the other cheek."

"I can't imagine how I'd feel if Alec went off with someone else," Lucy said. "But 'forgiving' doesn't come to mind."

"Nor to me," Julia said.

"I always thought I was the wronged one," Eve said. "Finding out Rex was still chasing other women was a terrible blow, but if he hadn't been with Audrey it would have been someone else. This is a small town and we all have to live in it. I don't think anyone else knew and Audrey certainly wasn't going to blab, so I swallowed my pride and got on with life. It took me a while to stop avoiding her in those years after I discovered her affair with my husband, but she's a hard worker, I'll give her that. When we ended up on the same committee, I buried the past and moved on. I guess it's Audrey that hasn't."

"She's certainly been a thorn in your side, and going along with Norma's accusation that you pushed her, that's very nasty," Julia said.

"It's certainly made it difficult for me to forgive her again ... but I'll try." Eve grinned. "Funny her calling us birds of a feather though. It's what we've become, isn't it ... the three of us."

Lucy shifted in her chair. "Yeah. I didn't really get what she was on about with that."

"We spend time together," Eve said. "We have some similar interests, like the museum exhibit ..."

"And Audrey disapproves of us," Julia said.

"Oh, I see." Lucy felt foolish. "It's that saying. Birds of a feather—"

"Flock together." The other two finished it with her.

Lucy laughed, Eve joined in and then Julia.

forty-one

Nine months later

It had been ideal autumn weather in Wallaby Bay for the whole weekend of the prawn festival – warm but not too hot. The sun was low in the sky, turning the plump clouds golden orange, and the sea breeze, barely more than a puff, gently ruffled the flags and pennants decorating flag poles and shop fronts through the main streets of town. Out on the bay and in the marina, thirty-nine prawn trawlers bobbed gently at anchor. They'd made a colourful display as they motored past the jetty two days prior, to begin the festival.

Julia and Glen were at the newly opened Jetty Seafood, seated at a table in the outdoor eating area closest to the beach.

"These chips are amazing," Glen said. He waggled one in front of Julia and she took a bite.

"Mmm!" she murmured as the hot salty chip crunched in her mouth.

"I'll have to find out where Alec gets them. Special caterer's packs, I suppose."

"No. He does them himself." Julia helped herself to another. "They're hand-cut chips; that's why they're so good."

"Great food and wine." Glen raised his glass. "A magnificent ending to a really well-organised weekend."

Julia took a sip of wine and groaned. "For once I'm not busting to get back to work this week."

"What! Don't tell me workaholic Julia wants some extra time off."

"It's been full-on this last month. All the new students and I've got two extra to mentor as well as leading the research facility, which is ticking along extra fast at the moment."

"I need to get back but you could always take a day off, work from home if you need."

"Mmm! I might. But then your office is next door to mine and I find that distracting."

"I thought you quite liked that arrangement."

"I do."

Glen had bought them a lovely place in what Adelaideans called the leafy suburbs. Instead of feeling overwhelmed by the house he'd chosen for them, she'd fallen in love with it. The rooms were light and airy and there was a magnificent garden that felt like a park outside her office window. Glen had turned a bedroom into a large office for himself, given he worked at home most days. There was a spacious guest suite that Eve often used when she came to visit, and Glen had made some headway with his daughters and was hopeful they would visit soon. The location gave Julia easy access to the university. She'd insisted the house be in Glen's name only. She'd kept her unit in Adelaide with her long-standing tenant but paid most of the utility bills for the place she shared with Glen.

"What are you smiling about?" He studied her, a smirk lurking on his lips.

"How good we are together."

He pretended to choke.

She leaned in and kissed him, the salt on his lips adding to her own. She'd admitted it to him, and at last to herself, living with Glen made her very happy.

Lucy only had time for a quick glance at the view as she wove her way back through the thinning crowds to the shop.

"Lucy, hi!"

She turned and smiled as Jess came towards her, pushing a pram.

"Hello. How's our little girl?"

"Sleeping at last."

Lucy bent over the pram and smiled. Wisps of hair fluffed around the sleeping baby's face. Her rounded cheeks were the softest pink and her rosebud lips moved gently in and out. Lucy's heart melted at the sight of her. She'd been surprised how clucky spending time with Jess and the baby had made her.

"She's adorable." Lucy straightened. "Are you coming up to the flat later?"

"On our way soon. I'm just waiting for Chris. He was trying to find a safe park for the Torana."

"I saw you go past in the parade this morning while we were setting up."

"How's it going?" Jess asked. "I hear you've been busy."

"We've been run off our feet. We're almost out of everything so Alec's going to close soon. I just dashed out to get some milk for later." Lucy lifted the container in her hand. "I'd better get back and help Alec. See you soon."

Lucy moved on. She and Alec had become great friends with Jess and Chris. And Lucy and Jess had become especially close since the baby was born. She'd come early and there'd been feeding issues. Lucy had been glad to be the calm voice of common sense for her friend when she'd needed it. A close female friend of a similar age was a new experience for Lucy.

Speaking of friends, a few steps ahead of her she saw another familiar figure.

"Eve!"

"Hello, I was just heading your way."

"Julia and Glen are already there. They've saved you a spot."

"I just have to get the dog back. Some children have taken her for a quick walk on the beach." Eve pointed below where Lucy could see a couple of teenage girls with a small white fluffball dashing between them.

"Poppy and Noah will be glad she's with you. And I'm glad I've caught you before we're all together." Lucy drew Eve to one side, out of the walkway. "I've got a surprise and I wanted you to know before we tell the others."

Eve's eyes lit up.

Lucy leaned closer. "Alec and I are getting married."

"Oh, Lucy!" Eve yelped and a few people looked their way. "That's wonderful news," she said, more gently this time, and Lucy was wrapped in a hug, one that she appreciated beyond words.

Eve let her go and looked at her hand. "Is there a ring?"

"Yes. It's beautiful but I didn't want to wear it while I was working and before everyone knew. We told Noah and Poppy first and Alec's mum and dad but ... I wanted to tell you next."

Eve's smile was wide as she cupped Lucy's cheek with her hand. "I'm so happy for you."

"We've brought her back." The two girls arrived with one of them holding the panting dog.

"There are dog water bowls by each table," Lucy said. "I'll see you soon."

Lucy went to turn away but Eve pulled her back and kissed her cheek. "See you soon."

Lucy smiled then hurried away as tears brimmed in her eyes – tears of happiness for the overflowing joy in her life.

As Eve thanked the girls and put the dog back on the ground she caught a last glimpse of Lucy as she dashed across the carpark to the Jetty Seafood building. Their friendship had deepened since Lucy had stopped being her nurse and home help. They caught up regularly when Eve was home, and Eve had even had Poppy and Noah to stay overnight on a couple of occasions. Like she'd become Julia's pseudo-mother so long ago, she felt she filled a similar role for Lucy. It was a role she cherished. Eve loved her sons dearly but they were a long way away and it was refreshing having younger women in her life.

"What on earth is that?"

Eve looked around. Gert was beside her, wiggling a finger at the dog sniffing at her feet.

"This is Dixie." Eve scooped the fluffy animal into her arms. "She's a miniature poodle."

Gert scratched Dixie under her chin. "Who does she belong to?"

"A couple Helen recommended me to. They've had to go to Adelaide for a few weeks. He's having treatment and they're already paying enough without the worry of dog care so I've got Dixie."

"For nothing, I suppose."

"I can afford to look after one little dog for a few weeks."

"You're very popular with dog owners. You hardly seem to be without a dog in your care these days."

"I enjoy it." Eve ruffled Dixie's soft curls and put her back on the ground. "And like grandchildren, I get to give them back."

"You don't have to shout any more, you know, Eve." Gert brushed a hand over her ear. "Since I've got these hearing aids everyone seems so loud. I think I'll need to get them turned down."

"I hear they take a bit of time to get used to." A bit like shoulders. Eve still didn't have full mobility of hers. "I was on my way to Lucy and Alec's seafood place."

"Me too. I'm so happy for them. I hear they've been busy as fleas this weekend with the prawn festival."

"The whole town has. It's been a roaring success."

The two set off together towards the freshly painted building with the huge sign declaring *Jetty Seafood*. On the way they stopped to look at a group of people crowded around someone dressed in a prawn costume.

"At least Audrey got her big prawn," Gert chuckled.

"She got several. They've been a hit giving away free trinkets to the kids and handing out information to the adults. They're easy to see."

"Yes, but thankfully not at the museum. I missed the official opening last week but I popped in yesterday and it's amazing. A real credit to you."

"A credit to the committee."

"But it was your foresight." Gert patted Eve's arm. "And a lot of your money. A wonderful legacy."

"Thank you, Gert. And thanks for donating the money for the beautiful conference table."

"I think Tom would have been happy to know he'd be the centre of all the meetings held there. He sold plenty of insurance to fishermen over the years."

"I'll look after him for you once you've moved," Eve said.

"Thanks, but he's coming with me."

Eve stilled.

"Look at your face." Gert chuckled. "I'm not digging him up. But I didn't put all of his ashes in the ground. I still have a small urn in my bedroom. A small part of Tom will come with me to Adelaide next week."

"Good on you." Eve linked her arm through Gert's, relieved her old friend was more like her former self these days. Gert had got used to managing without Tom, she was happy about her move to Adelaide and Eve believed life had to be better for her with improved hearing. It had taken a while for Gert's house to sell, but finally it had and settlement was next week. She'd been living between Wallaby Bay and Adelaide but on Friday she'd be leaving permanently with the last of her possessions.

"Gosh, it's busy," Gert said as they neared the Jetty Seafood outdoor eating area. The loud burble of voices reached them along with the thrum of music playing from a speaker.

"Lucy and Alec will be happy with the patronage but they'll be glad this is just a trial run. Alec's only been home three weeks and they've been working flat out to be ready for the prawn festival. They plan to close and finish the fit-out and renovations ready to reopen in September."

"They've got level heads, the pair of them, and the backing of Helen and Kon's experience. I hope it goes well for them."

Eve caught sight of a man waving to her from a table close to the sea. "Look, there's Glen and Julia."

"Oh, they're here too?"

"Yes. They've been here all weekend."

"Julia's done so well for herself, hasn't she?" Gert said. "Pam would be proud."

"Yes, she would," Eve said as Gert strode ahead.

Eve stalled, bothered by a twinge of sorrow. Tomorrow Julia and Glen would head back to Adelaide, then Gert would soon follow, and she'd be on her own again.

Dixie tugged at her lead, trying to reach some spilled chips. Eve picked her up and tucked her under her arm. "None of this self-pity, Dixie. I've got you for company, haven't I?"

"Mummy, is that lady talking to her dog?"

Eve smiled at the little girl being shushed by her mother and wove her way through the tables to meet the others.

"We've got you a drink," Julia said.

"And some chips to cover the liquor licence rules." Glen waved his hand over two bowls of chips that were no longer full.

"Lucy said they'll close soon and we'll go upstairs to eat in their flat," Julia said. "They're going to bring up a selection of food from their menu."

"It's a pretty good menu for—"

Julia gave him a dig.

"Ouch! What was that for?"

"You were going to say for a little place like Wallaby Bay."

"No. I was going to say for a couple who've barely had time to prepare for this weekend. I thought they might just stick to fish and chips, but they've also got prawn cold rolls, fish sliders in squid-ink rolls, and I like the sound of the spicy prawn stir-fry."

"Jetty Seafood was never going to be just about fish and chips," Eve said. "Alec is trying to make sure the produce is local if possible and ethically sourced. Spiro and I have been helping point him in the right direction with suppliers. There will be different dishes depending on what's available and they both want prawns to feature strongly on the menu."

"I'll vouch for Lucy's prawn dishes," Julia said. "She cooked us prawns every which way when I accidentally defrosted a few kilos last year."

"Accidentally," Glen chuckled. "Doesn't sound like you, honey."

"Glen just thinks because he's taken over most of the meal cooking that I can't cook."

"You're an excellent cook." Glen pulled Julia in close and kissed her. "When you dial Uber Eats."

"Exactly." Julia took a sip of her wine.

Eve smiled. She enjoyed seeing Julia so happy. Her work was both challenging and rewarding and her life with Glen spirited but content.

"Look at that sunset," Gert said and they all gazed seaward. The sky was a blaze of orange. "That's one thing I'm going to miss," she said sadly.

"You'll see them from my place when you come back for visits," Eve said. "My front verandah is perfect for sunset viewing."

"When it's not windy," Gert chuckled.

"Like tonight," Julia said. "It's almost balmy."

"It's so good to see you all." Lucy reached down to give Eve a hug then went round the table to each of the others.

"You must be exhausted," Julia said. "But you've had a great soft opening for Jetty Seafood."

"Yes," Lucy said. "It's been amazing and everyone's said they can't wait for us to open fully."

"Looks like the place is almost cleared out now," Glen said.

Eve looked behind her. The last stragglers were leaving and Alec was pulling the gate closed on the outdoor eating area.

"I'll take you all upstairs," Lucy said. "Helen and Kon are there with the children and Jess and Chris have just arrived. Bring your glasses with you."

They all followed Lucy around through their private back yard and trouped up the wooden stairs.

There were welcomes all round again and Poppy and Noah, dressed in their pyjamas, were beside themselves with excitement at all the visitors crowded into their living room. Poppy asked if she could play with Dixie, and with all the commotion Eve thought it a good idea for the dog to go into the bedroom with the children.

Spiro and Mary arrived and the volume went up another notch.

"How's your shoulder, Eve?" Mary asked.

"Much better than it was," Eve said. "You're looking well. How was your holiday?"

"Wonderful. Have you ever been to the New South Wales northern coast?"

"Byron Bay once."

"It's lovely all along the coast there. We both feel so relaxed. You look good too, Eve." Mary smiled. It was a soft, kind smile.

Eve had to admit one of the benefits of selling the business was an easier relationship with Mary. They no longer fought over Spiro. Not that Eve had ever seen him as anything more than a friend and business partner but Mary had viewed their relation-ship differently.

"I know it wasn't easy to give up the business," Mary said. "But we're all better off for it, don't you think?"

"Mary, bring your phone," Spiro called. "Helen wants to see some photos of our trip."

Mary smiled again and moved away. She'd been right — it hadn't been easy to give up the business and when Eve looked out at all those boats on the bay, longing still tugged at her heart.

"Oh, look at that view." Julia came to stand beside her in front of the big window.

"I never tire of it." Lucy had stepped up on her other side.

Eve turned her gaze north along the coast. She couldn't see her home from here but she knew it was there waiting for her to return. There'd been suggestions from others, Gert and Verity, that she move into one of the new apartments being built in town but she was happy out there. Lonely sometimes after her visitors left, but happy. She'd drawn a line in the sand and instead of wanting things to go back the way they'd been, she was taking the opportunity to make a new way forward. And it seemed to her that Julia and Lucy were doing that too.

Eve smiled and held up the glass she hadn't taken a sip from yet. "To our beautiful Wallaby Bay."

"To new ventures," Julia said.

Eve's heart warmed with joy as Lucy and Julia both slipped their arms around her.

"To birds of a feather," Lucy said.

They laughed and raised their glasses.

Alec called out over the chatter. "Lucy, can you come here a moment, please?"

She winked at Eve and went to stand beside him.

"I hope everyone has their glasses charged because we have a special announcement."

The bedroom door flew open and Poppy and Noah tumbled out with Dixie at their heels.

"Mummy and Daddy are getting married!" the children chorused.

There was an explosion of noise – congratulations, laughter and toasts to the future while all around them the room turned to gold, bathed in glorious light as the sun set over Wallaby Bay.

acknowledgements

This book was written during 2020 when the world as we knew it was turned on its head — a tricky time for everyone in one way or another. I work from home so that was nothing new but I found the creative process quite difficult when we were being bombarded by regular pandemic updates — I had to hide myself away both physically and electronically.

It was no wonder then that the trying times we faced seeped a little into my story, which is not about the pandemic but rather focuses on the challenges life can dish out. It's how we deal with those challenges that make us. We've all had to adjust to a new reality, and in particular the medical profession have become frontline "soldiers". Through Lucy's story, in some small way, I wanted to pay tribute to that.

The action in this story takes place in and around the town of Wallaroo where I live but we are a small community so I made up a new name, Wallaby Bay. All the people and places within the story are fictitious. Wallaroo does have a beautiful beach, many coffee shops and places to eat, and a fantastic nautical museum, but if you come to visit you won't find any of the other venues in the story. Eve's house and the cafes are all made up. You will find plenty of real places to stay and dine and you will see a few prawn boats at the marina wharf or out in the bay and there are plenty of places to serve you up a meal of delicious Spencer Gulf king prawns.

Many years ago my first teaching role was at Kirton Point Primary School, Port Lincoln, and the logo on the school uniform was a local prawn boat, the *Tacoma*. Later we moved to Yorke Peninsula and settled in Wallaroo. The Spencer Gulf prawn fleet is based between these two places. I've wanted to include some reference to this important local industry for some time and then along came Eve and *Birds of a Feather*.

I'd like to thank several people who helped me with my background research for this story. I've eaten many delicious prawns over the years and know a little about the industry but to dig deeper I was helped by Jim Waller (honoured in 2019 by Spencer Gulf and West Coast Prawn Fishermen's Association for his long-serving contribution to the industry) and Leon and Anita Martin. All three spent time with me talking about the industry and answering my many questions. Rob and Tony let me aboard their prawn trawler to ask more questions and poke my nose into nooks and crannies. They were all so generous with their time and knowledge and I'm most grateful. For more info on this industry go to www.spencergulfkingprawns.com.au

It was such fun to include another famous South Australian in my story, the Balfours frog cake. This sweet treat is a cube of sponge cake, topped with a dome of creamy filling and coated in a smooth fondant icing. Each head is cut by hand with a hot knife to form the mouth and finished with two hand-piped black dots for eyes. In the early days they were always green but now you can get pink and chocolate too. These delicious little cakes have been produced for more than ninety years and are a favourite from my childhood. If you're visiting SA pop into Balfours Café City Cross and try one of these special treats.

The life of a research scientist is a totally different world to mine and I had help from a couple of sources. Several years ago Professor Susan Clark spent time with me answering questions about possible scenarios for a character in a story that never eventuated, but the useful background info was perfect for this one. More recently my daughter-in-law, Sian, put me in touch with Dr Samia Elfekih. Samia read my early passages involving Julia and helped me develop her character as a research scientist. Big thanks to these awesome women in science whose suggestions helped me greatly. If you'd like to know more about their work you can find them at www.garvan.org.au/people/suscla and people.csiro.au/E/S/Samia-Elfekih

When it came to background on FIFO life I want to thank my young friends Gemma and Brodie O'Brien and Michael Hilder. They all devoted time to answering my many questions, which was much appreciated.

When I needed clarification on police procedures I was grateful for my friend in the force who cast her eye over that scene; thank you, Sarah.

All of these people were immensely helpful but, as always, I am a writer of fiction and love to elaborate, so any discrepancies between my story and reality are down to me.

This book is dedicated to two very special women, Margie Arnold and Mandy Macky, booksellers extraordinaire, with around sixty years of service to the industry between them. I first met them through their respective businesses, Meg's Bookshop in Port Pirie, which Margie runs with husband Mark, and Dymocks in Rundle Mall, Adelaide, which Mandy ran with husband Bruce.

I was in my early days as a teacher/librarian and we've been friends ever since. When I began writing, their encouragement helped sustain me, and when I finally had a book to share, they both supported me with launches, promotions and by keeping stocks on their shelves. We've had many launches, tours and events since and I am most grateful for their support and friendship as I know many other local authors are. Recently Mandy received the 2021 Lloyd O'Neil Award for outstanding service to the Australian book industry. As I write this, Mandy and Bruce have just retired and I wish them well for their next chapters and look forward to new beginnings with Dymocks, Rundle Mall. You can still find Margie and Mark at Meg's. If you're ever in Port Pirie make sure you call in and say hello.

A big thank you also to the many other booksellers I've met along the way and the librarians who have continued to hold events in all kinds of ingenious ways and, of course, to you, dear readers. Thank you all for devoting your precious reading time to my books and for sharing your joy with family and friends. Word of mouth is still the best way to discover new reads.

I am so lucky my stories have found a home with the fabulous team at Harlequin/HarperCollins. As always a big thank you to my publisher, Jo Mackay, and my editor, Annabel Blay; I love that we've travelled so much of this journey together. Big thanks also to eagle-eyed proofreader Annabel Adair, peart publicist Natika Palka, Mark Campbell and his talented design team, with accolades for cover designer Debra Billson, Jo Munroe and the marketing team, Karen-Maree Griffiths and the sales team, book juggler Johanna Baker, and the rest of the crew of talented people headed up by Sue Brockhoff who carry out the many tasks needed to bring this book to readers. I know it's been a particularly tricky working environment for you all this last year, but as usual you've come up trumps.

Once again a big thank you to my writing buddies for chat time and sharing the highs and lows and to my dear friends and family – you are my magic. Without your support there would be no books written, I can assure you. Extra hugs for the various people who've had shoulder injuries over the years. Your pain has been my gain. And special love to my home team, Daryl, Kelly, Steven, Harry, Archie, Dylan, Sian, Jared and Alexandra. Book fourteen … who'd have imagined it?

book club questions

- At seventy many people are looking to retirement. Why do you think Eve's not?
- How would you describe Eve and Spiro's relationship? What about the relationship between Mary and Eve?
- Julia appears to take an instant dislike to Lucy. Why do you think she does?
- Eve tells Lucy she has the right temperament for nursing, but Lucy no longer wants to be a nurse. Do you think she'll return to that type of work? Why or why not?
- Julia appears to keep her relationship with Glen at arm's length. Why do you think that is?
- Lucy thinks she's failed to be the best mother she can be. Do you agree? Could she have done anything differently?
- Eve said that by trying to protect her sons from the tough times in life she wasn't helping them and that it's how we deal with the lumps and bumps of life that make us. Discuss.
- What does family mean for each of the three women, and how has it affected their friendship?

- Eve finds a way to forgive Audrey. Do you? Why or why not?
- 'Birds of a feather flock together' is an old saying. What does it mean and how does it relate to Eve, Julia and Lucy?

talk about it

Let's talk about books.

Join the conversation:

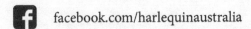 facebook.com/harlequinaustralia

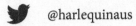 @harlequinaus

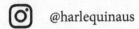 @harlequinaus

harpercollins.com.au/hq

If you love reading and want to know about our
authors and titles, then let's talk about it.